DEATH
BEFORE
DAWN

DEATH BEFORE DAWN

AN INSPECTOR CECILIE MARS THRILLER

MICHAEL KATZ KREFELD

Translated from Danish by Nina Sokol

SAGA
EGMONT

For my wonderful wife, Lis, the light of my life

Published in 2024 by Podium Publishing
www.podiumaudio.com

DEATH
BEFORE
DAWN

PART I

The moth's wings illuminated by the glow of the fire.
Swarming in unsteady pathways.
Towards the flames you now come so near.
Consumed by the fire before you're aware.

1

The darkness cloaked him as he looked over at the apartment complex on the opposite side of the street. It was 11 p.m. and Saxogade was deserted. The piercing cold kept most people indoors. Only a few had passed by in the hour he had been sitting in his car. He hadn't paid any attention to them; he had been fully focused on the apartment on the first floor. The ceiling light was turned on in the living room, sending its glow out to the balcony. Contrary to the neighbouring balconies, no satellite dish had been installed on the low railing, which meant that he had a clear view of the living room through the narrow balcony door. A clear view of Kristina Sand. He had observed her walking back and forth. She wore a white T-shirt that accentuated her breasts. He had seen her long hair flutter as she turned around. Twenty minutes ago, he had caught a glimpse of a wine glass in her hand, and he was thinking that she must be having a party. Her private party because he knew that she was alone up there. All alone. Kristina came into view again. Standing in front of the balcony door. She sipped from the glass. Was she wearing jeans? Maybe leggings? He wasn't sure. No matter what, the outfit accentuated her gorgeous long legs. She was swaying her hips back and forth to the beat of the music she listened to, he guessed. He reached for the button to the side window and rolled it down. He had naïvely hoped that he would be able to hear what she was playing, but all that reached him was the distant sounds of the city. He rolled the window back up and turned on the radio. The music they were playing was heavy and noisy, and he continued pushing the dial buttons until he landed on some older pop. It sounded like Britney Spears. Maybe Kristina was listening to the exact same tune . . . "*Oops! I did it again,*" sang Britney.

What a coincidence, he thought as he stomped his foot to the beat of the music and looked up at Kristina. After a while, she closed the thin curtains.

He felt disappointed, but then she started wriggling to the music behind the curtain. In the silhouette, she danced sensually, her hips swaying. His private dancer. It was a gift to him. Just as much as it was a sign. One of many that had recently appeared, and which had led him down the path to her. "Kriistiinna," he whispered to himself. He turned off the radio and looked back towards the light up there. She was like a firefly fluttering about a single light bulb. Drawn to something it can't comprehend. Like Kristina was drawn to the music and her movements. Like he was driven by certain instincts growing stronger and darker within. Instincts that were inexplicable but that he knew he would have to obey to feel whole. He grabbed the leather briefcase on the passenger seat. He considered whether he ought to check the contents one last time, but he saw no reason why he should keep postponing this. Now was the time for the whole thing to be executed. That which had always been in his mind. That which had rushed through his veins. He opened the car door and got out. It had started to rain, and the raindrops bounced off his long black nylon coat. He pulled up the collar and started to cross the dark street, keeping a firm grip on the handle of the leather briefcase. When he reached her building, he found her name on the door entry phone and pushed the button.

2

Cecilie made a sharp turn at the corner in her black Golf and continued down Istedgade. Vesterbro was just waking up on this piercingly cold Monday morning and there was a lot of traffic. She beeped impatiently and tried to edge her way around the line. When that didn't work, she turned on the flashing blue lights, forcing the cars in front to make room for her.

"Damn, Heino, did you just let out a fart?" Henrik asked from the back seat. The older, grey-haired colleague waved his hand back and forth in front of his nose.

"Not at this very moment, if that's what you meant," Heino answered, rubbing his hipster goatee while smiling innocently.

"But as in two seconds ago? Cecilie, Heino is breaking wind," said Henrik, moving his big hulk of a body away from Heino. Cecilie sensed the stench and rolled down all the windows.

"This is the last time I'm giving you a lift. Next time you'll have to drive yourselves. Joakim?"

"What?" said Joakim, sitting next to her, the Homicide Unit's newest and youngest member. "I haven't let out any farts."

"Dammit, Joakim, a briefing?" she said, sending him a glance. The black Ray-Bans and the open shirt were already irritating her.

"Woman who has been killed. Saxogade number 11, first floor," he said while noisily chewing his gum. "A resident found her after he had noticed that the front door had been ajar for more than a day."

"And that's all?"

Joakim spit the chewing gum out of the open side window.

"I haven't been given any more information."

"Joakim isn't a trusted employee, boss," Heino said ironically.

Cecilie shook her head and turned at the next street on the left.

"Isn't this it?" she asked.

"No, and this is a one-way street. Saxogade is the next street over," Joakim answered. "I can drive."

A car approached them at a very high speed.

"Boss, oncoming car," Heino said.

Cecilie activated the blue lights once again. The driver quickly swung to the side and made room for them to pass.

"Let's hope it's not Sonja who was killed," said Henrik.

"Who?!" asked Joakim.

Henrik shook his head.

"*Sonja from Saxogade.* Come on, am I the only one who remembers that television series?"

Heino crossed his arms. "Shit, sometimes I forget how old you actually are. Isn't it time for you to retire soon?"

"Yeah, in two years. And I'm already counting down the days till I won't have to look at your ugly face anymore."

Cecilie rolled up next to the patrol cars and the forensic detectives' station car, which were blocking most of Saxogade. At the entrance door, a couple of officers were standing together with a few curious citizens who had positioned themselves behind the red-and-white crime scene tape. Cecilie turned off the engine and snapped her fingers.

"Okay. Playtime's over, boys. And, Joakim, remove those goddamn sunglasses before I stick them up your ass."

Both Heino and Henrik held back a laugh as Joakim hurriedly put his sunglasses in his shirt pocket. They got out of the car and Cecilie looked up at the apartment on the first floor. It was cold as hell, so she zipped up her leather jacket. At that moment, she noticed some small glimpses of light coming from behind the curtains. It looked as though the forensic detectives were busy taking photographs of everything at the scene of the crime. She sensed her heart pounding as she approached the building.

No matter how many murder cases she had been involved in, it would never feel normal. Cecilie greeted the two officers and looked over at the entry phone and the name next to the apartment on the first floor. They all continued into the hallway.

"What about the guy who reported it? What apartment does he live in?" Cecilie asked no one in particular.

"I have no idea, but I'll find out," said Heino. "I'll start ringing doorbells."

Cecilie and the others went up to the apartment, where the door was wide open. The forensic team had put out a cardboard box with protective plastic overshoes, which they put on.

"It's almost like a house viewing," said Joakim.

Cecilie ignored him and walked through the hallway, past the small kitchen and into the living room. Everything was neat and tidy and there was no indication of a violent struggle. She greeted the two forensic officers, who were both wearing blue coveralls. Cecilie looked around the living room, which was neatly decorated with plenty of matching throw pillows and little knick-knacks. A single woman in the big city, she thought. The individual who had lived here had better taste than she did. Ole entered the living room. He was dressed in white coveralls with a corresponding hood that made him look like an astronaut.

"Goddammit, Cecilie," the middle-aged medical examiner exclaimed with a big smile. Cecilie stuck her hand out and they fist-bumped.

"I didn't think you walked among us mortals any longer," said Ole.

"What do you mean? Did you think I had croaked?"

"No, of course not, but since they had appointed you head of Homicide, I assumed you were far too busy mingling with the bosses at police headquarters, attending fancy receptions and things like that."

"That would suit me well, wouldn't it?" she said ironically. "It's good to see you, Ole. What do you have for me?"

"Not a pretty scene," Ole said, resembling an undertaker rather than an astronaut now. "Follow me."

Cecilie and Ole went into the adjacent bedroom with Henrik and Joakim at their heels.

"Fuck . . ." said Joakim at the sight, instinctively covering his mouth with his hand. On the bed in front of them lay the corpse of a woman with her arms and legs fastened to the bedposts. She was almost naked; all she was wearing was a girdle and white pantyhose that were drenched in blood. The skin of her stomach was perforated to such an extent that her intestines and viscera lay bare in the abdominal cavity, and her womb and inner thighs were lesioned with wounds. Her face had been disfigured into a bloody, shrivelled mass. A semi-stifled sound came from Joakim, who was struggling to keep his lunch down.

"Are you okay?" Cecilie asked.

"I . . . I . . . I'll try."

"The last thing I need right now is to worry that you'll throw up all over the crime scene. Go downstairs and help Heino with the witnesses."

Henrik took him by the shoulders and managed to nudge him out of the bedroom.

"What can you tell us, Ole?" Cecilie asked, positioning herself next to the bed together with the medical examiner.

"As you can see, numerous cuts in the stomach region, the groin area, and the face. We won't know the precise number until we've examined her more thoroughly. But I have roughly counted the first thirty cuts."

"And the weapon?"

"A large knife, perhaps several different knives. It looks like the stab wounds differ from one another." Ole pointed out two different cuts on the victim's groin.

"And the time of death? Any idea?"

Ole nodded. "It's more than twenty-four hours ago."

"Last night?"

"I'll be able to estimate it once we take her in."

Cecilie looked around in the small room.

"Have we located the weapon?"

"Not as far as I know."

"So, he's taken it with him . . . Bloodied up, we can safely presume?"

"Yes. This was a messy business."

"And yet there are no traces to be found, neither in the living room, the hallway, nor the stairwell?"

"Forensics might still manage to find some, but you're right. Taking the degree of violence into consideration, it is truly noteworthy that there are absolutely no traces to be found in the rest of the apartment. He must have been very careful."

"How did this happen?" she asked, looking at Henrik.

Henrik folded his arms over his chest and looked at the corpse. Pondering for a moment, he said: "There is no indication of a break-in. She must have let him in, or he must have had a key. There are no signs of a fight in the living room. Maybe they ended up in here rather quickly?"

Cecilie nodded in agreement.

"A single woman. Vesterbro at nighttime. If we assume that the crime took place at night, who would she have dared open the door to?"

"Someone she knew. A friend, a boyfriend, maybe an ex-partner. Murders committed out of jealousy are violent. We've seen that before."

"Indeed we have. As soon as we have her ID in order, we'll check out her social circle. Preferably today."

"Roger."

Cecilie looked around. She noticed the clothes that were neatly folded on the chair in the corner. A white T-shirt, a pair of black leggings, and woollen socks.

"Could he have pacified her? Before tying her up?"

Ole nodded.

"Aside from the many lesions, there are no other indications of physical violence. Neither in the form of head trauma nor signs of defence."

"Cable ties and sexy underwear. Could it be a sex game gone wrong?"

"I'll know more once we—"

"Get her in," Cecilie concluded his sentence. She bent down and looked at the deep slits around the victim's wrists.

"It seems like she struggled to free herself."

Ole squatted down and carefully examined the marks. The long skin abrasions and the repeated wear patterns indicated she may have struggled for a long time.

"No matter how it started, whether she voluntarily went along with being tied up or not, at some point she must have screamed for help."

"That goes without saying, yes."

"So why didn't anyone hear her? Why wasn't she found until the day after?"

"He could have covered her mouth, used a pillow?" Henrik answered.

Cecilie shook her head.

"With all that violence? He had been in a state of volatility. He had stabbed someone multiple times. He had nothing on his mind other than annihilating her."

"I agree with Cecilie," Ole answered. "A lot of energy was put into this murder. It looks like a blood frenzy."

She took out her little Maglite from her belt and shone it on the victim's face.

"Hold it straight, Ole."

Ole took the light from her hand and Cecilie took out a pair of disposable gloves from her pocket.

"What are you going to do?"

Cecilie didn't answer. Instead, she put two fingers inside the victim's mouth. She rummaged around a little until she grabbed hold of something, which she started to pull. A slimy sound came from the throat when she managed to get the piece of material out. She looked at the lace panties that matched the victim's girdle.

3

It was past noon by the time Cecilie returned to the Criminal Investigation Division on Teglholm Allé. Together with Heino, Henrik, and Joakim, who came plodding along behind her, she continued into the cold and grey building. As they were walking up the stairs, Heino turned to Joakim with a smirk on his face.

"So let me just see if I got this straight. You threw up? Right in the middle of the crime scene?"

"Like hell I did," Joakim answered, his gaze fixed on the steps.

Heino slapped Henrik on the back. "Henrik, did he throw up or didn't he?"

Henrik smiled back. "I'm pretty sure I saw a little vomit on the corners of his mouth."

"Fuck both of you," said Joakim, extending both arms. "I had a rough weekend. I was just a little hungover, that's all."

When they reached their floor, Cecilie turned towards them. "Joakim? Heard anything from the dog patrol?"

Joakim took out his iPhone and checked it.

"No, nothing new. They're still making the rounds in the neighbourhood. I also got uniformed officers to go through all the rubbish bins. They'll call as soon as they're done."

"I doubt they'll find the murder weapon," said Henrik. "The murderer seems too clever for that."

They continued walking through the open office space, which was buzzing with activity. A younger detective, whom she knew was working on a fraud case, approached Cecilie and was about to say something.

"Not now," she said, sending him a glance that made him moonwalk away again.

"You two . . ." she said, addressing Heino and Henrik.

"We're off to a great start. Everything's going according to plan, boss," said Heino, sending her a reassuring smile.

Cecilie frowned. "A woman has just been murdered, so, no, right now everything's going to hell."

"You know what I mean. We're on the case just as we always are. As soon as Forensics and good old Ole get back to us, then—"

"What about the neighbours?" she asked, noticing her shortness of breath.

"Like I've already said: the ones who were home and who we got hold of had neither seen nor heard anything. The witness who discovered her, Yusef Hasan, didn't have anything to add either. He was still shaken up. He was crying uncontrollably."

"Was he, now?" she asked with a hint of suspicion.

"We'll go out there again when people start coming home from work."

"Check up on the ones you already have, Heino. The murderer could just as well be one of them. Including the sobbing Yusef."

"I'm about to check out the registry."

"Well, then fucking run already," she answered, stopping in front of the door to her office.

"And Henrik, you—"

"I'm working on her closest circle; we've already worked our way to the family. We've got it all under control, Cecilie."

"I hope so," she answered, and went into her office. She shut the door behind her and let out a deep sigh. It was as though the world had gone mad. Nineteen murders had taken place since she had taken over the office from Karstensen. Each one more vile than the last. In two-thirds of the cases, the murderer had been a part of the victim's closest circle. The rest were either gang-related or had occurred in the city nightlife. It was getting to the point where it was hard to say what was more dangerous: going out or watching *Dancing with the Stars* at home with your family. In six of the murder cases, they still hadn't found the murderer. These numbers explained why she hadn't yet settled properly in the boss's office. It still looked like it did when Karstensen had left it, except for the fact that all the pictures of his grandchildren on the desk and all the old trophies won in shooting contests had been removed. She wished she had had time to do more about it. Not so much out of vanity or for the sake of cosiness but more to rinse out Karstensen's regime. Send out a signal that new, fresh vibes were on their way to the division.

Cecilie went over to the big mahogany table overflowing with old case folders and sat down. The worn-out chair with the shabby upholstery creaked ominously underneath her. As soon as Henrik found the closest relatives, she would contact them herself. She skimmed through her notes. Kristina Sand. Poor Kristina Sand, who was now being transported to Ole for an autopsy. And the poor Sand family, who didn't yet know what kind of grief was about to hit them. In most of the murder cases, Cecilie was the one who went out to visit the loved ones. She never had much of a chance to say anything to them. It was as though her very presence warned them about what had happened before she even had a chance to open her mouth. It was very rare that anyone broke down in sobs like you saw in films. Most often they were just at a loss for words. But their gazes spoke volumes. The light in their eyes was somehow shut off. She would never get used to it. Someday, when she was going to retire, it wouldn't be the macabre murders that would haunt her as much as the loved ones who were left behind.

Someone knocked on the door while opening it at the same time. It was her secretary, Jane, who came with the position she had taken over. Jane was in her mid-forties and always elegantly dressed and wore make-up that was just as discreet as her velvety soft voice. If Cecilie was ever going to wear something other than jeans and a leather jacket, Jane would be her unattainable idol.

"I'm very busy, Jane, so—"

"Then you're not going to like this."

"What?"

"John Nyholm and the Independent Police Complaints Authority are here."

"What is the IPCA snooping around for *now*? Isn't this the third time this month?"

"Not just snooping. They have taken Anders Bjerg to court."

Cecilie leaned forward in her chair. "Say what? What the hell do they think Andy Boy's done? Taken money from the cookie jar?"

"If only this was about cookies." Jane leaned forward confidentially and lowered her voice. "As far as I know, it's about euphoriants."

"Shit. Something discovered here in this division?"

"I don't know anything more."

"Why the hell wasn't I briefed about this before?"

"You were out, and your presence is not required. The Police Federation is down there too."

Cecilie got up from her chair. "Where is John, that cocksucker?"

Jane smiled shyly at Cecilie's language.

"They are all sitting in Meeting Room 4. But, like I said, there is no need for you to—"

"Like hell I won't," Cecilie said, and she swept out the door.

4

Without knocking, Cecilie entered Meeting Room 4. It had the desired effect, and all eyes shifted in her direction. Anders smiled with relief at the sight of her, as though she were the miracle he had been waiting for.

"Cecilie, they are totally out to get me," he said with an accent that revealed he came from the rougher neighbourhoods in the outskirts of Copenhagen. With his scruffy hair and dark under-eye circles, he looked like someone who hadn't slept for days, which could very well have been the case if the accusations against him turned out to be true. Sitting next to him was Jette of the Police Federation. She hadn't slimmed since they last saw each another, and her facial tics hadn't become fewer.

"Hi, Cecilie, I wasn't certain . . . if you should be present. But this is only preliminary . . . and there's no requirement for—"

"That's okay, Jette. It was probably the IPCA that should have given notice."

"We did," John Nyholm answered, and continued with a stiff smile on his lips. "The Commissioner has been notified."

She sent John a cold glance.

"Was it really necessary to inconvenience him? My office door is always open."

"I will make a note of that," John said, brushing his pale hand through his thin hair. Cecilie shifted her gaze to John's colleague, who resembled him, only he had slightly more hair on his head. The two detectives from

IPCA wore identical suits and each sat with a notepad in front of him. Both of them were in every way as far from the image of the average police officer as you could possibly imagine. She couldn't recall his name; was it Karsten, Kristian, or Klaus? Kenneth! Yes, that was it. Kenneth and fucking John Nyholm, who were always so damn busy trying to find dirt on her employees, as well as on her.

"So, what's this all about?" she asked, holding out her hand in a gesture of irritation.

In response, John pushed a plastic sleeve across the table in her direction. Cecilie took the plastic sleeve and saw that it contained the lab result of Anders's urine test. She cast it aside.

"Have any comments, Anders? They say they found coke?"

Anders leaned forward eagerly in his chair.

"I sure as hell do. As I've already explained to these two," he said, pointing at John and Kenneth, "it happened in connection with a case."

"Which he doesn't wish to elaborate on," said John.

"And rather stubbornly so," Kenneth added in his squeaky voice.

"That sort of thing is confidential. Even for you IPCA boys," Anders snarled.

"I can inform you that Anders and a detective colleague are investigating a few narcotics cases with connections to the gangs in Vesterbro and Sydhavnen. It's dangerous work," Cecilie said.

"I'm sure it is. I just don't see what that has to do with the result of the test," John said in a cold voice.

"In any way shape or form," Kenneth added.

"No, that's because all you two do is sit behind your fucking desks while the rest of us are out in the field, risking our lives. How exactly did this happen, Anders?" Cecilie asked.

"You know, the way that sort of thing always does," he said, rubbing his eyes. "We—me and Jeppe—were at PussySkin talking to some people. Some big shots who we can hopefully send behind bars for a shitload of years. And there was a party." He extended his hand. "Russian girls, vodka, champagne, and nose candy. In that sort of situation, you try to blend in as much as possible, okay? You gotta look like the clientele or you're dead."

"There's a difference between looking like the clientele and being the clientele," John said, pointing towards the plastic sleeve.

"A big difference," Kenneth said.

"So, when did your meeting take place?"

"The meeting? Well . . ." Anders said, scratching his head. "Last Thursday."

"And when is the test from?"

"Yesterday," John answered.

"That's a long time to have coke in your blood," Cecilie said, looking at him with a serious gaze.

Anders shrugged. "I know. It must be because I'm not used to it."

John snorted. "That's not quite how it works."

Kenneth nodded in agreement.

"What about Jeppe's test? Jeppe Fries?" Cecilie asked, looking at John.

"Nothing, negative," John answered.

"As in zero per cent," said Kenneth.

Cecilie put her hands at her sides and looked down at the floor as she let everything she had heard properly sink in. Anders said something or other, which she didn't hear. She sensed John staring at her with his mousy gaze. This was some serious shit. Finally, she looked up.

"I assume that the IPCA will take the case to the prosecution. Meanwhile, you're going to be suspended, Anders. Clean out your locker."

"I'm going to be what? Cecilie, for Christ's sake, you can't do that. You know damn well how it is. You can't seriously mean you're going to sacrifice me to those idiots?"

"You heard what I said."

Anders got up so quickly that his chair fell over.

"What . . . what . . . about all the crap you've done? How many times did we have to cover your ass?! Huh?! You've never walked the line. You've also showed up to work high. Because we've got to tackle all the shit we see!" he shouted, on the verge of a fit.

"Go home, Anders. Now," Cecilie said.

"This is my bloody life! And you're taking it away from me because of what? One little test? Would you be able to pass it? How are your stats today, boss?"

"Are you done?" she asked, staring him down.

He shook his head. "I've got so much dirt on you. If I were to pipe up about all the gangster shit you've done, believe me, you'd be finished."

"We're all ears if you have anything you'd like to add to your case . . . or to anything else for that matter," said John, crossing his arms.

Anders turned towards him. "Something to add? For you guys at the Independent Police Complaints Authority? If you can get your girlfriend here to suck my balls," he said, pointing to Kenneth, "then I'll give you the entire sausage." He grabbed his crotch and squeezed his member.

"Do you think you can find your own way out, or will I have to ask someone to help you?"

Anders edged his way past Jette and made his way to Cecilie.

"You'll pay for this." He gave her a shoulder as he passed her. "Sooner or later."

After Anders left, Jette got up. She seemed shaken by the whole episode and quickly said goodbye. John and Kenneth packed up their things and Cecilie noticed that they also had identical briefcases.

"I assume you know the way out?"

"Yes, of course. This place has got quite a speedy revolving door," John said. "It was quite a surprise to find out that you had managed to push Karstensen out."

"I haven't pushed anyone out. Karstensen retired, end of story."

"Yet still, it was rather unexpected that you would take over the position as the new head of Homicide. You've given the title a whole other meaning."

"Yes, everything taken into consideration," Kenneth added.

"And what consideration might that be?"

John tapped his briefcase. "Anders wasn't totally off in his accusations."

"My tests have always been negative. But if you've got something you want to accuse me of, then go ahead. Shoot, John. Or has the gunpowder got a little wet, as usual?"

"We both know who's been protecting you."

"I had no idea anyone was," she answered cheerfully.

"But even the Minister is operating on borrowed time. Talk soon."

She watched as John and Kenneth disappeared out the door. Both John and Anders were right: She was living on borrowed time. Sooner or later, it was all going to catch up with her.

5

The sun was setting across the Nordvest neighbourhood and Cecilie was stuck in the rush-hour traffic. The six-lane highway that meandered like a snake across four levels was clogged up with motorists honking their horns. The radio was playing Mary J. Blige's classic "No More Drama," which couldn't be further from the truth, considering her situation. Cecilie's stomach grumbled, reminding her that she had missed lunch again. She was tired, hungry, and sad. The visit she had paid to Kristina Sand's mother in Valby had been draining. The elderly lady with the grey poodle in her arms had dropped her cigarette on the doormat in shock upon receiving the news of her daughter's death. Cecilie had bent down and put out the cigarette so it wouldn't start a fire in the corridor. She wanted to be sure someone would come by and got Kristina's mother to call up a friend. Cecilie had tried to get some information on Kristina Sand and her circle of friends. Was there a boyfriend or friend they should contact? But the mother knew nothing. Due to an argument they'd had, she hadn't been in contact with her daughter the last few years. To her despair, she couldn't recall what the argument had been about.

Tomorrow, Cecilie would pay Ole a visit at Forensics and get the full pathological story. All the gory but necessary details. Heino and Henrik were in Saxogade talking with the neighbours who they initially hadn't been able to get hold of. NC3, the National Cyber Crime Centre, had received Kristina Sand's laptop as well as her mobile phone, which they were in the process of unlocking so they could read the contents. In that sense the investigation was rolling on wheels and there was a 99 per cent chance that some idiot stood at the end of the tracks. A wimp who seemed innocent at first glance, like he didn't have it in him. But when you pushed the right buttons, he would unveil a frothing and uncontrollable rage within.

She made a turn and drove among Bellahøj's dilapidated high-rises. Prestige buildings from the sixties that had been abandoned by the rich elite a long time ago. Instead, the neighbourhood suffered from gang wars and increasing unemployment among the residents. Nevertheless, Bella was, for better or for worse, her home. Cecilie found a vacant parking space in front of her entrance and got out of the car. She was about to lock it when she heard a voice behind her. "Ce-cil. Ce-cil," it said. And she already knew who it was. No one other than the president of the tenant association, who pronounced her name as though it were a cigarette brand.

"What's up, Omar?" she said, turning around. With her short stature, she was always sure to get a crick in her neck every time she spoke with Omar, who was exceptionally tall. Omar looked down at her.

"We have problems. Big problems."

Omar was in his mid-fifties, weather beaten, and had a thick black moustache. Some claimed he had once been a pirate, others that he had been in the Somalian National Intelligence and Security Agency. Cecilie believed neither of the stories. She thought Omar was a nice guy, though a bit zealous at times. He had taken the title of the president of the tenant association as though he were Bellahøj's uncrowned king, which meant that he treated Cecilie like his own private police force.

"What's wrong now? Was somebody cycling on the pavement? Or didn't sort the rubbish properly?"

"I know you're making fun of me. I understand Danish humour. But this isn't funny."

"I see," Cecilie said, yawning.

"Somebody's seen that the pushers have returned," he said, pointing in the direction of the park just behind them. "That's not good."

"No. Call the police, then."

"Are you crazy, Ce-cil?" he asked, his eyes opening wide. "If the municipality gets word of it, we'll end up on the ghetto list."

"Omar, I'm pretty sure that isn't how it works."

"That's precisely how it works. And it would be a great tragedy to end up on that list again. For all of us. Very shameful. You must do something."

She took a deep breath.

"I just don't have the energy."

"Ce-cil. They respect you. They know who you are. They know you aren't afraid of anything. They know you've thrown gangsters out. And that you've done it alone."

"Well, not exactly alone," Cecilie said.

"It's true. We are very grateful. Everyone in the neighbourhood is. That's why it would be such a shame if the pushers come back."

She looked in the direction of the park.

"How many are there?"

"We don't know. Haven't been there. People have come to me and said that there are pushers in the park."

"Dammit, Omar, I'm off duty."

"Police never sleep. Isn't that what they say?"

"The only reason why this officer never sleeps is because people like you continue to bother me."

"This is important, Ce-cil," he said, giving her a serious look. "Very important for the neighbourhood. You understand?"

"I understand that I won't get any peace from you unless I start marching in that direction," she said, and started walking towards the park.

6

She continued down the path between the bare trees. It ran through the park to Bellahøj open-air stage where the pushers usually hung out. That is, before she and the division, in collaboration with Bellahøj Police Station, managed to kick them the hell out. It had been one of her top priorities after she took charge. She unfastened the button on the side of her gun holster. You never knew just how many of those bastards there would be or what mood they would be in. Cecilie knew quite a few of them. Both of the ones she had arrested as well as the ones she had bought coke from. After being appointed, she had come to the realisation that wanting to save the neighbourhood at the same time supporting those pissants through her consumption made very little sense. And it made equally little sense to actually give John and the IPCA a golden opportunity to nail her on a drug test. She had gone cold turkey. Which had been damn hard. But at least now the withdrawal symptoms were gone. The cravings, on the other hand, were a different story.

She reached Bellahøj open-air stage, where the leaves swept across the stone of the amphitheatre. Aside from a single guy sitting on the lowest row, shuddering in a black fleece jacket and black jogging bottoms, the theatre was empty. Omar had exaggerated the situation once again, but even a single pusher was one too many. That type tended to attract others, like a turd attracts flies. She continued across the grounds towards the guy.

"What exactly is it that you clearly don't understand?" she shouted gruffly.

The dark-skinned guy shifted his gaze from the ground and looked up. He was much younger than she had initially assumed, twelve to thirteen years old at the most but rather large in stature.

"Say what?"

"Don't act dumb. Empty your pockets."

The boy did as he was told and exhibited a couple of coins, a set of keys, and a phone.

"So where are you hiding the goods?" Cecilie asked, looking around at the stonework.

"Y-you misunderstand," the boy stammered. "I don't have any drugs. O-on the contrary."

"Contrary to what?" she asked irritably.

"I threw them out."

"You threw out the drugs? Where?"

"No, no . . . the pushers . . ."

"You did what?"

He put his things back in his pocket and displayed his hands. The knuckles on his right hand were grazed and bleeding slightly.

"One of them got a little too s-smart."

Cecilie couldn't help smiling. The boy seemed a little mentally underdeveloped.

"Am I to understand that you managed to chase the pushers out on your own?"

He shrugged his shoulders.

"They were just some boys from B-Bispebjerg, who were selling hash. Little fish," he said, and smiled.

"What's your name?"

"Allan . . . Pak-Paki Allan."

"Okay, Allan."

"No, Paki Allan. My mum christened me Allan because it sounds Danish. But everybody can see that I'm a Paki. My name is—"

"Paki Allan. Understood. My name is—"

"Cecilie. You're a policewoman. You're cool. I also want to work for the police," he said, sniffing. "It's my d-dream."

"Good for you," she said. "Next time anyone comes down here, you get hold of me instead of beating them up yourself. Otherwise, it could end very badly in more ways than one. All right, Allan?"

"Okay."

"But thanks for your help," she said, smiling at him as she was just about to leave.

"Cool song they made about you."

"What do you mean?"

Allan took out his phone.

"It's a big hit and has got a lot of likes. You're famous. 'Fucked My Brother,' it's called. Have you heard it?" he asked, turning the screen towards her. A music video that had been recorded in a car park in a gloomy neighbourhood played. A group of young men in black tracksuits were trying to look tough in front of a couple of pimped cars. Videos of Cecilie at various press briefings had been pasted in between the car park shots.

Fucked my brother. With three shots to the back of the head and a hole this wide. Right between the legs until he disappeared. But that's not all. Now she's in charge of the cops. Duck for cover, brother. This ho's power is strong.

Cecilie recognised the performer on the video; it was that bastard Como. He had clearly been going to the fitness centre since she last saw him in Vestre Prison. Como had developed muscles and an attitude, but aside from that, he looked like the same loser he'd always been. Not much better than his missing waste-of-space brother, who was missed by no one except Como.

"You're a star," Allan said in a genuine tone as she turned around and left.

7

Cecilie took the elevator, which smelled of urine, to the top floor. She unlocked the door and continued into the dark living room, where she turned on the light.

"Hey, Bob, miss me?" she said, and tossed her leather jacket on the chair. The life-size martial arts dummy stood with his bare chest and bulging muscles by the balcony door and glowered back at her. She jabbed it in its latex jaw, making the dummy sway on its pedestal.

"I missed you too," she muttered.

Cecilie put her hands in her pockets and stared out through the panorama windows. The only spectacular thing about her apartment was the view. Copenhagen lay literally at her feet. Her entire district plus the neighbouring police district. From her Fort Loneliness she could keep an eye on them all. She found her phone and searched for Como's ridiculous song on the internet. A staggering 107,000 viewers had already seen it and it was ranked number 1 on various platforms. The comments on social media were drenched in sympathy for Como and hate messages towards the police and herself.

She was convinced that no one outside the gangs would take Como's songs or accusations seriously. It was just one "fuck the police" song of many. And she doubted whether John or any of the others from IPCA would be listening to rap music in their spare time. She went into the kitchen and opened the refrigerator, which was gapingly empty, but there

were still a couple of pizzas in her freezer. Not quite of the same quality as Venezia's number 8 with shawarma, but it would spare her from
having to go out again. Cecilie turned on the oven. She thought about
Como's song once again. Considering the gang war that had been raging in the neighbourhood, perhaps it was a good thing that their hatred
was directed at her and the police as opposed to a rival gang. It had been
a nasty war that had taken its toll on the residents—the victims of stray
bullets and car bombs that demolished the area. When the gang war had
reached its peak, she managed to move it into the gang's own territory.
Now both gangs had retreated. Their members had either died, landed
behind bars, or fled. And Como's big brother, the handsome but dangerous Jeremy, the notorious leader of the Rebels, had vanished into thin air.
Yes, yes, she knew where he had been buried. Of course she did. Como's
song hadn't just come out of nowhere.

8

Cecilie looked for a parking spot in front of the Teilum building where the Institute of Forensic Medicine was located. When she reached the entrance without finding a spot, she parked the car halfway onto the pavement.

"Nice parking," Joakim said ironically.

She pulled the key out of the ignition and exited the car. "Let's get it over with."

"Isn't Ole kind of a strange guy?" Joakim asked as he followed her to the main entrance.

She shrugged her shoulders. "How would you feel if you were surrounded by nothing but corpses every day?"

"You think he ever tried to fuck one of them?"

"What?!" said Cecilie as she stared at Joakim.

Joakim smiled foolishly as he extended his arms. "You said yourself that he's surrounded by nothing but corpses day in and day out . . ."

"Which made you think that he'd screwed one of them?" She shook her head.

Joakim laughed.

"Can't you imagine him walking around all alone in the freezer room on a night shift and suddenly feeling a little horny? Then he sees this beautiful babe. She's dead, of course, but still a babe. He pulls the sheet off her and has himself a quickie. Puts the sheet back on, so no one would ever know."

"You're sick, Joakim. And from now on you'll keep your mouth shut, okay?"

"It was just a thought."

She announced their arrival at the reception desk, and they were directed along the hallway to the autopsy room, where Ole was at work. Inside the windowless room lay Kristina Sand's naked body on the autopsy table. All the blood had been rinsed off and in the clear light from the lamp, her skin shone in a yellowish tone, as if she were made of wax. In the corner, with his back to them, Ole sat writing on his computer. From the small loudspeaker on the table, Frank Sinatra's iconic voice could be heard singing "Summer Wind."

"Two seconds and I'll be there," Ole said as he continued writing.

Joakim leaned in towards Cecilie. "He's playing romantic music for the dead. I'm just saying . . ."

Cecilie elbowed him in his side. At that very same moment, Ole turned around in his chair.

"Good to see you, Cecilie . . . and Joakim?" he said, nodding. Ole turned off the music and got up.

"Yes, she's been subjected to a rather violent ordeal, I'm afraid. I think I can safely say this is one of the worst cases I've ever seen."

Ole positioned himself next to the steel table and looked down at the corpse. Now that it had been rinsed, the scars from the knife cuts were more clearly visible.

"Did the perpetrator cut the entire abdomen open?" she asked, looking at the oval cavity that reached from the corpse's midriff to her chest.

"I had assumed that might be a possibility," Ole answered, taking out a pair of latex gloves. "But it is the many cuts in the torso that have caused the skin to break and the abdominal cavity to be exposed."

Joakim cleared his throat and Cecilie sent him a look.

"I'm fine," he quickly said, even though he looked pale.

"We've counted fifty-six cuts in all. Executed by the same murder weapon. From various angles and to various depths."

"Depths?"

"It seems that some of the cuts have the characteristics of non-lethal lesions."

"What?"

"Primarily around the groin area," Ole said, pointing towards the vulva.

"Did he penetrate her?"

"With the knife, yes. There are considerable wounds to the abdomen just like the labia majora and labia minora pudenda have been damaged. Those on the right side are completely missing due to the many knife cuts."

"What's missing?" asked Joakim.

"Her labia."

Joakim regretted asking.

"Did he have sex with her?" Cecilie asked.

"Not in the conventional sense. And we haven't discovered any traces from the perpetrator. Neither sperm nor spit nor hair has been discovered on the corpse."

"Do we know whether the forensic detectives have found anything?" The question was addressed to Joakim. He shook his head. "Their report is on the way."

"Were there any nail scrapings on the victim?" Cecilie asked Ole.

"Nope, we haven't found that either."

"You said that there were non-lethal lesions around her groin. Was that where the perpetrator started?"

Ole looked at her with a grim expression.

"According to my estimation, he started off by putting her panties in her mouth in order to subdue her screams, whereupon he began penetrating the vagina with increasingly more force. Then he moved towards the stomach region with the knife. That's where most of the cuts are to be found."

"And the cuts on her face?"

"They are not quite as deep. Perhaps he was starting to lose energy."

"What a fucking psychopath," mumbled Joakim.

Ole nodded. "Like I said, it's seldom that we get anything in here as violent as this. However, we do see it. Especially when it comes to murders of partners."

Cecilie nodded. "What about the toxicological report?"

"Okay, now that's where it starts to get interesting," Ole said, his face lighting up in a smile that was a little unsuitable for the situation.

"The drug test was negative, and there was only a little alcohol in her blood, at a level of 0.3. What we did find was traces of ether."

"Ether?"

"Yes, Aither, son of Erebos and Nyx, god of space and heaven, according to mythology," Ole said, nodding learnedly.

"Thanks for the lecture," Cecilie said ironically. "The perpetrator pacified her with ether?"

"Exactly. I was also surprised. Usually, it's ketamine or GHB we find in the victim's blood when it comes to drug rapes and that sort of thing. This is new, or rather, it's old."

"We're dealing with an old-school criminal. Any idea why he chose to use ether?"

Ole shook his head. "You're the detectives. But aside from the fact that it's rather easy to access, it's not as practical as other anaesthetics. It has a brief effect, unless you anaesthetise the patient, or in this case, the victim, constantly and know how to dose it."

"Which she wasn't?"

Ole shook his head. "Not with those wear marks she has on her ankles and wrists where she was tied. No, she wasn't that lucky."

"What about the panties we found in her throat; did they choke her?"

"No, there is no sign of choking. I think that after her death he pressed them further down her throat."

"As a signature?"

"You're the—"

"Detectives. Thanks, Ole."

9

By the time Cecilie and Joakim returned to the Homicide Unit, it was past noon. Most of her detectives were in the cafeteria and the open-plan office was half-deserted. Heino and Henrik were among the few who were left sitting in front of their computers. Cecilie whistled loudly, catching their attention.

"We're holding a meeting now." She pointed towards her office.

Cecilie threw the autopsy report on the long conference table and stripped off her jacket. Joakim sat down heavily in the chair across from her and took out a piece of nicotine chewing gum. At that very same moment, Henrik and Heino appeared at the doorway. Heino quickly looked around.

"What you've done with the office is very cool, boss," he said ironically. "I see you've really managed to settle in."

"Yes, very feminine," Henrik added as he sat down between Joakim and Heino.

"Keep quiet and listen," said Cecilie. "We passed by Ole's office. And he told us a lot of the frightening shit we'll find in here." She pointed to the report. Heino reached out for it and placed it between himself and Henrik. The drawing on the cover of the torso with the numerous knife cuts clearly showed just how violent the murder had been. Cecilie gave them a short briefing of the contents and of the discovery of ether.

"Ether?" Heino said in surprise.

"Yes. Aither, son of Erebos and Nyx, god of . . . something or other," Joakim attempted to reply.

"Let's try going through the victim's profile," Cecilie said. "Heino?"

Heino turned on his iPad. "The victim is Kristina Sand, forty-one years old. Single. Resided at Saxogade number 11, the same address as the scene of the crime and where the victim's body was discovered. Until her death, she worked at Bendix Coiffure on Gammel Kongevej."

"Coi what?"

"At a hairdresser's—you know, where you go to get your hair cut," Henrik answered.

"She had worked there the last eight years," Heino continued as he scrolled down through the report on his iPad. "According to her colleagues whom I spoke with, she was well liked. The clientele consists mostly of older Frederiksberg ladies, so that may not be the most obvious place to find the perpetrator. Unless we think that the motive was caused by a bad hair day."

"What else did they have to say about her?" Cecilie asked.

"They described as her funny and extroverted. Kristina was always the one who arranged social events and the one you could always confide in."

"Did they know anything about her private life?"

"She didn't have a boyfriend, but she was dating."

"Did any of them know whom she was dating?"

"There didn't seem to be anyone steady at the moment and none of them knew anything about the ones that weren't."

"Tinder? Online dating?"

"We still need to hear from NC3."

"And Ismail hasn't been by yet?"

Heino and Henrik both shook their heads.

"Joakim, check and see if they've sent something. I can't believe it would take them this long to open her computer and phone. If there isn't anything yet, call Ismail and tell him to get off his ass on the double. Don't accept any excuses. This has top priority."

"On it," Joakim answered, and got up.

"What about the neighbours; do we know any of them?"

Henrik shook his head.

"None of them are in the registry."

"And not one of them could tell you something about her?"

"Most of them were on nodding terms with her, but no more than that."

"What about the people living opposite her?"

"Same thing," Heino said.

"But she did say she had seen Kristina with a man about a month ago."

"Did she give a description?"

"She said that he looked Danish, the same age as Kristina, nothing special. He could be anyone," he said, shrugging his shoulders.

"Yeah, including our murderer."

"That's true, of course," said Heino.

"Have Forensics found anything for us?" Cecilie asked.

Henrik shook his head. "The only traces in the apartment are those of the victim."

She looked at him in surprise.

"No traces of DNA that we can use?"

"Neither blood nor sperm. There weren't any fingerprints other than those of the victim either. They've searched everywhere."

Cecilie lowered her head as she thought. She started drumming the surface of the table with her fingertips. Shortly afterwards, she looked back up.

"Ole says that Kristina was anaesthetised but probably not for long periods at a time. A possible scenario is that the perpetrator gets access to her apartment building. He walks up to her door and knocks. She opens it and *boom!* He is standing there already with the ether and makes her unconscious. Then he drags her into the bedroom."

"How long does it take him?" Heino asked attentively.

"A couple of minutes. Maybe more if he continues administering the ether."

"Enough time to tear off her clothes," said Heino.

"Which were placed neatly on the chair," Henrik answered.

"Okay, so he places them neatly on the chair. He manages to tie her to the bed before she wakes up," said Heino.

"He also just manages to put her panties in her mouth before things really start to take off," Henrik added.

Cecilie nodded.

"Or she knew the perpetrator beforehand and let him in herself," said Heino.

"Because . . . ?" Cecilie asked with curiosity.

"It could have been a date. She was wearing sexy underwear and had consumed one or two drinks as the toxicological report indicates."

"A Tinder date," said Henrik, swiping his finger in the air.

"Precisely," said Heino. "He has managed to write his way straight into her pants. Kristina had no idea what kind of psychopath she was letting into her apartment. Maybe he first anaesthetises her in the living room or in the bedroom."

Joakim returned carrying a pile of transcripts. "I got NC3 to send what they had, and I printed the whole damn thing myself."

"Ismail isn't coming, then?" Cecilie asked.

Joakim shook his head. "Forget Ismail. What we have here is gold."

Cecilie had an idea why that asshole Ismail hadn't been by the division after her appointment.

"Gold? What do you mean gold?"

"We got a list of her social media accounts with corresponding passwords."

"Was she on Tinder?" Henrik quickly asked.

"Yes, you dirty old man, she was on Tinder."

"Dirty old man, what's that supposed to mean?"

Joakim ignored him. "But best of all," he said as he quickly skimmed through the papers, "are these copies of her text message correspondences with . . . Mark Holt!"

"Who's that?" Cecilie asked.

"Judging by Mark's text messages, he's a pretty naughty guy."

Cecilie took the papers from Joakim and quickly skimmed through them. The correspondence between them was more than a month old. There was no mistaking the wording: *Miss you. Need you. When can we meet, beautiful?*

The flirtatious messages concluded with an agreement to meet.

"I've found a Mark Holt in her Facebook friends," Heino said, nodding towards his iPad.

"Well, well . . ."

"What?" Cecilie asked.

"It seems that Mark-Loverboy is a married man. Wedded to Gitte Holt."

He turned the iPad in her direction. The photo in the top row of his Facebook profile was from a skiing vacation and showed a man in his forties together with a dark-haired woman and two small children.

"I love Facebook," Joakim said, rubbing his hands. "Thank you, Zuckerberg, for solving our case."

"These are only tiny leads, Joakim," said Heino. "It is possible to be unfaithful and a complete jerk without necessarily being a psychopathic killer."

"But it wouldn't be the first time that a secret love affair turned violent," said Cecilie. "Good work," she said, giving them all a nod.

"Henrik, will you find addresses on Casanova Mark? Both his workplace and his home. We're going to pay him a visit right now."

"Of course."

Jane knocked on the open door and entered.

"I'm sorry for disturbing you, Cecilie."

"What is it?"

"I want to remind you about the event tonight."

"What event?"

"The National Police Commissioner's annual reception for management."

Cecilie shook her head. "I don't have time for that."

"You can't say no to something like this."

Cecilie sent her a look. "I assume a murder case is an excellent excuse, even for the National Police Commissioner?"

Jane shook her head in silence. "Unfortunately not. Karstensen always attended them. I could give them a white lie, of course, say that you're sick, but . . ."

"What time will it be?"

"At six p.m. and in full dress. That means skirts for the female managers."

"Skirts?" she said, her mouth agape. "Seriously?"

"I'll let them know that you'll be attending," said Jane, and she disappeared out the door.

"Should Henrik and I deal with Mark Holt?" Heino asked.

"What?" she responded, disoriented.

"I was just thinking that you might need some time to get dressed, boss," he said, biting his cheek.

"Maybe also get your hair done," said Henrik with a slick smile.

"I think the National Police Commissioner would appreciate a little red polish on your nails," Joakim said, pointing at her hands. "You could use one of those beauty makeovers."

"Fuck you, fuck you, and fuck you," said Cecilie, pointing at each of them one after the other.

"Heino, you go to the neighbour's again and see whether his description matches Mark Holt's profile. Joakim, you keep putting pressure on NC3. We need more than this."

"Can't I switch with Henrik and go with you instead?"

"Nope. NC3."

"I thought we were partners," he said, extending his arms.

"Cecilie doesn't have a partner!" Henrik and Heino said at once.

10

Cecilie and Henrik drove straight on Englandsvej, where big-brand car showrooms stood side by side. Even further away from the city centre, they passed all the used car dealers.

"I presume that Holt Automobiles belongs to Mark Holt," said Henrik, pointing at the sign on the front of the building. Cecilie made a turn into the car park in front of the low powder-blue building. The owner had clearly tried to jazz up the place, even though the motley selection of cars for sale resembled the competitor's next door. Cecilie and Henrik got out of the Golf.

"It's still got a little Amager-daintiness to it," Henrik said, eyeing the building.

"Are we going to put Casanova Mark through the centrifuge?"

"That's what we're best at," Henrik answered, following behind her.

In the small showroom, there were three cars that were in slightly better shape than the ones outside. A thin young man emerged. He had an equal amount of beard growth and acne on his cheeks.

"Welcome," he said, giving them a big smile. "Perhaps you've already fallen for the Hyundai?" he said, pointing at the white car next to him. "It was selected as the Middle Class Car of the Year." He conveniently didn't mention in what decade.

"Is Mark Holt around?" Cecilie asked.

"He is in a meeting right now. But perhaps there's something that I can help you with?"

Cecilie managed to extinguish all his enthusiasm when she flashed her ID card in front of him.

"One second . . . and I'll . . ." he said as he immediately moved towards the counter and disappeared into the back. Shortly afterwards, a ruddy-faced man emerged wearing a light blue shirt with buttonholes that were about to burst. He finished chewing some food as he approached them.

"What's this all about?"

Henrik and Cecilie showed him their IDs.

"Mark Holt?"

"I can't escape that." He placed his hands at his sides, revealing a big gold watch around his wrist. "So, once again, what's this about?"

"It's about a case that we're investigating in which your name has popped up."

"What case?"

"One that we're in-vest-ig-ating," she said in her exaggerated school-teacher tone. She looked at Henrik. "Didn't I make myself clear enough?"

"It was perfectly clear," Henrik answered, and turned towards Mark. "This is a routine check. We'll be out of here in no time . . . maybe."

"Yes, maybe," Cecilie repeated.

Mark looked at them nervously.

"Well, if we can be of any help to the police, then . . ."

Cecilie frowned. "We? Who is we?"

"I mean, if I can be of any help."

Cecilie nodded. "Okay. You can."

"Do you know Kristina Sand?" Henrik asked.

Mark quickly shook his head. "Kristina Sand? No, that doesn't ring any bells."

"Ding-dong certain?" Cecilie asked.

Mark cleared his throat and looked away. "We have a lot of customers every day, so I might have met the person."

"Was that how you met? She was a customer here?" Cecilie asked.

"Like I said, I don't recognise the name. But if you tell me what this is all about, I may be able to better place her."

"The bell might ring then?" Cecilie asked.

"Yes . . . maybe."

"You're friends on Facebook. That's why I'm wondering why you don't recognise the name," said Henrik.

Mark laughed nervously. "I'm friends with many of my customers on Facebook. I just accept people if there's a friend request."

"Without knowing them?" asked Henrik.

"Of course," he said, extending his hand. "It's all so superficial anyway."

"I never add anyone I don't know," said Cecilie, looking at Mark. "Do you, Henrik?"

"Never," Henrik answered.

"Yeah, well, different strokes for different folks. Luckily, it's no crime." Mark tried to laugh, but only a cough came out. Over at the counter a woman emerged. She stood looking at them while she was eating a carrot. Cecilie recognised her as Mark's wife from his Facebook profile.

"Is that all?"

"Is that all?" Cecilie asked, turning her gaze towards him.

"Of course not. We didn't come all the way out to Shit Island, I'm sorry, to Amager, to hear about your Facebook profile."

"Do you have a Tinder profile?" Henrik asked him.

Mark dropped his jaw. "What kind of a question is that?"

"Everybody has a Tinder profile. There's nothing embarrassing about that."

"I'm not embarrassed. But I'm married, so I don't need that sort of thing."

Cecilie let out a hollow laugh. "There are many married men on Tinder. I have met a number of them. They all claim to be oh so happily married."

"I see. Fine. But I'm not on Tinder," he said very matter-of-factly.

"Are you sure?" she asked, squinting her eyes.

"One hundred per cent. And now I'd like to know what this is all about or else—"

"Or else what? We've already explained to you what this is all about," Cecilie said, smiling calmly at him. "It has to do with Kristina Sand."

"A person whom I don't know, so I think you've come to the wrong place." He looked at his gold watch. "Is that all? Because I'm in a hurry."

"I think the sandwich can wait," said Henrik.

"Mark, I hate it when people lie," Cecilie said, taking a step closer. "So, are you completely certain you don't know Kristina Sand?"

"Is there anything wrong, Mark?" his wife asked in the background.

Mark half-turned towards her. "No, just give me two minutes," he said, waving her away irritably. His wife remained behind the counter. Mark turned back to Cecilie and Henrik.

"Listen, the name doesn't ring a bell, but if you have a profile picture, then I might be able to remember whether she's been in the store."

"A profile picture? Okay," said Cecilie, and she opened her iPad. "This is her profile picture," she said, turning the screen towards him. Mark opened his mouth in shock. The picture showed Kristina Sand lying tied up and slashed on the bed. "Was this how you left her?"

"My God . . . what is all this?"

"This is Kristina Sand, your lover. Or, rather, former lover, considering the circumstances." She closed her iPad.

"I-I-I . . ."

"You-you-you better make sure you don't lie to me this time, Mark," she said, lifting her index finger.

"I had nothing to do with this. Why are you showing me this?"

"Mark?" his wife called. "Is everything okay?"

"Not now, goddammit!" he shouted back.

His wife looked at him perplexed before she disappeared into the back of the shop.

"Perhaps we should start over again?" Henrik asked, putting his hand on Mark's shoulder. "We'll gladly walk through that door again."

"Or we arrest you and take you down to the station," said Cecilie.

Mark held his hands protectively in front of him. "I-I've spoken with her a little bit. That's all."

"Where do you know each other from?"

"The Dubliner. I was in town with a couple of guys. At some point that evening we ran into Kristina and her two girlfriends." He quickly looked back towards the empty counter before continuing. "I talked to her, got her phone number, then I added her on Facebook. The whole thing was really stupid, and I immediately regretted it."

"You immediately regretted it?"

"Yes, I'm not that type at all."

"Mark, you're a shitty-little-liar type," Cecilie said, pounding him on the chest with a straight index finger. "Didn't you hear what I said? I hate wasting my time with compulsive liars."

"But I swear."

"Don't swear. Just tell me how these text messages came about." She opened her iPad and showed him a copy of the correspondence between him and Kristina.

"Your number and Kristina's. From what I can tell, you are both equally promiscuous. Explain!"

He buried his face in his hands. "I'm sorry. I had no intention of lying. I'm in a fucked-up situation. Do you understand?" he said, on the verge of tears.

"I have tears in my eyes. What about you, Henrik?"

"Yeah, cry me a river."

"We had a brief affair, but it stopped over a month ago. And that's the truth."

The phone in Cecilie's pocket buzzed. She took it out and saw there was a message from Heino: Kristina's neighbour had identified Mark as the man she had seen with Kristina.

"Affair, you said. How interesting. Did you fuck?"

"We slept together a few times, yes. I truly regret it. I've never done anything like that before."

"Mark, you could have fucked the Prime Minister, for all I care. Have you been in Kristina's apartment?"

Mark hesitated as he looked down at the floor.

"It's a simple question, but your answer will be crucial for your future. Were you in her goddamn apartment?"

"Okay, yes, but it was a month ago."

"What about the night of the day before yesterday?"

"The day before yesterday? The day before yesterday I was in Hamburg. I was down there to pick up a car," he exclaimed with relief. "I have the receipts from the hotel and the ferry, and the German customer can confirm the transaction." Mark pointed towards the office.

"Okay, Henrik, check it, will you?"

Henrik nodded, whereupon he and Mark disappeared behind the counter. Cecilie looked at Mark's wife, who was standing with her arms folded in front of her and following what was going on. Shortly afterwards, she turned towards Cecilie, and their eyes met. Her gaze said everything. The wife would forgive him as she had done so many times before. Swallow all her pride. And for what? So that everything would look Amager-fine.

11

It was close to the end of the workday, but the Homicide Unit was busy. Cecilie was sitting next to Henrik and Heino in the middle of the open space. One of the detectives in the division was celebrating their birthday and had given out cake. Joakim didn't hold back and balanced two pieces on his paper plate while his mouth was still full.

"There's enough for one piece each," said Heino.

"People are on their way home, and it wouldn't make sense to let it all go to waste," Joakim answered as the crumbs fell out of his mouth. Heino shook his head and looked at Cecilie and Henrik.

"Can we cross Mark pussy-chaser off our list?" Cecilie said, sipping her cup of coffee.

"Yes, Mark is out. Henrik has checked everything."

"Yes, in addition to the receipts of his stay, I got hold of the German salesman who could confirm that Mark *vass herrre*," he said with a German accent.

"Any news from Forensics, Heino?" Cecilie asked.

"No, or yes . . . Dahlstrup can confirm that none of the knives in the apartment were used as murder weapons."

Cecilie nodded. "I also lean more towards the theory that he brought his murder weapons with him. Together with the cable ties and the ether. Probably also some outerwear so he wouldn't get bloodstains on him. He is cunning."

"NC3 has returned with Kristina Sand's information file," said Joakim.

"And?"

"In the days leading up to the time of the murder, a phone call had been made to the hairdresser, to one of her colleagues whom we have already spoken with, and then to two different women, Jeanne Lauritzen and Claudia Nielsen. She is friends with both on Facebook. There is a picture of all three of them in one of the women's profiles."

"Mark Holt mentioned two of Kristina's girlfriends," Henrik said.

"Maybe it's the same two?"

"We have to talk with them," said Cecilie. She turned the coffee cup between her fingers as she continued thinking. "The perpetrator is in her circle of friends or on the periphery of it. Kristina was enjoying single life. Her going-out friends, Jeanne and Claudia, may know more."

"The party patrol," said Heino.

"Yup. I'm sure there were other lovers besides sleazy Mark. We need to find real Mark among her contacts."

"Murderer Mark," said Henrik.

"Precisely. Trawl the whole thing again and maybe"—Cecilie straightened her posture in the chair—"maybe we should get hold of the contacts she's deleted in the past few months. That should be a task for NC3."

"I'll contact them again."

"Boss, it's almost twenty to," said Heino.

"Twenty to what?"

"Twenty to the hour when you're supposed to be wearing a skirt and partying it up at police headquarters."

Cecilie put the cup aside on the table and closed her eyes. "Fuck, fuck, fuck."

"Yeah, you might get lucky. I think the National Police Commissioner just got divorced," Heino said, laughing.

Cecilie grimaced. "Nooo, stop, stop, I'm getting ugly pictures in my mind's eye. There must be a way to avoid that reception."

"It might be a good idea to show your face there," said Joakim.

"And this is coming from the man who dresses like a teenager and eats cake like a little kid. When the hell did you start being so grown up?" asked Heino.

"Joakim is right," said Henrik. "Let them know there's a new sheriff in town."

"Yeah, in a skirt," she moaned.

Shortly afterwards, Cecilie opened the small closet in her office. She saw that her uniform was on a wire hanger with a plastic cover. It must have been Jane who had ensured that it was all ready for her. The black pumps were shiny and polished. Cecilie took the uniform out of the bag and examined it. A few extra stars had been added to the shoulders. She couldn't recall the last time she had worn it. They usually only used their gala uniforms when someone was to be celebrated or buried. For the last two funerals, she had chosen to show up in her street clothes. That was the only proper way to honour her deceased police partners. Cecilie put on the uniform and got the skirt zipped up with great difficulty. After going cold turkey, she had put on a couple of pounds on her behind. You could say a lot about coke, but it helped you keep a slim figure. She looked at herself in the mirror hanging on the inside of the closet door. She thought she looked like a fat cow. Cecilie found some mascara in her pocket and put a little on her eyelashes. That didn't exactly improve things. But what the hell, it wasn't like she was going on a date. On the contrary, she was going to shake hands with a bunch of middle-aged men who didn't think she deserved her position.

"Fuck that," she said, putting her cap with the golden band and emblem on her head.

When she returned to the division, the only ones left were Henrik and Joakim. Cecilie extended her arms. "What do you say?"

Henrik gave her a round of applause. "That uniform suits you exceptionally well."

"I already miss my jeans."

"You look very distinguished. And awe-inspiring."

"Oh, stop, Henrik, but thanks for the compliment."

"Yeah, you've got pure class," Joakim said, nodding appreciatively. "Super nice."

"I feel like someone who's on the way to the gallows. See you tomorrow, if I survive," she said, sending them a thumbs up on her way out the door.

<h1 style="text-align:center">12</h1>

Darkness had fallen when Cecilie walked across the courtyard in the former police headquarters. The wind was icy cold, and she hurried towards the colonnade.

"Goddammit!" she exclaimed when she twisted an ankle in her high heels. She continued limping along the tall columns and headed towards the closest double door. When inside, she checked to make sure the heel hadn't broken and continued towards the Parole Hall. It had been a while since Cecilie had been to police headquarters. After they had moved the division for Crimes Against Persons, in everyday language known as the Homicide Unit, to Sydhavnen, it was only when all hell broke loose that she was ever called in here for a meeting. These were always nerve-racking, not only due to the scoldings but because the place, with its dark colonnades and marble floors with swastika-like patterns, seemed like something Hitler would have appreciated. Hitler and then the National Police Commissioner. Who were one and the same.

She entered the Parole Hall, which was packed with uniforms with numerous stars on their shoulders. More than she herself had obtained. Most of them stood with a glass in their hand, conversing. It was as though the voices were thrown around in the windowless room in an infernal squawking. Cecilie gasped for air. It was steaming hot in here. She looked around. There were no familiar faces and she felt like slipping away before anybody could spot her. She noticed the National Police Commissioner, who was standing further inside the hall. It was impressive that there were uniform sizes that fit his humongous body. He was in the company of Karstensen, who wasn't exactly slim either. The newly appointed Commissioner of Copenhagen Police, Palsgaard, who had taken over from Volmer Bangsgaard, and John Nyholm were standing right next to them. She was surprised that Karstensen had been invited now that he had retired, but perhaps that was more of an indication that the old boys tended to stick together. She thought that the politest thing to do would be to greet the National Police Commissioner and thank him for his invitation. At that moment, a young muscular man with a beard joined the group. They all greeted him warmly. Cecilie recognised him. His name was Ryan Jensen and he had been hand-picked from the Security and Intelligence Service by the National Police Commissioner and appointed as the head of the new Travel Team. Travel Team 2.0, as it had been announced. So far, the most impressive case they had managed to solve had been a few battering ram burglaries in the dark Jutland. For her sake, Ryan and his team could stay there, Cecilie thought, as she dragged herself over to the National Police Commissioner and his crowd of people.

"I just wanted to say hello," Cecilie said, extending her hand. The National Commissioner just stared as though he needed a moment to place her before greeting her.

"And thank you for the invitation. That was very kind of you."

"You're welcome," he said measuredly. Cecilie greeted everyone, encountering a wall of glances.

"I understand that we've got a nasty murder," said Palsgaard. "Are we any closer to solving the case?"

"We're working very hard on it."

"The murder in Saxogade?" Ryan asked.

Cecilie nodded.

"Look no further than her immediate circle of acquaintances, and I guarantee you'll find him there."

Palsgaard and Karstensen nodded. And the National Police Commissioner sent Ryan an appreciative glance.

"I would have solved that case in no time had it been on my watch," Karstensen said, winning a couple of smiles from the others. "But the reins have been passed on."

Cecilie smiled dutifully. At that moment, the musical event was announced by a middle-aged man at the opposite end of the room. The Ladies' Choir, the Police Sirens, swarmed in through the door and lined up in a row in front of the guests, who clapped and whistled at them. They were wearing the same uniform as Cecilie.

"I wonder what they're going to sing?" she heard someone ask behind her. Cecilie looked at John, who had positioned himself close to her.

"No clue," she answered in surprise.

"Perhaps some rap. Like the one that goes: 'Fucked my brother . . .' You know that one?"

Cecilie felt her mouth go dry. "I don't think so, no. I didn't know you listened to rap music, John." John smiled with his thin lips. "I listen to everything. Nothing escapes my attention."

She shifted her gaze away from him and looked towards the choir, which had begun to sing. It didn't sound good, but, on the other hand, it didn't sound terrible either. There was no reason for her to stand there fluttering in the wind, so Cecilie started making her way to the bar. She reached a couple of tables upon which stood several rows of wine glasses with red and white wine respectively. She considered asking the bartender for some mineral water, but John's comment had demanded something stronger. She took a glass of white wine, which she guzzled down. The wine was both sour and lukewarm, but it didn't prevent her from taking another one.

"Cecilie Mars?" the man standing next to her said. Cecilie turned around to take a look at him. He was her age and had just as many stars on his shoulders. Only he had more of a belly, which probably meant he sat behind a desk in some division or other.

"Simon Kyndby, National Police," he said, extending his hand. Cecilie greeted him.

"Have we met before?"

"I'd be lying if I said yes," he said, winking at her. "But I wish we had."

"And yet you recognise me?"

"Of course. You're famous. Everybody's talking about you," he said, giving her arm a squeeze.

"More like infamous," she said.

"Well, perhaps," he said, laughing as his eyes tried to catch her gaze. Cecilie looked up towards the choir.

"They sing pretty well, don't they?"

"I haven't the faintest clue. But it's always wonderful seeing women in uniform."

"Oh."

Simon leaned towards her.

"If you ever need to spar about anything, anything at all, my door is always open. Day and night. You can get my direct telephone number."

The choir stopped, and everyone applauded. Cecilie put her glass down and clapped her hands with them. She hoped that Simon would soon leave, but instead she felt his hand on one of her buttocks. Cecilie looked at him.

"Would you be so kind as to remove your hand before I break your fingers?"

Simon removed it immediately.

"Well, well, a little prudish, aren't we?" he said, and retreated.

Cecilie took another glass. This time she chose red wine, which wasn't any less sour. The applause began once again when the evening's speeches commenced. Cecilie smiled at the sight of the Minister of Justice, Beatrice Klerke, who unfolded her speech notes and cheerfully addressed the audience. Cecilie hadn't seen Klerke since the Minister had personally offered her the position as head of Homicide. Beatrice Klerke was perfectly aware of all the cases that John had attempted to get Cecilie nailed for. But instead of putting her on probation and charging her, Klerke had put the Independent Police Complaints Authority's investigation on hold and pensioned off Karstensen. Beatrice Klerke concluded her speech and received a round of applause. The National Police Commissioner didn't look too thrilled at the sight of all the attention the Minister was receiving at his event. After Beatrice Klerke had done the rounds of greetings, she continued towards the bar. Cecilie had a growing sense of panic the closer the Minister got to her.

"Hey," she said, and was already inwardly cursing herself.

"Cecilie, I'm very happy to see you," Beatrice Klerke said in her artificial voice as she smiled measuredly. There was a reason why she was referred to as The Ice Queen, only emphasised further by her steel-grey hair, her narrow face with the high cheek bones, and the impeccable laser-sharp suit that she always wore.

"Saame . . . to . . . you. Great speech," Cecilie managed to say a little nervously.

"Oh, it's just a bunch of nonsense and rigmarole, a blow job for the big shots," Beatrice Klerke answered. "Have you managed to settle into your new position?"

"Yes, absolutely. We're busy, but we'll manage," Cecilie said sheepishly.

"And how have they received you? All those rejected males?" Klerke nodded towards the National Police Commissioner and his party. Cecilie glanced over and saw that they were all staring.

"Well, I think they just have to get used to it. To me."

"That was a very diplomatic response," she said as she gave Cecilie's shoulder a little squeeze. "But you won't get far with that. It's always hard to seize power. Especially for a woman. All women in leading positions are pioneers. It's sad but true. We have to fight for our lives. Sometimes quite literally."

"The latter I know how to do."

"Which is why you were selected for the job. Remember: You're not alone. Have you considered joining one of the network groups for female leaders in the bureau?"

Cecilie shook her head. "Not yet. I don't think I've had enough time to familiarise myself with those options."

"You should. It would help you in so many ways," said Klerke. "Once again, it was very nice seeing you, Cecilie."

"Thank you. It was nice seeing . . ." Cecilie watched the Minister, who was already busy continuing her rotation of the guests. Cecilie caught sight of John, who stood glaring at her. This time she returned his gaze and kept it until John suddenly got terribly busy checking the tips of his shoes.

13

He sat in the dark car staring at the brown leather briefcase lying on the passenger seat next to him. It contained everything he would need tonight. Last time he had been fully confident. But it turned out he had forgotten some very essential things. He had overestimated himself. Been a fool. A pathetic little idiot. A baby. A dimwit. A loser. He hit himself on the side of the head to get his chaotic train of thoughts to stop. It was better to check the whole thing one more time. He opened his briefcase and took out the CD, which he inserted into the stereo system of the car. It was a mistake that he hadn't brought any music, but it was because of this that he had felt drawn to Britney's voice on the radio. She had sent him in the right direction with "Oops! . . . I Did It Again." Her affectionate girly voice now filled the car's interior as she moaned her way through the hit from 1999, "Baby One More Time."

He looked into his bag and pulled out the big Japanese Yaxell knife. The blade consisted of 167 layers of Damascus steel and glistened like the scales of a snake in the dark. He put the knife down on the seat and took out the glass with ether and the rag. He made sure that there was plenty. Anaesthetising the moths was an artform. They shouldn't just sleep their way through the whole thing. That was no fun. He placed the glass and the rag next to the knife and took out the bag with clothes. Clothes for him. And clothes for her. He hoped he had found the right size. From his observations he had noticed that she had put on some weight. He made sure that he had brought plenty of cable ties with him. It would be hell if one of them broke while she was struggling and he wasn't able to secure her back down again. That would ruin everything. He dug into the bag and produced a small leather case. This time he had managed to remember it.

"*Hit me baby one more time*," beautiful Britney sang. He unzipped the leather case and looked at the surgical instruments the dissection set contained. The scalpel, the pair of scissors, the tissue hooks—they were all there. He glanced into the briefcase and made sure that he had remembered the empty glass with the screw cap. Yes, it was all ready. Now it was just a matter of patiently waiting for the moth to appear. *Out with the butterfly net*, he laughed to himself.

14

It was 11 before Cecilie, one of the last guests, left the Parole Hall. She struggled not to stumble in her high heels. Why the hell did she have to have that last drink? Or the one before that? Luckily, the National Police Commissioner and his buddies had gone, so they hadn't been able to witness her increasing intoxication. Cecilie continued across the open rotunda. It was a bit warmer now, and the alcohol helped to brace herself against the cold. Perhaps she had some leftover pizza at home? her reptile brain started thinking. Or maybe she could drive past Venezia on the way? When she made it to the car park, she rummaged through her pockets for the car key. Suddenly, she was caught in the headlights of a parked car further ahead. Cecilie shielded her eyes with her hand as she looked for the key. When she finally found it, she dropped it on the ground. She bent down to pick it up as the car continued to blind her.

"What the hell does he think he's doing?" Cecilie mumbled as she managed to unlock the car door. There came a short honk from the car. She turned around and extended her arms. "What the hell's your problem?"

The side window rolled down and a gloved hand motioned her to come closer to the car. If it was horny Simon, she'd give him a piece of her mind. Perhaps actually live up to her threat of breaking his fingers. Cecilie looked in and saw a middle-aged man wearing a dark suit with a shirt and tie and resembling that which he, in fact, was: a driver.

"Okay, you caught my attention. What now?"

The window behind him rolled down and Beatrice Klerke's pale face appeared from the darkness.

"Do you have a moment?"

Cecilie sat down in the back seat of the Minister's car. It was wonderfully warm in there, and she picked up the faint scent of perfume. She breathed in hard through her nose and tried to appear as sober as possible.

"What'ss thisss all abouttt?" she said, slurring her words.

"A small tip," Beatrice said, tapping the folder with the brown cover lying on the seat between them.

"Something that involves me?" Cecilie asked, looking at the folder.

"Not this time, no, although I hear that John Nyholm is bombarding the prosecution and whoever else he can get hold of with accusations against you. He's not your biggest fan."

"Fuck John!" she said, and immediately covered her mouth. "I'm sorry, I apologise, it just burst out of me."

"I've heard worse curse words. But watch out for him."

"I already do. So, what's the tip?"

Beatrice Klerke's eyes grew narrow. "A rotten apple in Parliament."

"So your tip has to do with a politician?" Cecilie asked in surprise.

"Yes, unfortunately. An otherwise well-liked colleague from one of the opposition parties who has managed to slip up big time. And not just once."

Cecilie rubbed her temples. "Okay, but isn't there some sort of administrative procedure when it comes to politicians? The President of the Danish Parliament? The Executive Committee, waiver of immunity, and all that stuff? Maybe you need to contact your own people in the Ministry, or the prosecution?"

"No, I've got the exact right one. You. Aside from the fact that this conversation has never taken place."

Cecilie took a deep breath.

"Is this some sort of quid pro quo?"

"Quid pro quo? For what exactly?"

"What do I know? For placing me in Karstensen's job."

"As far as I'm concerned, that position has always belonged to you. You just needed help attaining it. Which I contributed to, entirely for free. What I expect in return is that you solve the crimes that come your way and go after the perpetrators, no matter who they are or how they land on your desk. I need a head of Homicide who doesn't fear navigating in very deep water. And who isn't afraid of going up against the biggest and strongest adversaries. Have I judged you correctly, Cecilie?"

"I'm not afraid of anyone. That includes politicians," she answered calmly. "What is the case about?"

"I assume you know who Mogens Berg is?"

"The leader of the Democratic Coalition. Who doesn't know that? He must be one of the oldest members of Parliament."

"There are still a few others who have been there longer than Mogens. But yes, he has a long history in Parliament. Even though I don't agree with most of his ideological views, I have to admit, he is a skilled politician."

"So what has he done? It must be pretty bad since we're sitting here. I mean, aren't sitting here."

Beatrice Klerke nodded. "It's a known fact that as a woman it is necessary to keep Mogens at a distance when he has a little something to drink."

"He's the tongue-in-your-ear type?"

"Sometimes more than that, but yes, that type."

"I thought that had petered out of most parties."

"We're trying. But it still resembles a pigsty if you ask me. When it comes to Mogens, things go deeper. He has his contacts in the police headquarters, among other things. Episodes that should be investigated are swept under the carpet. In other words, someone is protecting Mogens Berg. Which I, as the nation's Minister of Justice, cannot tolerate."

"That's understandable. But wouldn't it be better if you approached the National Police Commissioner yourself?"

Klerke shot a glance at her. "Haven't you been listening at all?"

"Yes, yes, but I just don't know how wise it would be for me to go up against the National Police Commissioner himself because of something that might have taken place at a Christmas lunch in Parliament. I am sorry if I disappoint you."

"I understand your concern. If I were in your position, I would have been scared to death. But we are talking about things that are more serious than what may have happened at a Christmas lunch." She drummed her fingers on the folder.

"Is that something I should see?"

"Only if you agree to take the case."

Cecilie looked out the window as she thought things through. The wisest thing to do would be to climb out the car. But if she did that, what would happen next time John Nyholm approached the prosecution with a case against her?

"If this conversation has never taken place, then there's nothing preventing you from briefing me about its contents. In summary."

Klerke nodded. "In summary? Mogens beats up prostitutes."

"Beats up? How? Are we talking S/M or what?"

"We're talking Mogens selects brothels with vulnerable girls. Immigrants, girls without residency permits. Girls who have already been exposed to this and that. He is utterly systematic in his way of finding them. Once he has found his victim, he starts destroying her. The assaults get nastier and nastier and start to resemble torture. Once Mogens has got tired of beating up his victim, he finds another one." Beatrice Klerke opened the folder and found a photograph, which she handed over to Cecilie. The picture showed a Slavic woman whose naked body was covered with big bruises. Her upper lip had been cut and one of her eyes was swollen and dark purple.

"Nikita is her name. Mogens's latest victim."

"Where did you get all this information?"

"I have a big network both inside and outside the division."

"How come none of them have ever spoken out about this?"

"Like I said, Mogens is good at finding the most vulnerable ones. The ones who think they don't have any rights, which they actually don't when their attacker is a man like Mogens. I know of a case where he managed to deport a woman who had tried to report him."

"So what else is in the folder?"

"So you have decided to proceed with the case?"

"If I determine that there is a case, then yes."

Beatrice Klerke opened the folder and numerous pictures poured out onto the back seat. "There must be more than twenty victims, each one more badly beaten up than the last."

It was a nauseating sight and Cecilie started boiling inside. "And all of these are his work?"

"Each and every one. Mogens knows how to swing his belt when he doesn't use his fists."

"Get them to contact me and I'll see to their reports."

Beatrice Klerke smiled forbearingly. "Don't you think you're being a little naïve now, Cecilie?"

"In what way?"

"If you're going to make an impact on a powerful man like Mogens, you'd better hit hard, or he'll just get right back on his feet and go for your jugular. You wouldn't survive a single day if you were to press charges against him based on this background."

"What did you have in mind, then?"

Beatrice Klerke moved closer. "He's gotta be caught in the act. Nikita has agreed to meet with him again."

"And risk getting beaten up again?"

"Yes."

"That's brave. Or stupid."

"It is the only way we can stop him. She is doing it because she doesn't want other girls to get into the same situation."

"How had you envisioned this was going to transpire?"

"When Mogens makes an appointment with her, you'll receive a text message with the place and time. From there it's just a matter of moving into arrest." Beatrice Klerke took her hand. "When Mogens is charged with this offence, which he won't be able to escape from, we'll get all the girls to come forward. Then suddenly their charges will carry much more weight."

Cecilie pulled her hand back.

"I . . . Mogens is your political adversary, isn't he?"

"And? Do you think this is just something I've thought up to get at him?"

"No, no, I'm just wondering if there is a better way to do this. A way that's more by the book."

"By the book? You? Cecilie Mars?" Klerke said, and laughed.

Cecilie shrugged her shoulders. "I want a fresh start in this new job. Do the right things in the right way."

"Good luck with that," Beatrice said drily. "The past won't get washed away, Cecilie. Sooner or later we'll all have to pay for our sins. The only thing that matters is whether we manage to do something halfway decent before that happens."

"Amen," Cecilie said in an ironic tone, and got out of the car. "I'm going to have to think about this."

"Cecilie, that text message will soon come. Then it'll all be up to you."

15

He stood in the dark low-ceilinged bedroom and put on the white coveralls. The heavy material rustled as he pulled the hood over his head and zipped it up. Together with the goggles and the mask that covered his face, his entire body was hermetically sealed. He was already sweating and sensed the moist heat spreading underneath his suit as it soaked his clothes. It was as though his own bodily fluids made the situation safe. It was like returning to the womb, protected by amniotic fluid, cut off from the outside world in a sensual calmness. Nothing could get to him here. No insults, no failure, no loss of dignity. In the suit he was safe. Nothing could slip inside of it, nor could it slip out, which was important when someone like him was keeping an eye on his DNA with the utmost care.

A distressed moan reached him, followed by the sound of a sigh coming from the bed. He turned around and looked at the middle-aged woman who lay strapped to the bed. Tine Larsen, fastened with cable ties to the four bedposts, still unconscious from the ether. He edged his way past the piles of clothes in the filled-up bedroom that was a mess just like the rest of the cottage. He moved the bedside table with the hideous lamp and the full ashtray away from the bed. Then he caught sight of a teddy bear at the headboard, which he had overlooked. He tossed it into the corner with the other stuffed animals that had filled the bed. Tine's eyelids, thick with a layer of blue eye shadow, started to quiver.

In a few seconds she'd open her eyes. He retreated from the bed so that he wouldn't be the first thing she'd catch sight of. He wanted to give her the chance to return to herself. Feel the confused sensation of regaining consciousness. Recognise the contours of her bedroom and understand that she was lying in a bed. Believe that the encounter with him had been nothing but a bad dream. Until she realised she was tied up.

Tine opened her eyes and gasped for air with a small snort. She attempted to get up, but her strapped arms and feet prevented her from doing so. The panic began to spread across her face, and she looked around . . . He couldn't have wished for a better scream. A primitive scream, all the way down from her midriff. A gurgling shout that grew increasingly louder. Tine pulled at the cable ties and the wrought-iron bed creaked.

"Tiiine," his voice could be heard saying through the close-fitting mask, "there, you woke up . . ."

"Let me go . . . !" she shouted before letting out a scream.

He shook his head lightly. "You know perfectly well that won't happen."

"Let me go, you psychopath. You fucking bastard!"

"Please try to stop cursing. You don't even know me. I, on the other hand, know you extremely well."

Tine tried to get loose, but instead, the cable ties cut deeper into her fleshy wrists.

"Help!" she cried, perplexed. "Help!" she sobbed loudly.

"I don't think anyone can hear you, Tine. Most people have shut their cottages this time of year. Your neighbours are sitting comfortably at home in their apartments, dreaming about next season."

"What the hell do you want?" she sobbed.

"To see to you," he said, and cocked his head. He looked at her naked, somewhat corpulent body that shone white in the darkness. The black fishnet stockings were a few sizes too small yet he still somehow managed to pull them on her. The result hadn't been pretty, and Tine's thighs looked like strung-up hams.

"What on earth have you been filling yourself with?" he asked.

"What . . . what do you mean?"

"Look at yourself, Tine. Even for a tired old lady you're in horrible shape." He leaned forward and pinched her stomach fat with his gloved hand.

"Haven't you been able to control yourself? Have you just stuffed your mouth, little piggy?" He gave a hard slap to her heavy breast, which rocked back and forth. "Quivering—like jelly."

"Let me go, I'm begging you," she cried.

He poked his finger into the fading tattoo on her upper arm.

"Why, Tine? Why have you blemished your body in this way? You were once so pretty."

Something awakened in Tine's gaze.

"Do we know each other?"

"Everybody knows you, Tine. Even though you are practically unrecognisable." He leaned forward and brushed her thick blue fringe to the side.

"Just look at you now. Isn't that something you do when you are twelve, and not fifty like you? And the nose piercing." He took hold of the ring in the wing of her nose and pulled it. Tine screamed when he tore it out. Blood streamed from the open wound and ran down her lips and coloured her teeth as she wailed. He threw the ring on the floor.

"Somebody should have removed that a long time ago. Only bulls wear nose rings, not heifers like you. Are you ready, Tine?"

She continued crying.

"I asked you something," he said, and walked to the foot of the bed where his briefcase lay. He opened it.

"For . . . for what?"

"For what? What do you think, imbecile?" he said, laughing. He rummaged through his bag until he found his phone.

"To have your picture taken, of course. Which you like, don't you, Tine?"

16

The voices from the apartment next door awakened Cecilie from a heavy dream. When they weren't fighting, they were fucking at the same loud volume. Her phone buzzed on the bedside table, and she tumbled out of bed as she picked it up.

"Cecilie speaking," she said as she stretched her limbs in the dark room.

"Morning, boss," Heino's voice said. "Are you up?"

She looked at the display on her screen—it was past seven—and thought she better lie, "Of course, I've just completed my morning workout."

"Boss, you don't work out in the mornings or at any other time of the day for that matter."

"Why are you calling, Heino?"

"We've just received word of a death in an allotment out on Amager. Some construction workers found a woman's body."

"Are there any indications as to whether it was a murder or an accident?"

"I don't know the details, but we've got a patrol out there. Should I bring Henrik or Joakim along?"

"No, text me the address and we'll meet there," she said, and hung up.

Cecilie walked over to the window and drew the curtains. The view was so depressing that she felt like closing them again. A grey rainy fog lay heavily across the landscape and erased the contours of the city.

Everything indicated that today was going to be just as cold as the previous day.

The couple next door had stopped fighting and it looked like that was going to be the only good news of the day. She checked her text messages on her phone as she went out to the bathroom. Beatrice Klerke still hadn't contacted her. Cecilie pulled off her panties and sat down on the toilet to pee. If the pictures of the abused prostitutes were real, there was nothing more that Cecilie would have liked to do than handcuff the bastard who had done it. It was more the way in which Klerke had confronted her with the case. The whole political agenda that was behind her approaching Cecilie. She didn't even know whether she could trust Klerke's story, that Mogens Berg was a monster who everyone was protecting. Including her boss. Cecilie started googling Mogens Berg. There were various pictures to be found from his political life that stretched across a few decades. Mogens resembled so many of the Parliament types. Flabby with bags under his eyes, which indicated far too many committee meetings. She read that a few years ago he had been the Minister of Transportation, a fact that she had missed completely. But then again, she wasn't interested in politics. She found a couple of his family pictures. In one of them he was standing with his wife, his grown-up children, and a handful of grandchildren. Cecilie shut off her phone and finished off in the bathroom. She still wasn't sure what she'd do when she received the text message from Beatrice Klerke twenty minutes later on her way down in the elevator. It was exactly as cold as she had imagined it would be and she started jogging across the footpath to the car park. When she reached the car, she heard a voice, "Hey, yo!" Cecilie spun around. Her hand was already on its way to the gun holster on her right side.

"Oh, it's you," she said.

Paki Allan stopped the scooter that just barely protruded under his big body. He sniffed hard. "On your w-way to w-work?"

"Yup," said Cecilie, continuing to the Golf, which she unlocked.

"Y-you've got more likes. It's going t-totally viral, that video."

"Delete that shit, Allan. Shouldn't you be on your way to school?" she said, opening her door.

"I guess. Or I c-could go with you?"

She sent him a half-smile. "Oh?"

"You h-have to get a head start i-if you wanna be good at something."

"Start by going to school."

"W-will we g-get to be partners then?"

Cecilie didn't want to ruin his cheerful mood. "I don't have any part-ners. But we could work together, catch some bad guys. But not until you've got a badge," she said, tapping the ID card that hung from a string around her neck.

"Does it have emergency response?" Allan asked, pointing at the Golf.

"Of course," she said, and got into the car. When she reached the end of the road, she glanced at the rearview mirror towards Allan, who had remained rooted to the spot. She briefly turned on the flashing blue lights. Allan extended one of his hands in the air and jumped with excite-ment, as if she had lit the Christmas tree in Copenhagen City Square for him.

The morning traffic through the city was a killer and it took forever to reach Nordvest and out to Amager Strandvej. When she finally got there, she turned at Vågestien, which was the address Heino had sent her. He was standing further down the road by a patrol car and lazily stuck his arm out the window. Cecilie parked in front of the entrance to the Amager Strand Allotment Association. The area was like a small oasis situated between the cold, newly built high-rise neighbourhood and the Prøvestenens industrial area by Øresund. It had been a while since the last time she was on Strandvejen, which had been at the opposite end, down by all the big, expensive houses inhabited by nouveau riche entrepreneurs and gangsters. A visit that she had tried to forget. Heino knocked on her car window and disrupted her thoughts. Cecilie got out of the car.

"I brought some coffee, but I managed to drink both cups. Damn, it's cold," he said, rubbing his hands.

"Is it that way?" she asked, pointing towards the tall gate to the allot-ment gardens.

"Yup, Konkyliestien. Patrols are down there to barricade the place off."

They walked through the gate.

"Which can't be that demanding a task. Is there anyone at all out here this time of year?"

"No, at least not legally."

They walked down the hard, narrow gravel road where the allotment gardens were situated side by side. Most of the owners had shut down their houses for the winter and the place resembled a ghost town.

"There seems to be some life in there," Heino said, pointing at a little red house where smoke was rising from the chimney. They continued down along the path until Cecilie stopped and looked around.

"Are you sure about the address?"

Heino took out his phone and checked it.

"Yes, Koralstien."

"You said Konkyliestien just before."

"We're already walking on bloody Konkyliestien."

"Are you sure?" she asked, sending him a glance as she started walking back to where they came from. Heino checked the map on his phone.

"I got it now. Boss, we have to make a right just over here. It's not a detour. Koralstien is just at the end of . . ."

When they reached Koralstien, they saw two uniformed officers standing together with a younger man in working clothes. One of the officers caught sight of Cecilie and greeted her.

"She was discovered in there," he said with a gloomy look.

"Is that the witness who discovered the corpse?" Cecilie asked as she looked over at the man in working clothes.

"Yes, he and a colleague were doing some roof work on one of the houses further down the road. An insurance claim that—"

"What was he doing in there, then?"

"Um . . . yes, well, he explained that they heard loud music coming from there yesterday. The same record was being played again and again. When they arrived here this morning and the music was still playing, he decided to go over and check that everything was okay. That was when he found . . . the corpse."

"And the door was open?"

"I . . . I haven't asked, but there were no signs of a break-in, so . . ."

"Okay. How many have been in there so far?"

"Only him and . . . us," he said, pointing at his partner. He was clearly struggling to get the words out. "She's . . . in bad shape. In the bedroom."

Cecilie opened the garden gate and looked towards the mailbox. TINE LARSEN, it said on the sign next to stickers with the rainbow flag and a pink unicorn. Below the little shed roof of a yellowing trapezoid sheet roof, there stood a chair next to a jar filled with a mountainous pile of cigarette stubs.

"'Happiness is not a destination. It's a way of life,'" said Heino, pointing at the sign with the text above the door. Cecilie pushed it open and entered the little kitchen, which was overflowing with dirty dishes.

"Looks like my place after the kids have been round," Heino said. They continued into the small living room, which, with the many pieces of furniture, resembled a junk room. Cecilie edged her way to the bedroom door. She remained standing in the doorway and looked over at the wrought-iron bed. Heino positioned himself behind her and they stared in silence at the corpse lying there. She could hear Heino's breathing change.

"You are kidding me," he said, letting out a heavy sigh.

"I'm sorry, Heino, but it's real."

"Do you see the same thing as me?"

"Cable ties on her ankles and wrists," she answered.

"Check."

"Naked except for a pair of fishnet stockings."

"Check."

"Injuries to her head, stomach, and groin. Presumably executed with a pointed weapon."

"Fucking check. Having one of those déjà-vu moments . . . looks like the woman we just found in Saxogade, doesn't it?"

"We have a monster on the loose," Cecilie said, walking over to the bed. "Who the hell does something like this?"

"Yet another bastard in the long line of sick bastards on the loose out there."

She looked around in the cluttered room. A jogging outfit had been folded neatly on the chair in the corner. "I bet he drugged her and undressed her, precisely the same way he did with Kristina Sand." Heino took a deep breath.

"Okay, so what the hell do we have here? There is no indication of a fight in the living room, no sign of a break-in, just like in Saxogade. He's managed to get in without any hindrance, drugged her, and then tied her down to the bed."

Cecilie lifted her index finger. "But first he removed her clothes, except for the fishnet stockings, and then he tied her down."

"And her panties?" Heino asked, pointing at the corpse's bloody groin.

"If it's the same son of a bitch, then we know where we can find them."

"Holy cow."

"Should I do the honours?" Cecilie shook her head and took out a pair of disposable gloves from the pocket of her leather jacket. She bent down over the corpse and looked at the mutilated face. She carefully forced the mouth open and stuck two fingers deep into the throat.

"Don't mind me, Heino," she said as she pulled the bloody material out from the corpse's mouth.

"Fuck, fuck, fuck, boss."

"Yes, fuck, fuck, fuck. I'll get in touch with Ole while you call Forensics. That is, Dahlstrup personally. We'll need him and all his little uniforms to come out here. They're going to have to find something we can use. I don't care if it means taking the whole house apart."

"Roger."

Cecilie walked through the living room and out the front door. The rain hit hard on the sheet roof.

"And, Heino," she shouted after him, "we're going to dissect all the allotment gardens out here too. Bring the dogs out."

"Roger," Heino said again, appearing in the doorway. "Should I get started on the neighbours? Ask who may have seen something?"

"Yes, but first get hold of the team," said Cecilie as she stepped out into the rain. She looked at the nearest high-rise building across the street.

"They have a good view of the allotment gardens from over there. We need someone to go over and talk with them. The car dealer down at the corner of Amager Strandvej and Prags Boulevard has a surveillance camera, like the Danish Transport Authority has one over at Femøren," she said, pointing in the opposite direction.

"Pretty impressive."

"What?"

"That you know where their cameras are."

"And your point is?" she asked coolly.

"Nothing."

"Then get your ass moving, Heino."

17

It was 11 p.m. They had been hard at work on Koralstien the last fourteen hours. Cecilie had set up her command stall under the lean-to roof. From there she could follow the development of clues and frequently get updates from her team. A flash tore through the darkness and at first Cecilie thought it came from the forensic team until another flash appeared from the street. She whistled to the two officers in the front garden and motioned for them to see to it. The officers ran out to the street and the next moment she heard an agitated voice talking about freedom of the press and a whole bunch of other things that faded away. The first couple of journalists had already crowded around the garden that afternoon. Cecilie hadn't told them anything other than that they were investigating a suspicious death. But the journalists weren't dumb. They could surmise from the number of officers and detectives on site that there was talk of a big case. "Cecilie," said Dahlstrup when he stepped out the door and took her aside. The head of the forensics team put down the hood of his blue coveralls and stuffed his latex gloves into his pocket. "We're leaving now. I promise to return soon."

"It turned into a long day. Did you find anything, Dahlstrup?"

"We found something, yes, but whether it's something you can use is, as you know, another matter."

He sent her a tired smile. She didn't know how old Dahlstrup was, only that he had been in the service for as long as she could remember.

"But does it look promising?"

He shrugged his shoulders.

"A bloodstain on one of the baseboards in the kitchen. It could derive from food or herself or the perpetrator."

"Anything else?"

"A footprint outside by the window."

"Most probably from the construction worker who found her or from one of the officers. Anything else?"

"Hair, and something that could be seminal fluid on a couch pillow. I've made sure that we bring the tracksuit from the chair in the bedroom. If the perpetrator removed it, he may have left traces. I'll ask the lab to double-check the Saxogade victim's clothes."

"Thank you, Dahlstrup. Fingers crossed."

"Let's hope the perpetrator has been sloppy. Goodnight," he said, and disappeared across the front lawn. Heino entered through the gate. He briefly greeted Dahlstrup and walked up to Cecilie.

"Anything new?"

"The car dealer, the one on the corner. I finally got hold of him. Had to go all the way out to Sundby, where he lives. He was cool. Returned with me and gave me the SIM cards to their two cameras facing Strand-vejen. They contain the last seventy-two hours."

"You know how to charm them, Heino. Well done."

"He also said that there is a scaffolding company at number 18 that he knows has surveillance. Maybe their recordings go further back. I'll check up on that tomorrow."

Cecilie nodded in approval and looked over at the open front door. It was dark inside and the darkness stared back at her.

"Is there anything we've missed?"

"Probably, but what are you thinking of?"

"Could he have followed her? Or waited for her to return home?"

"That would be too risky in a crowded building complex like the one in Saxogade, but here . . . ?"

"Yes, perhaps."

"Let's assume that he runs the risk. His modus operandi is that he attacks his victims outside of their homes and drugs them. Then he uses their keys and drags them inside while they're still unconscious."

"Tine Larsen seemed like a heavy lady. Kristina Sand was stocky."

"So what? He's strong. He's motivated. The adrenaline is pumping inside him."

Heino shook his head. "How about traces outside, then? If I were the perpetrator, I'd make sure to get inside as quickly as possible. Be in control of the situation."

Cecilie nodded. "Yes, it's probably very important to him to feel in control. But then the victim and perpetrator must have known each other. Otherwise, she'd never let him in in the middle of the night, would she?"

"What did Ole estimate as time of death?"

"Around midnight. Precisely the same as he concluded for Kristina's death."

At that moment, her phone buzzed. She took it out and looked at the display.

"Speak of the devil," she said, and answered the phone.

"That was pretty quick, Ole, even for you."

Ole moaned at the other end of the line. "You better come over right away."

"Do you have something for us?"

"Maybe," he answered, and continued to sigh. "I may have misinterpreted something."

"Misinterpreted? What do you mean?"

"The lesions, among other things . . ."

"You mean on Tine Larsen?"

"No, the other one . . . Kristina Sand."

"But aren't you doing an autopsy on Tine?"

"Yes, of course. That's how I discovered that my first impression . . . wasn't entirely correct," he answered reluctantly.

"But in relation to what?"

"Come on over and I'll explain it to you," he said, and hung up.

Cecilie put her phone back into her pocket and shook her head.

"What was that all about?" Heino asked.

"Ole has either lost it completely or he's onto something. He wants me to go in immediately."

"Now? Want me to come with you?" Heino asked, and yawned.

Cecilie shook her head. "No, you go on home, Heino. See you tomorrow."

Half an hour later, Cecilie parked in front of the Teilum building, which lay deserted in the darkness. In reception, the night watch was expecting her and sent her downstairs to Ole. The walk down the long hallway with the autopsy tables gave her goose bumps. From the last room she could hear the melody from Gershwin's *Rhapsody in Blue* through the half-open door, which didn't make it any less chilling. Cecilie pushed the door open and stepped inside. Ole was standing with his back to her in his white smock, which was lit up from the glow of the strong projector in the ceiling. On the autopsy table lay Tine Larsen's corpse, and on a stretcher next to her, lay Kristina Sand.

"Hi, Ole," said Cecilie. Ole turned around in shock.

"Oh my God, you gave me a scare, Cecilie."

"I didn't think you forensic medics were spooked so easily."

"I am," he said, as he turned down the music on his iPhone. "Come on over and have a look," he said, motioning her to come closer. Cecilie positioned herself next to Ole and looked down at Tine Larsen's corpse. Now that the blood had been washed off, the many cuts were clearly visible.

"What is it you want to show me?"

"Labia minora," he said, pointing towards the groin.

"Her labia?" Cecilie said, squinting her eyes.

"Don't bother trying to see them. They're gone."

"What do you mean?"

Ole took out a magnifying glass and held it towards the corpse's abdomen.

"Even though the abdomen has been damaged, it is still easy to discern the fine cuts."

"Are you saying that the perpetrator cut off her labia?"

Ole nodded. "Yes, and he's gone out of his way. He has used a surgical instrument, a scalpel, or something similar."

"And was that one of the first things that happened?"

"Yes. The scars from the knife cuts subsequently hit the scars from the scalpel, which are on each side of the vaginal opening."

"Jesus Christ," Cecilie said, trying to collect herself. "What did you mean when you said you had been mistaken in relation to Kristina Sand? Has she been through the same thing?"

"Both yes and no," Ole answered as he pulled Cecilie over to the stretcher. "Because the area around the groin is so damaged, I assumed that the missing outer labia on the left side of Kristina Sand's corpse was due to lesions deriving from the murder weapon. But upon closer examination," he said as he held the magnifying glass above her groin, "I'm quite certain that the perpetrator subsequently cut it off with the murder weapon."

"Is it the same knife that he used to murder them?"

"The same type, at least. His stabs seem more controlled. The angle seems more even on the ones given to Tine Larsen."

"More skilled," Cecilie said ironically.

"It would seem so, yes. This murder seems more targeted, but aside from that it's the same modus operandi in terms of the execution."

"And has he . . ." She shook her head before continuing. "Has he taken them with him?"

"We have examined the bodily orifices of both women for foreign objects and found nothing. I assume he did. Unless Forensics have discovered something on the scene . . ."

She shook her head.

"I remember the case you had with the guy who would hide the women's breasts that he had cut off in his freezer."

Cecilie nodded.

"Morten Pier Nielsen, but that was in his mother's freezer."

"Oh, that's right. Well, there you go," Ole said, giving a little smile. "I guess he isn't out doing this sort of thing again now."

"Morten is dead. I personally sent him to the Æsir gods for whom he was sacrificing the women."

Ole looked concerned. "I certainly don't envy your job."

"I don't envy your job either."

Ole shrugged his shoulders. "The dead are easier to get along with."

"Will you send me the report as soon as you're done?"

Ole nodded and turned the volume of the Gershwin piece back up.

18

It was approaching 10 a.m. In the Homicide Unit, Cecilie was sitting on top of Henrik's desk and the team had gathered in a semicircle in front of her. There was a campfire feeling about the whole thing. Cecilie sipped the coffee that Henrik had brought her in his own personal cup. WORLD'S BEST GRANDPA, it said. They had gone through Ole's forensic report on Tine Larsen and all the unpleasant details it contained.

"Do we still need the information from NC3?" Cecilie asked.

"We still need the last bit, yes," Joakim answered.

"And we have no idea what's on Tine's computer or phone?"

"I could try calling them again."

"I sure as hell am happy to hear that you could try again, Joakim. We need to find out whether there is a connection between these two victims. The perpetrator may frequent their mutual circle of friends."

"I've already checked up on her social media accounts," Joakim answered.

"And?"

"Tine wasn't particularly active, neither on Facebook nor on Instagram. She only had a few followers. There were no links to Kristina Sand or to any possible mutual acquaintances."

"Thank you, Joakim." Cecilie turned her gaze towards Henrik, who straightened up in his chair. "What did you find out there?"

"We found a couple of residents who live there all year round."

"What did they say about Tine?"

"It was a mixed bag. One of them said that there was often a lot of noise and parties at the house, while another one said that Tine Larsen tended to keep to herself. But an elderly woman down at Konkyliestien said that she had noticed a man lurking around in the allotment garden a couple of weeks ago."

"Did she have a description of the lurker?"

"Either an undertaker or a real estate agent."

They all looked at Henrik.

"She thought so because he was wearing a long black coat."

"You've got one of those too, Henrik. Have you made a career change?" Heino asked, laughing.

Henrik looked at him and shook his head. "Mine is a navy-blue Mulberry, not that I'd ever expect you to be able to tell the difference."

"But none of them had heard or seen anything around the time of the murder?" Cecilie asked.

Henrik shook his head.

"Maybe the scaffolders caught him on their surveillance camera," said Heino. "Their storage building is right across from the car park at the allotment gardens."

"Have you talked to them?"

"I called them. I'm meeting up with Danny at noon. It sounds promising. He says their surveillance system stores the old footage for a week before it is overwritten."

"What's that? Will it give you a hard-on?" Joakim mumbled, and got an instant middle finger from Heino in response.

"Great. Look through it yourself before sending it to NC3," said Cecilie.

"That's going to take a while," Heino moaned. "I also have recordings from the car dealer."

"Then start with the scaffolding company. What about the traffic camera further down the street?"

"I'm on it, boss."

"Not fast enough, Heino. Are you losing your touch?"

"What about the press?" Henrik asked. "They were humming around out there. They keep calling us to ask questions about the two cases."

"About Kristina too?" Cecilie asked thoughtfully.

He nodded.

"The rumour about a serial killer on the loose is spreading like wildfire."

Cecilie put her coffee cup down on the desk. "How the hell did that happen?" She looked around at them all. "Who spoke about this?"

They all shook their heads dismissively.

"Nobody from here, boss. We may be stupid, but we're not that stupid."

"It has to be an officer or a goddamn forensic expert." She shook her head knowingly. "Okay, Henrik, get hold of Dennis Juhl from *Ekstra Bladet*, and tell him something—anything—that they can all quote."

"What am I allowed to say?"

"Tell him that we're investigating all aspects, and that evidence shows no connection between those two cases."

Jane appeared, and both Heino and Joakim smiled like two tomcats. Cecilie silently considered the possibility of getting them both castrated.

"Jane? To what do I owe the honour?" Cecilie asked.

"The press briefing."

"I have just made a statement that Henrik will send out."

"I meant the press briefing at the Commissioner's office."

"I see. Now?"

"Yes, Palsgaard is waiting," she said, and disappeared again.

Cecilie jumped off the desk.

"I hate it when those high-ranking guys look down on us mortals," said Henrik as he fidgeted restlessly in his chair.

"Don't have a heart attack over it, Henrik. I think the Commissioner just wants to go out and beam in front of the press, which is all well and good," she said as she collected her things. "*Vamos*, boys. That's Spanish and means get your asses moving."

19

Commissioner Palsgaard's office had the city's best view of the dock and was kitted out with designer furniture from Philippe Starck. He had acquired the futuristic furnishings from a deceased police chief—a story that he was fond of telling to those who were privileged enough to obtain an audience with him.

"Good to see you, Cecilie," he said, getting up from the chair behind his desk. "I apologise for pulling you away from your work like this."

The combination of his bony body, steel-grey suit, and small round glasses gave him the appearance of a shark.

"Please, sit down," he said, motioning to one of the chairs in front of his desk. "You know Ryan from the National Police Travel Team," he continued, smiling at the man who was sitting in the chair next to hers. Cecilie nodded towards Ryan and sat down. Her brain was working at turbo speed. What the hell was the Travel Team doing here?

"We met at the National Police Commissioner's reception," Ryan said. Her smile grew wider as her inner alarm system began beeping loudly.

"It was an excellent evening," said Palsgaard as he sat down behind the Plexiglas desk.

"There were perhaps a few too many speeches. Our dear Minister tends to be a little long-winded," he said, smiling. "You look tired, Cecilie, are we working you too hard?"

"No, I'm fine, thank you."

"Excellent. Yes, well, I realise that taking the reins from Karstensen is quite a handful."

"I'll manage. The Homicide Unit isn't exactly unknown territory for me."

"No, not at all. Cecilie has solved many cases in her time," he said, looking at Ryan. "And demonstrated great courage."

Ryan nodded. "Yes, I've certainly heard about Cecilie . . . and all the cases," he added with a smirk.

"And the pressure on the Homicide Unit hasn't decreased with the last two murders, I presume?"

"We have it under control," Cecilie said.

Palsgaard shook his head dramatically. "It is terrible. Inhuman. Reading the details truly turns your stomach." He rearranged the autopsy reports on the desk in front of him. She was surprised that Palsgaard had received those, and even read them. It was all very unsettling.

"This is hard to swallow even for a seasoned gentleman like me. I can't even begin to imagine what it's doing to you, Cecilie, having just acquired your new position. And as a woman."

"I have had similar cases, but yes, it is violent. That's why both cases have our full attention." She shifted in the chair. "I understand from Jane that you'd like for us to hold a press briefing."

"Yes, yes, we'll get to that," Palsgaard said, raising his arm dismissively. "But first . . ." He leaned back in his chair. "Personally, I never did understand why the Travel Team was shut down, which is why I'm so pleased to see its restoration, Ryan. And that you have got off to such a good start."

"Thank you. It comes with quite a bit of responsibility," Ryan said, smiling with satisfaction.

"That's why I'm delighted to be able to bid you and your team welcome."

Cecilie looked from Palsgaard to Ryan. "Welcome? Here? To what? I don't think I understand."

"No?" Palsgaard asked in surprise. "Cecilie, we are facing a potential serial killer of the worst kind," he added dramatically as he banged his fist on the reports.

"I am aware of the seriousness of the situation, and I guarantee you that we have everything under control. Getting new people on board would delay the investigation. We don't need any help, but thanks anyway, Ryan."

"Cecilie, I know that you are all dedicated and extremely professional, but it's in everyone's interest to catch him as fast as possible," Palsgaard said.

"I agree. He's got to be stopped right now or we'll have another case . . ."

"Which is why the Travel Team is taking over as of today."

"Taking over?" she asked, her jaw dropping. "But this is our case. My case."

He waved his hand. "Cecilie, there's no time for sensitive feelings or hurt pride. We are a united entity. We step in for one another. You and your team have done an excellent job in this initial phase, so the A-team can now take over."

Cecilie tried to get over the shock. "The A-team? I'm sorry, but handing over the entire network of cases would take even longer."

"We are familiar with most of it," Ryan quickly answered. "We are already in dialogue with NC3 and Forensics, and the Medico-Legal Institute has continuously kept us up to date . . ."

"It would have been nice to know who had access to confidential information. Especially since it seems someone's leaked it to the press," said Cecilie.

"It hasn't been coming from here. My team is professional."

Cecilie looked at Palsgaard appealingly. "It's one thing to have the information but another to be at the crime scene, talking to witnesses . . . We have several promising leads . . ."

"All of which you will hand over to Ryan. As soon as possible."

"This is going to set the investigation back years."

"Do you have a profile of the offender?" Ryan asked.

The question caught Cecilie off guard. "A profile? No. We're still in the early stages of the investigation. Even though there's a lot to indicate that we're dealing with the same perpetrator, we can't be certain. But we do have an idea about—"

"I don't mean mere hunches. I mean a solid profile upon which the investigation can be based. Have you managed to produce one yet? Have you?"

She didn't answer Ryan but instead looked at Palsgaard.

"If I may give my honest opinion, it is far too early in the investigation to start profiling . . ."

"Our criminal profiler has more than enough information to be able to summarise a comprehensive profile of the offender," said Ryan, pointing at a document in front of Palsgaard.

Palsgaard banged his fist on the pile of papers again and smiled. "The A-team, Cecilie, the A-team. They know what they're talking about. You can rest assured that the case is in good hands."

She sensed the rage rising within, but tried to compose herself.

"And what conclusion has your profiler reached, Ryan?"

"That's classified."

"I thought we were supposed to be on the same team."

Ryan shrugged his shoulders. "I guess I can share what we're going to announce at the press briefing this afternoon. We are dealing with a person with psychopathic features, impulsive and uncontrollable behaviour, with very few social skills. His modus operandi has a religious motive."

"Religious?" Cecilie exclaimed. "Based on what?"

"The genital mutilation, among other things."

She shook her head. "There's no evidence for that."

"Our profiler, Niels Vogel, has developed profiles for both the FBI and the German Federal Police, so I think—"

"That he's got it all wrong," Cecilie said, looking at Palsgaard. "It doesn't add up."

Ryan continued undauntedly. "According to Vogel, the individual derives either from the Middle East or the east coast of Africa. Both places have a long tradition of female circumcision."

Palsgaard nodded in approval. Cecilie looked at them both.

"I'm sorry, but that is not what this is all about."

"And how do you know?" Palsgaard asked.

"Female intuition?" Ryan mumbled.

"Experience," she said, staring at Ryan. "So perhaps you and the Travel Team ought to live up to your name and move on."

She shifted her gaze to Palsgaard. "I ask you to let us continue with the investigation. This has nothing to do with pride. If I believed that Ryan or that guy Vogel were right, I'd be the first to hand over the case, but honestly, this whole thing sounds like bullshit to me."

Palsgaard folded his arms and for a moment, it seemed as though he had listened to her. Cecilie sent him a hopeful smile.

"You disappoint me, Cecilie. As a leader you've got to be able to see beyond yourself. See everything from above. Accept your own limitations and not stand in the way. It's an important ability."

"But this is going to cost—"

"I expect a smooth transfer of the case from you and your team to Ryan and the Travel Team. Is that understood?"

"Loud and clear," said Cecilie, looking down at the floor.

20

The following day, Ryan and his detectives had moved into the Homicide Unit's open office space. Cecilie made sure to place them near her office so that she could keep a proper eye on them. From her seat behind her desk and with her door a bit ajar, she had a full view of the entire crew. The four men on Ryan's team resembled him with their pumped-up muscles and macho attitudes. The group looked more like a gang task force than a team of homicide detectives. The men chatted as they set up their stuff. Heino entered her office.

"Have you seen them, boss?" he said, pointing.

"I've done nothing else all day. Move over a little," she said, waving her hand.

"Did you go through the video recordings?"

"Yes. Unfortunately, there wasn't anything of use, neither from the car dealer nor the scaffolders."

Heino walked over to the desk and turned towards the open door. "I feel like pissing on their computers," he said, scratching his goatee.

"I sure hope they get started soon. Our perpetrator isn't waiting for them to install their computers."

"You do know that this is their first murder case, don't you?"

"I imagine that the head of police knows what they're doing."

Heino looked at her briefly to see whether she was serious.

"This project is doomed to fail. The big steroid-fuelled pieces of beef have been brought in from every district around because the local sheriffs want a piece of the National Police Commissioner's prestige project." He shook his head.

"Did you watch the press briefing with that guy Ryan?"

"No, but I have seen what all the news sites are saying."

"*Muslim Serial Killer on the Loose*, it said on *Ekstra Bladet*'s site," said Heino. "That headline must have generated a couple of clicks. I expect all the crazies will start calling us, don't you think?"

"Calling *them*," she said, nodding towards the door opening. "*We* are not allowed to do anything. Which means more wasted time. And even more grit in the machinery."

"But we've got do something! Dammit, boss, we can't just sit back and watch!"

"What do you want me to do, Heino?"

"I don't know," he said, gesturing resignedly. "Some boss-like thing . . ."

"Like?"

"Shooting them in the kneecaps?"

"Lend me your gun," she answered ironically.

A dark-complexioned man with a beard and a huge blue parka went over to Ryan's table. Cecilie immediately recognised Ismail. The two men greeted each other, and Ismail tossed his jacket aside and sat down next to Ryan.

"What do you know, NC3 seem to have no problem showing their face now," said Heino. "Fucking Ismail. It's been impossible getting him to come out here."

Cecilie didn't answer. "Did you manage to get anything out of them?"

"NC3?" He shook his head. "They still haven't opened Tine Larsen's phone for us. We can only hope that she called her murderer. At least then there might be a chance that they manage to solve the case," said Heino.

When he left her office, Cecilie continued observing Ryan and Ismail from her seat.

Ismail glanced in her direction every so often, and when he got up ten minutes later and put on his parka, Cecilie also got up and slipped out into the open office. She caught sight of Ismail at the opposite end of the room where he was waiting for the elevator. She hurried through the office and just managed to step into the elevator before the doors closed. Ismail looked at her in surprise.

"Ce-Cecilie . . ." he stammered as the elevator began to move.

"Ismail, how wonderful to finally see you," she said, and pressed the stop button. The elevator jumped as it stopped.

"What are you doing?"

"I thought we could have a brief word with each other. It's been a while since you've been by here. And you never called back either."

"I'm sorry . . . but I've been awfully busy," he answered, his eyes fluttering.

"But not too busy to greet the Travel Team. Should I be jealous?"

Ismail tried to smile back.

"They insisted . . . and I had some time to spare. Besides, there was nothing on Tine's phone. Nothing that they could use if that's what you wanted to know."

"Wow, Ismail," she said, opening her eyes wide. "Are you sharing confidential information? I would never have guessed that about you," she said ironically.

"Dammit, Cecilie."

"What is it, Ismail?"

He took a deep breath.

"Do you really want to know why I've been avoiding you?"

"Very much so."

"Because I am afraid."

"Afraid? Of whom?"

"Of you."

His answer took her by surprise, and she smiled.

"And why are you afraid of me, Ismail?"

He stared at her in silence.

"You can speak openly."

"Oh?" he said sceptically as he looked around in the compact elevator. "You have no idea?"

"No, not really."

"Okay, let me give you a hint. The song that's playing everywhere on the internet right now, Como's song. Jeremy's little brother's song."

Cecilie squinted her eyes. "It's incredible how many people have started listening to crappy rap."

"I couldn't agree with you more."

"I mean, when even those tight asses in the Independent Police Complaints Authority are listening to it, then you know it's become a hit."

She gave him a serious look. "Has John Nyholm spoken to you?"

"I think John has spoken to everyone who could reveal something about you, Cecilie. On several occasions, even."

"And what did you two talk about?"

"About a gangster by the name of Jeremy who has disappeared. What do you think we talked about?"

"And what did you tell him?" she asked, taking a step closer towards him.

"Nothing. Not a single thing, but mostly to stay out of trouble myself."

"If you haven't told John anything, why are you so afraid to talk with me? Why have you been avoiding me?"

He looked down at the floor and answered in a subdued voice, "Because I'm afraid of what you did with the information I gave you."

"What do you mean, what I did?"

"Killed Jeremy, goddammit."

She smiled sheepishly.

"Oh, come on, Ismail. Are you being serious? I'm a cop, not a gangster. You know perfectly well that I abide by the law. Most of the time, at least," she said, winking.

"I'm no idiot, Cecilie. Christ, I thought you were going to arrest him."

"Well, it seems I didn't get a chance to before Jeremy disappeared. What exactly is the problem?"

"It was information that I gave you off the record. *Under the rose.*"

"Which I am very grateful for."

"Which I sure as hell regret now," he said, rubbing his beard. "If it ever gets out, if John and the Independent Police Complaints Authority find out about it, I'm finished. They'll fire me on the spot. My name will be dragged through the mud."

"Now stop with all the drama. If you just keep your trap shut, no one will ever find out."

"But I'm a fucking accomplice," he said as his voice cracked.

"In what?" she asked, shaking her head. "I honestly don't know what you expected to happen. Why would I ever go after a frigging gangster like Jeremy? Risk everything?"

"Revenge. Because he went after you first. Because he planted a bomb in your car, which, Troels, your partner, unfortunately took instead of you."

Cecilie placed her hand on Ismail's shoulder and gave him a hard squeeze through his parka until she could feel his shoulder joint. "Ismail, regardless of what you think, I am very grateful for what you did. If you hadn't given me that information, Jeremy would have gone after me next."

"But, Cecilie . . ."

"But, Ismail, everything resolved itself. Through divine intervention," she said, shifting her gaze up towards the ceiling of the elevator.

"Perhaps Jeremy fled and is now living his best life on a sandy beach. Perhaps Brothers knocked him off. Or maybe some of his own did. Maybe it was his brother who's now accusing me. No matter what, that case is buried. Deep into the ground in a safe place. Absolutely nothing will ever come to the surface. Do you understand what I'm saying, Ismail? Forget all about that case."

"Okay, I'll forget it, then. But, Cecilie?"

"Yes?"

"Promise me you had nothing to do with his disappearance," Ismail said.

She gave him a reassuring smile and told him everything he wanted to hear. "I had absolutely nothing to do with Jeremy's disappearance. Okay?"

21

The pink neon sign with the letters GRILL lit up in the darkness like a guiding lighthouse on Bellahøjvej. Cecilie parked the Golf in front of the white building where Bella Grill was situated. The smell of grease lingered in the street from the open door, which seemed to attract customers because the iconic fast-food place was full. Cecilie greeted the owner, Kurt, and continued into the adjoining room, where she found a vacant table. A few minutes later, Kurt came and wiped off the oilcloth.

"Long time, no see, Cecilie. Congratulations on the promotion."

She raised her eyebrows. "I'm guessing Omar has been by and spilled the beans?"

Kurt smiled. "The leader of the tenant association doesn't miss a thing. You look beat. A Carlsberg?"

"Carlsberg and a burger, thanks."

"With extra sauce?"

"I'll take the diet version," which at Bella Grill meant gravy instead of the usual bearnaise and doubling up on the cucumber salad. When Kurt went back into the kitchen, Cecilie took out her phone and checked her messages. The last one had been received ten minutes ago. The sender was anonymous, and the tone was formal, yet the message was clear. It included an address in Vanløse and a time. She searched for the address, which apparently accommodated a massage clinic. She found it on a website that said *Belarus-Beauty. Nikita will spoil even the most demanding gentleman.* The ad included the sexual services that Nikita offered and photographs of her posing in lace underwear. Cecilie recognised the girl from the pictures that Beatrice Klerke had shown her.

"It's chow time," said Kurt as he placed the tray with her beer and burger drenched in sauce.

"Thank you, Kurt, it looks good, as always."

"Incredible that you are so petite with that appetite of yours," Kurt said, smiling. "Enjoy."

Cecilie took a couple of sips of the ice-cold beer and started eating her burger. It was cooked to perfection. As she ate, she looked at the pictures of Nikita. The way she posed in the bed reminded her of the position in which they had found Kristina Sand and Tine Larsen. A thought struck her, and she started looking for the girls' phone numbers on a couple of the intimate massage sites, but none of them showed up. The investigation hadn't indicated that any of the victims made a living as a prostitute. It was solely the perpetrator who had displayed them in that way. Perhaps deriving from some S/M fantasy or other? She wondered whether Mogens Berg was on his way down the same path. She recalled just how beaten up Nikita and the other girls looked, and she started googling Mogens Berg again. She found a picture in which he was standing with the National Police Commissioner and the former Minister of Justice at an official event. She came across other pictures of Mogens Berg in the company of heads of states and prominent businesspeople. Beatrice Klerke had been right. If you were going to go after a man like Mogens, the best thing was to strike at full speed, or you'd be doomed. Cecilie had been on suicide missions before and had survived. She never held back from doing what had to be done to stop the monsters. She fought them by any means necessary, even those that were less lawful. That was why John was looking for dirt he could put on her, dirt that could put her behind bars. Expanding her alliance with Beatrice Klerke and gaining her favour might prove to be vital. And when the National Police Commissioner's gang had deprived her of the possibility to go after a psychopathic murderer of women, she could at the very least relieve the world of a sadistic bastard like Mogens Berg. Perhaps it was about time she showed them she could also play their game.

"Another Carlsberg, Cecilie?" Kurt asked, taking her plate.

"No, thanks. Anyway, I'm going to have a busy day tomorrow."

22

Cecilie was standing in the doorway to her office and was looking across the division. Over by the Travel Team, only Ryan and two of his colleagues had arrived. Ryan had not disclosed any of their findings and she had no sense of how far they had got in the investigation. Cecilie looked at her watch. It was a few minutes to 11, which meant another half hour before Mogens Berg would be at the address in Vanløse. Her plan was to begin the raid at around 12, when he would probably be in full swing. She looked over at her team. All the boys were working on their computers. Heino stretched and yawned. It would do him good to get out, Cecilie thought, and went over to them.

"Everything okay?" she asked.

The three of them looked up from their computers and nodded. Cecilie leaned forward and lowered her voice.

"I'm going out on some cop business and need some backup. Anyone interested in joining me? Henrik? Heino?"

"I'm *ready*," said Heino, and Henrik nodded in approval.

Joakim got up from his seat across from them. "What are we doing?"

"It's hush-hush, and we need people who can hold the fort here, Joakim," Cecilie answered.

"Yeah, it's only suitable for grown-ups," Heino said, receiving a middle finger from Joakim.

"Cecilie, fire Heino. You know I'm a better cop than him."

"Which is why I'm leaving you here as my deputy," she said, motioning the others to get up from their seats.

"Deputy?" Joakim said, leaning back heavily in his seat. "What am I supposed to say if somebody asks for you?"

"Say that we're investigating a tip. No," she said, shaking her head, "tell them we're having a performance review."

Heino laughed.

"A performance review sounds good. It sounds very boss-like, boss."

Half an hour later, Cecilie rolled down Jernbanegade in Vanløse with Heino sitting next to her and Henrik in the back seat. The street was empty and Cecilie searched the doors for the right number.

"This is outside our district, isn't it?" Heino asked.

"Heino starts getting tics any time we venture too far away from the hipster cafés."

Heino shook his head.

"Come on, boss, tell us what we're going to do. I'm going crazy," he said, shifting restlessly in his seat. Cecilie stopped the car and looked towards the narrow passage between two houses. She discerned a small and dilapidated rear building further down.

"I think we're here," she said.

"There's another road right around the corner," she said, pointing at the GPS. "You take that one, Heino."

"Roger."

"So what awaits us inside?" Henrik asked.

"Repeated assaults committed by the same customer towards a prostitute."

"Are we going to a brothel, boss?" Heino asked, surprised.

"The perpetrator is inside there right now," she said, and looked at her watch.

"Is there a connection to the two murder cases?" Henrik asked.

"Are we messing with the Travel Team in any way?" Heino asked as he lit up into a smile.

"None of those things. This is an independent case that belongs under the category 'Personal Crimes.' And we are the Division of—"

"Personal Crimes," Henrik finished her sentence.

"Okay, it sounds pretty boring," Heino said disappointedly.

They got out of the car and tore across the street. Heino continued around the corner, while Cecilie and Henrik walked through the narrow passage.

"Knowing you, something tells me this isn't going to be boring."

Cecilie didn't answer but continued towards the rear building. She opened the buckle of her holster and made sure that Henrik did the same. With their pistols down by their sides, they passed the dirty window with an OPEN sign and continued down to the blue front door. Cecilie carefully pressed the handle down and pushed the door open. They stepped inside the dark house in which there was the pungent smell of mould. It was eerily quiet and Cecilie motioned Henrik to follow her down a narrow hallway. As they approached the room furthest away, they heard a woman sobbing, followed by the sound of a man's deep voice. It was impossible to hear what he was saying and soon his voice was replaced by very loud smacking sounds and screams.

Cecilie placed her hand on the door and slowly pushed it open. Inside the small room, a naked woman lay on the floor. Her back and buttocks bore stripes of bruise marks. A middle-aged man, his chest bare and his back facing them, was standing over the woman. He was squeezing a leather belt in his hand. "Keep screaming, I know you can take more, can't you? You whore. Answer me, answer me, bitch."

Cecilie stared at the back of the man's head as she raised her gun. It seemed so unreal. As though it wasn't her aiming her gun. Cecilie felt a sense of fear take over. Cold sweat moistened her back. Her legs started to give way. If she didn't pull the trigger, she'd die. The woman on the floor looked up at her, her mouth open, as blood ran down from her upper lip. Suddenly, the man turned around and saw Cecilie. His flushed face was drenched in sweat. His eyes met hers. Wild and enraged. His yellowing teeth were bared in a hideous grimace. *Shoot him* echoed in her head. *Shoot the monster.* She began to squeeze the trigger. Noticed that the man froze. Saw his fear take over his gaze. Seeing that fear felt good. It dampened her own.

"Police!" Henrik shouted behind her. He pushed Cecilie to the side and grabbed hold of Mogens Berg. Henrik locked his arm behind his back and pressed him forward in a secure grip. Cecilie put her pistol back in her holster and took the cotton blanket from the bed. She placed the blanket around Nikita's shoulders.

"Are you okay?"

Nikita nodded.

"You can't just barge in here like this. It's a violation of my privacy!" Mogens shouted. "Let me go this instant!"

Cecilie helped Nikita sit up on the bed.

"This is a misunderstanding . . . the girl and I have an agreement . . . it's not what it looks like."

"Will you tell him his rights?" Cecilie said, looking at Henrik. Henrik nodded and told Mogens that he was under arrest. The blood rushed from Mogens Berg's face and his jaw fell to his chest.

"Now look . . . you can't arrest me . . . I do, in fact, have immunity, not that I need to put it in use. I haven't done anything unlawful."

Heino appeared in the doorway. "Everything okay?"

Cecilie nodded. "We'll need to send for an ambulance and a patrol car to drive him to—"

"Isn't that . . . ?" Heino said, trying to place him.

Henrik took out his phone and called up the station.

"Now, just wait a minute . . . do me a favour and call the National Police Commissioner . . . He can vouch for me," Mogens Berg said. Henrik got through to the station and asked for a patrol car and an ambulance to be dispatched to the address.

"Put some handcuffs on him and take him outside, Heino," said Cecilie. Heino got out his handcuffs and Henrik helped him put them on Mogens, who was writhing.

"You're all through! This is an assault!" Mogens looked at Nikita with pleading eyes. "Tell them it was a game, Nikita."

Nikita sent him a glob of spit in response.

Heino grabbed Mogens and dragged him out of the room.

"You're gonna regret this!" he shouted on his way out. "I'll see that you're fired!"

Henrik looked at Cecilie. "Are you okay?"

Cecilie nodded.

"For a moment there I thought you were going to pull the trigger."

"No, of course not. I'm no psychopath, you know." She half-smiled back at him.

23

Have you completely lost your mind?" Palsgaard shouted. She hadn't even managed to enter his office properly before he was rushing towards her with murder in his eyes. "Do you realise what you've done? It's all over town!"

She took a step back. "Mogens Berg is a public figure. The attention can't come as a surprise."

"Which is precisely why you don't pull a number like that."

"That's news to me, that we can only take on cases that the press won't hurl itself at."

"Stop twisting my words. I won't tolerate it."

"Sorry if you think that was what I was doing. My point was that we act on all offences that we encounter, regardless of the press."

"Which is the very heart of the matter. When you go after a high-profile individual like Mogens Berg, an elected official who has immunity, you better be one hundred per cent certain you are right."

"We caught him in the act."

"I see! Really? With a prostitute? Good going, Cecilie. Prostitution is, as you know, lawful in Denmark. Both buying and selling sex is something the individual is at liberty to do. The only thing you've managed to do is violate his privacy, as well as the whore's for that matter."

Cecilie nodded thoughtfully.

"But I assume that the abuse, the aggravated violence, the involuntary suppression and rape don't belong under the 'private' category?"

"Of which there is no evidence."

"We caught Mogens Berg causing bodily harm with a belt to the aggrieved. Furthermore, we have the emergency room's report describing the scope of the injuries. Just like we have interrogated the victim, Nikita Olinga. In her testimony, she explains that Mogens Berg has contacted her and exposed her to physical assaults on multiple occasions."

"The prosecution won't base a criminal case on the testimony of a Ukrainian whore," he snorted.

"She is from Belarus. And Nikita isn't the only one. We have already been contacted by more women who want to report Mogens Berg for similar—"

"You've what? The case has just come out. How is this at all possible?"

Palsgaard seemed shaken, which suited Cecilie perfectly well. She shrugged her shoulders. "He's a well-known face. Apparently, a serial criminal as well."

"Just take it easy," he said, holding up a cautionary finger. "Mogens Berg must be treated with respect. How many reports are there?"

"So far three. We're bringing them in this afternoon."

"Oh no you're not. This is stopping right now!" said Palsgaard.

"I don't see how. The man was caught breaking the law. There are women who, independent of one another, have stepped forward with similar accusations."

"You . . . you've got to go out with a disclaimer," he said in a panicky voice. "A statement that the accusations are being routinely investigated, but that there is no sufficient evidence for maintaining a . . . a . . ." He shook his head. "Mogens Berg has cooperated with the police regarding this case . . . voluntarily submitted an explanation. That's what you're going to say."

"Not gonna happen," Cecilie said, crossing her arms in front of her chest.

"That's an order!"

"Sorry, but I won't do it. I imagine it would be strategically unwise for anyone in the agency to defend the accused, who is under suspicion for having beaten and bloodied up at least four women."

The words clearly made an impression on Palsgaard, who gaped and resembled a punctured pufferfish.

"I'm certain that the Minister of Justice has already sent a request to the head of Parliament to nullify Mogens Berg's immunity," Cecilie said.

"The Minister?" Palsgaard asked, looking at her suspiciously. "How did this case land with you anyway?"

"A source . . ."

"And what source is that, may I ask? One from the streets or from politics?"

"Mogens Berg's sadism was well known among prostitutes. I received an anonymous call, which I responded to."

There was no mistaking the look in Palsgaard's eyes. "You have no idea what's at stake here. You are blindly going down a dark path that will lead to your own demise. I almost feel sorry for you. Do you really think this is about saving a couple of poor, vulnerable girls? Girls the rest of society couldn't care less about?"

"I care about the girls."

"But not that much, if you were to be perfectly honest. Really only because it pleases the Minister. And it means that you were notified by Beatrice Klerke."

Cecilie looked away.

"I know Klerke better than you do," Palsgaard continued. "We're all aware of her cynicism. But Klerke's days are numbered. That's why she's stooped to such an act of desperation. It's a shame she's managed to take advantage of you." He sent Cecilie a scornful smile. "This case won't be so easily forgotten and someone's going to have to pay for it. You can rest assured."

It was approaching nighttime and Cecilie looked out across the half-empty division. Ryan and a few members of the Travel Team were still sitting with their profiler, Vogel. The rumour about her disfavour with the management had already spread, and judging by Ryan's attitude he was satisfied with the development. Her phone rang, and she noticed the call was anonymous.

"Cecilie Mars," she said.

"Good evening, Cecilie, and congratulations on the arrest," Beatrice Klerke said.

"Thank you," said Cecilie in surprise. "We are busy with the investigation of Mogens Berg."

"I'm pleased to hear that. It's very good that we managed to stop his gross assaults. But speaking of the case, don't expect to see it through."

"What do you mean?"

"That the case will be taken from you."

"But they can't do that," Cecilie said in an upset voice, drawing Ryan's attention. She turned her back to him and lowered her voice. "That case can't just disappear."

"Of course not. God forbid, now that we have finally managed to catch him in the act. What I mean to say is that it will soon be handed over to someone else in the division. You will probably select someone yourself. Otherwise, it will most likely be Palsgaard who will be allowed to play boss and given the opportunity to delegate the task to someone. It can't hurt to throw him that bone," she laughed.

Cecilie supported herself on the doorframe. "I'm afraid I don't follow you at all . . ."

"There is no reason to waste your team's energy on a case that has already concluded. A case that will probably be prolonged. You have more important tasks to see to."

"I thought that it was an important case . . ."

"Not more important than the case about the two women who were murdered, which seem to be connected."

"The Travel Team has got those cases."

"You and your team will be taking over the cases starting from tomorrow. The Travel Team will be taking off."

"How did that happen?"

"Everything is connected, Cecilie. Everything is in play. Get used to it."

"Okay, thanks," she said, speechless.

"Thank yourself. But Cecilie, don't screw up now. I'm counting on you," was the last thing Klerke said. Cecilie put the phone away and turned towards Ryan, who was giving her a self-satisfied look. She sent him a friendly smile and shut the door to her office.

24

Cecilie had gathered the team in her office, where they were all sitting around the conference table. At one end of the room there was a whiteboard, and she had pasted notes and photographs from the two cases up on the far wall. For the first time, Cecilie felt as though she had properly taken over the space.

"Shit, it's just crazy that we've got the case back," Joakim said ecstatically as he clenched his fist. "I would have loved to have seen Ryan's face . . . or helped them pack up."

"But it entails a certain responsibility, don't forget," said Cecilie, pointing towards the far wall and the photocopied portraits of Kristina and Tine. "We can't waste a single second."

"But tell us how you managed to kick them out."

"Just concentrate on your job, Joakim," Henrik said with his arms crossed.

"Yeah, Joakim, concentrate on your job . . . see if you can keep up with what's going on," said Heino.

"It was after we busted that politician, wasn't it?" Joakim persisted. "Finally, Palsgaard realised what we're capable of, didn't he?"

"*We* busted Mogens Berg," Heino said, pointing at Henrik, Cecilie, and himself. "All you did was sit here all afternoon jerking off. By the way, Palsgaard is disappointed with your performance," said Heino.

"Fuck you, Heino," Joakim responded.

Cecilie clapped her hands to draw their attention.

"I have tried to get an overview of what Ryan and the Travel Team managed to investigate, which is, unfortunately, infinitesimal. It seems that they have been through most of the videos without any result."

"Fine, then we won't have to waste hours watching them," said Heino.

"Not quite. I don't think they knew what to look for. Which is why that will be one of your tasks, Heino."

"Roger." He sighed.

"See whether the individual the witness described as an undertaker is anywhere to be found. Maybe we can identify a licence plate if he turns up at the car park in front of the allotment garden. Or—"

"Look for anything suspicious. Got it."

Cecilie got up from her seat and walked over to the whiteboard.

"The Travel Team continued down the same path as us by matching the two victims' circles of acquaintances, which didn't garner them any results either. However, the Travel Team took it a step further by mapping out the two women's lives in order to find another common denominator, which is an interesting move."

"Did they get anything out of it?" Henrik asked, his arms still crossed in front of his chest.

"Yes and no. They certainly managed to establish that Kristina Sand and Tine Larsen had most likely never met each other. Neither in connection with work, recreational pastimes, or shopping patterns. Which suggests that the perpetrator didn't know the women beforehand."

"Perhaps we should take a look at what the file contains," said Heino.

"Excellent idea," Cecilie answered.

"The Travel Team has already profiled him," said Joakim, snapping his fingers. "We've gotta get hold of that."

"Do we get an extra bonus for having Joakim on the team?" said Heino.

"What now?"

"We're not dealing with a Muslim serial murderer here. Am I right, Cecilie?"

She nodded. "I doubt that the murders are religiously motivated."

"Though they fill up quite a bit of space in the statistics."

"Who does?"

"Well, not to sound racist or anything, but people with an immigrant background are overrepresented when it comes to sexual crimes," said Henrik.

"That may be," said Cecilie, "but in relation to murders of women in Muslim circles, they usually tend to be honour killings and have an entirely different modus operandi than what we've seen in connection with Kristina's and Tine's cases."

Henrik nodded.

"And it doesn't seem as though the Travel Team has had all that much success with that theory," said Cecilie. "They've done thorough research into the registry for sentenced sexual criminals with immigrant-sounding surnames, but they've all been removed from the list."

"Can't we put together a profile ourselves?" Joakim asked, waving his arms.

"Be my guest, Sigmund Freud," said Heino.

"Joakim is onto something," said Cecilie. "We can't be more off than the Travel Team's profile," she said, taking out a marker. She tested it to see whether it worked on the whiteboard.

"So, what do we know about him?"

"He is a sick pervert who likes to cut women open," said Heino.

"I think Cecilie wants us to be slightly more detailed," said Henrik.

Cecilie nodded. "In contrast to Vogel's theory, I don't think the perpetrator is impulsive, uncontrolled, with few social skills. I think that the clues from the scene of the crime suggest a person who is very much in control. Someone who has carefully planned the murders. He must also have been very persuasive since his victims let him into their homes."

She wrote a couple of key words on the board and then turned back around to face them all.

"Got any input?"

"I don't know. The whole thing seems so violent. So aggressive," said Joakim.

Henrik shrugged his shoulders. "He could be just about anybody, as far as I'm concerned. I mean, he may be organised and cunning, or maybe he's just lucky."

"Yeah, who knows how a psychopath like that thinks?" said Heino.

Cecilie put the marker down. "You guys really aren't very helpful, are you?"

"We're just telling it like it is. We need more information, more leads, more—"

"But this is what we've got. And we probably won't get more. And he's probably going to strike again soon. So what do we do?" Cecilie asked.

"He may have started long before this, which wouldn't be abnormal."

"Go on, Henrik."

"We could go back to the archive and look for persons who have been sentenced for violent crimes in the past. Perhaps something that has certain similarities to this, even on the smallest scale."

"I'm pretty sure I'd be able to recall a case like this even in the minutest scale," Heino said. "It would also be time consuming to have to go through the whole thing. We risk the investigation running into the sand."

"Heino is right. We've got to speed things up," said Cecilie.

"Maybe we should get our own profiler," said Joakim. "Find someone who's an expert on all this stuff. Some psychology nerd or other."

"Cecilie doesn't like psychologists!" Heino and Henrik said at once.

25

Evening was approaching when Cecilie left the office and drove out towards Bellahøj. On the radio, the Spencer Davis Group helped her get through the traffic on H.C. Andersens Boulevard with their song, "Gimme Some Lovin'." Absorbed in thought, she was only half-aware of the music and her fellow drivers. The question of how they were going to identify the perpetrator before he struck again kept repeating in her mind. He was a monster, just like all the other monsters who had been in her life. The ones from her childhood whom she had just barely managed to escape from. The ones from her youth who had sunk their claws into her. The ones from her work who had shown her evilness of all kinds. The monsters had different modi operandi and different desires, but it was as though she wasn't able to see their individual characteristics until she had caught them. Until then, they were a mere cloud of evil. Which was why the task of profiling him, of understanding him, seemed daunting. Just the mere thought of it made her stomach turn. Understanding would mean accepting. Acceptance was incompatible with her desire to kill them all. She thought about the episode with Mogens Berg. Was she about to shoot him? Would she have pulled the trigger had Henrik not intervened? When she got out of the car, she was greeted by the sound of a familiar voice.

"Ce-cil. Ce-cil."

"Hello, Omar," she said in a tired voice as she turned around towards the president of the tenant association.

"There are problems again, Ce-cil."

"Has the shit hit the fan?"

"Not the fan, the pavements. Little bandits are riding around on those pathways. It's not a bicycle path; it's a footpath."

"Honestly. What do you want me to do, Omar?"

"You're the police."

"Yes. But I'm not employed by the traffic police," she said with a smile on her lips.

"Ha ha, I get Danish humour," he said drily. "That's not funny, Ce-cil. We need law and order here. Or else we'll end up back on the ghetto list."

"I doubt that's going to be enough to get us on there again."

"It doesn't take much. Believe me. Brown people need only make half the mistakes that white people do."

"Well, guess it's a good thing there are still a couple of us palefaces around," she said, pointing at herself.

He frowned and gave her an angry look. "What's this about a Muslim murderer? Now it's our fault that the ladies are dead or what?"

"Forget what you've been reading in the newspapers, Omar."

"Not just in newspapers. Everywhere. It's a big problem for us. It could put us on the ghetto list."

She took a deep breath. "Omar, we're not going to end up back on any more lists. And as far as the sudden Muslim take on this case is concerned, there is nothing to substantiate that."

"Well, there is something to substantiate it for those who get shouted at and called ugly things in the malls. Ugly things at the swimming pool."

"There are idiots everywhere," said Cecilie. "Have a nice evening, Omar."

"We have to take care of the neighbourhood, Ce-cil!" he shouted after her.

Cecilie nodded as she walked down the path towards her apartment. Her thoughts had already returned to the case. Perhaps they were dealing with a murderer who hadn't committed any crimes before or had managed to remain under the radar. If that was the case, all they could do was sit and wait for him to make a fatal mistake, which meant more bodies on the autopsy table. But if he had a past, if he was in the registry, they desperately needed someone who could identify him. They needed a profiler. But not somebody like Vogel, who, despite his FBI background and international merits, was, when it came down to it, nothing but a cop guessing his way through it all. No, they needed someone who had knowledge of the dark side of the human mind. Someone who could identify a monster behind their façade. Someone who knew them intimately because they were around them every day. A monster guard. It wasn't that she hated psychologists, as the boys had said. She just hadn't had the best experiences with them. She opened the door to her apartment and stared at the darkness and the empty hallway. She suddenly knew where to look to find a personal profiler.

26

Slagelse is pretty boring," said Joakim, looking through the windshield as Cecilie drove them through the centre of town in the pouring rain.

"Slagelse or Plaguelse as H.C. Andersen referred to the town," Henrik said from the back seat.

"I had a cousin who once lived here, which didn't make her any less grumpy."

"I should have taken Heino with me. He's better company than the two of you put together," said Cecilie.

They continued towards the hospital and the psychiatric ward, where Cecilie parked in front of Sikringen, Slagelse's psychiatric institution for very dangerous inmates. They got out and the sound of the cars from the highway made a rumbling noise in the background.

"It's a nice place, despite everything," Joakim said, nodding towards the low main building of plastered brick.

"How many patients are committed here?"

"Thirty. They are the nation's most violent criminals, and they can't be committed anywhere else," Cecilie answered as she started making her way towards the main entrance.

"They have a hundred and twenty employees to care for them and each employee costs tax payers four million a year," she said, shaking her head. "But at least they can't harm anybody while they're here."

"Are . . . are we going to talk with one of them?" Joakim asked.

"Yes, of course, Hannibal the Cannibal himself," answered Henrik as he shook his head. He looked at Cecilie. "You think that professor guy can help us?"

"Preben Sommer? I certainly hope so. He's managed to produce an ocean of mental statements on persons who have committed sexual crimes. If our perpetrator is anywhere to be found in the registry, Professor Sommer may have done a test on him and be able to identify him."

In the reception area, they were received by a guard who, after having checked their IDs, led them to the conveyor belt where their outer clothes and possessions had to go through security. And then they all had to go through the body scan.

"It's almost like going on vacation," said Joakim as he gathered his belongings.

After a few minutes, Preben Sommer appeared.

"Welcome," he said, extending his arms. Preben was in his mid-fifties, with an unruly beard and an impressive head of hair. He led them down the pastel-coloured hallways to his office. When they were inside, Preben opened the door out to a small atrium courtyard and fished a pack of cigarettes from the breast pocket of his shirt.

"Why don't we step outside for a bit of fresh air?"

They followed Preben, who lit his cigarette. "This is my only vice . . ." he said as smoke billowed out of his mouth. "I was surprised to get your phone call, Cecilie. It's like a visit from a celebrity."

"How so?" she asked, thinking about whether Preben had watched Como's music video online.

"What with all the patients you have sent our way. You've got a small fan club," he said ironically.

"With Steen Holz as chairman?"

Preben Sommer laughed. "He's not nearly as bitter with you as he has been. Not after he got married in here."

"Married? Are you serious?"

"Oh yes," said Preben, taking a drag of his cigarette. "To twenty-year-old Mona from Thy. She was previously seeing one of our other inmates. I suspect Mona of having a father complex, which she lives out by way of middle-aged serial killers." He lifted one of his hands in the air. "That's not a professional assessment though."

"Who's Steen Holz?" Joakim asked.

"One of my former colleagues who had a penchant for killing his patients and who Cecilie managed to stop."

"Not just his patients," Cecilie mumbled. The thought of Steen Holz didn't bring anything good. The jerk, who deserved more than anyone else to get a bullet, had managed to screw with her brain.

"Oh, so that's why you don't like psychologists," said Joakim.

"Only the ones who commit murder," Cecilie rushed to say, and smiled at Preben Sommer.

"Did you get a chance to look at what I sent you?"

He nodded. "I think your notes make more sense than Vogel's profile." He shook his head. "Where the hell do they find people like that? And what is the basis for his conclusion? Tarot cards and astrology?"

"No idea. But that's why we need help from an expert," she said ingratiatingly. "So we know who to look for."

"The last time I made the rounds in our division, everyone was there. So it can't be any of mine who have been busy. Would you like a cup of coffee?"

Cecilie shook her head. "No, I'd rather have your help."

Preben lit another cigarette with the stub he was holding between his fingers. "I've been following the cases and together with your descriptions, it's clear to me that it is the same perpetrator who is responsible for them both. But what did you think I could help you with?"

"Perhaps you recognised the modus operandi from a former patient or from your job at the Medico-Legal Institute and your knowledge of psychiatric reports."

"Oh, right," he said, running his hand through his hair before shaking his head. "Not really, but then I don't really think of it in that way. I mean, when I help evaluate an accused person, we keep the individual in question under close observation. We pose questions on the basis of a very specific area just to see whether the person is fit for punishment."

"But the cases? Do you remember the things they were accused of?" Henrik asked.

"Preferably not," he answered, taking a huge drag. "I have to be able to sleep at night, right?"

"Okay, I had hoped you would be able to help us. We're under a time constraint."

"I'm sure you are," said Preben as he blew out some smoke. "This guy can't seem to stop himself."

He bent down and put out the cigarette in the flower bed. "But maybe you're right. He could perhaps have been here at some point." He tapped the breast pocket of his shirt as though to make sure that there were more cigarettes in the pack. "Maybe Niko can help you?"

"Who's Niko?"

"Nikolaj Jacoby, a gifted young psychologist who is affiliated with us." He snapped his fingers. "Maybe he could even make a profile? I'm certain he could make one better than Vogel's. He has a special connection with our patients. But he isn't the most extroverted person in the world. He's got his own ideas . . . about the police, among other things. But by all means, you should ask him."

"Great," said Cecilie. "And where do we find Niko?"

Preben checked his wristwatch.

"He's probably still down at the gym. He's running a class on mindfulness yoga for a group of inmates."

"Mindfulness yoga? It almost seems as though we're at a real prison," said Cecilie, smiling. "Can we speak with him when he's finished?"

"Yes, of course," said Preben, lighting another cigarette. "If he wants to, that is."

27

They had to wait for Nikolaj Jacoby for an hour. Long enough for Cecilie to suspect him of deliberately making them wait. Finally, a male nurse came to get them and brought them to Nikolaj's office. It was smaller than Preben's and didn't have a terrace door and atrium garden, but it did have the same combination of pastel colours on the walls. Nikolaj was sitting behind his desk and busy taping his broken glasses frames together. He was in his mid-thirties, sun-tanned, and muscular. There was blood on his T-shirt and there was a wad of cotton in his left nostril. Nikolaj looked up at them. "Three officers? Are you sure that's enough?"

"It's like with the blind, the deaf, and the mute. That which one of them doesn't grasp, the other two register," Cecilie answered.

"And you're the leader, I take it?"

"Cecilie Mars," she answered, showing him her ID badge.

"The new head of Homicide. Preben has already warned me."

"Are you all right?" Henrik asked, pointing at his bloody T-shirt.

"This is nothing."

"I didn't know that yoga could be so dangerous. What happened?" Cecilie asked.

He looked at her for a brief moment. "We all transformed into carnivorous orcs. That's at least what one of the patients experienced."

"An inmate did this to you?" Cecilie asked, pointing at his nose.

"Could we make this short? I have a busy day."

"Of course," Cecilie said, and continued. "We have two identical murder cases in which the two female victims were tortured and stabbed to death in their homes. We need help to identify and stop the perpetrator before he strikes again." She waved the folder that contained a copy of her notes and Vogel's report in the air. "You might recognise the modus operandi from a former patient. Perhaps you could make a profile of the murderer for us based on this information, which we can build on. Preben recommended you," she quickly added.

Nikolaj smiled coldly. "Which is Preben's way of passing on the buck. I have absolutely no experience in developing profiles."

"He said that you have a certain sense, a certain connection to the inmates—"

"Really? Is that what this looks like to you?" he interrupted, waving his broken glasses. "And in terms of giving away former patients, I believe that is crossing an ethical line. Perhaps also a legal one."

"Crossing a line?" Cecilie asked, half-smiling. "We already share registry information with the prosecution, just like we exchange reports on those accused with you—including the psychiatric reports that have been created. I'm thinking that we're on the same side?"

"That all depends on the eyes looking at it. I personally don't have any desire to conduct a witch hunt against any present or former patients."

Cecilie took a deep breath. "I can't really see how the investigation of a sadistic murderer could be interpreted as a witch hunt."

"Nikolaj, we're pursuing a serial criminal who is going to strike again soon," said Henrik, looking at him pleadingly.

"We desperately need all the help we can get," Joakim added. "So we can catch him."

Nikolaj looked back at them all. "Which is why you're wasting your time here. We watch our patients carefully and none of them are allowed to leave."

"Then let's focus on the ones who have been allowed to leave here and the ones you've sent to have a mental examination," Cecilie suggested. "We need to know whether any of them could possibly match—"

"I understand the assignment. And I repeat: I will not partake in a witch hunt against previous patients. Aside from a few individuals, they are a vulnerable group of people who have served their punishment and who are just trying to get on with their lives."

Cecilie's patience was about to reach its end. "I'm sorry if we've offended anyone, but your patients are men who have committed violent assaults, and one of them may possibly be the one we're looking for right now." She squinted her eyes. "In relation to 'getting on with their lives,' the recidivism rate speaks for itself."

"We clearly don't agree. What a surprise, huh?" he said, putting his glasses back on. "I don't know about you, but I've got other things I've got to see to now."

"And what, precisely, would that be, Doctor?" Cecilie said, provoked. "Have you ever managed to cure anyone? I mean for real? Or do you know that your patients won't ever seriously change their ways?"

Some of Nikolaj Jakoby's self-satisfied façade began to dissolve. "I . . . I get them to take responsibility for their actions so they no longer feel imprisoned by their obsessions and self-destructive patterns. For everyone's sake."

"Tell that to the victims' loved ones," Cecilie said in an ironic tone.

"Come on, Nikolaj, take a look at this and help us," said Henrik. He took the folder from Cecilie and handed it to Nikolaj. Nikolaj sat motionless.

"Forget him," Cecilie said, taking back the folder. "He's been in the wrong company for far too long." She turned towards the door. "I apologise for wasting your time, Doctor. When we catch him, we'll make sure to send him here so he can attend your yoga class. Thanks for jack shit."

"What an arrogant jerk," Cecilie said, marching back to the Golf. Both Henrik and Joakim struggled to keep up with her. When she reached the car, she banged her hand against the roof.

"What a bloody waste of time this was!"

"What do you think we should do?" Henrik asked.

"Do I look like somebody who has a Plan B?" she asked, getting into the car. After they had been sitting in silence for a little while, she looked at Henrik in the rearview mirror. "We have no choice but to go through the entire archive. Maybe focus the search on those who live in the metropolitan area."

"That's still quite a bit to go through. But yes, good plan."

"We could also go back and break his glasses again," said Joakim.

"That's the best suggestion you've had in a long time," said Cecilie as she started the engine.

28

When they had returned to Teglholmen an hour later, they ran into Heino on the staircase leading up to the Homicide Unit.

"I've been trying to get hold of you, boss," he said excitedly.

"We had an appointment with a doctor. What's up?"

"You're not going to believe this."

"Did you find something on the surveillance cameras?"

He looked at her perplexedly. "Oh, those? No, not yet."

"What, then?" said Cecilie, passing him.

Heino grabbed her arm. "The Travel Team has returned. They've set everything back up while you were gone."

"Say what?"

"I asked Ryan the Clown what they were doing, but he didn't say a word. However, I did overhear somebody say something about a search. Do you think they've got our case back?"

Cecilie didn't answer but continued up the stairs. With giant strides, she walked through the division and headed directly for Ryan.

"I gotta hand it to you, Ryan, you certainly live up to your name what with all this flying in and out you do. So the question is, what the hell are you doing here again?"

"Cecilie, nice to see you too," he said, leaning back in the office chair. "You look like you're busy. Have you managed to solve the case?"

"We just need to clean up after you guys, but, yes, it looks promising. So I'm going to ask you again: What are you guys doing here? I don't recall inviting you over."

"A new case," Ryan said, smiling roguishly.

"Is this my cue to ask which of my cases you think you're taking over?"

He crossed his legs lazily. "A disappearance case."

"I have no idea what you're referring to."

"The report is with Palsgaard. He has asked us to see to the investigation."

She lowered her hands to her side. "Independent of us?"

"Independent of you," he said, pointing at her.

"And why would he do that?"

"Because the Independent Police Complaints Authority is involved," he said, having difficulty concealing his smile.

She sensed her pulse rise and her cheeks turning red. "Is John the one who's initiated this? And who's the missing person?"

Ryan held up one of his hands dismissively. "I can't comment on that. You know how it is when the Independent Police Complaints Authority is involved."

"Is someone in my division being investigated? If so, I have a right to know about it."

"I think you know who the arrow is pointing at."

"Are you really so gullible, Ryan?" she said, shaking her head. "John's always been out to get me."

"I know nothing about that."

"I know what this is all about."

"What's it about, then?"

"John is trying to create a bullshit missing persons case regarding the disappearance of a gangster named Jeremy. Am I right?"

Ryan looked away. "No comment."

"Fuck you, Ryan. Are you really going to waste your time on this? Is this why you became a cop? To throw mud at your colleagues? To be John's . . . bitch?"

"I don't see it as a waste of time. On the contrary."

"So this is your way of getting revenge because we got the case back?"

"There's no talk of revenge here; we're just doing our job. Turning every stone. Digging until the truth comes out. Digging real deeeep," he added jovially. The men on his team laughed.

She looked around at them. "I see. It's a loser's case, created by men with small dicks. I don't know the size of yours, Ryan, but I think I can make a sound guess. We, on the other hand, are dealing with a real case," she said, pointing behind her to her team. "A case that has up until now cost two women their lives. If you or any of your people start messing around with our investigation or stand in the way of it, there are going to be serious consequences."

Ryan yawned. "I'm shaking already. But right now, we've got a search to see to." He got up from his chair and towered over her.

"Search? I thought it was a missing persons case."

He looked down at her. "People have a tendency to disappear in all sorts of ways. Some in small bits and pieces. Dahlstrup and his uniforms are already at the address, waiting. There isn't much that gets past those nerds' noses."

Cecilie looked at Ryan and the investigators. At that moment, Henrik and Heino went over to her. "Everything okay, Cecilie?" Heino asked.

"Everything is as far from okay as it could possibly be." She looked at them both. "Keep a close eye on those assholes. Don't speak to them about anything without conferring with me first. Is that understood?"

"What's this all about? Are they taking over the case again?" Henrik asked.

"No, but they could fuck up the whole thing anyway," she said, and started walking away.

"Where are you going?"

A few minutes later, she knocked on the door to Palsgaard's office. She didn't wait for him to answer but walked right in. Palsgaard looked up with surprise from his seat behind his desk. She looked around quickly and determined that they were alone.

"You can't possibly be serious."

Her straightforward manner threw him off. "About . . . what?"

"About planting the Travel Team in the middle of my division with some bullshit crap investigation."

"Watch your tone, please. What is your problem, Cecilie?"

"My problem is that having those clowns running around is creating a sense of unease in my division."

"Well, if there's no reason to feel uneasy, then there's nothing to worry about. But from what I understand, there's talk of a very serious case."

She sent him a scornful look.

"About what? A case that John Nyholm wants to nail me for?"

Palsgaard leaned back in his chair. "I can't make any comment on that, but you are getting warmer."

Cecilie stared back at him. "So now it's the Independent Police Complaints Authority and John who are running the show? I didn't see that one coming."

"John doesn't decide anything."

"Fine, then I'll ask you to stop this, for the sole reason that it is disruptive to the division's work."

He leaned back and pointed at her with a straight finger. "Remember who started this. I warned you. It's impressive how many people's toes you've already managed to step on."

"Is that so? Had I known that there were so many crybabies running the agency, I would have turned down the position. Charge me already, so I know what I'm being accused of."

"I imagine that will happen soon enough. Until then, we'll just have to wait and see how the whole thing develops."

"The Independent Police Complaints Authority and the Travel Team are going to look like the biggest fools when they get absolutely nowhere after all their efforts."

"Well, they seem firmly determined."

29

Cecilie drove the Golf down the broad pathway that cut through Bellahøj Park towards the open-air theatre. *Fuck John. Fuck Palsgaard. Fuck Ryan and fuck missing Jeremy*, she thought. She stopped the car and observed the human figures prowling around on the plateaus in the dusk. The pushers had returned and so had the customers. Just the sight of it tickled her nostrils and she felt her heart pounding faster. The body never forgets its craving for drugs. Believing anything else is just plain stupid. People had turned up in large numbers over there. Alarmed by the sight of the car, they stood like deer caught in the headlights. When she turned on the blue flashing lights, the customers started to run while the pushers remained calm. It'd take more than some blue lights to make them flee. Just like it had taken more than ordinary police work to stop the gang war between the Rebels and the Brothers. Jeremy's disappearance had laid the foundation for peace. It had stopped the war and created a sense of safety for the neighbourhood's inhabitants. Jeremy's disappearance. Jeremy hadn't merely disappeared. He was dead as a doornail. Exactly like Troels, her former partner. *You don't murder a cop*, she thought as she bit her lip, *you just don't*. Especially not a cop like Troels. Troels, who had been just as pure as all the snow she had shovelled into her nose. Troels, who had a little daughter, a wife, and a single-family detached house. Hard-working, loyal Troels, who had known about all her faults and had still kept his mouth shut. Should Jeremy have got away with killing Troels unpunished? Ruining a family? Making a child lose her father? Hell no. When the tele-information had indicated that it had been Jeremy who had used his phone to activate the bomb that had killed Troels, she had seen that justice was served. End of story.

She opened the glove compartment and took out the rubber baton, which she hid in the sleeve of her leather jacket. If you hesitated, you died. She had been completely calculating that night in Jeremy's house on Amager Strandvej, which was also why Dahlstrup and the uniforms would never be able to find any traces leading to her. What was she afraid of? Had her new position as a boss made her soft? Robbed her of her ability to navigate the streets? All that political and scheming shit she had to navigate was of zero help here. She opened the car door and got out. The pushers stirred like a flock of crows, considering whether it was worth the effort to flee. Cecilie walked into the gleam of light as she headed towards the amphitheatre. The pushers clearly recognised her and started to retreat towards the park behind them. Just one remained. He turned around to his colleagues and extended his arms. "What are you running away for, chickens?"

Cecilie calmly climbed up the stone terraces towards him. The pusher, a huge oaf, looked down at her. "You've gotta be the shortest cop I've ever seen. Don't you think you'd better leave?" He stood with his hands at his sides and with a big smile on his lips. "Or did you come all the way up here to suck dick?" he said as he moved his hand between his crotch and gripped hold of his balls. Cecilie stopped at the terrace below him and leaned her head back.

"You must be new. Is this your first day on the job?" she asked.

"My what?"

Cecilie calmly slipped the baton from her sleeve and down into her hand. "Since you don't know who I am."

"Yet another dyke cop?"

"Wrong guess," she answered, and swung the baton at the man's knee. It made an unpleasant sound, and he bent forward. She grabbed his hoodie and pulled. The pusher stumbled down the stone terrace and continued falling down the next couple of steps. He rolled around as he remained lying on his back. Cecilie walked down to him while swinging the baton.

The man moaned and tried to get up. His nose was bleeding after his head blunted the blow. "You . . . you . . . fuck . . ."

Cecilie swung the baton and hit his face. The man howled and grabbed hold of his jaw, which was now out of joint. She hammered the baton down on his body with some thorough blows to the kidneys, which knocked the wind out of him.

"Let's see what you've got in your pockets," Cecilie said, bending down and searching them without finding anything. "Are you really that gross?" She stuck her hands down the man's pants. "That's gotta be the smallest dick I've ever come across," she said, pulling her hand back out. "On the other hand, you've got plenty of dope," she said, holding a small plastic bag with white powder in front of his face. "So, how much've you got here? Twenty, thirty grams?" She put the bag in her pocket. "Running around with your entire stock—how dumb can you be? It really must be your first day." She let the tip of her baton rest on the tip of his nose. "And it's your last day too. Am I right?"

The man nodded, terror-stricken.

"So, what are you waiting for? Get your ass out of here." The pusher limped away while holding his broken jaw. Cecilie walked back to her Golf. She sensed the adrenaline in her body. She hoped she had managed to send a signal to the pushers that would make them reconsider whether Bellahøj Park was such a great place for them after all. But as long as there were customers, they'd continue to swarm around the park like flies around a turd. Next time there would be more who would stay behind. And the next time after that, they'd be carrying knives. And the time after that, firearms. It was a vicious spiral until one of them was brought to their grave. Then the whole thing would stop for a little while. Her phone was vibrating in her pocket.

"Nikolaj Jacoby . . . yes, we met at . . . I know who you are, Doctor. Anything new from psychopath land?"

"I'm sorry that we got off on the wrong foot."

"Okay," she said, leaning against the car. "That makes two of us. How can I help you?"

"I was under the impression that you were the ones who needed my help."

"Do you already have a few suspects lined up?"

"Like I said, I don't want to stigmatise anyone. Which is why I want to help you in creating a correct profile."

"Excellent! Hopefully one that's better than Vogel's."

"Preben showed me Vogel's report. I can already rule out the possibility that the murders are religiously motivated and based on female mutilation rituals."

"We agree on that. But just out of curiosity, what makes you so certain?"

"The fact that ninety-seven per cent of all serial killers murder within their own ethnicity or religious faith. The remaining three per cent can be ascribed to random circumstances or a perpetrator who is out of control. Your perpetrator seems controlled in all his phases. I'll start putting something together for you."

"Sounds very interesting."

"Not yet. And it's still incomplete, but I'm thinking that there is enough to provide the basis for a meeting."

"It's good to have you on board, Doctor."

"This may be overdoing it, but I would like to help you connect the dots."

"Thanks for calling, Nikolaj."

She got into the car and turned off the flashing blue lights. She smiled to herself. Maybe they still had a chance of finding the perpetrator before it was too late.

30

Cecilie was standing in the Homicide Unit's kitchenette and swallowed some ibuprofen. She hoped the pills might help get rid of the headache that had been nagging her all morning. It was 11:30 and Nikolaj was probably going to show up any second. He had sent a text message saying, *Don't expect too much*, which had only whetted her appetite even more. At that moment, Ryan entered, holding his empty coffee cup. When he saw her, he stiffened for a brief moment, but continued and got himself another cup from the coffee machine. She put her glass down. "Have you found your missing gangster?"

"It looks very promising."

"So Dahlstrup and his uniforms found something you could use?"

"No comment," he said, sipping his coffee.

"In other words, you didn't find jack shit. How did John Nyholm take it?"

"We have other leads," Ryan quickly said. "A . . . very interesting lead, in fact."

"Wow," she said sarcastically. "Well, good luck." She returned to her office and shortly afterwards, Heino was standing in the doorway. She waved him in with the pen she was holding.

"Wasn't that doctor supposed to come at half past?" Heino asked.

She looked at her watch. "Yeah . . ."

"He's now five minutes late."

"I know how to tell time, Heino. He's probably on his way."

Heino scratched his goatee. "Is everything okay with that guy Ryan? He's always looking at you in a funny way."

"Oh? Is there anything new from Forensics? About the search they made at Jeremy Cox's house on Amager Strandvej?"

"The uniforms didn't find anything . . . other than a hash pipe."

Cecilie threw the pen on her desk.

"That sure won't get them far."

"But I heard something from one of the guys in Bellahøj who I play basketball with."

"Someone from the gangs?"

"Oh no, he's much too soft for that," he said, smiling.

"So, what'd you hear?"

He lowered his voice. "That the missing gangster's car has been parked there for months."

Cecilie tried to look unaffected. "So it was seized?"

"Yup. A big Porsche Cayenne, turbo. A real rocker's vehicle. Without a tracker, and a fake licence plate, of course."

"But how does that add up?"

"It turns out that it was stolen and that at some point it turned up in a case about a hash sale."

"I see," she said, crossing her arms. "Have they arrested anyone in connection with the case?"

"During the operation, the pushers managed to flee. It wasn't until several hours later that a patrol unit found the abandoned Porsche over on Ægirsgade. Bellahøj seized it and the car ended up in storage as the investigation continued at a snail's pace. They still haven't managed to find the gangsters."

"And do Ryan and the Travel Team know anything?"

"Yes, but not until now, as the leasing company has complained, and Bellahøj then saw who was on the contract. They were the ones who contacted Palsgaard, who then sent it directly to the Travel Team."

"But that just confirms the theory that Jeremy's disappearance was gang-related."

Heino looked away.

"What? Do you know something?"

"No, no . . . I don't know anything . . . It's just that . . ."

"That what, Heino? Talk to me."

He extended his arms. "It's that crappy rap song about you that has been spreading around. It seems like everyone has heard it and believes in the nonsense."

"Maybe they should listen to some schlagers instead."

"Schlagers are great, boss. I'm merely telling you what I know. I've got your back," he said, and smiled. "I won't let anyone throw mud at you." His confidence made her feel ill at ease.

"Thank you. Let me know as soon as Nikolaj shows up, okay?"

"Roger," Heino said, and left her office.

Cecilie massaged her temples. The two ibuprofens weren't nearly enough for her headache. She had driven that Porsche. With Jeremy's stone-dead corpse lying next to her. She had known all along that it was just a matter of time before Jeremy's car would show up. She had just been lucky that it hadn't happened until now. She had left it in Nørrebro with the key still in the ignition, knowing perfectly well that it would get nailed. She had hoped that the thieves would contaminate it with their DNA or, even better, that the car would be disassembled and the parts sent to Poland. But apparently it hadn't managed to get that far. She thought back on that night. She had been very careful. She had wrapped him in the plastic mat she had spread out in his fitness basement, where she had shot him. Not a single drop of blood had been spilled in the house, nor in the car. She had wrapped him up like a mummy. She had been wearing one of Forensics' coveralls. She had driven through the city in the middle of the night, like a blue flamer wearing that outfit. She had been careful, but . . . her head was pounding in tandem with her concerns, which were mounting. Perhaps she should have burned the car? Driven the piece of junk to Amager Fælled and lit it up. But she knew why she hadn't done it. The burning of a vehicle signalled that someone had committed a crime that they were trying to cover up. Everyone would have been able to deduce that not only had Jeremy disappeared, but he had also been killed. This was much better. Time is always on the side of the perpetrators. It gives them better odds. It gave her better odds. There was a knock on the door at that moment and Heino appeared once more.

"The psycho's here. Can we call him the psycho? I'm asking on behalf of Joakim."

"You can call him whatever the hell you like; just get your asses in here on the double."

31

Nikolaj cautiously smiled at Henrik, Joakim, and Heino, who were standing side by side with their arms crossed.

"Good to see you, Nikolaj," said Cecilie, who returned his smile. "And thank you for taking the time to help us. We really appreciate it."

"Of course," he said, hugging the leather briefcase he was holding in front of him.

"We look forward to reading your profile. Please, take a seat," she said, pointing towards the conference table.

"Thank you," he said, but remained standing. "Just so you know, I didn't bring a physical report with me."

"What do you mean? Haven't you made a profile for us?"

All eyes were on Nikolaj.

"Yes, that is, fragments of it. It's all in my head."

"But we need something concrete," said Heino.

"Which you already have."

"What do you mean?" asked Cecilie.

"That you have the same information that I have looked through. The reports from the scene of the crime, the ones from Forensics, all material from those two cases."

"Yes, of course, but we need someone like you to put together a profile based on that information," Cecilie said.

"Like that guy Vogel," Heino added, "just better."

"Sorry, but I'm unable to provide you with that."

"Okay, but then why did you come?" she asked disappointedly.

"To tell you that you already have the answers in your own minds," he said, giving them an encouraging look. "Take off your shoes," he said as he removed his trainers.

No one did as he said. Instead, they all stared at his polka-dot socks. The left one had a hole in it.

"Perhaps we could start off by taking the chairs and sitting in a circle?" he asked unabashedly.

"What had you envisioned was going to take place now?" Cecilie asked.

"Have you ever tried guided meditation?" he asked, smiling to each one of them.

"I doubt that," Cecilie answered for them all.

"I have," said Joakim, lifting his hand in the air.

"You have? When the hell was that?" Heino asked.

"That's totally irrelevant."

"Hell no. When was it?"

Joakim shrugged his shoulders. "I'm a little bit afraid of flying. So I took a course that's supposed to help."

"Afraid of flying? Did it work?"

"I haven't flown since. But I guess it has."

Heino shook his head.

"Nikolaj, I don't think this is a good idea," said Cecilie.

"I think it could work," he said, pushing his glasses back in place.

"What could work?"

"That we find the answers together. That we create a profile of the perpetrator together through meditation."

The room was silent until Henrik cleared his throat. "Should I continue checking the archives?" he asked, looking at Cecilie. Both Joakim and Heino started getting ready to follow him.

"Look, I understand your scepticism," said Nikolaj. "But it's actually pretty simple. You've got all the answers yourselves. You've got the experience, and you have all the knowledge you need from the reports from the two cases. My job is to facilitate it so that those two things can come together. There won't be any voodoo involved whatsoever," he said, smiling.

"Okay," Cecilie said, taking a deep breath and removing her shoes.

The others cast sidelong glances at one another, whereupon Joakim and then Heino and finally Henrik followed suit.

"Thank you, Cecilie," said Nikolaj. "The first thing we need to do is create a safe space."

Cecilie snapped her fingers impatiently. "Get those chairs over here so we can make that circle!"

A few minutes later they were sitting in a circle, holding one another's hands. Aside from Nikolaj, they all seemed very ill at ease at the intimacy being forced upon them.

"I ask that you close your eyes and take a few deep breaths," he said in a subdued voice. They did as he said and Nikolaj continued speaking in the same monotonous tone. "There is a person out there who is murdering people. There is a person who can't stop himself from doing it. He murders women who live alone. He murders them in their homes. He leaves no traces. No traces whatsoever. There is a person out there carrying a knife. A knife he uses to kill them. The murders are different, but the knife is the same. Why does he use the same type of knife?" The question lingered in the air without anyone answering it. "Because it means something to him," Nikolaj answered. "With the knife he has power. There is a person out there who enjoys exercising power with the help of weapons. What other weapons does he use?"

Again, no one answered, and Cecilie opened her eyes, squinting. "A scalpel," she said, and shut her eyes again.

"There is a person out there who uses a knife . . . and a scalpel."

"And ether," said Heino.

"Ether isn't a weapon," Henrik mumbled. "Per se . . ."

"It's part of his arsenal," Nikolaj said.

"Ether, a scalpel, a knife. In that order. Very methodical. The ether paralyses, the scalpel amputates, and the knife kills them. So why ether?"

"That's what he had lying around, I guess," said Joakim.

"That's one possibility, yes. Any other ideas? Henrik?"

"I've got no clue. It seems old-fashioned and clumsy to me."

"Just like you," said Heino without getting any applause.

"No matter what, it's important to him. Maybe it's supposed to be old-fashioned? As a part of his fantasy? So there's a person out there who fantasises. What does he fantasise about?"

"Violence," said Heino.

"Sadism," Joakim added.

"And misogyny," said Henrik.

"Yes to the first two possibilities. Why misogyny?"

"Because he kills them, of course. Mutilates them," Henrik answered.

"Maybe you're right. Maybe there's something else at play. There is a person out there who cuts off women's labia. There is a person out there who was clumsy in his first attempts but who became more skilled the next time."

"I think it seems pretty hateful," Henrik answered.

"No. He sees them as nothing but objects," said Cecilie.

"I think you're right. There is a person out there who sees women as objects. There is a person out there who sedates them with ether and cuts off their labia."

"He is a collector," said Cecilie.

"The kind that collects insects and kills them with ether," Henrik mumbled.

"Yes," Heino exclaimed. "Damn, the old man's right."

"So he sees them as insects?" Henrik asked sceptically.

"Or just as objects in his fantasy world," said Cecilie.

"There is a person out there who collects women's labia before killing them with a knife. Does he do anything else?"

"He ties them to the bed," said Heino.

"There is a person out there who ties women to beds. Women wearing underwear. Is it their own?"

"We don't know. Maybe," Cecilie answered.

"The size basically fits."

"Like the amount of ether is suitable for sedation. Like the scalpel is suitable for amputating, like the knife is suitable for killing. He has brought the clothes."

"In which case I guess he knows their size beforehand?" said Heino.

"So, there is a person out there who observes them," said Nikolaj, chanting.

"It's all part of his fantasy. He observes them, he dresses them up . . ."

"He films them before he . . . he starts cutting them and kills them," said Joakim uneasily.

"There is a person out there who fantasises about spying on women, breaks into where they live and dresses them up, to then get a trophy. A person who can break in and exit without leaving any traces. How?"

"He knows what he's doing. He's intelligent but sick in the head," said Joakim.

"He knows the territory. And he knows what to say to get in," Heino added.

"That may be a part of his profession. He knows how to talk to people. He can gain access," said Henrik.

"Exactly," said Nikolaj. "Access to two grown-up women's homes, access to their trust. He is an intelligent being. An authoritative being. He has a friendly, reliable-looking appearance. What makes them let him in? Their vulnerability? His authority? What does he claim to be?"

"A psychologist," Joakim said, half-jokingly.

"A landlord or janitor," said Henrik, "which means he is in closer vicinity to them."

"But have you found him close to the vicinity? No. Then think in broader terms. A mover, message service, taxi driver . . ."

"Taxi drivers. We've got several of them in our registry . . ."

Suddenly, Cecilie felt very hot. She couldn't breathe and the air was much too heavy. The voices of the others got all mixed up as they tried guessing the perpetrator's profession, how he had entered the women's homes, his sexuality, why he didn't ejaculate. Cecilie saw all the cases she had had before, all the monsters. She saw Jeremy among the paedophiles, the rapists, and the murderers. He stood in the basement of his magnificent home, staring into the barrel of the pistol she was holding.

A frozen moment until she pulled the trigger. She saw the hole that the projectile formed on his forehead. A small black hole. She saw him tumble onto the plastic she had lain on the floor. Cecilie let go of Niko-laj's and Heino's hands and opened her eyes.

"Anything wrong?" Nikolaj asked, looking at her with concern. She shook her head.

"No, no, please continue," she said, getting on her feet. "I just need to make a phone call. I'm sorry . . ."

32

As soon as Cecilie reached the restroom, she doused her face with water until she couldn't breathe anymore. Gasping for air, she looked at her reflection in the mirror. Her mascara was a little smudged and she looked like a drowned mouse. Her personal waterboarding had neither managed to block out the images of the serial murderers nor the sound of Nikolaj's chanting voice that haunted her mind. That little cunt had managed to throw her off and meddle with something within her that shouldn't be meddled with. She had had her fill of psychologists in her mind, most recently the serial killer Steen Holz, that bastard, and that hadn't ended well at all. She fixed her mascara with a couple of paper towels. Why the hell couldn't Nikolaj just deliver a profile report to them? She put her mascara back in her pocket and felt the small plastic bag with coke that she was still running around with. What were the lyrics to that popular song? *I don't like the drugs, but the drugs love me.* She was tempted. Mostly because she knew that a quick line would calm her racing thoughts. But she didn't need calmness; she needed to be sharp. She took a couple of deep breaths. Freaking out now was completely out of the question. "Pull your shit together, Cecilie, or innocent people will die," she warned herself. When a moment later she stepped into the hallway, she almost stumbled over Ismail. His blue parka acted as an airbag and prevented both of them from losing their balance.

"Damn, Ismail, where did you come from?"

"Cecilie," he said, trying to smile.

"Got anything new for us?"

"You might say that."

"Great. Shoot. We need all the help we can get," she said, giving him a big smile. "We've literally sat in a circle holding each other's hands trying to find answers."

"Huh?"

"Forget it; what've you got for me?"

He shook his head. "You misunderstand. I've been to a meeting with them," he said, pointing behind them towards Ryan and the Travel Team.

"About what?"

"That car they found. You know, Jeremy's Porsche . . ."

"Yeah, I know," she said irritably. "It was a frigging freebie from Bellahøj Station. But why'd they call you?"

"Why do you think?"

"I have no clue. So why?"

"I have to track the car's routes. Find out where it was driven."

Cecilie's laughter sounded hollow. "Do those idiots really think they can trace Jeremy that way?"

Ismail shrugged his shoulders. "'The place where the dog lies buried,' was how Ryan put it, so yes, they probably do."

"But there's no tracker in it."

"And you know that because . . . ?" he asked, sending her a look.

"Since when has a gangster had a tracker in his car?"

Ismail lowered his voice. "So it's not that you had anything to do with it, right?"

"Why are you asking me that, Ismail?"

He quickly looked around. "Because I need to be certain, as in one hundred per cent certain, that you didn't have anything to do with Jeremy's disappearance."

"Haven't we been though all of this before?"

"That's very possible. And I'd be more than happy to go through it one more time in order to ensure that this doesn't lead me into the arms of a biker whom you've disposed of."

"Gangster."

"Huh?

"Jeremy was a gangster, not a biker."

"You know, it worries me every time you refer to him in the past tense."

"Not as much as it worries me that you work for Ryan. That asshole's only got one thing on his agenda, and that's to get me nailed, Ismail. And you're helping him. Do you see where I'm going with this?"

"This is my fucking job," he said, lifting the yellow shopping bag he was carrying.

"Going grocery shopping for him? What's in the bag?"

"What do you think? The infotainment system from Jeremy's car." Ismail opened the bag and showed her the unit that lay on the bottom with various wires sticking out of it.

"Because?"

"Because gifted people like me know how to extract data from the hard drive."

"What kind of data?"

"Just about everything, from what kind of music was being played to where the car was driven. That kind of data."

"From the infotainment system?" she said, her mouth agape.

"Precisely. So, is there anything you'd like to tell me before I get started on it?"

"I don't know; what would that be?"

She continued through the division and looked towards Ryan, who was staring at her. She felt like giving him the finger but composed herself. *Fuck!* a voice within her was screaming. She could have kicked herself a million times. She had up until then managed to be very careful. She had thought of everything. Just not of the bloody infotainment system. Was Barry White now going to give her away? But when it really came down to it, what were Ryan and his stooges going to get out of it? What if Ismail found a whole bunch of routes? It wouldn't show who had driven them. It could have been anybody. And it didn't show where the dog was buried. There was no reason to panic. *No panicking here*, she tried to convince herself as her heart pounded away.

33

Cecilie went to work early the next day. She was pretty bleary-eyed after having spent most of the night searching the registry for potential suspects. When she reached the division, she was surprised to find the boys already sitting there behind their computers, working.

"Good morning," she said as she placed her bag on the closest desk. They all looked up from their screens and responded to her greeting.

"So, have we got wiser since our session with Doctor Nikolaj?"

"A little, maybe," Henrik said, forthcoming.

Cecilie nodded.

"I don't know how much weight we should put on Nikolaj's input, but hopefully we managed to turn the whole thing on its head."

"I thought he was cool enough," said Joakim.

"Cool won't get us anywhere. We've got a perpetrator who we've gotta catch," said Heino.

"That's the spirit, Heino. But do you guys have any leads?" she asked, looking over at his screen.

"We've got two suspects," Heino answered.

"TWO? That's pretty impressive."

"We were also up late working. Some more than others," Henrik said, sending Joakim a glance.

"Okay, show me what you've got."

Henrik picked up some printed photos from the table and turned them towards Cecilie.

"This guy, Lars Munck, thirty-eight. Despite his surname, he's about as far from holy as you can get. He's got several cases behind him, nineteen to be exact, that all have to do with indecent exposure, primarily in the city's parks. Vigerslevparken, Valby Parken, Søndermarken, even in The King's Garden, so he's even a little royal," said Heino.

"Apparently, he can't keep his pants up when female joggers pass by him," said Henrik.

"He's got tons of fines, plus a suspended sentence of four months wasn't enough to stop him either."

"I'm sorry, but that sounds a little lame compared to what we're facing," said Cecilie.

"Yeah, I know, but things started to escalate with him," Heino quickly said. "In 2017, he assaulted a woman with . . . ether. He left her naked in a thicket."

"Rape?"

"No, but he was sentenced with assault and attempted rape."

"He got two years," Henrik.

"And is he free?"

"He's free and lives in Valby. I've got his address here," Henrik said, waving a piece of paper.

"We haven't found anyone in the registry who's used ether up until now, so maybe . . ."

"Okay, we need to pay him a visit. Who's the other one?"

Joakim got up and walked over to the whiteboard. Cecilie looked down at his feet.

"Excuse me, Joakim, but why are you barefoot?"

"Oh, I don't know," he said, shrugging his shoulders. "I thought it was kind of cosy yesterday when we all took off our shoes. It feels kind of nice without socks."

"He's a total imbecile, and this is the final piece of evidence," Heino said, pointing at Joakim's feet.

"Okay, what've you got?" Cecilie asked.

"Michel Bagger, fifty-five years old," he said, attaching it to the whiteboard with a magnet. "He's spent many years in jail. His criminal record contains everything from rape to attempted murder."

"Aside from the fact that he's obviously dangerous, how is he relevant in connection with our perpetrator?"

"The fact that his victims have mostly been women. The times he has committed acts of violence and rape have been in connection with break-ins. In the last case, he waited until the victim had returned home and tied her to the bed and raped her for about twenty-four hours. He injured her with a knife, among other things, which he used on her face."

"Okay, he might be interesting."

"Michel spent some time at Sikringen before ending up in Vestre Prison, so maybe Nikolaj knows him?"

"And is he free?"

"He was released under six months ago."

"We'll need to visit him too."

"So who's going to pick up who?" asked Heino just as he was about to get to his feet.

"Hold your horses a minute," said Cecilie as she signalled him to sit back down. "We're not done. With all due respect, I think that you've come up with some interesting candidates, but we've also got Emil here." She took out her tablet from her bag and showed them an archive photo of a young red-haired man with protruding eyes.

"And what has Emil done?" Henrik asked.

"Emil Bråby and I go back a long way. It annoys me that he didn't pop up in my mind earlier. He was one of my first cases."

"That is a long time ago, boss."

"Thanks, Heino. Anyway, Emil had a tendency to kidnap the dogs that supermarket customers often leave to wait outside while they're shopping. The first ones he kept for a few days before letting them go. But when that wasn't enough for him, he started slitting their throats and placing the dead bodies of the dogs here and there in the neighbourhood."

"Goddamn bastard," Henrik said, shaking his head.

"Henrik is a dog lover . . . in case anyone didn't know," said Heino.

"A few years later, when we ran into him once again, he had dropped the animal abuse in favour of spying on women in the apartment complex he lived in. He even broke into the apartments of those women who lived on the ground floor. He'd climb up on their balconies and enter through the balcony door."

"Did he rape them?" Joakim asked.

"He made do with stealing their underwear. We found a whole pile of underwear and bras at his place."

"I assume it didn't just stop there, boss?" Heino asked.

"For us it did. But I checked him in the registry last night and saw that our colleagues in Århus had the pleasure of having to deal with him."

"What had he done?"

"He attacked his ex-girlfriend on Christmas Eve. According to the records, he forced her to put on the lace underwear he had bought for her as a present and then raped her afterwards."

"So, where is he now? Are we going to Jutland?" Heino asked in a worried voice.

"No, no, don't worry. We have to go to Ikea. In Gentofte."

"That's already exotic enough for Heino. Does he sell beds?" Joakim asked.

"No, he works for a trucking company. He transports furniture to people."

"So, they employ somebody like that in their company? That's not particularly reassuring," said Heino with his arms crossed.

"That's why you should always have a trailer so you can do your own moving."

"So who will we be going to first?" Heino asked.

34

The building where Lars Munck lived was located between the hairdresser, Jeanne d'Arc, and Goga Butt Grill in Folehaven. The low yellow buildings were situated close to the intersection of Gammel Køge Landevej and Ellebjergvej and you could hear the roar of heavy traffic. Cecilie thought that either the inhabitants had to be deaf or wished that they were. When she reached the second floor with the team, she knocked hard on the door of Lars Munck's apartment. It took a little while before it was opened.

"Yes?" said Lars, staring vacuously at the heavy police presence. He was rather heavy-built and was wearing a loose T-shirt that was struggling to conceal the size of his stomach.

"We're from the police, Lars, may we come in?" she said, and pulled out her ID card.

"It's . . . it's not such a good time. I'm actually pretty busy," he said, touching his greasy hair that was gathered in a small ponytail.

"We can also do it at the station."

A mottled cat appeared at his feet. It purred as it rubbed against his legs.

"Is there someone who can see to the cat? Interrogations like this tend to take time."

"Come inside," he said, and turned around. They followed him into the dark hallway, where the stench of cat piss stung their nostrils. Lars supported himself against the wall as he limped into the room. Cecilie directed Heino and Henrik to the kitchen and bathroom, respectively, while she and Joakim followed Lars.

"So, what happened to your leg?"

"Oh, nothing," he said, and sat down at the round dining table. He took the cigarette machine and started rolling a cigarette.

"Nothing? You've got a terrible limp," Cecilie said as she quickly cast a glance around in the living room, which looked like a bomb had hit it.

"I fell on the staircase."

"When?"

"A couple of months ago. Why?" he asked, having just lit his cigarette, whereupon he blew some smoke in their direction.

Cecilie looked over at the computer standing on a table in the corner, which was on. The screen saver had a picture of the cat, which was still crawling around Lars's dirty feet.

"It must have been a pretty bad fall since you're still limping."

"They had to give me twelve screws to put it all back into place," he said, pulling up his jogging bottoms and showing the wound from the twelve screws in his lower leg.

Joakim turned his back to him and faced Cecilie. "It can't be him. He wouldn't have been in any shape for it."

"What were you doing on the computer?"

"Nothing."

She went over to the table and took hold of the mouse. The screen-saver disappeared and a window to a gambling website opened.

"You could just say you're gambling instead of lying."

"Yes, yes, of course."

"What have you been placing your bets on?"

"Nothing. I haven't really gambled today, not yet."

Cecilie clicked her way to the search engine, where a long list of porno sites emerged.

"'Anal pain, slave bitches, spanking teens, rapists in the woods,'" she read aloud, and clicked on the last page, which led to a cheaply produced porno film with two men who were having rape-like sex with a girl in the woods. Cecilie turned towards Lars. "So, that still turns you on? Women getting attacked. Humiliated. Raped."

Lars fiddled around with his cigarette while looking down at the floor.

"It's just something on RedTube. It's not illegal. I don't even know why I watched it."

Heino and Henrik entered the living room.

"Find anything?" Cecilie asked.

They both shook their heads.

"Should we take him and the computer with us?" Heino asked.

"Waste of time," Cecilie answered. "Let's split."

Lars looked up from the floor. He fiddled with the cigarette before stubbing it out in the overflowing ashtray.

"You've got no right barging in here. Damn bitch," he added. The last words were mumbled.

Cecilie stared at him. From the computer could be heard the screams of the young girl as the men whipped her with their belts. Cecilie felt like giving Lars a hard slap on his podgy face. Instead, she reached for the screen and pulled it down to the floor. Lars sat with his mouth agape, staring down at the broken screen, which had gone black.

"You're more than welcome to file a complaint," Cecilie answered.

After they had left the building, Henrik looked at her. "Where to?"

"Let's drop by Ikea," Cecilie said as she unlocked the car. Joakim sat down in the seat next to her and the next moment they were rolling out into the chaotic traffic on Ellebjergvej with Henrik and Heino following behind them. They continued on the beltway northward towards Gentofte as Tessa rapped them through the rush-hour traffic with her song "Ben." When they finally reached the storage house where the Danish and Swedish flags were waving side by side, Cecilie parked in the spot in front of the loading platform. From there, she and Joakim had a clear view of the delivery vans that were lined up and waiting for the customers. Heino and Henrik were parked on the opposite side, close to the exit and ready to block the road. There was quite a lot of activity, and the moving vans replaced one another pretty quickly, but Emil had not turned up. Most of the drivers were either of African or Middle Eastern descent, so Cecilie figured that spotting the red-haired Emil would be pretty easy.

"They have milkshakes!" Joakim said, surprised.

"Who?"

"Heino and Henrik. They're sitting there slurping milkshakes," he said, pointing. He took out his phone and called Heino.

"Did you get milkshakes?"

"Yup," said Heino.

"From McDonald's?"

"You're going to be a big detective someday, Joakim."

"Damn, that's so unprofessional. We're actually on duty," he said, and hung up. "Isn't that unprofessional?"

"It's okay," Cecilie said.

"Should I pick some up?"

"No time for that," she said, and got out of the car. She continued towards the moving van that had just pulled in. Joakim followed behind her, and from the corner of her eye, she could see that Henrik and Heino were on their way.

"Emil!" she called out, making the lanky driver in his work clothes turn around. Emil's red hair had faded since the last time she saw him and the bags underneath his protruding eyes were now dark.

"It's been a long time."

Emil didn't recognise her, but when he realised that he was surrounded, it seemed as though he understood what was at play.

"Too bad you don't remember me. I usually manage to make a lasting impression," Cecilie said, taking out her police badge.

"Fuck this," he said, shaking his head and turning around to leave. He bumped into Heino, who stopped him with two hands on his chest and turned him around towards Cecilie. Emil took a deep breath.

"I'm at work, you know? What do you want?"

"To talk to you. Hear what you've been up to lately."

"Trying to earn a pretty penny; what does it look like? So whatever this is about, it's going to have to wait. We've got customers," he said, pointing to the line.

"I'm sorry if our visit doesn't fit better into your schedule, but unfortunately there's an individual on the loose who's murdering women."

"However, first he gives them sexy underwear to put on," said Heino.

"Does that sound familiar?" Joakim asked.

Emil looked around at them. "You don't think it's me? You're way out of line if you do."

"What's goin' on, Em?" asked a pumped-up, dark-complexioned man wearing the same work clothes as Emil. The man gave Cecilie an aggressive look as he towered over her.

Joakim pulled at his sleeve and showed him his badge. "Don't you have a couch you have to move?"

"Damn cops," he said, and disappeared.

"I've read about that case, and it sounds creepy," Emil said, extending his arms. "But I have nothing to do with it. I swear."

"It'll take a little more than that to convince us. Have you ever met Kristina Sand or Tine Larsen?" Cecilie asked.

"Never . . . that is, I have no clue who they are."

"Have you delivered goods to them?" Henrik asked.

"Was that how you met them?" Heino added.

"I . . . I don't know."

"You don't know?" Cecilie asked, taking a step closer to him. "It doesn't look too good, Emil. I know what you've done before, both to pets . . ."

"Which is damn gross," Henrik interjected.

". . . and to your ex-girlfriend."

"I . . . I've had problems, it's true, but that's all in the past. I don't think I've been to those places, or I'm pretty sure I haven't . . . Where did you say they lived again?"

"Amager and Vesterbro."

"I've never delivered anything to Amager, but maybe Vesterbro . . . a while back. We usually deliver up here, north of Copenhagen."

"Must be perfect for you having a job like this," Henrik said, stepping closer to him. "Where you can get into people's homes, to all those single suburban housewives. Have you snatched some panties lately?"

Emil looked around nervously.

"I think we'd better take him in so we can get to the bottom of this," said Cecilie, and she looked at Henrik. He pushed his jacket aside and rummaged for the handcuffs in his belt.

"This job is really important to me," said Emil, sending Cecilie a desperate look. "I play by the book now . . . pretty much. You can take a look at my schedule. You can see my routes; it's all in the log. It covers the past six months."

He pushed his way past Henrik and to the open side door of the van. When he returned, he extended a tablet to them. Heino grabbed it from his hand and started scrolling through the pages. A little while later he looked up and shook his head.

"On the face of it, it doesn't look like he's been to those addresses."

"That's what I was trying to tell you. Can I please go back to my job now?"

Cecilie looked at him thoughtfully.

"Henrik, Heino, Emil is going to get off work early today so he can show you around his home."

"Oh, come on," said Emil as he threw back his head. "I can't just leave. What am I gonna tell my partner?"

"I don't give a shit," said Cecilie. "You can tell him you've got diarrhoea or that the police are searching your apartment because you raped your ex-girlfriend. It's up to you."

"Fuckin' hell," he said as he ran his hand through his hair.

"But, Emil, if we so much as find a single piece of lace underwear at your place, it sure as hell better be in your size or I'll charge you for double murder. Is that understood?"

Emil nodded and voluntarily went with Heino and Henrik. A while later, Cecilie drove off with Joakim, who had gone to get milkshakes for them both. The GPS was set to find the address in the Sydhavnen neighbourhood, where Michel lived. Their last suspect on the list. Cecilie drummed on the steering wheel. Joakim looked at her.

"Do you think they'll find anything at Emil's place?"

"Maybe. Once a panty sniffer, always a panty sniffer. But no matter what, he didn't have anything to do with those murders."

"How can you be so sure?"

"Emil may be an incorrigible bastard, but he's not a monster. If you've met enough of them, you start to recognise their stench." She rolled down the window and continued along Enghavevej. Half an hour later, they knocked on the door of the dilapidated terraced house. Since no one opened, Cecilie looked through the dirty kitchen window.

"What the hell are you doing?" a man behind them who had entered the front garden asked. Cecilie recognised him from the picture. Michel was dressed in a worn windbreaker and stood holding a bag of bottles with a cigarette dangling from the corner of his mouth.

"Michel Bagger?"

"And? Who told you to come here and look through my windows? Get the hell out of here!"

He started to approach them with clenched fists. Cecilie took out her badge, which made Michel snort. "So, is this when I'm supposed to piss my pants in fear?"

"Preferably not. We want to talk with you."

"Go fuck yourself, dyke cop," he said, and pushed his way past Cecilie and Joakim. Cecilie placed a hand on his shoulder.

"Either we talk here or at the st—"

Michel dropped the bag and whirled around. Cecilie took a step back and just managed to evade his clenched fist. "How about a taste of this, bitch!" he hissed, and attempted to hit her again. Once again, Cecilie managed to evade the blow. Michel hurled himself at her and dragged her down with him on the grass. He landed heavily on top of her and knocked the wind out of her. His blows rained down on her until Joakim managed to pull Michel away. Cecilie got on her feet and helped Joakim turn Michel on his stomach. She placed her knee on his back as Joakim managed to fasten his wrists together.

"Police brutality!" Michel shouted.

"Are you okay, Cecilie?" Joakim asked.

She wiped the blood from her upper lip. "Yes, forget about it."

She pressed her knee even harder against Michel's back as she pulled one of his arms. "Lie still!" Michel let out a howl.

35

Y ou look like one of those ladies who's had something done to their lips," said Henrik as he stared at Cecilie from his seat.

"Botox, they get Botox injected," said Heino, nodding superciliously. "It's the latest fashion."

"Well, I guess I've become fashionable, then," said Cecilie, who was sitting on the edge of the table. She touched her lip and felt the swelling. It was still sore after yesterday. Fortunately, nothing had happened to her teeth.

"So, when are we going to headquarters to interrogate him?" Heino asked as he impatiently drummed his fingers on the surface of the table.

"I'm thinking we should give him time to properly cool down in there. That never hurts an interrogation. Did your visit to Emil's place yield any results?"

"No, we didn't find anything other than old underpants and a half-dead hamster. I don't wanna know what he's been doing to it."

"What about the search in Michel's home?" Henrik asked.

Joakim said they had to dig their way through loads of junk, but there had been nothing to be found. Heino looked past Cecilie and out across the division.

"What's the psycho doing here?"

Cecilie turned halfway around.

"I've invited him in to witness the interrogation. Can't you just call him Doctor or Nikolaj?"

"Are we suddenly sensitive now? I didn't think you liked him," Henrik said.

"Is he single, boss?" Heino asked.

"Shut up, Heino," she hissed.

Nikolaj came over and greeted all four of them.

"Good to see you, Nikolaj. Thank you for taking the time to talk to us."

"Of course," he said. He looked at her swollen lip but didn't say anything. "Even though I doubt that I can be of much help."

"Well, since you have some background knowledge of the suspect, I don't think that's true."

"I'm sorry that you've been using my input to look only in the registry to find the perpetrator. That wasn't really the intention."

"You yourself emphasised that he had a past," she answered.

"Which you can safely say Michel has," Henrik added.

"Have you gone after others in the registry?" Nikolaj asked.

"This one's our best bet," Cecilie answered evasively.

"What was your assessment of him at the time?" Henrik asked.

Nikolaj put his hands in his pockets. "It's a long time ago and I only helped out in relation to the investigation. But Michel had definite narcissistic characteristics and lacked empathy. And he tended to display externalising behaviour."

"In other words, a complete psychopath," said Heino.

Nikolaj shook his head. "Not in medical terms."

"He's done some pretty crazy stuff."

"In my experience, it is often healthy individuals who commit the most bestial crimes."

"See, now that's why I want you on the sidelines to observe the initial interrogation."

"Why?"

"To see whether Michel fits our perpetrator's profile."

"I'll do my best."

Cecilie got up from the table. "Should we get going, then?"

Ryan appeared from the opposite end of the division.

"Cecilie, do you have a moment?" he said in a semi-loud voice as he continued towards her.

"Not really, Ryan. We are on our way to interrogate a suspect." She enjoyed throwing those words at his face.

"It's just because I'm going to need some manpower soon. So can I borrow some of your men?"

"For what?" she asked, crossing her arms.

"To question potential witnesses. Do a little canvassing in the neighbourhood, that sort of thing."

"What neighbourhood?"

"Bellahøj."

She felt her rage growing. "My hood?"

He shrugged his shoulders nonchalantly. "Yes, if that's what you want to call it."

"In connection with what?"

"We have a suspicion that Jeremy's earthly remains are located there."

"On what grounds?"

He held his head high. "As you know, we found his car and I've had NC3—"

"Yes, I know . . . had them check the infotainment system. And what does that have to do with Bellahøj?"

"Among the registered routes, we found one that went from his house on Amager Strandvej across the city to a location in Nørrebro. But there's an interesting stop along the route. A whole twelve minutes near Utterslev Mose, the boglands close to Bellahøj."

"I see. And why is that interesting?"

"For various reasons that I can't get into now. But there are some deep lakes in the bog, aren't there?"

"I'm afraid you're asking the wrong person. I've never bathed there," she answered ironically.

"Me neither. But we're getting the divers out to search them."

"You plan to search a whole bog because your suspect stopped to take a piss?" She sent him a contemptuous glance. "What does the head of police think of you spending such resources? I can't remember the last time we had that sort of thing at our disposal," she said, looking at Heino and Henrik.

"Me neither," said Henrik.

"It's already been approved," Ryan said triumphantly.

"Yes, of course it has. Don't get your feet wet." She turned around and walked through the division with the others following on her heels.

"Divers!" she said, shaking her head. "Goddamn Travel Team!"

She did not like the look on Nikolaj's face, so she looked away.

36

Cecilie and Henrik sat across from Michel Bagger and his court-appointed defence attorney—a middle-aged woman who looked as though she had just woken up—in the windowless interrogation room at police headquarters. A camera sent a signal to the room further down the hallway where Heino and Nikolaj could follow what was going on. Michel had been examined by a doctor, who had put his left arm in a sling after the arrest.

"I'm not saying a single word to you before my complaint has been noted," he said, looking at his lawyer. "You have to go after them, dammit. They're total Nazis. The bitch sprained my arm."

Before the lawyer had a chance to respond, Henrik interjected, "As I've already informed you, Michel, you're being charged with resisting arrest and assaulting a police officer, according to Penal Code § paragraph 119, and disorderly conduct."

"Hey, I'm the one who was assaulted, on my own property, man!"

"You could have answered our questions nicely and calmly."

"Hey, I didn't get a chance before that dyke attacked me," he said, pointing at Cecilie.

"We're going to talk with you about your activities and movements," said Henrik as Cecilie remained silent.

"Activities and movements?" Michel sneered.

"Yes. Where you have been, what you've been doing. Simple questions like that."

"Oh no, it's not simple at all. It's fucked up, is what it is. Because you tricked me and now I've been trapped, again!"

"There are no traps here, and absolutely no one here is trying to trick you. Furthermore, you've got your court-appointed lawyer right here to make sure that everything is done in a correct manner."

Michel looked at the lawyer disapprovingly. "As though that's gonna do any good. What the hell is it that you wanna know? The size of my cock or what?" he asked, staring at Cecilie. She looked back at him with an expressionless gaze. She wasn't at all present in that small room. The only thing she could think about was Ryan and the divers who he had planned to send into the lake. Goddamn Ryan had tried to provoke her. His request to borrow her men had been a test. To see whether she would blink. Had she blinked?

"Cecilie?" Henrik asked, trying to get her attention. She signalled with a wave of her hand for him to continue.

"Very well, then," Henrik said, and cleared his throat. Cecilie disappeared back in her thoughts and only listened with half an ear. Michel explained. Michel whined. Michel swore. She stared at the midget. A little drunkard who was now sitting before her, ungroomed, smelly, dishevelled, and whose set of teeth was brown. A boasting asshole who hadn't accomplished a thing in his life other than causing pain and suffering for other people. He had raped before, and if given the chance, he'd do it again. Driven by a callous desire. He was like a dog humping someone's leg. During the next half an hour, Michel answered all of Henrik's questions about his whereabouts. It could all be boiled down to him either being at home, at the local pub, or with one of his loser friends who'd give him an alibi. Regardless of her loathing for him, she knew it was all a waste of time.

Michel leaned back in the chair and belched. "This is all about those dames who were ripped up, isn't it? I heard about them on TV."

He seemed proud to have been associated with a high-profile case.

"But it wasn't me. Those two bitches were too old for me to get it up. I do, after all, have a little taste." He let out a small hoarse laugh. "So, too bad, you've got the wrong guy. Are we done here?"

Henrik was at a loss for words and looked at Cecilie. She made no response but continued to stare at Michel's forehead and the imaginary bullet hole she was trying to plant there.

"Did he fuck them first?" Michel leaned forward in his chair defiantly. "I think he gave them a real workout with his cock, am I right?"

He nodded, looked towards Cecilie, and licked his lips. "I think he fucked them violently as they were screaming. Did he fuck them in the ass? Did he finish all over them?" Michel gestured with his hand. "Did he come on their faces, all over their boobs? Before cutting them off?"

White foam appeared in the corner of his mouth and excitement was painted all over his eyes. Cecilie took a deep breath and leaned towards him. "That's precisely what the perpetrator did. Right down to the tiniest detail of what you just described."

"Really? I bet they deserved it. If only he'd done it to you."

"Well, he didn't. And we're sitting here now. And you are giving information that corresponds with the situations of the two murders. Which only reconfirms my suspicions about you."

"Say what?" he said, straightening his back. "What the hell do you mean, bitch?"

"That I've got enough on you to charge you with both murders."

"Christ, that was just something I said. I don't know jack shit about it."

"It sounded like a confession to me," she said, smiling coldly. "And considering your past, I think we've got ourselves an excellent case."

"What?" He desperately turned to his defence attorney, who still didn't seem to have woken up.

"Say something to that bitch. Defend me, for Christ's sake!"

The attorney yawned. "They can charge you with whatever they want. But that doesn't mean it's true. That'll be up to the judge."

Cecilie got up and Henrik followed suit.

"We're done for today. But, Michel, you should probably get used to small rooms. Enjoy yourself at Vestre Prison." She turned to the lawyer. "I would probably advise your client to go into voluntary isolation. The prisoners aren't too friendly to woman killers. We'll keep in touch."

When they were out in the hallway, Henrik looked at her. "You didn't mean that seriously, did you? I mean, about charging him?"

"Hell no. I just wanted to watch him shit his pants."

"Well, you certainly succeeded in that," Henrik said, smiling.

"We'll let him stew in custody and charge him for resisting arrest."

Henrik nodded.

37

When Cecilie and Henrik had gone a little further down the hall-way, they joined Heino and Nikolaj.

"Damn, what a provoking son of a bitch," said Heino.

"We followed the whole thing even though the sound was pretty bad."

Cecilie looked at Nikolaj. "Sorry for having wasted your time. Michel Bagger clearly isn't our man."

"I'm happy to hear that you think so. Was there any particular reason why you had to intimidate him like that?"

They all looked at Nikolaj in surprise.

"You did hear what he said, didn't you?" Cecilie asked.

"Yes, and?"

"That asshole was explicitly throwing dirt at the victims."

Nikolaj nodded. "Being unsympathetic isn't a crime. There was really no reason to go after him like that."

"The man had a defence attorney at his side. Everything was done by the book."

"What happened to his arm?"

"He jerked off too much. What do I know?" Cecilie said, gesturing with her hand.

"It sounded to me like it happened during the arrest."

Henrik gave Heino a nudge. "Cecilie, we're going to go back and organise Michel and that paragraph 119 charge."

Cecilie nodded briefly to the two of them, who disappeared, whereupon she turned back to Nikolaj.

"Are you his lawyer, or what?"

"Merely a concerned citizen, and anyway, you invited me to listen in on it."

"There is no reason to be so concerned for Michel. Believe me, the best way to handle guys like him is to treat them like a yellow dog. Let them know who's in charge."

Nikolaj smiled. "Not according to my experience or international studies, for that matter."

"What do the studies say?"

"That therapy, compassion, even the tiniest bit of understanding can transform people like Michel considerably."

"Yeah, just like you can train a tiger to jump through hula hoops, but it's still a tiger. And in Michel's case, a nasty motherfucker."

She started walking.

"Cecilie?" he called, and she turned around. "Where does all that anger come from?"

She looked away. "I don't know. I've never asked any of those bastards."

"I meant your anger."

The question took her aback, but she didn't show it.

"Hey, there's no anger here. I'm as happy as can be," she said, extending her arms.

"I mean it. You seem stressed, and a little burned out."

She took a few steps towards him. "Is that Palsgaard speaking now? Someone from the top brass?"

"What are you talking about?" he asked, shaking his head and trying to smile. "It was just from sheer interest."

"For my well-being?" she asked with suspicion.

"Um . . . yes?"

"Listen, I am perfectly fine, okay?"

"It would make sense if you were stressed regarding this case. And wasn't there another one you were talking about earlier? It must be stressful being you. If you ever need someone to talk to, then—"

"Then your couch is available?"

"My what?"

"Your couch. Isn't that what you lie on when you go to a psychologist, or is that just a cliché?"

"We could talk about it over a cup of coffee. It wouldn't have to be any more complicated than that."

"Thanks, Nikolaj," she said, squeezing his arm. "I appreciate the offer, I think. But, really, I'm fine, okay?"

"Okay . . . but you've got my number."

"I've got your number."

When she returned to Teglholmen, she rushed through the division while casting a glance at Ryan and his team through the corner of her eye. They were still there, which was a good sign because it meant that the dive hadn't come about that day. She was going to have to put a permanent stop to it before too much reached the surface. It was time to return Beatrice Klerke's numerous calls and ask for help. The situation couldn't be much worse, she thought, and disappeared into her office. And yet . . .

"Ismail. What the hell are you doing here?"

She threw her bag on the conference table, next to which was a chair he was sitting on, waiting for her. His big blue parka enveloped him like a turtle shell as he shook his head in discouragement.

"I can't do this anymore, Cecilie. I can't take it anymore."

"What do you mean? What's happened?

"The infotainment system."

"Oh, that."

"Did you throw the body into the lake?"

"What are you talking about? Of course not. They're really screwing with your head, aren't they?"

"No, they're not screwing with my head. But I'm not stupid, Cecilie!" he said loudly before composing himself and subduing his voice. "I'd understand. I'd understand if you killed him. But then we've got to say it. Tell it like it is before they find his body. You've got to confess."

Cecilie stood with her arms folded. "What can I say to make you understand that I've had nothing to do with Jeremy's disappearance?"

He shook his head. "I don't know. Not anymore."

"Okay, let's say that I had killed him, which I haven't. But if I had, it would never affect you. You're not guilty of anything. You gave me the information that indicated Jeremy's involvement in Troels's death. I never got a chance to interrogate Jeremy before he disappeared. And that's that."

Ismail looked down at the floor. "I'm not like you, Cecilie. I can't just block it out. I know he was a son of a bitch who maybe deserved it, but I just can't live with it. I wish I could. I honestly do." A tear rolled down his cheek.

"Do you intend to go to Ryan and tell him all of this?"

"Yes . . ." he said faintly. "But at the same time, I can't bear the thought . . ."

"You're in a nasty situation, huh, Ismail?" she said as she sat down on the edge of the table.

They sat in silence. Cecilie extended her hand and caressed his black spiky hair. "You are in quite a dilemma. But, Ismail, look at me."

Ismail lifted his face and looked up at her. "They won't find anything, okay?"

"I hope not. Or I'll . . . I'll probably have to tell it like it is . . . Do you understand?"

She didn't answer him. Instead, she looked at the black bullet hole that seemed to take shape on his forehead.

"Of course, I understand."

38

It was 10:30 p.m. and Cecilie was the last one left in the division. The humming sound from the fluorescent tubes was replaced by the cleaning woman's pottering further down the hallway. Cecilie stared out through the panoramic window towards the empty car park in front of the building. She looked at her watch impatiently. She had agreed with Beatrice Klerke to meet at 10 p.m., and now she was starting to get nervous that the Minister might let her down. Either because more important things had turned up or as a punishment for the fact that Cecilie hadn't returned her requests to meet in a more private setting. However, Beatrice Klerke had responded quickly to Cecilie's invitation. A pair of headlights lit up the dark street, and shortly afterwards, a big black Mercedes pulled into the car park. Cecilie recognised it as Klerke's official car and rushed to get her bag and jacket. A few minutes later, she stepped out of the main entrance and continued towards the car park. The middle-aged driver was standing in front of the car, in his thin black suit, shivering. It was clear that he had been sent outside, which hadn't suited him at all.

"The Minister is waiting," he said, without making any indication that he was going to open the car door for her. When she sat down in the back seat, Klerke looked up from her papers. She pushed her gold-rimmed reading glasses down the bridge of her nose and smiled at Cecilie.

"You've been ghosting me. Isn't that how young people put it nowadays?"

"In which case I wouldn't know," Cecilie said, smiling back at her.

"Oh, you're young enough," Beatrice Klerke said, placing the papers in a big leather briefcase that she put aside on the floor. She took off her glasses and folded them.

"Shall we go right to the heart of the matter or waste our time on foreplay?"

She placed her hand on Cecilie's thigh.

"Um, I . . ." Cecilie managed to stammer.

Beatrice removed her hand. "Of course, not literally, God forbid."

"Let's get to the heart of the matter," Cecilie said, and quickly smiled.

"Why have you suddenly contacted me? Has the Travel Team got in the way of the investigation? Not that I've been following it closely, but you and your team seem to have got a little stuck."

"We've talked with a few suspects . . . and have got several leads we are pursuing, even though it's a little slow going, that's true," said Cecilie, meandering a little.

Beatrice Klerke shook her head. "I'm not the one you need to tell that to. It's your closest manager you need to convince. Results create power, Cecilie. While a lack, thereof, is a direct ticket out in the cold. I know what I'm talking about."

Cecilie nodded. "The only thing is that the Travel Team, especially Ryan, they take up a lot of space in the division and are creating unrest."

"Well, put them in their place, then," said Klerke, frowning as much as the Botox in her forehead allowed her to. "I thought you had managed to outmanoeuvre him a long time ago. I made sure the case went to you."

"For which I am very grateful, but it's meant that they've started to look into an old case, the sole purpose of which is to damage me."

"What case?"

"A case about a missing gangster that they want to put me on the hook for."

"I see. Because you didn't manage to find him, or . . . ?"

"No, someone who they think I let disappear."

Beatrice squinted her eyes. "As in actually disappearing?"

"As in dead and gone, as they say."

"It's concerning that you are even sharing something like that with me."

"But—"

Beatrice lifted her hand. "No matter what, it is a case that is in every way damaging to you and could damage me politically. It's free ammunition for my opponents. It will have to be buried as quickly as possible."

"I couldn't agree more. It's just hard when the Travel Team is busy pulling it up to the surface."

"What do you mean?"

"They have recruited divers to investigate the lakes in Utterslev Mose, which is the last place I want them to search."

"Damn, Cecilie," Klerke exclaimed, and looked away.

It became quiet in the car. Cecilie was sweating profusely and desperately wanted to roll down the window. Beatrice Klerke looked at her again.

"How certain is it that the case would resurface?"

"It's a small bog. I can't imagine it not resurfacing."

"You're going to have to work this out, Cecilie."

"Yes. But I don't know how. That's why I'm asking for help. For a divine intervention."

Beatrice snorted. "Flattery won't get you anywhere."

"I'd be very grateful if it were possible to do something."

"*Grateful* is a cheap word that desperate people throw around at random."

"Perhaps I could repay you at some point?"

"Oh, really?"

"Yes, of course," said Cecilie, who was just about to grab hold of Klerke's hand but stopped herself.

Beatrice sent her a sidelong glance. "Very well. A problem has actually just appeared."

"Something that I can be of any help with?" Cecilie asked in a forced voice.

"Our former political spokesperson, Helge Sundvald, is about to get into our good graces again."

"The name doesn't ring a bell," Cecilie said, unzipping her jacket. The Mercedes was beginning to feel like a sauna.

"Well, he's also been tucked away in the back row. Shielded from the surveillance of the press while he was busy cleaning up his act."

"Did he manage to do that, then?"

Beatrice Klerke made a gesture of regret. "Yes. Just like he has managed to get a proper hold of his base. They see him as the prodigal son who has returned."

"But that must be a good thing, right?"

Beatrice looked at her as though she was an imbecile. "Don't you know anything about the realities of Parliament?"

"Apparently not."

"Well, let me explain it to you, then. The Parliament consists of a hundred and seventy-nine narcissists who are trying to nose out the popular feeling better than the neighbour they are sitting next to. Your worst opponents are the other members of your own party. Especially those who are eyeing the same positions as you. And Helge is about to get lined up with his own constituency."

"What are you referring to?"

"There are rumours that our idiotic Prime Minister, my party's leader, is planning a reshuffle in the near future, and in that reshuffle, Helge will be appointed as the new Minister of Justice."

"Wow."

"Wow indeed. We can't let that happen. Neither for my sake or for yours, for that matter. Helge, that holier-than-thou douchebag, wants to clean up the Ministry and the agency. Expose all the skeletons in the closet. Find a scapegoat," she said, poking Cecilie on her thigh.

"But what is it you want me to do?"

"Isn't that pretty clear?"

"Not really."

"Use Helge's weakness to our advantage," she said, touching her nose and sniffing.

"He still isn't clean?"

She shook her head dismissively.

"Oh, no, he's as clean as a lamb. He's found Jesus."

"Well, that'll make it somewhat difficult, won't it?"

"So? Difficult, did you say? Since when has that been a hindrance?"

Cecilie gave a little smile. "I can't just plant drugs on him."

"I'm not telling you what you should or shouldn't do. But I need Helge to disappear, at least from the political landscape. Can you ensure that, Cecilie?"

Cecilie hesitated.

"If he's guilty, then yes. Otherwise . . ."

"We're all guilty of something! Look at it as justice finally catching up with Helge, just with a slightly delayed effect. He's broken the law numerous times with his drug abuse and each time someone covered for him."

"Yes, but . . ."

"Even if the representative government and the inviolability of the political system means absolutely nothing to you, then consider just how many individuals from your neck of the woods would have been given the same chances as Helge's been given." She stared at Cecilie intensely.

Cecilie looked down at the floor. "I don't need to hear any more reasons; I know when I'm being played."

"Good, then play along."

"Sorry. I can't go after innocent individuals. I'm not cut out for it."

"Well, then what use are you to me?" Beatrice Klerke exclaimed.

Cecilie looked at her. "I can help with so many other things . . ."

"But this is what I need. And you need me."

"I'm sorry, but . . ."

"Fine. You're nothing but a burden to me, then. Get out of my sight," Beatrice said, looking at her as though she were a piece of excrement.

"Get out! Now! Get lost!"

Cecilie stepped out of the car. The driver quickly shut the door and got behind the wheel. A moment later, the Minister's car was gone.

"Fuck," Cecilie heard herself shouting. Beatrice Klerke was crazier than her.

39

The low white terraced houses in Kongelundsparken lit up in the glow of the moonlight. It was here, among young families and pensioners, that she had chosen to hide. From his position at the tall birch trees on the green common area, he looked at the buildings straight ahead of him. The cold and the rain kept the inhabitants indoors and he could stand there unbothered and without the risk of being seen. Byrupsvej number 111; this was where Lizzette had settled down. She had been difficult to locate. She wasn't on any of the social media platforms like Instagram, Facebook, or TikTok. Her name change had blurred her identity. Camilla Toft had become Lizzette Morning Star. One of those spiritual numerologists must have worked overtime. He had been forced to dig very deeply to find her and had risked being discovered in the process. But it had been well worth the risk now that he had succeeded. She was going to help him make his collection complete. He had prepared well. He had bought a camera with a built-in flash. A camera that could take proper pictures. The ones he had previously taken with his iPhone had come out too fuzzy. And that had compromised the pictures not only aesthetically but also in terms of the level of detail. They had been sloppy and not at all representative of his collection. Which tormented him. It was important to go out of your way when doing things, no matter what they were. As a collector you would be judged not simply by the content of your collection, but also its quality. His collection would be marked by his own development. The way he had cut into the subjects. Fumbling at first, and then later becoming gradually more experienced, to finally exhibit a professional knack. At least, that was his ambition. Which was why he had purchased a pair of surgical scissors that allowed him to make deeper, more precise cuts. He had also obtained a vaginal pump that he could place above the vulva to create pressure. In that way he could press the blood out of the labia and the clitoris, which would grow during the process. The enlarged genitals would make his work so much easier. Perhaps he would manage to cut off the entire clitoris this time. The mere thought of it made his heart pound faster. This could truly be huge. A collection of real significance. His collection.

Lizzette's balcony door was opened. He was too far away to be able to see whether it was her, but her pronounced curves and her slightly bent posture indicated that it must be her. He knew that Lizzette was divorced and lived alone and that she had a grown-up daughter who had settled down somewhere in Jutland. Vejle, he thought. Lizzette also had a little dog to keep her company. A balding mutt, whose breed he didn't know. As she stood swaying in the doorway, Lizzette managed to let the dog out into the small garden. *Are you drunk, Lizzette? You little drunkard. Are you boozing all alone? Now, that's really very sad,* he thought. A downfall from the heights of the past. The rain was clearly too much for Lizzette, who shut the door and left the dog out there alone. This was the moment he had been waiting for. He quickly crossed the lawn with his briefcase under his arm. He continued towards the gate in the low fence and carefully opened it. At that moment, the dog let out a bark. He squatted down as he found one of the small Danish meatballs that he had brought with him in his pocket. Kötbullar from Ikea. He himself had fallen for them and luckily, the dog seemed to feel the same way. He gave the dog one more as he grabbed hold of its collar and pulled it out of the garden. A few minutes later, Lizzette opened the terrace door and stared out into the darkness.

"Molly? Mo-o-olly. Molly, dammit." She looked around as the rain made her T-shirt wet. "Well, you can stay out, then. Mum's going back inside."

He was squatting with the dog in his arms as he held its snout closed. When the terrace door was closed, he let it go. The dog started whimpering and licking his fingers. He felt like squeezing it to death. Watching the light disappear from its round eyes. Instead, he let it go and got to his feet. He gave the dog a hard kick and it howled as it sprinted away. Then he continued around the end of the house and to the main door on the opposite side. Now was the time. The evening had made it clear to him. It was time to expand the collection. *Do your best. No, do your utmost.*

"*There's no escape, I can't wait. I need a hit, baby, give me it,*" little Britney sang to him.

It was early in the morning when a middle-aged woman wearing a pink tracksuit stopped, out of breath, by the entrance to Lizzette's home.

"Hey, Molly-girl, what's with you?"

Lizzette's little dog was sitting drenched in front of the main door, trembling from the cold. The woman went over to the dog and rang the doorbell.

"Have you been sitting out here all night?"

The dog whimpered in response and scratched impatiently at the door to be let in. When the woman rang the doorbell three times without anyone answering, she pushed the door handle down and peeped in.

"Lizzette, it's Jytte . . . Are you okay?"

The little dog slipped inside and since no one had answered, she followed it. She called out a few times as she walked through the house.

"Where could your mother be, Molly?"

She returned to the hallway where the little dog was on its way up the stairs to the first floor.

"Lizzette?" she called, as she remained standing. No one answered and the stillness in the house was unnerving.

"Lizzette, are you there?" Jytte asked in a concerned voice.

At that moment, the little dog appeared on the landing, and in the next second it came rushing down the stairs.

"God, Molly," Jytte said as it ran between her legs and continued to its basket, where it huddled in the corner. Jytte looked at the dog and noticed with alarm the blood on its paws and around the corners of its lips. She looked back up towards the first floor and she slowly began to climb the steep staircase. When she reached the landing, she once again called Lizzette's name, even though she knew deep down that she would get no response. She continued towards the bedroom at the end of the hallway and looked in through the open door. A shrill wail came from Jytte, who stumbled backwards and hit the wall. Her legs were unable to carry her, and she slowly slid to the floor, where she remained sitting. Jytte stared dumbfounded into the bedroom. From a hook in the ceiling above the bed, Lizzette was hanging naked from a dog leash and had a dog collar around her neck. Her stomach had been ripped open and her intestines hung heavily from her abdomen. On the floor, there was a pool of blood in which the outline of Molly's paw prints could be discerned. Jytte tried to call for help, but no sound came out of her mouth.

40

From her balcony, Cecilie looked out across the neighbourhood, which was just awakening. Her sweaty body was steaming in the biting cold. She had just completed her sparring round with Bob. In the living room behind her, the boxing dummy could still be seen swaying back and forth after the last hammering blows she had delivered to it. Cecilie almost hadn't been able to close her eyes after her meeting with Beatrice Klerke. The Minister's explosive outburst had come as a surprise to her and had revealed a dangerous side to Klerke. Her demand for a quid pro quo was almost as absurd as Cecilie's wish that the Travel Team be discontinued, which just showed how stressful a situation Klerke was in. It was a matter of survival for them both. If Klerke was removed, Cecilie could just as well drown herself in the same bog into which she had dropped Jeremy's body. Cecilie thought about the kinds of secrets Klerke was hiding. How she had attained power. How she had fought all the way to the Ministry. She had to have several skeletons in the closet, no doubt about that.

Twenty minutes later, Cecilie was standing next to the Golf and unlocking the door. From the opposite end of the car park, Paki Allan came zipping over on his scooter. She didn't have time for the kid today, but when she saw his black eye, she decided to stop after all.

"Hey, what happened to your eye? Did you get into a fight?"

"I walked into a door. A door by the name of Hash-hassan," he said, stopping on his scooter.

"You've gotta be careful with those kinds of doors."

"I know. But the id-idiot and his brother d-deal in the park. Have you seen how many pushers . . . that come there now?"

"Allan, dammit."

She looked at the boy, who despite his big size, was still a child. "I've told you to stay away from that. I'll take care of it."

"You will?" he asked, looking at her sceptically.

"Yes," she quickly said. "I promise. But you've also got to promise me not to get yourself mixed up in all of that. It's not good for you."

Her phone rang, and she answered it. It was Heino, who sighed heavily. "We have another case, boss."

"Where?"

"Kongelundsparken. A woman was killed with a knife in her home and found naked by a neighbour. Sounds like our perp, doesn't it?"

"Text me the address," she said, and hung up.

"Are you going to turn on the lights?" Allan shouted after her.

She didn't answer but instead raced out of the car park.

It wasn't hard to see where the scene of the crime was among Kongelundsparken's identical white terraced houses. The many police officers and patrol cars and the throngs of curious residents in front of number 111 gave it away. Cecilie pushed her way through to the barrier. It was always the same thing: The flashing blue lights of the sirens attracted people. The only difference between now and the past was that these days the spectators would uninhibitedly film it with their phones, like they would at a concert.

"Expand the perimeter," she said to the officers, who were getting pushed back towards the entrance. "It's a crime scene, goddammit!"

"Cecilie," Heino called to her from the open front door.

She checked the door frame on her way over to him. "No sign of a break-in, or what?"

"Nope, no sign. The modus operandi is identical to what we've seen before." They entered the hallway. There were forensic officers and police everywhere. Far too many, she thought.

"Get rid of the ones who have no business being here, Heino. Where is the deceased?"

"Upstairs," Heino answered, pointing towards the staircase. Cecilie carefully avoided the small yellow flag markers that Forensics had placed by the bloodstains on the stairs. When she reached the bedroom, Ole, wearing his white coveralls, was standing next to the body, which was hanging by a dog leash from a hook in the ceiling. The ceiling light that had evidently been hanging from the hook was now standing below the window.

"Hi, Ole," Cecilie said. "This looks pretty familiar, doesn't it?"

"Yes, to a worrisome degree."

Cecilie looked at the naked woman whose intestines hung out from the open cavity in her stomach. The sight of the abused body was nauseating, and she was forced to swallow her saliva.

"The same modus operandi?"

"I'm guessing she was killed around midnight like the other two. Judging by the cuts and stab wounds, it would seem the same type of murder weapon was used. In comparison to the two earlier murders, this one differs due to the long cuts that opened the stomach."

"He deliberately opened her this time?"

"It would seem so, yes. By and large, I would say that the whole thing seems more calculated, more professional, if you can describe something like this in such terms."

"What about the injuries to her groin?" Cecilie asked, pointing to the dried-up blood surrounding the flesh wound by the woman's vagina.

"The cut marks look very deep this time."

Cecilie walked over to the bed and looked up towards the lamp hook the corpse was hanging from. "Was she strangled in that?"

"We'll find out later, but there is nothing to really indicate that. My guess is that he didn't hang her up there until post mortem and perhaps first cut open her stomach."

"What do you base that on?"

"There are no abrasive marks around her neck," he said, pointing. "However, there are marks on her wrists and ankles, which indicate that she was tied up and was trying to get free."

Cecilie looked at the marks on one of the ankles that were strewn like bloody ribbons across the faded tattoo of a French lily. A couple of cut-up cable ties hung from one of the bedposts.

"And what about her panties?" she said, pointing to the victim's mouth.

Ole nodded. "The same as the other two, yes."

"So aside from the hanging this seems to be the same modus operandi." She looked at the thin dog collar on the victim's neck, upon which there was a name in glittering brass. "Who's Molly?"

"The deceased's dog," said Heino, who appeared in the doorway. "It was sitting outside and whimpering when a friend of the deceased passed by this morning. Henrik is getting her statement now."

"Let me know when we can bring her with us," said Ole, pointing at the corpse.

Cecilie nodded. "The sooner the better. We'll keep in touch, Ole," she said, and went downstairs with Heino.

"So how did he get in?" she asked while they were standing in the hallway.

"The dog was outside. In theory, she could have met him while she was walking the dog. Maybe he assaulted her or managed to sneak in behind her."

Cecilie took a quick look around. "It was raining all evening and all night, but I don't see rubber boots or an umbrella or anything like that."

She went into the living room and looked towards the balcony door, where one of the forensic officers was busy securing traces.

"Were the curtains drawn?"

"No, they were open. And there is no indication of a break-in on the door," he responded.

Cecilie looked out the window towards the small garden plot and the large green area behind it.

"That would be a good spot to watch her from, over there by the trees. We're going to talk to all the neighbours. Some of them may have seen something in the weeks leading up to this."

"Roger. I'll also check up on what kind of surveillance cameras there are in the area."

"We need to take her computer and phone with us today."

"Joakim and Forensics are busy gathering it all together," said Heino, pointing at the items on the dining table. Cecilie went over to it. Aside from two tablets and a phone, there was a set of keys as well as three boxes containing her personal papers. All of them were things that would hopefully help them piece together a picture of Lizzette's life. They still hadn't managed to find any connections between Kristina and Tine; however, Kongelundsparken wasn't situated far from Tine's allotment house. *It wouldn't be the first time that a madman was running around on Amager*, Cecilie thought as she removed the lid from the foremost box. The contents surprised her. There were about a dozen or so erotic magazines of an earlier date. She quickly skimmed through them. Aside from a couple of *Special* magazines and an issue of *Boobs*, there were also some German publications.

"What the hell's this?" Cecilie asked.

"It looks like something Joakim could have brought with him from home."

At that moment, Joakim entered the living room. "What does?"

"Where did you find the box with these?" Cecilie asked, waving the magazine in her hand.

"In the china cabinet, along with the other boxes," Joakim answered.

"Am I the only one who thinks that it's strange for a middle-aged single woman to have porn magazines lying around?" Cecilie asked.

"I don't know, my mum's pretty up to date when it comes to that stuff," said Joakim.

Heino wrinkled his nose. "Please, spare us the details of your mum's desires. No, boss, you're right. It is strange."

Cecilie put the magazines aside on the table and Heino grabbed the top one and skimmed through it.

"Have you been through the rubbish bins?" Cecilie asked Joakim.

"They are in full swing with the ones by the entrance and the common ones further down."

"Boss? There's something here that's a little spooky," said Heino with the magazine in his hand. "Check it out," he said, turning the magazine towards Cecilie and Joakim. On the picture, a naked girl was posing with a red dog collar around her neck. She was pulling the leash herself. "It resembles the corpse upstairs. Is that just a coincidence, you think?"

"What does the caption say?" Cecilie asked.

Heino turned the magazine around and started reading out loud, *"Hot-blooded Camilla says, 'Strong men who know what they want turn me on. I'm ready for anything.'"*

Cecilie looked at the picture once again. She noticed a tattoo on the girl's ankle, a French lily.

"That lily, do you recognise it?"

Heino's face turned chalk white.

"Fuckin' hell. That's . . . that's the deceased, that's Lizzette, though a much younger version."

41

Cecilie had pictures from the crime scene in front of her together with the medico-legal report that Ole had delivered to them that morning. Next to the report lay all the magazines they had found at Lizzette's place. Cecilie had retreated to her office while the team was in full swing with the investigation. She had a hard time focusing, mostly because Ryan and the Travel Team had gone to Utterslev Mose boglands to observe the divers. She couldn't get the thought of Jeremy's impending resurrection out of her mind. She had tried to call up Klerke earlier, but now she was the one being ghosted. Cecilie hadn't changed her mind but had hoped that she could make herself so indispensable that the Minister would decide to save her after all. But it seemed that her value was decreasing. She needed to get a grip on this whole thing, so she took out Nikolaj's number, even though she had serious doubts as to whether he was the right one to confide in. Nikolaj sounded happy that she had called, and when she asked when he had time to meet, he said, "Give me an hour."

They agreed to meet at Bella Grill, which, aside from being her safe haven, was also situated only 500 metres from Utterslev Mose. A fact she was sure a psychologist would have a field day with. Cecilie was sitting at her regular table and looked up when Nikolaj entered.

"Mmm, the alluring smell of trans fats," he said, smiling.

"What?"

"Nothing," he answered, and sat down. "Do they serve coffee in here?"

"Of course. Anything to go with? The fries are good."

"I think I'll just stick to coffee."

Cecilie ran up to Kurt behind the counter and returned with two cups of black coffee.

"How's it going?" he asked, sipping the coffee and grimacing.

"To hell."

"Tell me all about it. I imagine your job must be a horrible strain."

"Most certainly. But we're not here to talk about me."

"Oh? But I thought . . . ?"

"No, we'll take that another time lying down . . ." She smiled at her slip of the tongue. "Well, you know what I mean."

"Of course," Nikolaj quickly answered. "But what did you want to meet about, then?"

"There's been another murder, most probably the same perpetrator." She took her bag from the chair next to her and found the pile of pictures taken at the crime scene, as well as Ole's autopsy report.

"The latest victim is Lizzette Morning Star, fifty-nine years old, divorced. Up until her death, she lived alone in Kongelundsparken on Amager." Cecilie spread the pictures out on the table, and Nikolaj automatically moved back in his chair.

"My God, that's severe," he mumbled, putting a hand up to his mouth.

"Yes, it's pretty intense. She was stabbed to death with a knife, most likely by the same perpetrator who killed Kristina Sand and Tine Larsen. The autopsy report shows that the same type of ether was used to sedate her. She has fewer cuts to her torso and face compared with the other two victims. On the other hand, the perpetrator chose to rip her stomach open this time."

Nikolaj swallowed hard as he stared at the pictures from Lizzette's bedroom.

"Are you all right?" Cecilie asked.

"Yes, go on."

"As with the two previous cases, the victim's labia were removed. According to Ole, our forensic pathologist, this time it was done with a pair of surgical scissors size twelve. Her clitoris was also cut off. According to Ole, the perpetrator's skill has improved considerably."

"Excuse me," said Nikolaj as he got up and rushed to the bathroom. Meanwhile, Cecilie checked her phone. Still nothing new from Beatrice Klerke or from Heino regarding the divers' investigation. A few minutes later, Nikolaj returned as pale as a ghost.

"I'm sorry. Can we go outside? I'm afraid . . . the smell of fried fat doesn't help me here."

"Of course," said Cecilie.

She packed everything up and they went out to Bellahøjvej.

"So, how can I help?"

Cecilie leaned against the wall as the cars whizzed by. "The boys are mapping out her life and movements. But the fact that she wasn't on any social media platforms makes it somewhat difficult. Her neighbours describe her as private."

"Did she have a job?"

"She had an interior decorating shop on Amagerbrogade."

"And the perpetrator could have met her there?"

"Yes, maybe, we're looking into that too. But I have another lead that I think is more interesting."

"What's that?"

"During our little . . . session, you know, we talked about the perpetrator's motive. How the modus operandi might fit into his fantasy . . ."

"Yes, of course."

"You suggested that he might be filming them."

Nikolaj shrugged. "I didn't base it on specific evidence, but yes, I'm sure he enjoys observing his victims since he dresses them up. The voyeur part of it plays an important role for him. That's what leads him to . . . the rest . . . to the collecting element," he said, and looked like he was about to throw up again. She took the *Special* magazine from her bag.

"In 1982, Lizzette was nineteen years old and she was posing for this magazine. Back then, her name was Camilla." She showed him the picture.

"Okay," he said, surprised. "Are you sure it's her?"

"Lizzette's daughter confirmed that her mother was a former nude model and that she changed her name back in the noughties. The tattoo on her ankle is identical to the one we found on the corpse."

"Interesting," he said, and cleared his throat. "How . . . did you manage to find that magazine, if I may ask?"

"You may. Lizzette had a whole box full of them. Apparently, in her younger days, she gladly removed her clothes both here and abroad. The question is whether the perpetrator knew about this picture and tried to recreate it before he killed her."

"That is not impossible. It would fit his profile very well. What about the other two victims? Have they also been nude models?"

"We haven't got that far yet. But if that's the case, it'll be the first thing that we've managed to find that connects the victims to one another."

Nikolaj studied the picture. "You said she had a bunch of other magazines? Why is this specific picture important to him?"

She shook her head. "I've no idea. Maybe it turns him on? It's kind of S/M-like. What with the dog collar and leash."

"Yes, but it's also rather innocent. Compared with the hardcore pictures you can find on the internet." Nikolaj looked up from the magazine. "I think there's a definite link between the picture and the recreation of it. There is an equal amount of loathing and fascination involved in this for him."

"In what way?"

"Fandom and destruction go hand in hand. His collection of labia is the ultimate exertion of power. But it's also a way to obtain that which is inaccessible. Preserve that which is perishable."

Cecilie put the magazine back in her bag. "I'm going to have to ask you whether you've come across anyone who fits this profile."

"No, not individuals. Seen from above, the whole thing seems pretty Oedipal. Which then includes half of Denmark's population."

"That's quite a man's view," she said, smiling.

He kicked a couple of stones on the ground. "Now, I'm not a great fan of Freud, but your perpetrator may be. According to Freud, all religions, morals, social structures, and art derive from the Oedipus complex, which is at the same time the core of all neuroses."

Her phone rang, and she saw that it was Heino.

"I'm going to have to take this. Thanks so much for your input. I really needed to pass this by someone."

"Anytime. You're always welcome to call, about this or anything else," he said.

She walked towards her car.

"What's up?" she said into the receiver.

"The latest report from the Travel Team." He sighed. "Rumour has it they've found something out in Utterslev Mose."

"Thanks, Heino," she said, and hung up. It was now time to revisit the bog.

42

The thin, rainy mist that hung over the boglands of Utterslev Mose erased the contours of the surrounding trees. Until 1920, the bog had been a part of Copenhagen's fortification but had long since been transformed into a recreational area with big lakes and islets lush with birdlife. An idyllic place by day, but by night, it was a sketchy area that most people chose to avoid. If the darkness didn't fill one with fear, then the assault and rape statistics should have. Cecilie stood with a small crowd by the lake across from the crime scene on the opposite side of the bank. With the help of Bellahøj Station, the Travel Team had barricaded the area, and she could see Ryan strutting around among the uniformed officers. Four divers sat resting by the water's edge next to a pile of old shopping trolleys and rusty bicycles. But that wasn't the only thing they had managed to bring to the surface.

Ole stood behind them together with some paramedics by the barrier they had set up. Cecilie guessed that it was Jeremy's corpse that lay underneath the white sheets. Most probably enclosed in the tarpaulin she had draped him in. It had been heavy having to drag him from the trunk of the Porsche and out to the water. As she stood observing the scene before her, she wondered whether there had been more suitable spots in the bog. But the truth was that, due to that frigging infotainment system, they would have found him no matter what. The only excuse for her miscalculation was the fact that the murder had taken place during her coke period.

Ryan turned around and gazed over at the crowd of people. Cecilie ducked. It would be unfortunate if he caught sight of her there. She desperately took out her phone to check to see whether Beatrice Klerke had sent her a text message, but she hadn't. She thought about the kind of reaction she could expect from Klerke once the news that Jeremy's body had been recovered hit the headlines. Would Klerke make do with distancing herself from her or should Cecilie prepare to get attacked? Maybe Klerke was ready to sacrifice her to prevent her opponents from beating her to the punch. To prove herself strong and assertive.

"Ce-cil, what are you doing here?" she heard someone behind her say.

Cecilie started and looked at the president of the tenant association.

"Damn, Omar, you made me jump."

"Shouldn't you be with them?" he said, pointing to the opposite side of the bank.

"It's not my case."

"It's all our case."

"Is that so? Since when have you joined the police force?"

"That's not what I mean, Ce-cil. Body in the bog, bad for the neighbourhood. We'll get on the ghetto list again," he said, looking at her with an expression of admonishment. "Do you know who it is?"

"Why are you asking me?" she replied. "How the hell should I know?"

Omar put his hands in his pockets. "You're the police."

"Like I said, it's not my case."

"I think it's that gangster they've been searching for. The one they sing about in that rap song. That's what I think."

"You have a right to your opinion."

"Is it him?" he asked invasively.

"I have no idea, Omar. Why don't you ask them yourself if you're so damn curious?"

"If it is him, then it ended badly."

Cecilie nodded. "That's the first sensible thing you've said."

"Bad for the neighbourhood, Ce-cil."

"Yeah, yeah, I know, we'll end up on the goddamn ghetto list. I heard you the first time."

"I'm serious. The pushers are also back, dealing in the park. Making everybody nervous," he said with a sombre look.

"I threw them out."

"They've come back."

"What the hell do you want me to do?" she asked, extending her arms.

"Fix it, Ce-cil," he said, as though it were a given. "Fix it the way you always do."

"The way I always do is just as dead as that guy down there," she said, pointing across to the opposite side of the bank where two paramedics were carrying the stretcher with the body bag to the ambulance.

"I'm worried about you. I'm worried about you and the neighbourhood."

She didn't respond.

PART II

Time passes like seagulls over a junkyard fly.
In the palace of the rich in unison all monsters lie.

43

Cecilie was sitting on Heino's desk and sipping her coffee. She looked at her team. All the boys looked beat behind their computer screens. They had practically been working round the clock the last few days. Jane approached them. Her semi-transparent blouse had a stimulating effect on Heino and Joakim, who both eagerly smiled at her.

"Palsgaard wants to see you, Cecilie."

Cecilie could deduce that the conversation was either going to be about the dead gangster or about why they hadn't had any breakthroughs yet with the case.

"Tell him I'm in the middle of a meeting but will come as soon as I'm done."

"Okay," Jane responded, lifting her plucked eyebrows. "You know how he hates waiting," she said, and disappeared with Heino and Joakim's gazes following her.

"Boys, try to rest your eyes a little," Cecilie said, putting the coffee cup down on the desk. "How far have we got?"

"Almost none of the magazines we found at Lizzette's exist anymore," said Henrik, pulling away from the table. "It seems like the heyday of gentlemen's magazines is long over and done with. Aside from a few anniversary and special issues, the last of those kinds of magazines to be published was in 2014."

"Which makes it hard to know whether Tine or Kristina had been nude models," Joakim added.

"But they are old enough for it to have been a possibility?"

"Yes, if we assume that they were the same age as Lizzette when she was doing it, that is, around twenty or so, then they could have been in the magazines in the noughties or back in the nineties."

"Or maybe even earlier. The minimum age was different back then," said Henrik.

"But how probable is it that all three victims were nude models?" Heino asked, throwing his pen on the desk.

"What about Lizzette's ex-husband? It's not uncommon for a family member to be involved in these kinds of cases."

"What information do we have on him? Do we know him?"

"A businessman, owns four, five taxis. He's been previously charged for VAT fraud and tax evasion."

"That doesn't make him a murderer, but check him out anyway," said Cecilie.

"And what about the Ikea guy? I still think there was something off about him. Anyone can fiddle around with their shifts. Is that enough of an alibi?" Henrik asked.

"I don't think it's him, but check him out again. What about Tine Larsen's background?"

"Her parents are dead, but I've located an older sister who lives on Falster," said Joakim. "She might be able to tell us whether Tine has been a nude model, but she still hasn't responded to my phone calls."

"We could send Heino down to pay her a visit," said Henrik.

"Falster?" Heino asked, looking very uneasy. "I've got enough to do here."

"You'll have to delegate that one out among yourselves," said Cecilie, jumping down from the table. She cast a sidelong glance over at Ryan's empty chair. "There's no time to waste."

Which was true. She knew that Ryan was at Teilum right now, being briefed in Ole's office. While a couple members of his team were ransacking Jeremy's house one more time. As far as she had been informed, the technical department was busy breaking apart

Jeremy's Porsche into tiny smithereens. Cecilie put on her leather jacket.

"Where are you going, boss?"

"To Valby to talk with Kristina's mother. Maybe she can tell us whether her daughter ever worked as a nude model."

"Do you want one of us to come along?" Henrik asked.

"No, thanks. Probably best that we don't show up in full force."

"And if Palsgaard asks for you?"

"Tell him I'm on my way," she said, winking.

Half an hour later, Cecilie parked in front of Lillian Sand's house on Toftegårds Plads. She hoped that Kristina's mother had got past the initial shock since last time she had been there and had delivered the unpleasant news of her daughter's death. Lillian opened the door holding a silver-grey poodle under her arm and a cigarette hanging from the corner of her mouth.

"Yeah?" she said, blowing a cloud of smoke into the hallway.

Cecilie took out her ID card and introduced herself. The poodle began barking so loudly that it echoed through the hallway.

"Keep quiet, Tiki," Lillian said, putting the dog down. She shoved it with one of her legs and the dog disappeared into the apartment with a bark.

"I do remember you. I'm not that old, you know. Did you catch my daughter's murderer?"

"We're working very hard on it."

"I read about another case in *Ekstra Bladet*. Was that him again?"

"We're trying to find out."

She took a drag of her cigarette. "Well, he isn't hiding out here."

"I know, but I've come to get some help. May I come inside?"

"No, it's not a good time," she said, crossing her arms, her cigarette still sticking out.

"I have a few questions about your daughter."

"What questions?"

"They may seem a little bizarre, but we're looking for leads," Cecilie said, trying to ease her into the questioning.

"Maybe you should ask me more directly. I'm not that sensitive."

"Good, I'll dive right into it, then," Cecilie said, smiling. "Has Kristina ever worked as a model?"

"Oh, was that all it was? Well, that was many years ago."

"What kind of model?"

"I think you already know the answer to that. The nude kind."

Cecilie suppressed her enthusiasm. This was the connection they had been looking for.

"Did she work for different magazines?"

"Yes, of course. Why else would you allow yourself to be photographed without a stitch of clothing?" She frowned with her charcoal-black eyebrows. "But no porn, or anything gross, if that's what you're insinuating."

"I'm not insinuating anything. Do you remember when it was?"

Lillian shook her head as she tried to think. "I guess it started when she was around twenty. She was still living at home."

"How did she get into it?"

"She was discovered on the street. I wasn't too happy about it. And her father was totally against it." She took a drag of her cigarette. "But it was her decision."

"And for how long did she work as a model?"

"Only for a few years. She found out that that line of work wasn't really her cup of tea."

"How? Had she had any unpleasant experiences?"

"They tried to push her to go further each time. The pictures always had to be more and more daring so there would be something new to look at." She shook her head. "She refused to go along with it. Oh, and then there were the letters."

"What letters?"

"Men who wrote to her."

"Were they fans?"

Lillian giggled. "You could call them that. But they always came with all sorts of gross offers. Some of them had . . . well, you know, masturbated on the writing paper. Left stains."

"What did you do with the letters?"

"Threw them out, of course! Made sure that Helmer, my husband, didn't see them."

"Do you still have any of the magazines she appeared in?"

"God no!" she said, rolling her eyes.

"And none of the pictures that were taken?"

"No, no, not at all," she answered decisively. "Or, no, wait here." She shut the door as though to ensure that Cecilie didn't follow her. A few minutes later, she returned with a stack of black-and-white photos in A5 size.

"These are from the test shots," she said, handing Cecilie one of them. In the picture there was a young girl with long hair, sitting naked on a chaise longue with her side to the camera.

"I always thought that one was so beautiful. Very innocent."

"Yes, I understand. Kristina is beautiful in that picture."

"It was the only time I came along."

"You were there when it was taken?" Cecilie asked, handing the picture back to her.

"Yes, Kristina was terribly nervous. But he was nice enough, the photographer. He was the one who took most of the pictures from then on for the magazines."

"Do you remember his name?"

"No," she said, shaking her head. "But he was rather well known back then. That's what Kristina said. He's also taken pictures of actors and singers, but not naked. I remember he wore a silk scarf around his neck and had loose wrists. Gay, no doubt. Not that I care what people are," she said, shrugging her shoulders.

"But you don't remember his name?"

Lillian turned the pile of photos around and pointed at a small stamp with the photographer's name and address. "Torben Wøllund, on Burmeistersgade, number 12. Yes, that's right. That's where he had his studio."

Cecilie took out her phone and got a picture of Kristina's portrait and of the stamp on the backside. She recognised the name. It was the same photographer who had taken the pictures of Lizzette.

"Thanks so much for your time, Lillian. That's all for now."

44

When Cecilie returned to the division, she just managed to walk through the door when Jane discovered her like a terrier. The secretary looked above the rim of her glasses.

"He is in a state of raging fury, Cecilie. I'm just saying."

"Who is?" Cecilie asked as they continued down through the division towards Henrik.

"I think you must know."

"Tell Palsgaard that I'll be there in five minutes," Cecilie said, brushing her arm. She stopped in front of Henrik's desk.

"What's new?"

"Palsgaard has been here shouting for you."

"I heard." She looked at the empty seats where Heino and Joakim normally sat. "What's new?"

"Joakim went to Falster to locate Tine's sister and Heino is tracking down Lizzette's ex."

"Heino is wasting his time."

"Oh? Sounds like you've found something?"

She nodded and sat down on the edge of his desk. "Kristina's mother confirmed that her daughter was once a nude model."

"Bingo."

"Yes. That's no coincidence."

"At the same time as Lizzette, or what?"

Cecilie shook her head. "No, they were both in their early twenties. If you do a little math, you can assume that Kristina's career was around the year 2000."

"As opposed to Tine, who posed in the eighties," said Henrik.

"Which doesn't create a direct link between the two cases."

"You're wrong. They had the same photographer."

"Interesting," Henrik said, lifting his eyebrows. "Maybe he knows something?"

"Yes, maybe he does," she said, smiling.

"Do you consider him to be a suspect?"

"Maybe. It'll be interesting to see what Joakim comes up with."

Henrik's phone buzzed on the desk.

"What have you found, kid?"

"Cecilie!" someone yelled from the opposite end of the room. Cecilie turned halfway around and caught sight of Palsgaard, who was energetically waving to her like a traffic cop. All he needed was a green vest.

"What does Joakim say?" she asked Henrik as she sent Palsgaard a thumbs up, which only annoyed him even more.

"Cecilie! NOW!"

"Tine had also been a model," Henrik said to her.

"Great! Ask him who the photographer was." She could no longer stretch it and had to go.

Palsgaard shut the door to his office behind them. Ryan was lounging in a chair in front of the desk with his legs crossed. He greeted them with a dry smile as Palsgaard marched to his desk and sat down behind it.

"Considering the gravity of the case, it is quite remarkable how scant your briefings are."

"I'm sorry, it's been very busy. I meant to drop by here much earlier," she lied, and sat down in the other chair facing Palsgaard's desk.

"We have a management that expects results and a press that has to be kept at bay so that they don't start coming up with their own stories. Being a leader is a delicate balance, Cecilie. You are no longer one of the boys."

"I will make note of that," Cecilie answered, trying to conceal her smile at his choice of words. "So, where do we stand?"

"We have a number of leads that we are looking into."

"What you have are three unsolved murder cases. You have interrogated a number of suspects, I understand?"

"Yes, and Heino is actually interrogating someone right now while the rest of us are busy investigating new leads."

"Oh? And what are they?"

She glanced at Ryan. She didn't want to let him in on anything.

"Huh, Cecilie?"

She felt forced to reveal that all three victims had been former nude models.

"Nude models? Weren't they all middle-aged? When would that have taken place? Back in the Stone Age?" Palsgaard asked, receiving a smile from Ryan.

"It happened over the course of several periods. That's what we're investigating. Like I said, it is new information."

"New? It seems far-fetched to me." Palsgaard leaned back and folded his arms over his chest. "Ryan has had more success with his investigation."

She sensed that they were both expecting a reaction from her. But she remained silent. Palsgaard didn't give a damn about her investigation. What he was about to say was the real reason why she had been asked to meet in his office. "Last week we found the missing person in Utterslev Mose. He hadn't just been out to take a piss as you had suggested," said Ryan.

"Congratulations. Guess you and your team are ready to fly off, then?" Cecilie asked.

"Oh no. Now the real investigation begins. We need to uncover who dumped him there."

"You are welcome to look in our files of gang members, both his and the Brothers'. I imagine that Bellahøj Station can be of assistance as well."

"Bellahøj is already assisting us very well."

"Well, everything's fine, then," she said, extending her arms, mostly to signal that she wanted to get back to work.

"I can't help but wonder why you haven't inquired about the cause of death," Palsgaard interjected.

"It's not my case."

"At least, for professional reasons."

"I have enough to see to. However"—she turned her gaze to Ryan—"if he drowned with his fly unzipped, then he probably took that piss after all."

"Shot in the head. Liquidated," Ryan answered sharply.

"He was also in a dangerous line of work."

"Yes, but the victims in that line of work tend to get mowed down, typically with various weapons and a whole lot of random shots."

"And?"

He straightened up in his chair. "A shot at close range indicates that the perpetrator was able to get up close to the victim. Which further indicates that the individual had a close relationship with him."

"Well, you'll have to talk with his family, then check his closest circle of friends. That was what you advised me to do," she answered sarcastically.

"His brother, Como, has an idea of who it could be."

"Really? Who?"

"You!" he said, pointing at her dramatically.

Cecilie smiled disarmingly. "Oh yes, of course."

"It's a serious accusation, Cecilie," said Palsgaard, staring at her through his tiny round spectacles.

"It most certainly is," she answered.

"Do you have anything to add?"

"Aside from the fact that the accusation is ridiculous?" She shook her head thoughtfully. "Oh yes. Is Como a reliable witness or is he a gangster like all the rest of them?" She got up from her chair. "It's well worth considering before you take the case to the prosecution, Ryan. But that's merely a professional piece of advice. Was there anything else?"

None of them answered. She smiled at Palsgaard. "I'll be sure to keep you regularly updated. I'm sorry about the lack of communication on my part."

Palsgaard looked at her like a shark that had smelled blood, but he remained silent. Something told her that she had failed to pass their little test. When she returned to the division, she immediately got hold of Henrik.

"What did Joakim say?"

Henrik turned his chair. "You survived?"

"Oh yes, no problem," she retorted. "What did he say?"

"That the sister could confirm that Tine had worked as a nude model and later as a stripper. Until a hip injury prevented her from continuing."

"You're kidding me, right?"

"That's what the sister said. Unfortunately, she didn't have any nude photos or magazines from then lying around."

"Okay, but did she know who had photographed her?"

"No, a bunch of different people."

"We need to track down that photographer—Torben Wøllund."

45

TW Studios was situated in Burmeistersgade in a low, worn-down factory building. Cecilie parked in front of the entrance and got out, as did Henrik. A few kids were riding around on scooters, but otherwise the street was empty. A faded sticker above the doorbell was the only visible indication of the company's existence. Cecilie pressed the button. A moment later, the door was opened by an older man in his seventies. He wore a wrinkled white shirt and a silk scarf around his neck. His long grey hair had been combed back and gathered in a small ponytail. A couple of chunky gold rings matched his sturdy bracelet.

"Torben Wøllund?"

The man nodded and Cecilie introduced herself and Henrik.

"May we come inside?"

"What's this about?"

"We just have a few quick questions."

"Well, as long as they're quick," he said, opening the door wide so they could come in.

They followed Torben into the bare room where his photo studio was situated. Aside from a dining table full of photo gear and a few robust lamps, the room was practically empty.

"Do you want coffee?" he asked, pointing to a kitchenette that was cluttered with used cups and utensils.

"No, thank you."

"Has anyone made any complaints?" he asked in a nasal voice as he stuck his hands into the pockets of his white jeans. "And I don't mean complaints regarding the quality of my pictures."

"Has anyone had reason to complain?" Henrik asked.

"Never. I've never had the urge to expose my member to any of the girls, like some of my colleagues have. I swing the other way, so to speak."

"You have nothing to fear, then."

"You never know in these Me Too times," he said, turning one of the gold rings. "You'd be amazed how far some of the girls are willing to go to get in the limelight. Or to get revenge if they don't succeed." He shook his head. "They aren't exactly little angels."

"Do you still take pictures of young girls?" Cecilie asked.

"I've had to expand my repertoire a little," he said in a tired voice. "I take photos of everything from pin-up girls to school portraits."

"School photos? That's quite a jump, wouldn't you say?"

"Not really. Except for the fact that the kids are wearing more clothes and have a higher IQ. I also take graduation shots, preschool, high school. You have no idea how much parents are willing to spend on their offspring. The kids are totally absorbed by it. They know exactly how they want their pictures taken."

"We want to ask you about some former models, whether you remember them. You'll have to look years back."

"I see. You do realise how many I've photographed through the years, don't you?"

Cecilie opened her folder and took out a couple of magazines.

"You've brought some literature with you."

She handed Torben a *Special* magazine. "Lizzette Morning Star. Perhaps you remember her? Her name was Camilla Toft when you photographed her."

Torben looked at the photos with a crooked smile. "It was so innocent back then. Oooh," he said, frowning.

"What?"

"Look at all the shadows. It's not one of my better series," he said, handing the magazine back.

"But do you remember her?"

Torben shook his head, and she handed him a few more magazines. Torben skimmed through them and shook his head. "I don't recall her at all. But taking all those photographs through the years sort of blinds you. The only things you register in the end are whether the model is a blonde or a brunette, whether her breasts are big or small, and whether she's got pubic hair or not."

"What about this one? Kristina Sand. She was here with her mother for some trial shots." Cecilie showed him pictures on her phone.

"Hmm. That looks good. I must have been sober that day. Notice the way the light falls on her shoulders."

"But do you remember her?"

"There may be something about her, but I could be confusing her with another. But let me see if she's in the collection."

"The collection?" Henrik asked.

"Why yes. Come along," he said, as he opened the door across from them. "Denmark's biggest horny file," he said with irony. "Cunt-boob pictures over six decades. But at least they are my cunt-boob pictures."

He lit the bare bulb in the narrow storage room.

"Wake up, girls, we have guests."

The boxes stood side by side on the shelves with the year of reproduction indicated on the front of each box. Torben quickly found the box with Kristina's trial photograph. It contained various folders with both paper pictures and negatives.

"Kristina Sand, model number 01848." He started pulling several boxes down from the shelves and began looking through them.

"Have you saved all of them?"

"Almost. I also have a couple of hard drives after we started photographing digitally. I think that's all I have with her," he said as he spread about twenty pictures out on the floor. "Some of it isn't bad at all," he said, self-satisfied.

"Do you recognise that?" Cecilie asked Henrik, pointing at some pictures of Kristina posing in a garter belt and a pair of thin white stockings.

"Yes, it looks like the same set of underwear as the one we saw at the crime scene."

"What?" Torben asked, disoriented. "The scene of the crime?"

Cecilie didn't answer.

"We're also looking for Tine Larsen. But I assume the name is too ordinary—"

"Tine Larsen." He nodded and looked down at the floor. "I've also taken pictures of her. But she was recently murdered. Brutally, if you believe the papers. But what's that got to do with—"

"Have you had any contact with her?" Henrik interrupted him.

"No, she was raving mad."

"Why do you remember her?"

"Because she was raving mad. She had no boundaries. She also supported herself as a stripper and perhaps more than that back then."

Torben started looking through his boxes and found a number of pictures of Tine, which he handed to them.

"She was beautiful, I'll give her that. But damn she was crazy."

"The same fishnet stockings," Cecilie said to Henrik. "It's no coincidence."

"What's this all about?" Torben asked, sweeping his hand over his thin hair.

"I think someone's copying your pictures, Torben," said Cecilie.

"What? That's illegal as hell. Let me see."

"It's rather violent," she said, clenching the phone close to her chest.

"I want to see them."

Cecilie showed him the picture of Lizzette hanging from the ceiling in her bedroom with her stomach ripped open. Torben took a few steps back and was about to tumble over the boxes. "My God . . ."

Cecilie put the phone away. "Perhaps we'd like that cup of coffee after all."

Torben nodded and rushed out. Cecilie leaned in towards Henrik. "Judging by Torben's reaction, I find it hard to believe that he sought out his former models to take the final pictures for his collection."

They sipped instant coffee in Torben's kitchenette. Torben's hands were shaking. "Am I in any danger, do you think?"

"We haven't given that a single thought. But do you have any suspicions?" Cecilie asked.

He shook his head. "No. There's always been jealousy among us photographers, but nothing like this, not at all."

"Then I don't think you have anything to worry about. Has anyone contacted you lately? Perhaps in connection with Tine Larsen's death?" She locked his gaze.

"No, no, not at all. Only the usual freaks."

"Freaks?"

"Some of the fans, especially back then, who didn't know when they crossed a line."

"In what way?"

"Some of them would spy on the girls." He pointed at the photographs. "You know, stalkers, but it was many years ago."

"Anything that was ever reported?"

"Not by me. That was part of the game. The girls were cool about it too. Over the years it's mostly collectors who have contacted me. From Denmark and abroad."

"What type of collectors?"

"They collect everything that has to do with the girls. Old underwear, magazines, and original photos . . . The negatives are in high demand. They're willing to pay a high price for them."

"Why?"

"The negatives are unique. They provide the ultimate sense of ownership. I've had a couple of break-ins. The last one was no more than six months ago."

"Did they steal anything?"

"Some gear and a computer."

"Do you have any information about the collectors who've contacted you?" Henrik asked.

"No, I don't want to talk with them at all. I always just hang up."

"You've never sold anything to anyone?"

"No, never. This is my collection. Besides, it would be unfair to the girls," he said, shrugging. "But some of my colleagues don't share that view. There's a big market on the internet. Plenty of websites where you can buy almost anything."

"Next time someone calls about the pictures, make sure you get their information. Then call me," said Cecilie.

"Of course. You think it's the same person who's killed all three of them? Are you certain I'm not in any danger, then?"

"Not unless you start posing yourself," Henrik said wryly. "Remember to give us a call if anything comes up."

Torben nodded.

46

Cecilie and Henrik returned to Teglholm Allé, where she parked the Golf on the small square across from the investigation department. She had only just got out of the car when a young man approached her. She recognised him. He was a journalist from *Ekstra Bladet* whom she sometimes provided with information. A middle-aged photographer followed behind and began taking pictures.

"Hi, Cecilie, do you have any comments?"

"Regarding what, Dennis?" she asked, not slowing down her pace.

"The accusations against you."

"As far as I'm concerned, I haven't been accused of anything, so, no, I don't."

"Friends and family of the deceased, Jeremy Cox, accuse you of being involved in his murder."

Cecilie and Henrik crossed the street with Dennis and the photographer on their heels.

"Is that so? I'm not aware of any charges."

"His brother, Como, has written a song about the murder where he references you."

"Oh well, in that case there might be some royalties to be gained," she said, trying to smile as if full of energy. "I'm afraid you'll have to excuse me," she said as she picked up the pace.

"Just a final comment on the press conference that was held?"

Cecilie stopped and looked at him. "What press conference?"

"The one at police headquarters, an hour ago. Your own boss and the guy from the Travel Team briefed us. Didn't they mention that to you?"

"Oh—yes. Yes, of course," she lied.

"You've been suspended, or what?"

"No, that's . . ." Cecilie said, hurrying inside the building. "Have you heard anything, Henrik? Did you know there was supposed to be a damn briefing?" she asked as they continued through the hallway.

"No, I would have told you if I had."

A moment later, they were in Cecilie's office. She grabbed the remote control on the conference table and turned on the TV.

The News Channel, which broadcasted live TV 24 hours a day, showed a news item from Jeremy's funeral procession. Masked gang members were walking behind the hearse together with Como and some other members of the family. The procession was closely guarded by uniformed police who had turned out in full force. Shouts could be heard from the many hangers-on directed at the press and the officers.

"There's a surprising number of participants," Cecilie said, looking at the screen with concern. "I hope our colleagues manage to film all those bastards for the record."

"I thought the Rebels had practically dissolved. But it seems that Jeremy's funeral has managed to draw out a crowd," said Henrik.

"Good thing, then, that it's only a one-off event," Cecilie said, trying to conceal her concern. The numerous hooded participants were a frightening image. With the pushers' return to the park and a rearmament of the Rebels, Bellahøj could easily become the scene of a new gang war. In which case, getting back on the ghetto list would be the least of the residents' worries. The news item from the funeral was interrupted by another from the press conference at police headquarters, which had been held a few hours earlier. Cecilie looked at Palsgaard and Ryan standing side by side. They were asked to respond to the rumours that a senior employee on the police force had been involved in the murder of Jeremy Cox. Ryan responded that all leads would be investigated and that no one was above the law.

"We will take the necessary steps, and the Independent Police Complaints Authority is already involved in the internal part of the investigation," Palsgaard added.

"Has the police officer in question been suspended?"

"For the present, no."

"As head of Homicide Investigations, is there a real risk that she will influence the investigation?"

"We are working with watertight bulkheads. Which is why the Travel Team and the Independent Police Complaints Authority are the ones seeing to the investigation."

Cecilie turned off the TV and threw the remote control aside. She tiredly rubbed her temples. "It seems pretty intense, Cecilie," Henrik said, mostly to break the silence.

"Our line of work is pretty intense."

"But are you all right?"

She smiled dully.

"All right is an exaggeration."

"It's unfair as hell. You're the most decent and genuine officer I've ever met."

"Thanks, Henrik," she said, looking away.

"They've got nothing on you. It's so unfair." He placed his big bear paw on her shoulder. She quickly patted his hand.

"That's nice of you," she answered uneasily. She was almost on the verge of confessing everything to him. Not that he would applaud it or understand it, but then at least she wouldn't have to keep lying to him.

"What'll happen if you're taken off duty . . . with the case, I mean?"

"The Travel Team will take over, I presume."

"Damn, we can't let that happen."

"I couldn't agree with you more," she said, pulling herself together. "Henrik, we need to track down the sites where the magazines were bought, find out who bought what. We have to get Ismail moving on it."

"I'll see to NC3."

"And I need to call Nikolaj again."

"The doctor?" Henrik said with suspicion as he scratched his head. "I doubt we have time for his meditation therapy."

"I agree. But he's able to see things we can't. And we need all the help we can get."

When Henrik left the office, she took her phone and wrote a text message to Beatrice Klerke: *I need help! Now!*

She got no response. Cecilie considered calling her, but couldn't seem to bring herself to do it. Nikolaj, on the other hand, wasn't nearly as difficult to get hold of. He immediately responded to her message and suggested that they could meet tonight, preferably at his place. She couldn't judge what lay behind his invitation, but they agreed to meet the next day at her office. He sounded disappointed and said he would try to fit it into his schedule.

A few hours later, she drove home to Bellahøj. She continued to the park and rolled down the pathway. She reached the open-air theatre, where about a dozen pushers were standing with their customers on the stone terraces. Cecilie turned on the flashing blue lights, which was enough to send the customers fleeing. She got out of the car and none of the pushers so much as budged. A baton wouldn't be enough to drive them away, so she unzipped her jacket to have better access to her holster and the tear gas in her belt. A whoosh could be heard going through the air. A stone hit the ground in front of her and rolled towards her feet. Cecilie unbuttoned the holster on her belt as a warning. Yet another stone whizzed through the air, indicating to her that they had ignored her warning. Before she managed to do anything else, a new rock hit the hood of the car with a crash. Cecilie turned around. This was a war she wouldn't be able to win. She got into the car and started backing up. Cheers could be heard coming from the pushers followed by yet another crash from a rock that hit the roof of the car. She could either contact Bellahøj Station and get them to send out a couple of patrol cars or she could get the emergency force to come out in full riot gear. However, neither one of those possibilities would solve anything in the long run. The battle was doomed from the start. The pushers had returned for good.

47

The team had been busy working most of the day and the boys would have to continue for quite a while yet. Cecilie looked at them from the doorway to her office: her team, like small ants methodically working their way forward. She was going to miss them. Heino walked over and handed her one of the two cups of coffee he was holding.

"Thanks," she said, taking a sip.

"So, what did Lizzette's ex-partner have to say?"

"Zilch. But you knew that would be the case, didn't you?"

"It never hurts to look into all possibilities."

She turned her gaze to the empty seats that the Travel Team normally occupied. "Any idea where they all are? I don't recall seeing any of them today."

"I think they're busy setting up a new base at police headquarters."

"At headquarters?"

"Yes. Close to the prison. I'm guessing it's more convenient for them when they start their interrogations."

"Have there been any arrests?"

He shook his head.

"It must be the calm before the storm. What about the doctor?" he asked, nodding towards Nikolaj, who was walking between the tables with his arms crossed. "What did you invite him here for? He makes me nervous."

"I thought maybe he could contribute something. But I may be wrong."

"So far he's only contributed with a moan while looking over my shoulder."

"Moan?" She gave him a quizzical look.

Heino groaned loudly. Cecilie concealed a smile behind her cup and jabbed his side.

"Cecilie, I'm seriously tired of having to look through old men's magazines," Joakim said, stretching behind his computer.

"If Joakim has got tired of looking at porn, I think we can safely conclude that we've been through the entire internet," said Heino.

"Porn? My mum watches stuff that's much worse than these soft-core magazines."

"We don't want to hear about you and your mother," said Heino. "You've clearly got an unhealthy relationship."

Cecilie walked over to them. "What's the status?"

"On the various forums we've seen references to thirteen magazines that Kristina appeared in, nineteen that Tine has been in, and in Lizzette's case an entire twenty-six. Several of the picture series are repeats, which matches up with what Ismail found on different sites," said Joakim. Cecilie looked over at Ismail, whose gaze was directed at the screen as his fingers danced across the keyboard.

"Ismail?"

"Yeah?"

"Status?"

"Candyland."

"Please explain."

"Candyland is a vintage Danish site where I have located the largest number of magazines for sale."

"What about the pictures that the perp seemed to imitate?"

"Yeah, you can buy those there too," he said distractedly as he typed away.

"It would be great if—"

"If we tapped into their client base to see what's been sold to whom. I'm on it, Cecilie."

"Cool. Have you contacted the seller?"

Ismail shook his head. "You asked for 'fast,' didn't you? I'm already past their firewall." He shook his head tellingly. "There isn't much security here."

"Not to be a party pooper," said Heino, looking around at them all. "But what if the perp bought the magazines back in the days when they were published and didn't go nuts until many years later? Isn't that a possibility, Doctor?"

Nikolaj adjusted his glasses. "Everything's possible."

"That's not plausible," said Henrik. "Why would he start murdering now?"

"Because he's gone nuts, like I said."

"None of the victims are *young* young," said Joakim, getting up from his chair. "Have you thought about that? Maybe he hates his mother."

"Why does he keep bringing up his mother?" Heino asked, shaking his head.

"Am I right, Nikolaj?" Joakim persisted.

"Yes, the murderer could be driven by an Oedipus complex," Nikolaj answered. He had positioned himself behind Ismail and was looking over his shoulder, which apparently didn't please Ismail, who moved to the side and looked at Cecilie.

"I've found four Candyland customers who have bought magazines with Kristina Sand and Lizzette Morning Star within the last two years," said Ismail, and he took a sip of his Red Bull. "But only one bought magazines with all three victims."

Cecilie put down her coffee cup and went over to him.

"And is it with the photo series that—"

"Yes, exactly those pics," said Ismail. He stopped for a moment and pointed at the screen and a row of columns.

"It's the same modus operandi. He's bought six magazines at a time, including the magazine in which Kristina, Tine, and Lizzette appear, respectively. It seems like he's trying to cover up his purchases."

"Can you see when they were bought?"

"Last year, with a few months' interval. The dates are listed there," he said, pointing at the screen.

"Do you have a name and an address?"

"Only a username so far. He calls himself Mr. Troglodyte."

"The hermit," said Nikolaj.

"Yes, that's what it means."

"We need to get as much information as possible on him," Cecilie said doggedly.

"Should I contact the seller or dig deeper?" Ismail asked.

"Whatever's faster."

"Then I'll start digging," said Ismail as he attacked the keyboard.

"Has anyone come across the name in the various forums?" she asked out into the room.

They all shook their heads.

"We were solely focusing on finding the magazines in which the victims had appeared," said Henrik.

"Then we'll start from scratch," said Cecilie. She sat down in front of the closest computer and started searching in the biggest forum, Vintage Lover. The interest among the collectors was as huge as Torben Wøllund had said. They asked around for magazines and pictures of pin-up girls from the past and helped one another find specific features, like big breasts, blondes, redheads. The girls were treated as objects just as much back then as they are now. Cecilie glanced up from her screen and noticed Nikolaj trotting around aimlessly. She regretted inviting him here.

After half an hour, Heino clapped his hands. "Boss, I found Troglodyte, or whatever he's called, in the forum, The Escort. He's asking for magazines with Camilla Toft."

"Is anyone responding?"

"Oh yes, quite a few. The thread is long. They are listing magazines in which she appears. There's even one who says he'd like to see them and the other Danish girls now in their more mature years. Troglodyte asks for her online profiles and her private address."

"Has anyone responded?"

"Only to say that she changed her name to Lizzette Morning Star. They had a good laugh about that in the thread."

"When was this thread created?" Cecilie asked.

"Eight months ago."

"Ismail, can we get behind their profiles?"

"Maybe via their IP addresses, unless they have a Tor browser, in which case they appear anonymously. Plus, I don't think you're going to find Mr. Troglodyte."

"Why not?

Ismail took another sip of his Red Bull before answering.

"His username on Candyland is Donald Duck. I think it's safe to assume that it's made up."

"What about payment details?"

"I can tell by the card number that it's a prepaid credit card without any personal information. And before you ask what the delivery address is, he's used three different delivery points. One on Amager, one in Frederiksberg, and the last one was in Nørrebro."

"All of them are most likely kiosks without much surveillance," Heino said dejectedly.

"Nevertheless, we still need to talk to the owners," said Cecilie, biting her lip. She knew that there was a 99 per cent chance that nothing useful would come of it. But they might be lucky. "Mr. Troglodyte is our perp."

"I can't see his IP address," Ismail said as he continued typing. "He is using a Tor browser to move around in the forums, just as I assumed."

"Maybe somebody knows him? Maybe we can contact the other users?" Henrik suggested.

"That would take time, which we don't have. Plus, there is nothing that would indicate that there are any personal relations between them," said Cecilie.

"Cecilie's right. They're all just jerking off behind their own screens."

"Does that mean we've hit a dead end, boss?" Heino asked, looking over at Cecilie, who was staring into space.

"Cecilie?"

"What, Heino?!" she asked irritably as she extended her arms. There was a telling silence between them.

"I think I may have an idea," said Nikolaj.

"Please, no sitting in a circle for a séance now, Doctor, with all due respect," Heino interrupted him.

"If you have a suggestion as to how we can identify Troglodyte, then by all means, tell us," Cecilie said tiredly.

"Probably not in connection with the perpetrator."

"What then?"

"His next victim."

48

Nikolaj pulled the whiteboard over to them. If he hadn't yet managed to catch their attention, then the screeching sound of the tiny wheels did it. He found a marker and, like a schoolteacher, turned towards Cecilie and the team. "Whenever I talk with my patients, the inmates, we talk a lot about their actions . . . their crimes. Most of them don't know why they acted the way they did. Not even the most deliberate and controlling ones. What they articulate instead are statements of momentary situations: for example, 'I got angry,' 'I snapped,' 'she provoked me to do it,' et cetera. But when you as a psychologist are dealing with a patient who has repeatedly committed the same acts of violence, a profile of the victim gradually becomes apparent."

"Haven't we already tried to make a profile of him, Doctor?" Heino asked impatiently. "Cecilie, shouldn't we go out and visit those kiosks?"

She hushed Heino.

"Sorry, but I don't see where this is heading," said Henrik.

"Well, as a matter of fact, it's pretty simple," said Nikolaj, waving the marker. "What does it take? What sets the perpetrator off? How do the women manage to unintentionally draw his attention? In other words: How do you become eligible to be a part of his collection?" He paused and it seemed as though he had managed to catch their attention again.

"Continue," Cecilie said, giving him a nod. Nikolaj smiled back.

"Victim number one," he said as he started writing on the white-board. "Kristina Sand, forty-one years old. Hairdresser on Gammel Kongevej, residing in Vesterbro. She started her career in modelling in 2001 when she was twenty-one years old."

Nikolaj turned back around towards them. "The picture that you presume the perpetrator took his inspiration from is from a September issue of *Special* from the same year. Victim number two," he said, and started writing on the whiteboard again, "is fifty-year-old home care aide Tine Larsen. She was unemployed when she was murdered. Resided on Amager. She started her modelling career in 1994 when she was twenty-two years old. The picture from which the perpetrator got his inspiration is from the September 1995 issue of *Expressen*. The latest victim was Lizzette Morning Star," he said as he continued writing away on the whiteboard. "Her former name was Camilla Toft, fifty-nine years old, shop owner on Amager, where she also resided. She debuted in 1982 at nineteen years old. The picture that was the source of his inspiration was in the magazine *Journal* from September 1982." Nikolaj turned around and looked at them. "What triggers our perpetrator?"

There was a glaring silence.

"Young teenage girls who have now become MILFs or granny types," Joakim answered.

"The doctor didn't ask what your personal preferences are," said Heino.

"Joakim may be right," said Nikolaj, waving the marker in the air. "But just to play the devil's advocate, the girls were physically very different. Lizzette was shapely already back then. Kristina was thin. We have two brunettes and a blonde. On top of that, there is an eighteen-year age difference between the victims, so—"

Cecilie cleared her throat. "Sorry to interrupt you, Nikolaj, but I'm afraid we're delving into details we've already been through. I can't really see how this is going to lead us to his next victim."

Nikolaj twirled the marker between his fingers.

"You can't? You can find a good part of the answer on the whiteboard."

"Sorry, but I don't really see it."

"Me neither," said Henrik, crossing his arms.

Ismail was about to say something but then regretted it. Nikolaj quickly picked it up. "Ismail, you were about so say something?"

He shook his head. "No, I'm such a nerd with these things . . ."

"Fine, let's be nerds together," Nikolaj said, smiling at him encouragingly.

"The pictures that the perp has got inspiration from are all from the same month—they're all from September."

"Exactly!" Nikolaj said with great enthusiasm. "Just like they are also each from their own decade."

He turned around and started drawing circles around what he had written. "Kristina is from the noughties—2000 to 2010, Tine is from the nineties, and Lizzette is from the eighties. Yet another pattern."

"Isn't that a little far-fetched?" asked Heino.

"All collections consist of a group of objects that, combined, create a common meaning for the collector. But not necessarily for outsiders. Check out what's being requested in the forums you've thoroughly examined. In my view, it makes very little sense for someone to be willing to pay five thousand Danish kroner for an old men's magazine while the collectors think it's a bargain and an invaluable addition to their collection."

"Let me get this straight," said Cecilie, looking at him sceptically. "Do you believe that our perpetrator is driven by his hatred to specific months and decades?"

"No, no, no. On a psychological level he's driven by other impulses that are apparent through his violent actions. But an implicit systematisation is part of his narrative. It is the foundation for the mission he has created. And to a lesser degree for his self-perception. Without the system, the whole thing collapses. His impulsive outpouring of violence is controlled by his intellect."

"I can't follow you at all," said Joakim.

"And I'm far from convinced," said Cecilie.

"I agree, boss. All of this could just as well be a bunch of random coincidences," Heino said.

Nikolaj shrugged his shoulders. "How many girls have appeared in these magazines in the last forty to fifty years? Ten thousand? Fifteen thousand? And he 'randomly' chooses one from each decade and from September?"

"But the magazines are different," said Henrik.

"Maybe an important element of his collection is that each model has to come from a different magazine, and from each decade, and that they have to be connected by the month of September?" Nikolaj suggested to them.

Henrik threw his pen aside and looked as though he had given up. "I think you've lost me as well now, Doctor."

"You started off by saying that you could perhaps identify his next victim," said Cecilie.

"Point in the direction of."

"Okay, so what direction is that, then?"

Nikolaj smiled once again. "The seventies. Porn and the sexual revolution. That's got to be the only decade that's left."

"There were also magazines being published in the teens," said Joakim.

"Okay. Then the seventies and the teens," said Nikolaj. "But the seventies is my best guess."

"That's a lot of models to go through," said Heino.

"Not if you limit the search to the September issues," said Ismail.

Henrik nodded. "In the seventies, *Special* was the only magazine around, but it was also published weekly."

"The first issue came out in 1972, which means there are thirty-two potential victims," said Ismail.

"Several of which may have passed away due to natural causes, or the magazines may have used foreign models, who will be harder to track down."

"No, it doesn't seem like the perpetrator is a big traveller," Joakim added. "The three victims are from the Copenhagen area."

"Which might further reduce the number of victims down to a handful. It might not be such a dumb idea after all," said Henrik, nodding approvingly towards Nikolaj.

"What do you think, boss?" asked Heino. "How much time do we have until he strikes again?"

"The interval speaks for itself," said Nikolaj regretfully. "His ability to get away with the crime is probably motivating him even more. I'm guessing within the next couple of days."

"Which means that he's already spying on his next victim," Cecilie said, getting up from her chair. "Henrik, we'll go to Torben Wøllund's archive and do some digging around. The rest of you start searching on the internet for models and photographs from back then, everything that can point us in the direction of those girls. Ismail, get hold of the people behind Candyland and see if they can help us track down the old issues from the seventies and the teens."

She took her leather jacket from the back of her chair and pulled it on. Nikolaj smiled at her, and she nodded to him approvingly. Inviting him here hadn't been such a bad idea after all.

"Henrik, get off your fat ass so we can get going," she said.

49

She was his next September girl. She lived up there in the high-rise that jutted straight up in the darkness. A light was on in her window on the second floor, one of the few in the entire building. There was a cold light in the kitchen, which he could see looking up from the car he was sitting in. She could just as well have put in a red light bulb in the ceiling, that little whore. Signalled who she was. He was just about ready to include her in his collection. His collection of girls. Small, rare beings from each epoch in which they had had their heyday. Where they had arisen from their pupa stage and spread their wings. And now, so many years later, he had recreated them in their time capsules. Immortalised them one last time with his camera in a carefully organised tableau. Almost like a sorrowful reference to the heyday of their youth.

"Oh, my collection," he thought out loud and turned up the volume of the car's stereo. Britney Spears was singing the number "3."

"*One, two, three*," Britney sang with her high-pitched voice. Britney had also got older, even though the producer tried to maintain her girlish sound. Create a time capsule for them all.

"*Let's just do it you and meee.*" A man appeared at the window on the second floor. The sight came as no surprise. He was far from the only one who visited her. The whore was selling herself more than ever these days. *Shared by many eyes, now by many cocks*, ran through his mind. He envisioned her labia. All wrinkled and leather-like. Glistening from the sperm of numerous men. He caught himself in the middle of the vulgar thoughts she had awakened in him. He sensed a blend of horniness and white-hot rage. An urge to destroy her. Remove the power she had over him. He sensed that it was going to be intensely violent. He would penetrate and devour her. He'd give himself plenty of time to enjoy the terror in her eyes. Not rush himself like he had the other times where things had been over and done with far too fast. This time he'd register every single detail. The sounds that she made, her muscle spasms, her scent, sense her skin turning warm, feel her pulse increase, watch her incontinence when he cut into her sex. The way he had cut into the others was almost embarrassing. As though he had been afraid that they wouldn't die. That he didn't have the ability to kill them. He had grown wiser. The real art was keeping them alive. The human body is fragile. He would first cut into her limbs. Big slashes with his knife, but not deep enough for her to bleed to death. Afterwards, he'd take care of her face. It was interesting to see how few cuts it took to make a person unrecognisable. If you cut off the nose and cut the mouth all the way up to the ears, then all human traits would disappear, and the face would resemble a punctured football. This time he'd start with her ears, then her eyelids, the nose and lips. Little by little he'd remove her facial characteristics. Reduce her to a creature without an identity. A pile of unidentifiable flesh. He would stop the bleeding and awaken her back to life every time her body sent her into shock. He would cut off her breasts and, as the very last thing, remove her labia. Remove her pussy and place it into a glass.

He snarled into the dark, sensing his pulse rise. But he knew that he had to compose himself in order to not let his sense of excitement get to his head. The real art was not leaving a single trace for the subhumans in protective suits to find. Suits that he himself wore during his visit. At that moment, the light up there was turned off. Britney had stopped singing and he felt the darkness envelope him inside the car. A lonely sort of darkness. He felt like masturbating but regained his composure. Not here, not now. Not until he had penetrated her with the knife would he permit himself to touch his member and come in the nappy he was wearing.

50

It was 10:30 p.m. and Cecilie was sitting with her team, devouring pizza as though it would be her last meal.

"When did Nikolaj leave?" she asked.

"Several hours ago," Joakim said with his mouth full of pizza.

"So what did you two get out of talking to Candyland?"

"Claus Melby, who owns the site, was very helpful. So tomorrow we'll have everything he can get hold of from the seventies," said Heino.

"We only need the September issues, and it should have been today."

Heino nodded. "Those were the ones I meant."

"Then make it clear," said Henrik, grabbing a slice of Hawaiian pizza.

"What about the issues from the teens?" Cecilie asked.

"He'll make sure we've got those too. But he said that they'd be a little more difficult," Heino said.

"Why?"

"Because they aren't purchased as much as the older magazines."

"On the other hand, I've found the names of a couple of photographers from back then. A Palle Iversen and a Tommy Mortensen," said Joakim.

"And what do they say?" asked Cecilie.

"Unfortunately, we haven't managed to get in contact with either of them yet."

"Well, that's quite some detective work you've managed to produce,"

Henrik said in an ironic tone of voice as he almost dropped a piece of pineapple on his shirt.

"What about Torben Wøllund? Has he taken any shots of anyone from the teens?" Heino asked.

Cecilie shook her head. "No . . . that is, yes, but he's lost the hard disk with the girls from back then."

"And is he to be trusted?" Heino asked.

"Who is, when it comes down to it? But at least Torben found a couple of models for us in his archive," said Cecilie, lifting up the two folders with fading nude pictures lying among the half-empty pizza boxes.

"So, so far we have two women who match our victim profile. They are both September models and from the seventies."

"Who are they?" Joakim asked, craning his neck to get a better look at them.

"Vinnie Pettersson from Høje Gladsaxe. She made her debut when she was sixteen, back in 1976 in a September issue," said Cecilie. "In a maid's uniform."

"They had a different view of what the minimum age should be back then."

"I've already run her through the system," said Ismail, nodding towards his laptop.

"Cool, Ismail," said Cecilie, impressed. "Find anything on her?"

"Bad girl," said Heino.

"Has she worked as a prostitute?"

"You said 'has worked.'" They all looked at Ismail, whose arms were extended. "Tracking down her ad was as easy as pie," he said defensively.

"You're on a streak, Ismail," Cecilie said.

Ismail turned the computer around.

"Massagespots.dk. This is where she has her ad," he said, pointing at the screen.

They all huddled closer together to be able to see it better. "'*Grandma with go,*'" Heino read out loud. "Must be something for you, Joakim."

Below the caption there were a couple of photographs of a mature, big-bosomed woman posing in different styles of underwear. Cecilie took the folder with the photographs that Torben Wøllund had taken and held them up next to the screen. Despite the many years that had passed, it was still possible to detect some similarities.

"The same thin lips and crooked nose," said Heino. "It's Vinnie offering a little fun and games."

"According to the ad she's offering quite a bit more than that," Ismail said, turning the laptop back towards himself.

"Did you get a chance to check out the other one . . . Helle Jørgensen?" Cecilie asked.

He nodded. "Yes. But she's not quite as exotic. She lives in a terraced house in Vigerslev together with her husband, Ove, and their son, Paw, forty-two."

Heino laughed. "That's like Joakim. He hasn't left home yet either."

"Yes, I have," said Joakim, offended.

"Well, that's certainly a new development, then."

Cecilie hushed them both and asked Ismail to continue.

"Both Helle and Ove are pensioners. I wasn't able to find anything on the son."

"So, we don't know him?"

"No, he's totally clean."

"When was Helle a September model?" Joakim asked.

"Back in 1973," Ismail answered.

"Damn, that's ages ago."

"So, what's the plan? Do we contact and warn them?" Henrik asked.

Cecilie wiped her mouth with a napkin and threw it into an empty pizza box.

"I have no intention of doing that."

"But what, then?"

"Until we track down all the September models, these are our best chances of catching the perp."

"It could take a long time, couldn't it? I know that Nikolaj said that the perp might strike in a couple of days, but do we believe that?" Heino asked.

"I'm thinking that it's highly likely. Maybe he's sitting outside right now, staring at either Vinnie or Helle while he's getting ready to make his move," said Cecilie, looking around at them all.

"Ole had estimated the time of death for all three victims to be approximately midnight." She checked her phone for the time. "It's almost eleven o'clock."

"Damn," said Joakim, taking a deep breath. "Okay, who's coming with me to Gladsaxe?"

"Of course you feel the urge to go there and spy on a prostitute," said Heino, rolling his eyes.

"Well, come with me, then, Heino," he said, giving him a thumbs up.

"I'll go with Joakim and see whether Vinnie's receiving any male visitors tonight."

Cecilie shook her head. "You two are going to Vigerslev to keep an eye on Helle Jørgensen and her family. And you're to stick together the whole time. This guy's dangerous."

"Only for those who are between eighty and half dead, and who used to strip in their youth," Heino said, getting up. "I think even Joakim'd be able to handle him."

"I'll put him across my knee," Joakim said, laughing.

"Hey!" Cecilie said, banging hard into the table. "I mean it. No monkey business. Don't underestimate that asshole. We're not losing any colleagues. You're going to watch out for each other," she said in a grainy voice.

"Easy, boss. We'll be sure to watch out," Heino said, patting her on the shoulder.

"Yes . . . for each other . . ." Joakim added.

51

Forty-five minutes later, she was sitting with Henrik in the Golf in front of the old apartment complexes in Høje Gladsaxe. Aside from a couple of troublemakers riding around on scooters, there wasn't a soul in sight. Judging by the many dark windows, most of the inhabitants had settled down, including Vinnie Pettersson on the second floor. Henrik unbuckled his seat belt and pushed the seat back to give him more leg room.

"We should have brought some coffee with us. And some snacks."

"Can you make do with a piece of chewing gum?" she asked, taking out a pack of gum from her chest pocket. Henrik dismissed it with a wave of his hand while she took a piece. She sent Heino a text message and asked how things were going. *Nothing happening in Vigerslev*, was his response.

After they had been sitting there for an hour, she could hear Henrik snoring. The way he was sitting there, with his mouth open and his head tilted to the side, he resembled a little boy. She waited yet another half hour before terminating the stakeout. She wrote to Heino that they could go home, and he responded by sending a yawning emoji. When shortly afterwards she started the engine, Henrik awakened.

"Yeah?" he said, disoriented.

"It's almost one thirty. I don't think he's going to show up tonight. We'll return tomorrow night."

"Sounds like a good idea," he slobbered.

At that moment, she saw a figure run across the car park in the direction of the apartment complex where Vinnie lived.

"Did you see him?"

"See who?" Henrik asked, looking drowsily out the windshield towards the empty area.

"Someone was running towards the apartment complex."

"Should we check it out, or do you want to call backup?"

In response, she opened the door and got out of the car. Henrik followed behind her, and together they headed towards the high-rises. It was quiet, only the sound of their footsteps echoing into the night. Cecilie unfastened the belt of her holster.

"Are you sure you saw someone?" Henrik asked.

She walked over to the entrance of Vinnie's building and leaned against the window pane in the door. The dark staircase seemed empty. She took hold of the door handle. The door was locked.

"Let's take a look around. Meet you on the opposite side," said Henrik.

"Are you sure?"

He tapped his gun in his holster before disappearing around the corner.

Cecilie continued down the narrow pathway between the apartment complexes. The tall shrubbery enveloped her in the darkness and she couldn't see where she was going.

Cecilie stopped and searched for her little Maglite. At that moment, a click could be heard behind her, a sound she knew all too well. She slowly turned around and stared into the barrel of a short-nosed revolver.

"You," she said flatly. The hand that was holding it was shaking, making the barrel dance before her face.

"So, what are you doing here?" she asked, trying to seem calm.

"I've come to kill you," said the feeble voice of Como. He was wearing a much too large black hoodie that made him look a lot smaller than he actually was. Two boys were standing behind him wearing hoodies identical to his, trying to make themselves look big. She wondered whether they were the same troublemakers whom they had seen riding around on their scooters earlier.

"I see. Isn't it past everybody's bedtime?" She was hoping that the boys would get provoked and intervene so that the revolver would be lowered. But the boys remained standing.

"Knock her off, Como," one of them said.

"How did you find me? Do the Rebels hang out here?"

"I've got bros everywhere."

She smiled contemptuously. "I'm assuming those two idiots aren't fully fledged members, 'cause if they are, you sure are in a sorry state."

One of the boys stirred, but the other one pulled him back and held him.

"Put away the gun, Como. Before things go seriously wrong," she said.

"Shut the fuck up. I'm gonna knock you the hell off, you understand?"

He placed the muzzle against her forehead. "You're a dead bitch now."

She sensed her pulse rise. Where the hell was Henrik?

"Believe me, you don't want to be a cop killer."

"Oh no? Try me."

"You sound pretty determined," she said.

"Shoot her, Como."

"Yeah, before the other cop shows up."

Como pressed his finger against the trigger but then hesitated.

"Got any fucking last words? Before I blow your brains out?"

"Yes . . . about your brother."

"My brother?"

"Isn't that why you're here? That goddamn song you made that has been playing over and over again?"

"It's the fucking truth."

"Yeah, okay, maybe, but only part of it."

"Bitch, got something you'd like to confess? Like that you killed him. He fucked you and then you killed him."

"No, it was the other way around as far as I remember, Como."

"Say what?" Como shouted. "What the fuck are you talking about?"

"I was the one who fucked him . . . Sorry, but your brother was pretty useless in bed."

"Fuck you, whore!" he said, pressing the muzzle harder against her forehead.

"But I think you, on the other hand, have more to offer," she said, winking at him.

Como looked at her perplexedly. "Say what?"

"Remove the gun and I'll give you a blow job." She licked her lips. It was enough to throw Como off.

"What the hell?" he said, taking half a step back. She quickly raised her arm and hit the gun away from her forehead. It went off with a bang as the projectile whizzed past her. Cecilie grabbed hold of Como's wrists and forced the hand holding the gun away from her. With her other hand, she hit his larynx. Como let go of the gun and gasped for air. She kicked his legs from under him, making him land heavily on the tiles in front of her. The two boys stared at Cecilie, paralysed, as she picked up the gun.

"And what about you two?" In response, the boys fled down the path.

"Cecilie?! Are you okay?" shouted Henrik, who came running from the opposite direction, waving his gun in his hand.

Cecilie turned around and nodded. "Everything's fine."

She squatted down in front of Como, who had caught his breath.

"Como, Como, Como," she said as she shook her head. "It's seldom you come across someone who's too dumb to be a gangster. But you sure do take the prize. Don't you know what the punishment is for killing an officer? Got any idea?"

"I . . . don't give . . . a shit," he sputtered.

"Oh?"

"You can just lock me up . . . I'll just . . . get out again . . . and knock you off."

She poked him in the chest with her gun. "Who said anything about locking you up? Why would we waste our time doing that?" She moved the gun up to his forehead.

"Cecilie . . ." Henrik said faintly.

She tightened the trigger. "Do I have your attention, Como? Just a nod'll do."

Como nodded.

"Your brother was a worthless piece of shit who didn't deserve to be born. Just like you, who should have remained a blob on the ground of that courtyard where your mum chose to get fucked." She tapped the muzzle hard against his forehead. "They found your brother with a bullet through his head. Do you want the same treatment, Como? Do you want to play gangster?"

"I-I-I . . ." he stuttered.

"'I-I-I' isn't really the right answer when you've got a gun pointed at your head. Are you a gangster or not?!"

"Nooo!" he sobbed.

Cecilie grabbed his hoodie and pulled him to his feet. "Then stop all this. Stop thinking you owe your brother, the gang, or any of the other assholes anything. Is that understood?"

"Yes . . ."

"Oh, and one last thing, stop that gangster-rap shit. You'll only end up becoming a target yourself. It'll only be a matter of time before some layabout thinks he can move up the ladder in the streets if he knocks off famous little Como." She nudged Como and he dashed off.

"You let him go," said Henrik, staring at her.

"Yes, what the hell else should I have done?" she said, putting the gun in her pocket.

"He tried to kill you."

"Yes, because he thought I had killed his brother."

"I don't think the motive matters so much. It was an attempt to kill you."

"I think it matters a great deal. Hopefully, Como will think better of it."

Henrik frowned. "As in not go to the Independent Police Complaints Authority or testify for them?"

She looked away. "It's got late, Henrik; maybe we should start heading home."

"You know you can always count on me if you need to. Right, Cecilie?"

At that moment, her phone buzzed. She took it out of her pocket and saw that it was Heino.

"What's up?"

"Boss! I've been trying to get hold of you . . . It's really bad—"

"Are you guys okay?" she interrupted him.

"Yes, we're okay . . . but he's managed to strike again."

"What!" she said. "You were supposed to keep an eye on her!" she shouted out into the night as she started walking. "How in hell could that happen?"

"It isn't Helle Jørgensen who's been killed. We got a message from the officer on duty. They also tried to call you."

"Where did it happen?"

"In Bellahøj. Your hood." She slowed down the pace as she let it seep in.

"Send me the address and we'll meet you there," she said.

52

Even though it was 3 a.m., a small cluster of residents stood bathed in the blue glow of the ambulance vehicles in front of the police barricades. It was the same scenario as the one they had seen back when the gang wars had caused havoc and people were attracted to the sirens after every single murder. Cecilie parked the Golf in front of the closest patrol car and got out.

"Ce-cil. Ce-cil, what's happening?" a voice could be heard behind her.

She turned halfway around as she continued towards the barricades. "Omar, not now, okay?"

"So many officers here, not good." Omar grabbed her sleeve to hold her back.

"Hey, buddy!" said Henrik, nudging him away from Cecilie.

"But this is important, Ce-cil! You have to listen to me!" he said, looking at her desperately. The uniformed police at the barricade had caught sight of Omar. Cecilie stopped and looked at him.

"Take it easy, Omar. I know you're worried about the neighbourhood and about that frigging ghetto list. But we've got a murder case. Someone was killed up there," she said, pointing towards the building. "Okay?"

"I'm sorry, Ce-cil, but my"—he looked down at the ground—"but Farida . . . my oldest daughter lives in that building on the second floor."

Cecilie looked at the crowd behind him where Omar's wife and the three younger children stood tired and dispirited in the dark.

"We are worried. She doesn't answer the telephone. The police say nothing."

"Okay, Omar," she said, patting him on the shoulder. "Take it easy. I'll get back to you as soon as I know something."

Cecilie pulled up the barricade tape and continued towards the apartment building, where she was met by Heino. He was as pale as a ghost.

"Boss, I was just up there. It's bad. As in bad bad. Worse than the others."

"Is that possible?"

When she reached the apartment on the second floor and entered the bedroom, she had to agree with Heino.

"Goddammit," Henrik mumbled behind her. "Goddammit."

In a dried-up pool of blood lay the corpse of a naked brown-skinned woman in the bed. Her body had been ripped apart, and both her breasts had been cut off. They lay next to the torso in a neat row of dried-up pieces of flesh on the bed. Cecilie looked at the disfigured face and she realised that the pieces of meat on the bed were the murdered woman's ears, nose, lips, and eyelids. Ole was standing next to the bed in his white coveralls. Cecilie greeted him.

"Looks like our man has been at it again."

"Do we have any idea who the victim is?"

"The apartment belongs to Farida Muhamed," Heino answered behind her.

"Fuck, why her?" Cecilie said, feeling her throat constrict.

"Are you all right?" Ole asked, looking at her with concern.

"Yes, yes, of course."

"Someone you knew?" Henrik asked.

"I've seen her in the neighbourhood. I know her father."

"The one who came over to us downstairs?"

Cecilie nodded and looked at the corpse's bloody sex.

"Same modus operandi?"

Ole nodded. "Just like in the other three cases, he cut and removed part of—"

"Okay, thanks," she interrupted him. "When did this happen?"

"My guess is approximately forty-eight hours ago."

"Get her in as fast as possible and send me a report tomorrow morning."

"Of course, Cecilie."

She turned towards Henrik and Heino. "Why her? Why in hell did he choose her? It doesn't make any goddamn sense. We should have, we should . . ." She shook her head in despair.

"We couldn't predict this," said Henrik. "No one could."

"Henrik's right. The man's a psycho. He's capable of anything," said Heino.

"We better get a move on. Check her apartment. Talk with the neighbours. Somebody must have seen something, somebody must have frigging heard something. This hasn't transpired quietly," she said, pointing behind her towards the corpse. "Has he stuffed her mouth with a pair of her panties like he did with the others?"

"No, there are no foreign objects," said Ole.

"It makes no bloody sense," she repeated.

"Where are you going, boss?" Heino asked.

When she stepped out from the entrance, she saw Omar standing by the barricade. She couldn't see his family anywhere. Perhaps they were standing further away among the spectators. She hoped this was the case. Delivering Omar the bad news was going to be hard enough in itself.

"Ce-cil?" he asked quizzically.

"Come here, Omar." She pointed towards the furthest spot in the barricade where no one else was standing. She held the barricade tape up so that he could step inside.

"Did you get hold of her?" he asked. There was panic in his voice. "My wife call and call her."

"I'm so sorry, Omar."

Omar stared at her vacantly as he slowly opened his mouth.

"Is it . . . is it my . . ." He was unable to continue the sentence. Instead, he squatted down and placed both his hands on his head. A quiet sob could be heard coming from him and Cecilie bent down and stroked his shoulder.

"What happened?"

"She's dead."

"How?"

"She was killed."

He threw back his head and looked at her. "I want to see her."

"No, Omar, you can't, not now."

Omar got on his feet. "I want to see my daughter."

"Omar, I'm sorry. But Forensics are working on collecting traces up there," she quickly said.

"I have to see her . . . See my Farida."

"Listen, Omar, you can't."

"Two minutes, Ce-cil," he said, looking at her urgently. "She's my daughter."

He tried taking a step towards the building, but Cecilie put her hand on his chest.

"I know . . . but you can't see her. Not like that."

He looked back at her. "What happened to her?"

"It's bad, Omar, very bad. So you're going to have to help me out here. Do you think you can do that?"

"What do you want to know?"

"Just a little bit so we have something to work with. Day-to-day things. Little pieces of information. Where she worked, her interests, who she hung out with, friends, whether she had a boyfriend, what she was doing the last few days. Can you tell me those things?"

"No, I . . . it . . . it . . ."

"Of course, I didn't mean to pressure you, but once you are able to, I'd like to know. It's important," said Cecilie.

"No, that's not why."

"Why then?

"Because I haven't been in contact with her."

"Okay, for how long?"

He looked away.

"Many years. My wife had number . . . but I forbade any contact," he said, choking back his own tears.

"Why?"

Omar wiped the tears from his face. "We fought . . . I threw her out . . . I threw my daughter out . . . to this." He broke down in sobs and Cecilie squeezed his arm. "It's my fault that she's dead, Ce-cil."

"Omar, of course it's not your fault."

The ambulance crew came out carrying a covered stretcher and gasps could be heard from the crowd. Omar looked up. "Farida?" he said, and freed himself from Cecilie.

"Omar!" she shouted as she grabbed hold of his arm. Omar pulled his arm back and hit Cecilie in the face with his elbow.

"Fuck," she said, and placed her hands on her eye. Before Omar managed to reach the stretcher, two officers were on top of him and managed to wrestle him to the ground. People started shouting and pushing themselves past the barricade. They tried to help Omar, which meant that more officers came. There were some scuffles between a couple of the big boys and the officers. Cecilie stood from a distance, observing it all: Omar in handcuffs, being dragged off, his dead daughter on the stretcher and an entire neighbourhood that was falling to pieces.

53

The night's defeat and the tragedy in Bellahøj loomed like a heavy blanket over the investigation division. The mood matched the pouring rain that was coming down in buckets outside the panorama windows. Cecilie sat on top of Heino's desk as Heino and the others took the seats surrounding her. It was late morning and they had all been home to get just a few hours of sleep.

"I swear, your eye is getting more and more blue," said Joakim as he looked at Cecilie.

"Does it hurt?"

Cecilie shook her head.

"You ought to press charges against him."

"First, his daughter was just killed. Second, it wasn't on purpose."

"Cecilie has turned into the forgiving type," Henrik said, sending her a glance which she didn't return.

"Poor guy. Poor family," said Heino.

Cecilie nodded. "I picked up Omar this morning from detention and drove him home."

"Did he say anything?" Heino asked.

"My fault, my fault, my fault." She took a deep breath. "I was grateful it's only a five-minute drive from Bellahøj Station."

"You said that he wasn't communicating with his daughter. That he had thrown her out," Henrik said.

"Actually, Farida herself moved out as soon as she turned eighteen," Cecilie said. "That's what her mother said."

"You spoke with her mother?" Henrik asked.

"Only very briefly when I dropped off Omar."

"Did she say anything else?"

"Farida had always managed on her own, had a full-time job, and was always on top of things."

"What was her job?"

"Working as a receptionist at a veterinary practice in Skovlunde."

"She was even an animal lover," Joakim said in a sad voice.

"Do we know what the conflict was between her and her father?" Heino asked.

"From her father's perspective, Farida had got a little too fond of the Danish lifestyle: guys, dancing, and drinking."

"And so the family cut her off?" Heino asked.

"According to her mother, they would exchange text messages, but months could go by between messages."

"How well do you know Omar?" Henrik asked.

"What do you mean?"

"Well, what type of guy is he?"

"You mean whether he's the 'my daughter screws Danish boys so I'm going to kill three women' type of guy?"

"I was just asking," said Henrik, folding his hands in front of him.

"We're not going to waste our time on Omar or on some stupid theory about Muslim honour killings. We'll save that for the Travel Team."

"Did I hear you say the Travel Team?" asked Jane as she approached them.

"Yes, why?" Cecilie answered.

"Because they are sitting in Palsgaard's office together with two gentlemen from the Independent Police Complaints Authority and they want to talk with you."

Cecilie looked at her in surprise. "Is Palsgaard there too?"

"And the National Police Commissioner."

They all looked at Jane in bewilderment.

"To talk with me?" Cecilie asked, pointing to herself.

"Apparently so, as in now," Jane answered.

Cecilie hesitated for a moment before answering. "We're in the middle of a criminal investigation briefing. Tell them I don't have time."

"Do you want me to tell that to the National Police Commissioner?" Jane said, looking at her in disbelief. "I don't think that's going to be all too popular . . . So what do I say to them?"

"That I'm on my way," Cecilie said, taking a deep breath and looking around at the officers. "Now, where were we?"

Ismail looked like someone who had just been given a death sentence and both Heino and Henrik looked at her with concern. She clapped her hands. "Let's return to the case! What did the neighbours have to say?"

"The usual," Heino answered, clearing his throat. "No one had seen or heard anything, except for the upstairs neighbour who noticed loud music coming from Farida's apartment on the night of the crime. But nothing that had made any particular impression on him—he just turned the volume up on his own stereo. Like he said, there's always someone or other who's being noisy somewhere in the building."

"What about the witness who discovered her?"

"She's a friend of the deceased who lives in the neighbouring complex. She couldn't understand why Farida had given her the slip and hadn't returned her calls. The two girls had keys to each other's apartments. So when she returned home after her night out on the town, she decided to check up on Farida. The woman is receiving emergency crisis counselling."

"What about video surveillances in the neighbourhood?" Henrik asked.

Cecilie shook her head. "The landlord set up cameras everywhere a couple of years ago so we'd feel safer, but within a day they had all been broken. They tried to put up some new ones, but the same thing happened again. So it pretty much ended there."

Cecilie's phone buzzed. She saw that it was Ole and answered it.

"What've you got for us, Ole?" she asked, putting her phone on speaker.

"I'm through with the autopsy. I'm sending the report to you now, but I just wanted to give you a summary."

"Shoot. I assume we can conclude that the perp is the same?"

"It's certainly the same modus operandi. But we've found a larger amount of ether in the victim's blood than in the others."

"Which means?"

"It's hard to say, but I have a theory."

"Of course you do, Ole. And what is the theory?"

"He wanted to prolong her death. He most probably let her float in and out of consciousness while he was performing the amputations."

"What would the motive for that be?"

"I have no idea. I'm neither a detective nor a psychologist, but he prevented her body from going into shock. The many lesions on her torso and on her limbs aren't particularly deep either. Just like the few stab wounds that there are weren't fatal."

"So he preferred to cut her up?"

"I'll leave that for others to determine. All I can say is that there are no fatal lesions to be found. Nothing that can be termed as causing death."

"So she bled to death instead?"

"Um . . . not quite."

"Well, what, then? What was the cause of death?"

"Cardiac arrest."

"As in she died from sheer fear?"

"That's not the technical term, but yes. The mind probably gave up before the body. Again, I'm no psychologist or detective, but I think that may have been the perp's intention."

"Thanks, Ole," she said, and hung up.

They all looked at one another in silence.

"Our perp is developing," Henrik said, leaning back in his chair, which made a screeching sound.

"Yeah, just when you thought that it couldn't get viler," said Joakim, his eyes moist.

"Why Farida?" Cecilie asked out into the room.

"Yeah, it's really tough that it's hitting you so close to home," said Heino.

"No, I mean, why her?" Cecilie asked, jumping off the desk. "To use Nikolaj's words, what compelled him to choose her? How old was she?"

Ismail looked up from his computer. "Farida had just turned thirty."

"In the noughties and in the teens, she would have been somewhere between eighteen and twenty-eight years old."

Henrik looked at her in surprise.

"But you don't seriously think that she, with her background, has ever been a nude model, do you?"

"There are many black . . . I mean, dark-skinned models," said Joakim, "so why not?"

"But isn't she also Muslim?" Henrik asked.

"A small cultural rebellion?" said Heino.

"Could that be the reason for cutting ties with the family?"

Cecilie nodded in agreement.

"Did you get an answer from Candyland about the magazines that came out in the teens, Ismail?"

Ismail shook his head. "They haven't got back to me. But since most magazines stopped publishing in 2014, I imagine it should be pretty easy finding the September models."

"Well, make it happen, then, Ismail. We need those magazines today."

Jane returned and gesticulated that it had to be now. As in right now!

"Two minutes," said Cecilie, and she turned to the rest of group.

"You continue, then, no matter what happens," she said, pointing to herself.

"Good luck," said Henrik.

"Can we talk?" Ismail asked, swallowing.

"It'll have to wait," said Cecilie, walking towards her office. When she got inside, she felt the sense of panic spreading throughout her body. She had to get Klerke involved. The Independent Police Complaints Authority couldn't stop her now. Not with the murder of Farida and that psychopath still free. Who cares what happened to her afterwards. She took the phone and dialled Klerke's number, then someone knocked at the door.

"I don't have time, Ismail," she said irritably, and turned around.

"Are you all right, boss?" Heino asked.

"Of course," she said, locking her phone. "What's up? I'm in kind of a rush."

"Not that it's any of my business," he said, smiling, "but is it the guy they fished out of the lake they want to talk with you about?"

"Not that it's any of your business," she said, and smiled, "but most likely, don't you think?"

He nodded. "Henrik said the brother tried to kill you last night. He pulled out a gun and everything . . . Is that true?"

"Henrik talks too much."

"The old man's worried about you, and I am too."

"Well, at least I'm still alive, as opposed to Farida."

Heino nodded. "I want you to know that I've got your back. No matter what happens," he said, looking down at the floor. "No matter what."

"Thanks, Heino."

"And we'll be sure to get him, boss," Heino added, as though he could read her thoughts.

She nodded. "Yup. Thanks. Now beat it, Heino."

When Heino had slipped out the door, she called Klerke again. But the Minister didn't answer.

54

Cecilie entered Commissioner Palsgaard's office and looked at the crowd sitting in his uncomfortable Philippe Starck chairs, staring at her. The National Police Commissioner had taken Palsgaard's seat behind the desk and left Palsgaard to sit down together with the others.

"I apologise for the delay, but I had to finish up a briefing," Cecilie said.

"Yes, and as far as I understand, it's been quite an eventful night. Sit down," the National Police Commissioner said monotonously. He gestured towards the vacant chair across from Ryan, Palsgaard, John, and his assistant, Kenneth. The chair resembled the gallows more than anything else, Cecilie thought as she sat down.

"Yet another femicide has been committed by the perpetrator?" said the National Police Commissioner with his characteristic nasal voice.

"We assume so, yes."

"Four murders and no suspect?"

The National Police Commissioner leaned his huge corpus across the table. "And he cuts off their labia. Is that correct?"

"Yes, that is correct."

"And you have arrested a Muslim man from the area?"

"The victim's father was naturally affected by the situation and so there was a little disturbance as a result. We chose to put him in detention for his own sake."

"I'd check him out thoroughly if it were my case."

"I agree," said Ryan.

"We're working based on a different theory," Cecilie said, smiling diplomatically.

"Well, that isn't the case we wanted to talk with you about anyway."

"No? Which one, then?" Cecilie asked, and already regretted her challenging tone of voice.

"Ryan? Will you?" asked the National Police Commissioner.

"Or perhaps you, from the Independent Police Complaints Authority, would like to do it instead?"

Ryan and John were so excited they practically spoke all at once. Ryan won the battle.

"We've received an official report from Como Cox, who is accusing Cecilie of threatening him and attempted murder."

"Attempted murder?"

"Yes, you allegedly followed him to Høje Gladsaxe and threatened him to keep quiet in connection with the case about his murdered brother, Jeremy Cox."

"Why would I do that? That case has nothing to do with me," she said, staring back at Ryan.

"There are mixed views on that. But can you confess to seeking out Como Cox?"

"Como, who is a regular criminal and on every level an unreliable witness . . ." she said, looking around, "threatened me with a gun on a surveillance assignment."

"Why didn't you arrest him then?"

"We had a murder to see to, so I had to let him go."

"Carrying a loaded gun?"

"Confiscated. It's in my office and will be sent to the stolen goods department."

"It's against regulations to have a weapon lying around," said John Nyholm.

"To a great degree," Kenneth added.

"It could have disciplinary consequences." John looked at the National Police Commissioner. "I request that we suspend Cecilie Mars and the colleague who witnessed the episode and should have intervened or filed a report to the Commissioner"

"Keep Henrik out of this, John," she said coldly.

"Sorry, but the case is rather clear," said John.

"Crystal clear," said Kenneth.

"Are there others in that division who witnessed this?"

Cecilie didn't answer.

"If so, we'll have to suspend them as well," John added.

She tightened her fists. "There is a man running around out there who has murdered four women and you're worried about a procedural mistake?"

"I don't think you understand the gravity of this Cecilie," said John Nyholm instructively.

"That is clear," Kenneth added with a little smile.

"Como has admitted that aside from this accusation, as well as the accusation against you of the murder of his brother, he also wishes to report other crimes that you have committed . . ."

"Including the smuggling of phones in prison to gang members, the possession and distribution of cocaine, as well as blackmail and violence," said Kenneth. "Como has a vivid imagination. Is he going to write more songs about that?"

She looked at the National Police Commissioner. "This isn't the first time that criminals have accused me or one of my detectives. It's usually a desperate attempt to evade a charge or get revenge for something," she said, extending her arms. "The Independent Police Complaints Authority and the Travel Team ought to be aware of that sort of thing instead of wasting everybody's time with it."

"Como Cox's account is backed up by various pieces of forensic evidence," said Ryan, "and by the witness account of a confidential colleague at NC3."

Oh no, Ismail. The thought shot through her mind as she looked at Ryan, seemingly unaffected. "Technical pieces of information? Indicating what? That Como sings off-key?"

"The colleague at NC3 admits to have given you confidential information indicating that Jeremy Cox was the one who was behind the

bombing of your service vehicle, which resulted in the death of your partner, Troels."

"We are constantly collaborating with NC3, and it was my case, so
what's the problem?"

"That the colleague retrieved tele-information without any legal basis
and shared it with you, which is considered a misconduct that can result
in serious penal charges for the individual in question. The fact that you
didn't file it is also considered a misconduct," said John.

"More procedural mistakes, John? I was the one who requested
the information. If there wasn't any legal basis for that, the individual
shouldn't have to pay a price for it."

"It's not just that, Cecilie," Palsgaard said. "The question is more
what you did with that information."

"Nothing."

"The employee has expressed concern in that regard," said Ryan, adjust-
ing his diving watch. "Serious concern. Considering that Jeremy Cox was
liquidated shortly afterwards, it raises a number of questions. Troels was your
colleague. You had a personal relationship with Jeremy Cox and—"

"Impressive, Ryan!" interrupted Cecilie, who was having a hard time
sitting still from sheer rage. "I sense that you are establishing a motive.
Try walking out the door and doing some proper investigating. I'm sure
you would find a lot more." She turned her gaze towards the National
Police Commissioner.

"The only reason why I didn't go further with the information was
because the suspect disappeared before I got a chance to confront him
with it. So there was no longer any reason to pursue that lead."

"Other than for the sake of law and order," the National Police Commissioner said unctuously.

Hypocrite! Cecilie felt like shouting, but she remained silent as he continued. "I think you are withholding crucial information on this case. If it
were up to me, you'd be charged with the murder of Jeremy Cox."

Cecilie looked at him perplexedly. If it were up to him? What the hell
did he mean by that? He was the one who bore the most number of stars
on his shoulders in that room. He had the power to throw her straight in
jail if he so much as disapproved of her appearance.

"But . . . ?" she ventured to ask.

"Beatrice Klerke, the Minister of Justice."

Cecilie smiled, relieved. Had Klerke managed to pull some strings after all?

"Yes, what about her?"

"When was the last time she reached out to you?"

Cecilie's sense of relief had been short-lived.

"I don't think I understand."

"Well, I'd advise you to do so because I am a very impatient man," he thundered.

"It was at police headquarters, at the reception . . . I greeted her then."

"I see. And was it there that she ordered you to go after Member of Parliament Mogens Berg?"

"I haven't been ordered to—"

"Stop. Think very carefully before you answer. What you say can have grave consequences for you and . . . for several of your colleagues. I will, if necessary, suspend your entire team, your whole division if I must, to get to the bottom of this."

She sensed everyone's gaze on her. The National Police Commissioner's, Palsgaard's, Ryan's, John's, and that of his assistant, Kenneth, who just sat there picking his nose.

"Am I to understand that this case is now getting first priority?"

"Absolutely. I expect everything to be put on standby." He looked around at his colleagues, who bowed their heads at his gaze. What he was offering was a tight deadline. A quick fix of sorts. Ryan and John didn't really have a part in it. If those two didn't nail her, things would look very bleak in their careers. They could say goodbye to ever attaining stars on their shoulders. She smiled to herself. In the apartment complex where she had grown up, it was a standard rule for the kids that if anyone threatened to beat you up, it would never happen because then they would have done it already. Applied to the National Police Commissioner's threats, it meant that as long as he thought there was a possibility for him to get at Klerke, she would be safe. Whoever had tipped him off, probably one of Klerke's political rivals, the individual wouldn't be satisfied with nailing a frigging cop with coke on her fingers and a skeleton in the cupboard.

"I don't recall receiving those orders," she said. "But I may be mistaken."

"How?" The National Police Commissioner's face turned scarlet red, and he looked as though he was in serious danger of having a stroke.

"And if the meeting here is going to continue, I imagine that there really should be a lawyer present or, at the very least, lovely Jette from the Police Federation," she said, smiling.

Shortly afterwards, Cecilie returned to the division. They were all staring at her as though she were Christ resurrected from the dead.

"Is everything okay, boss?" Heino asked.

"Absolutely," she said, nodding. The adrenaline was still pumping through her body and making her throat dry. "Couldn't have gone better."

"Were they hard on you?" Henrik asked.

She shook her head and looked around. "Where's Ismail?"

"He left a little while ago. He said there was something urgent he had to see to at NC3."

"Urgent? I see," she said, thinking that Ismail had probably fled. "What about Candyland?"

Joakim waved at her to come over.

"I have at this very moment just scanned in these pages. It's the September issues from four Danish magazines that were published until 2014."

"We'd better open those," she said.

Henrik and Heino got up from their seats and went to look over Joakim's shoulder.

"Nothing beats looking at pictures of naked ladies with your colleagues," said Heino.

"I bet that's been a wet dream of yours for a long time now," Cecilie answered, making them all laugh. The laughter subsided when Joakim opened the file from 2011 and a dark woman emerged. She had her father's high cheekbones and sharp nose and Cecilie was able to recognise Farida from the pictures on her Facebook profile.

"Do you think the family knew?" Joakim asked.

"What does it matter? She's dead now," Heino answered.

Except for the fact that it did matter, Cecilie thought. The press was soon going to learn about this, and Farida's past would be on full display for the world to see. And parts of that world were both closed off and conservative to such an extent that Omar and his family would be ostracised. The President of the Tenant Association's time was starting to run out just like her career and freedom.

Cecilie sat down heavily in the chair. They'd soon return, the National Police Commissioner and his gang. As soon as they had found more to pressure her with or persuaded some of her colleagues to testify against her, they were all one another's executioners.

55

The Muslim section at the Bispebjerg Cemetery, situated between the German and Catholic sections, was filled with a little under 100 mourners for Farida's funeral. It seemed as though the neighbourhood's residents had come to pay their final respects, alongside her family and friends. Representatives from the Muslim community, civil services, and the feminist movement had used the tragedy to make their mark with speeches outside the cemetery. They all agreed that the politicians didn't care and that the police merely stood by and watched while women and minorities continued to be attacked. The emergency force had turned up in large numbers but had remained in the background and at a considerable distance. Cecilie followed the ceremony together with those who had shown up at the gravesite. She recognised many of her neighbours, who stood with their heads bowed. They looked grief-stricken, as though the tragedy had hit them personally. She had impressed upon the team that they should keep quiet about the discovery of the nude photos, but of course it was just a question of time before word would get out. The only thing she hoped for the sake of the family was that it wouldn't happen in the course of the next three days when they would, according to custom, open their home during their grieving period. To her surprise, she caught sight of Nikolaj, who was standing under a tree a little further off from the rest of the procession. They hadn't spoken with each other since the day he had visited the division. Cecilie was about to walk over to him when someone tugged at her sleeve. She turned around.

"Allan," she said, surprised, as she looked at the tall boy in the hoodie.

"Cecilie," he answered, and gave her a big smile. "It's . . . p-p-pretty bad," he stammered.

"Yes, Allan, it sure is."

"The pushers have also returned."

"Yes, I know," she said absent-mindedly as she looked over at the tree where Nikolaj had been standing. She looked around, but now he was nowhere to be seen.

"Are you looking for witnesses?"

"Witnesses?" she asked.

"T-to the girl's death?"

"Yes, of course," she said, nodding. "You always do in cases like that. It's very important."

"I'd like to b-b-be a w-w-witness . . . it s-s-sounds exciting," he said, sniffling.

"Then you have to have seen something that the police can use," she said instructively.

"I have seen a car. A black car. One like yours."

"A Golf? Okay, Allan, where?"

"In front of the girl's house."

"You mean the car park?"

"Yes."

"But there are many cars parked there, aren't there?"

"A man was sitting in the car . . . a white man . . ."

She looked around once more for Nikolaj. "A man, okay, and what was he doing in the car? Was he keeping an eye on the apartment where the girl lived?"

Allan sniffled. "He talked on the t-t-telephone."

"I see . . ." she said, smiling indulgently. "Thanks, Allan, I have made a note of it."

Shortly afterwards, the ceremony was over, and the funeral guests started leaving the cemetery. Cecilie remained standing and waited for Omar to walk past her.

"My condolences, Omar," she said when he reached her. He looked at her with a dejected gaze.

"Ce-cil," he said, nodding. He had grown a million years older since the last time they had seen each other.

"I'm so sorry. I wish we could have prevented it."

Omar shook his head. "What kind of a person am I?"

"Don't blame yourself."

"I'm the one who moved the family to Denmark. I was the one who said we'd be safe here. I was the one who said as long as we mind our own business and follow the laws, everything will be fine." The tears rolled down his face. "I was the one who pushed her away. What kind of a father pushes his own daughter away?"

"I'm certain that she knew deep down that you loved her."

He shook his head. "How could she have possibly known that?"

She leaned towards him and lowered her voice. "Omar, it's not your fault, just like it isn't Farida's fault. No matter what comes out or what people think, it's the murderer's fault. Only him, Omar."

He nodded.

"Thank you, Cecil. I have always seen you as my Danish family, my Danish friend."

"Thank you," she said, quietly smiling. "I know it won't bring back Farida, but we are doing everything we can to catch him."

Omar looked across the cemetery with a vacant gaze. "I appreciate that. But how will he be punished?"

"He'll get life. Or he'll get detention."

"So he'll get out again?"

"He won't get out again. He'll stay behind bars for the rest of his life."

"Behind bars, yes, getting three meals a day and his own TV. Is that really a punishment? In Somalia you're a rich man if you can afford those things."

"I know, it does seem very unfair. But it's the law."

Omar looked her straight in the eyes. "Kill him, Ce-cil. If you get the chance, kill the bastard. You'd be doing us all a favour. I beg you, by my daughter's grave . . . kill that monster."

"I can't promise you that, Omar, you know that."

"Why not? Is this any different? I know what you're capable of. We all do. You take care of the neighbourhood. Take care of us all."

"Omar . . ."

"The world is run by monsters," Omar said, and started walking.

When Cecilie had reached the car park at Bispebjerg Square ten minutes later, she ran intro Nikolaj.

"I thought I saw you there," she said, greeting him.

"I saw you standing with the girl's father," Nikolaj said. "I didn't want to disturb you."

"It's a very nice gesture that you came, but I'm a little surprised to see you here."

He put his hands in his jeans pockets and looked down at the ground.

"Well, you know . . . I felt I was a little to blame."

"To blame? For what?"

"For steering you in the wrong direction. But I was certain the perp would go after one of the models from the seventies."

"I think we all did. But you might still be right," she said with concern.

"Did you find the models from the seventies?"

She nodded. "Yes, there's one in Høje Gladsaxe and one on Vigerslev."

"Okay, who are they?"

"Vinnie and Helle. One's a prostitute, the other one is a pensioner. Why?"

"Just curious, that's all. Am I the only one who gets a dry throat after a funeral?" he asked, nodding towards the opposite side of the square. Cecilie turned around and noticed the bodega with red awnings further down.

"Are you offering a beer?"

"Only the first one."

56

The tobacco smoke hung heavily over Jeppe's Bodega, which was half filled with guests who were sitting in red plastic booths. At the far end, the mood was jovial among some older men who were playing darts. However, the cheerful mood couldn't overpower Rasmus Seebach, whose voice could be heard from the jukebox, singing "Millionaire." Cecilie and Nikolaj had found a booth away from the other guests.

"I'm sorry, we could have gone to another place," said Nikolaj.

"Don't worry about it. I invited you to coffee at Bella Grill," she said as they toasted the half pints of tap beer they had both ordered along with two Gajol shots.

"See, they've even got red-and-white-chequered tablecloths," she said, stroking the laminated surface with her hand. "Had it been any fancier, I would have rushed out the door."

"Well, that's certainly something we have in common," he said, taking a sip of his beer. "Are you all right?"

"With what?"

"After everything's that's happened. Or is happening," he corrected himself, and looked at her with concern.

"Well, if I wasn't, I should have chosen another job other than running the Homicide Unit."

"Why did you choose to become a police officer?"

She smiled a little. "Yes, why did I? I'm sure it had to do with wanting to catch bad guys, help the defenceless, make a difference, maintain justice, and not least get a little excitement in my day-to-day life. What about you? Why did you become a psychologist?"

"Make a difference, help the defenceless, get a little excitement in my day-to-day life," he said jokingly.

"Yeah, right. Be honest."

"Honest?" he asked, looking her in the eyes. "You want to know why?"

"Yes, of course."

He took his shot glass and clinked it against hers, signalling that they should empty the glass.

"Is the story that intense?" she said, emptying her glass with him. They chased it down with beer.

"No, there are people who've grown up in much worse situations than I have. But I had a rather dominating and bipolar mother. She tended to take her mood swings out on me. Both in her depressive moments and her maniacal ones. On top of that, she tended to run into the wrong guys. Men who harmed her and who she didn't have the wherewithal to protect me from."

"Damn, that sounds intense."

"It was in certain periods. There were also good moments and happy memories. But to get back to your question, I had a need to understand my mother. Why she treated me the way she had. Which, in a roundabout way, meant that I started studying psychology. And I discovered something that I was good at. I got the highest average in my class. The rest is history, as they say."

"Interesting. I'm thinking that you could have applied your abilities doing something else besides wasting your time on criminals," she said.

"You're tough, Cecilie," he said.

"I live off catching them. I see what they actually do," she answered, and drank from her beer.

"That's fair. But human suffering comes in many forms. Extroverted aggression and criminal behaviour don't make those individuals less sick. They have just as much need to be cured as anyone else."

Cecilie leaned back in her chair.

"Are you trying to save them, Doctor?"

"I try to do many things, but I think saving them is beyond my expertise. Instead, I try to understand the roots of the illness." They ordered another round of shots and immediately emptied them.

"Well, Cecilie, what was the real reason that you decided to work for the police? I sense that it was for more personal reasons."

She looked down at the table. "No, I don't really know . . ."

"My guess is that it was a violent experience of some sort, maybe that someone close to you had a traumatic experience."

"You're fishing, Doctor," she said, and looked up.

"Am I close?" Nikolaj said, laughing.

She turned her beer glass. "I was raped when I was in high school." She placed her hand on his and stopped his stream of words. "It's okay. We can talk about it."

"I'm sorry to hear that. Was he your age?"

"No, an old pig who had nothing better to do with his time."

"I'm sorry you had to go through that."

"Don't be. I got over it a long time ago."

She took a sip of her beer and looked over at the jukebox that was playing "Susan Himmelblå."

"I'm thinking that all our experiences influence us. Influence the choices we make. Make us who we are today. Don't you think so?" Nikolaj attempted.

She turned her head towards him. "I don't think about it so much anymore. The asshole is dead, and I've moved on." She took a sip of her beer.

"Are you sure?"

"You've seen the kinds of cases we work with, what we go out and find."

Nikolaj nodded.

"I've seen abused and murdered children. I've seen people mutilated and tortured in the most grotesque ways, the latest being Farida. I've faced the biggest psychopaths who've tried to kill me. Each and every neighbourhood in Copenhagen reminds me of a murder case. I've seen what horrors people are capable of doing to each other over nothing. I think that that, if anything, has shaped me."

"Has it made you harder?"

"I was hard from the beginning. But yes. The world is run by monsters, which is, by the way, what Omar said to me after he asked me to kill his daughter's murderer."

Nikolaj nodded. "A father in grief, that's understandable. But do you really feel that the world is run by monsters?"

"I think we all contain some evil in us. That we all possess the ability and the desire to harm others, though our motive, what triggers us, may vary."

"You should have become a psychologist," he said, clinking her glass.

"I don't think so."

"Oh yes," he said, cheerfully. "From a scientific point of view, you're right. There is proven evilness in us all."

"Are you kidding me?"

"No, have you heard of the D-factor?"

"Only if D stands for death."

"Not quite. The D-factor, or D-score, is the term for the dark personality traits that describe the extent to which we strive towards our own goals at the expense of others."

"What are those personality traits?"

Nikolaj lifted his hand and counted on his fingers as he listed, "egoism, Machiavellianism, feelings of superiority, self-promotion, narcissism, malice, psychopathy, sadism, and scrupulousness. Through a test you can map out a person's dark sides. See what parameters you belong to."

"And which parameters do you belong to, Nikolaj? I'm certain that you've already taken it."

"Believe me, you don't want to know," he said roguishly, and took a sip of his beer.

"And where do you think I'd belong? Do I belong under most of the categories?"

He shook his head. "No, I see you as an empathic person. You care about your surroundings, the people in your neighbourhood, and not least your colleagues. Probably also your family. Your boyfriend?"

She smiled. "Very smooth."

He ducked his head. "Sorry, I'm not very good at this sort of thing. So, do you have a boyfriend?" he asked, looking her in the eyes.

"No, I'm bad at relationships. It comes with the job. Many of my colleagues suffer from it as well. And I tend to fall for the wrong types on top of that."

"Really? I can't imagine that."

"No? Just ask the Travel Team or the Independent Police Complaints Authority," she said coolly.

"What do you mean?"

"That the last person I dated, sorry, screwed, has been fished out of a lake with a bullet through his head. But I think you already know that, Nikolaj."

He nodded. "There are lots of rumours going around about it. So, how do you feel about that?"

"I would have preferred it if he had stayed down in that lake."

He looked at her in surprise.

"Just a joke," she said, smiling. "So, how's your dating life, Doctor?"

He rolled his eyes. "Nonexistent. Which probably also comes with my job."

"Well, I guess it's pretty impressive, then, that we two ended up here."

"So you think of this as a date?" he asked, laughing.

"Why not?" she asked, looking around. "I've dated worse people in much gloomier-looking places. Should we play a round?" she asked, pointing at the dart board, which was now vacant.

They ended up playing several rounds. And before they knew it, the heavy-set bartender with the red suspenders was ringing the bell. "Last call!" he shouted, which they took advantage of.

"Damn, I'm drunk!" said Nikolaj as they walked down the stairs supporting each other.

"I don't feel a thing," Cecilie slurred.

"Want to share a taxi?" he asked.

"Where do you live?"

"Amager."

She giggled. "I'm off to Bellahøj, so we'll have to part ways."

"Yes," he said, swaying. "Well, it was f-fu—"

Cecilie pulled him in for a kiss. He returned her kiss and pressed her against the wall. They caressed one another as the light in the bodega was turned off.

"I want you," she said in his ear. "Right now."

"Here?" he answered, looking around.

She pulled him towards the nearest entrance and pressed all the buttons on the entry telephone. A resident buzzed them in while others asked who they were.

"Come," she said, pulling him into the entrance. She tore at his belt, and he started unzipping her jeans.

"What if someone sees?" he asked, laughing.

"Well, it'll be bloody embarrassing, won't it?" she said, laughing as she helped him pull down her pants.

57

Cecilie could hear a constant ringing sound through a distant fog. The sound was infernal, and she wanted it to stop. But instead, it continued until she opened her eyes. It took a little while before she realised that she was lying in her bed. Once again, someone rang the doorbell, and the sound drilled deep into her hungover brain. She picked up her phone to see what the time was but was instead confronted with a message from Jane saying that she had a meeting in Palsgaard's office today. The doorbell rang once more.

"Oh, go to hell," she said, getting up out of her bed. She walked through the living room, where her clothes were lying in a single straight line from where she had taken them off the night before. *Fuck, fuck, fuck*, she thought when, for a split second, the previous night's events flashed through her brain. Through the spyhole she could see a blue parka jacket that was much bigger than the person wearing it and she opened the door.

"Ismail? I thought you had fled after ratting on me to John and the other bastards."

"I'm sorry to disturb you," he said, looking down at the doormat.

She suddenly became aware of the fact that she was only wearing a pair of panties and a wrinkled T-shirt.

"That's the least you should apologise for. They want to suspend me now on account of what you said." She waved him inside and Ismail followed her obediently through the entryway.

"I mean, I can handle a shitty gangster like Como, but it's quite a different story when one of NC3's nerds rats on me."

"I'm sorry."

"I even think that the white judiciary is willing to disregard your brown skin and consider you a reliable witness."

"I just told the truth."

"How could you when you don't know what it is?" she asked, feeling nausea rising. She regretted having invited him in. "If you've come to ask for forgiveness, I am hereby giving it to you. Have a nice day."

"I didn't come here to be forgiven. Not by you, anyway. I know I made a mistake when I handed over the tele-information, but that was solely to protect you from Jeremy."

"So that the Independent Police Complaints Authority could slaughter me afterwards? Thanks for nothing."

"They came to me, not the other way around!" he said despairingly as he extended his arms. He resembled an overfed blue penguin as he stood there flapping in his much too large parka. "They had all the evidence. I had to tell them what I knew. All I said was that I had shared the information with you. They wanted me to say a whole bunch of other things as well. About you and Jeremy and how you had killed him. They wanted me to open your phone, your computer. I said no to everything . . ."

She lifted her hand and stopped his stream of words. "I know. You did what you had to do, Ismail. It's just that I'm in a shitty situation now. Which is unfortunate as fuck because we finally might have a chance to actually catch that perp."

"Really? How?"

"I think he still needs a model from the seventies to complete his collection."

"You think that either Helle or Vinnie will be his next victim?"

"Yes, and if I get removed, the whole thing will get fucked up by Ryan and his Travel Team. They might go after you as the perp," she added sarcastically.

"Me?"

"Well, you're a Muslim."

"Hindu."

"Okay, my bad."

He looked down at the floor. "I'm sorry we didn't get to Farida before it was too late."

"Me too. I can see her apartment from my balcony," she said, shaking her head, which worsened her hangover. "I need some coffee. How about you?" she asked, walking out to the kitchen.

"I don't drink it."

"I've run out of Red Bull and Coke, so you'll have to make do with water."

"I'm not thirsty."

Cecilie poured some water into the kettle and got out some Nescafé and a mug from the cabinet. He picked the edge of his sleeve as he tried to find the words. "The reason why I came over is because I might have found something that may lead to the perp."

She quickly looked at him and accidentally spilled Nescafé granules next to the mug.

"And you waited until now to announce that? Okay, well, shoot, then."

"Not before you tell me the truth. Did you kill Jeremy?"

"I've already told you that I didn't. Tell me what you know."

She swept the coffee off the table with her hand and poured it into the mug.

"Did you?"

She gave him a suspicious look. "Was this Ryan's idea? Or John's? What did they do, wire you up?" She grabbed the zipper on his jacket and zipped it down.

"Hey? What the hell?" Ismail cried out. Without hesitation she tore open his shirt and checked his chest.

"Hey, the phone!" she said, reaching for it. "Are you recording our conversation?"

"Hell no," he said, showing her that the phone was off. He modestly stuffed his shirt back down his trousers. "I came on my own initiative because I've found something important."

"Tell me what it is, dammit."

"Not before you tell me the truth. Did you kill him?"

She was about to lose her patience. "It doesn't matter what the hell happened to that damn cop killer, Ismail."

"I think it does."

"Does it?

"Yes."

"Well then, get this into your head. If Jeremy weren't dead, he would have gone after me, the war in the neighbourhood would have continued, it would have spread to other areas, more innocent people would have been killed in the bullet exchanges between the gangs, more young people would have been recruited, more pushers would have come to finance the war, which would have meant more junkies on the streets, more crime, more prostitution, more of all the crap Jeremy stood for."

"Why were you seeing him?"

"I wasn't seeing him. I took advantage of him to get closer to stopping the war. He, on the other hand, tried to take advantage of me, and when he didn't succeed, he tried to kill me with a bomb. And in between those events we screwed once or twice . . . end of story."

"End of story because you killed him?"

"Yes, goddammit!" she shouted. "Until I shot a frigging bullet through his head, okay? Is that truth enough for you? Is it, Ismail? Do you think you can stand to hear the truth?"

Ismail didn't answer. He looked unusually sad. As though she had punctured all his illusions about her. Cecilie took a deep breath. "What you found on Jeremy wouldn't have held up in court, Ismail . . . Jeremy would have got away with killing Troels. Sorry, but in my world that sort of thing isn't to be tolerated."

"You killed him," Ismail said reflectively. "Precisely the way you want to kill this perp now?"

"Huh? No," she said, shaking her head and feeling her hangover returning. "I hope to put him before a judge. I do. I really do," she repeated.

He stared at her. "And there's nothing within you that wants to kill him?"

She returned his gaze. "Yes, every fibre in my body. But that doesn't mean it's going to happen. I want to prevent him from mutilating and killing other women."

"I don't know if I dare trust you," he said, sighing.

"Ismail, I'm not a psychopath," she said, extending her arms in a conciliatory gesture.

"No?" Ismail asked faintly. "If I tell you this, it has to go by the book. It has to go through the right channels. It has to be official."

She nodded impatiently. "Of course; now tell me what it is."

"Do you understand, Cecilie?"

"I understand, Ismail, by the book, the official channels."

He crossed his arms and remained silent.

"If you don't trust me, then at the very least tell our team before the Travel Team takes over. Which will most likely be later today."

"It's a dilemma for me."

"What is?"

"That I don't dare trust you, but that I can't go to any of the others either."

"Why not?"

"Because I think the perp is a cop."

58

Cecilie leaned against the kitchen table and looked at Ismail. It was as though her hangover had disappeared.

"Did you just say *cop* or am I hearing things?"

"That's what I said. When I have to extract personal information from one of the registries, I usually go the back way." He shrugged his shoulders. "Everyone does in the NC3. It's the easiest way in and you have smooth transitions between one registry and another without having to constantly log in."

"That sounds efficient and not exactly legal."

"Who you are to judge?"

"Fair enough. What did you find?"

"By going behind the system, you get access to the continual activity log, which registers all the searches that are made. Not surprisingly, there has been a lot of activity on searches dealing with the four victims. And it culminated around the times of the murders."

"You could follow our login?"

"Yes, not just yours and the team's but also Palsgaard's and the members of the Travel Team's, who have been following it very closely."

She lifted her eyebrows. "And I thought they were fully preoccupied with finding dead gangsters. So far you haven't revealed anything out of the ordinary."

"I'll get to that," Ismail said, clearing his throat.

"What's unusual is that the same IP address searched Lizzette Morning Star's name three months before her death."

"Okay. Now that's interesting. What information was the search for?"

"Her address and name change."

"Normally, it beeps and makes a racket if someone makes an unauthorised search. Why not here?"

"Because a case number was filed immediately afterwards, which closed it again."

"But if the search is following a case, then there's nothing interesting about it, right? Do you know what case she was involved in?"

"Of course. Battering ram burglaries in towns like Herning and Løgumkloster."

Cecilie looked at him in surprise. "That's far away from Amager and Lizzette's profile in general."

"Yes, it doesn't quite match up with a middle-aged woman who owns a decorating store on Amagerbrogade."

"And those battering ram burglaries were investigated by the Travel Team?"

"Yes, the search was done from one of their IP addresses."

"That is . . . interesting, but still," Cecilie said, smiling. "As little faith as I have in the Travel Team, I still find it hard to believe that the perp is one of them. There must be an explanation. A wrong case number . . ." She noticed that Ismail remained silent.

"What else did you find?"

"It's not the only search that is a little curious. There was a search on Farida in the same period. Several months before her death."

"From the same computer?"

"The same IP address, yes. Just affiliated with another case number."

"What case?"

"A stolen goods case from Viborg that was connected with the battering ram burglaries and the same circle of people. It's a very smart way of getting around the security system. Under the set of criminal offences, there are thousands of different searches in a group of people of about two hundred different CPR numbers. The searches for Lizzette and Farida were well hidden there."

"Except they weren't for you, Ismail. That's impressive."

"Well, I am one of the best in NC3."

"Do we have a suspect among Ryan's people?"

"No."

She looked at him in surprise. "What do you mean? I thought you said that the IP address belonged to one of the Travel Team's computers."

"The IP address from which the search was made belongs to Ryan."

Her mouth fell open. "Fuck."

"Yes."

"And you're a hundred per cent sure?"

He cocked his head. "Like I said before, I'm one of NC3's best, if not the best."

"Ryan, that cocksucker," Cecilie said out into the kitchen. She sipped her coffee, which had turned lukewarm. "An officer can at any time of day knock on the door and deceive his way into someone's home," she said rhetorically. "The only thing he'd have to do is show his ID card and say that he's got some important information. Perhaps about a sudden death."

"That would explain why he was able to get into their homes without leaving a single trace."

"Do we have any evidence?"

"It's all here," he said, tapping his shoulder bag containing his computer. "So, what do we do?"

"We have to get hold of Allan."

"Who?"

"A boy from the neighbourhood. He told me he had seen a man in a car in front of Farida's apartment complex. It seemed insignificant when he told me, but if he can identify Ryan, it would support everything you've discovered so far."

"And what then? What do we do afterwards?"

She let the question linger in the air. "I need to put on some clothes," she said, and left the kitchen.

Ten minutes later, they started searching for Allan in the neighbourhood, but he was neither on any of the walkways nor the ball courts. Cecilie wished she had known where the boy lived or what his surname was. But considering that he was always in the vicinity whenever she drove from the car park, she guessed that he lived in the northern part of Bellahøj.

"Maybe we should drop it, Cecilie? He could be at home or in school."

"School is probably the last place, but you're right," she said, and continued towards the Golf and let herself into the car. "Let's get out of here." She had an idea and turned on the flashing blue lights.

"Is that really necessary?" Ismail asked as he covered his ears. She let the sirens sound off a little while longer before turning them off.

"Most of the troublemakers in Bellahøj run away when they hear the sirens, except for Allan. He likes the sound and the flashing blue lights."

And sure enough, Allan came whizzing by on his little electric scooter.

"Hi, Allan, good to see you," Cecilie said, getting out of the car.

"What is it, Cecilie?" Allan asked, hopping off his scooter. "H-h-has the m-m-murderer struck again?"

"No, don't worry. I just needed to find you."

"Me?" Allan asked, his eyes brightening.

"Yes. You want to be a witness, right?"

"Y-yes, very much."

"Good. Last time we talked, you said you had seen a white man in a car close to Farida's front entrance door. Do you think you'd be able to recognise him?"

Allan looked at the ground, a little uncertain. "M-maybe?"

"It's all right if you can't, but I want to show you a picture." She got out a picture of Ryan from his Instagram profile and showed it to Allan.

"Have you seen him before?"

Allan looked at it. "Y-yes, I've seen him before."

"Are you sure? It's very important, Allan. Take another look," she said, trying to conceal her enthusiasm.

"Yes, h-he was d-down by the lake when they f-fished out that b-body, right?"

Cecilie nodded. "Yes, Allan, that's right, that's well spotted. But is he also the one you saw by Farida's apartment?"

Allan hesitated. "Well . . . well . . ."

"You have to be a hundred per cent certain, Allan. Was it him?"

"I don't know, Cecilie. I think, m-m-maybe. It w-w-was raining, and I couldn't s-s-see him very well."

"That's perfectly fine," she said, patting him on his shoulder.

"W-w-was I a good witness?"

"Yes, of course you were. Talk to you soon." She opened the door to the Golf.

"B-b-but the car, Cecilie. It looked just like yours," he said enthusiastically.

"Yes, you've said that. A little black vehicle, right?"

Allan nodded energetically. "Y-yes, a police car."

"A what?" she said, letting go of the car door. She walked over to Allan. "How do you know it was a police car?"

Allan laughed. "Everyone in the n-n-neighbourhood knows what a p-p-police car looks like, even though it doesn't say 'police' on the side of it."

"How?" Cecilie wanted to know.

"Little a-a-antenna on the roof. Blue lights by the radiator and on the side-view mirrors and in the back," Allan said, pointing to the lights on Cecilie's Golf.

"Well spotted again, Allan. Did you get the licence plate as well?"

"No, should I have?"

"No, that's fine."

Cecilie and Ismail got into the car. She moved the gun in her holster, which caught Ismail's eye. "Through the official channels, Cecilie, you promised."

"Of course, I have no intention of putting a bullet through his head . . . yet."

She changed gears and drove off.

59

Cecilie and Ismail had just entered the division when Jane came rushing out to meet them.

"They're waiting for you, Cecilie. As usual, I might add," she said with a little smile.

"Who besides Palsgaard is there?"

"John and Kenneth from the Independent Police Complaints Authority."

"What about Ryan?"

Jane shook her head.

"Perfect," said Cecilie, smiling at Ismail. When they reached Palsgaard's office, Cecilie knocked on the door and entered with Ismail. She briefly greeted Palsgaard behind the desk as well as John and Kenneth, who had pulled some chairs over.

"This is a formal meeting about your situation, Cecilie," said Palsgaard as he pointed at Ismail as though he were a dog who had accidentally lost its way.

"We have important new developments. That's why Ismail is here too. It is, however, confidential information. Perhaps it would be best if it were only you and John who remained?"

John snorted. "Everyone in the Independent Police Complaints Authority are trusted colleagues, including Kenneth."

Kenneth smiled nervously. Cecilie looked at Kenneth. He resembled John, though a younger and paler version.

"Okay, stay, then."

She turned her gaze to Palsgaard. "We have a suspect for the four murders. Solid evidence that could lead to an arrest today."

"It's no longer your case, Cecilie," Palsgaard answered, folding his arms.

"Now, listen, Palsgaard!"

Cecilie's outburst clearly took the Commissioner by surprise, yet he remained silent.

"I'm sorry," she said, extending her hands apologetically. "But this is important. We have found evidence that indicates that the perpetrator is a senior police officer."

Palsgaard and John quickly sent each other a glance that could be interpreted as disbelief.

"What kind of evidence do you have, then?"

Cecilie recapitulated everything that Ismail had told her, about how the searches on Lizzette and Farida respectively had been done months before their deaths and later attempts had been made to conceal them. And that the searches had been made from Ryan's computer.

"From Ryan's? And you're certain of this?" Palsgaard asked, looking at Ismail.

"Yes," Ismail answered. "One hundred per cent."

"It matches up with the modus operandi that an officer would be able to contact the women and trick his way into their homes," Cecilie said energetically, and continued in the same upbeat tone. "We also have a witness who saw a plainclothes officer car parked in front of Farida's apartment complex where the driver observed her several days before the murder took place."

"And has the witness been able to identify Ryan?"

"No, the witness wasn't certain. But there may be others in the area who've seen something. We want to investigate as soon as possible," she said, nodding eagerly. "I suggest we arrest Ryan and place charges against him today."

Palsgaard gave her a vacant look and the office became completely silent.

"Is he at headquarters or at home?" Cecilie asked. "I'll send a team out to get him."

Palsgaard smiled stiffly. He reached up and adjusted his small round glasses. "Your survival instinct never ceases to amaze, Cecilie."

"What do you mean?"

"That you are apparently willing to do anything to get out of a muddle."

"This is solid evidence. It's not just something that I've made up. Ismail came to me and presented me with this."

John moved forward in his chair. "It seems to me that Ismail has a tendency to find things for you, convenient things, doesn't he?"

John looked at Ismail, who flinched. "I . . . I found it in the data log."

"Why hasn't anyone found it before you?" asked Kenneth.

Ismail scratched his beard. "It was concealed between the other cases."

"I see, and how, then, did you gain access to the data log?" John asked.

"Did Cecilie assign you to do it? Or was it on your own initiative?" Kenneth added, moving forward in his chair. "According to the strict protocol for the entire registry security system, a disciplinary case has to be initiated before those kinds of steps can be taken." Ismail looked down at the floor as he clutched his briefcase.

"I understand your silence. Those are quite a few crucial questions to consider," John said, smiling indulgently. "But during our last conversation I was under the impression that we had established a trust of sorts. Where you expressed a willingness to cooperate. Which is why this surprises me, Ismail."

"This has nothing to do with Ismail," Cecilie snarled. "Everything that has taken place was under my orders, and that's as far as it goes, John!"

"In which case I'm afraid you have a little reading up to do, Cecilie," he responded, crossing his arms. "Ismail, I'm going to have to suspend you so that we can get some clarity on the previous situation as well as this new one. It seems as though there have been some serious breaches committed in terms of data security."

"Data security?" Cecilie asked, looking at Palsgaard. "We have a possible perpetrator on the loose and the Independent Police Complaints Authority decides that now's the time to come up with some sort of civil service accusation?! We need to do some investigating and I need Ismail."

"What you need is to take it easy," Palsgaard said in an admonitory tone. "And to not let your emotions get the better of you. Once you have done that, I suggest you contact the Police Federation and a lawyer."

Cecilie placed her hands at her sides. "Are you suspending me?"

"Yes, that's why we've called you into this meeting."

She stared at him in disbelief. "But . . . but we have evidence indicating that—"

"For good reason, I am not aware of what you have or don't have. That is solely your claim. Which, together with the charges being filed against you, will be investigated."

"And what will happen in the meantime? Who's going to prevent another murder from being committed?"

"That's none of your concern."

"But I am greatly concerned, so who's going to take over the investigation?"

Palsgaard remained silent.

"Could I at least be permitted to hand over this new piece of information to my team?"

"First of all, you no longer have a team, and second of all, we're not going to start a rumour mill," Palsgaard said very firmly.

"A rumour mill?" she repeated, fired up. "The Travel Team is taking over? Tell me it isn't true!"

"At the request of the National Police Commissioner himself," he said, smiling.

She looked at him pleadingly. "Palsgaard, you've got to go back to the National Police Commissioner and notify him about this so he can reconsider his decision."

"I'm afraid it's over, Cecilie."

Cecilie shook her head as she tried to consider more options. "Klerke? Is she still the one you want to get at?"

"That ship sailed ages ago. Another missed opportunity on your part." Palsgaard smiled knowingly to John and Kenneth. "As far as I understand, the Minister's days are numbered."

The meeting was finished, as was her career. She was ordered to hand everything over. Her phone, ID card, and her service pistol. Ismail had to hand over his computer. Together with Ismail, she was escorted by two police officers through the entrance hall. She turned to one of them.

"I'd like to go past my office and pick up a few personal items."

"Sorry, Cecilie, but we have been instructed to see both of you straight to the door without any stops."

"What are we going to do, Cecilie?" Ismail whimpered.

"I have no idea."

He shook his head helplessly. "I should never have gone along with you. I've been suspended! What will my family say?"

"Tell them it's sort of like a vacation."

"That's not funny, Cecilie."

"Don't you think I know that? We need to call Heino or Henrik."

Ismail cast a sidelong glance at the officer walking next to him and lowered his voice. "But we're not allowed to pass on information. We'll be punished."

"Well, they can't exactly suspend us twice, now, can they?" she asked as they were sent out the door.

"But we could get a longer prison term," said Ismail as he stopped on the pavement.

"We'll worry about that when the time comes."

"But I'm already worrying about it now!"

"The most important thing is that we get hold of Heino or Henrik. We've got to warn them about Ryan and get an investigation going."

She took out her private phone and called up Henrik. The call went directly to his answering machine. The same happened when she tried to call Heino.

"What are those two clowns up to?" she said, looking up towards the windows on the first floor. She tried to call Joakim, but all she got was a silly jingle and Joakim singing, "*Just leave a message*."

Cecilie crossed the street to the car park.

"Where are you going?" Ismail asked.

She received a message from Heino: *We are all sitting in a meeting with Palsgaard. This is some real terrible shit, boss!*

She wrote back to call her as soon as he could and got out her keys.

"You didn't give them your car keys?" Ismail asked, staring at the keys in her hand.

"Nope."

"But don't you think it's illegal to take the car while you're suspended?"

"Probably. Want a lift?"

Ismail shook his head. "I've broken enough laws for today. I'm taking the subway."

"It's up to you."

Ismail remained standing.

"Cecilie, you're not going to go after Ryan. You're not going to shoot him, are you?"

"What do you take me for? A complete psycho or what? Anyway, I don't have my service revolver anymore," she said jokingly. She didn't tell him that she hadn't handed over Como's gun but had instead taken it home.

60

The darkness had settled across Valeursvej in Hellerup, where the stately white houses stood side by side. Aside from a few dog walkers who had passed by in the last hour, everything was very quiet in the fashionable neighbourhood. The silence was broken when a limousine-size Mercedes emerged on the street. The clear glow from the headlights cut through the night as the car continued down the road. When it reached number 2, the driver stopped and got out of the car. He opened the back door and Beatrice Klerke got out with her arms full of documents and her black Gucci bag hanging over her shoulder.

"Thank you, Sørensen. See you tomorrow at seven."

"Goodnight, Mrs. Minister," he said, and returned to the car and drove off.

Beatrice Klerke struggled to open the gate when she heard a voice behind her.

"Need some help?"

She turned around in shock as she saw the dark figure emerge.

"How long have you been standing there?"

"A couple of hours now. You work late," Cecilie answered.

"I'm surprised you haven't run away. I heard you got suspended."

"Where was I going to run off to?"

Klerke scrutinised her. "Well, certainly not to my place. I can't help you, Cecilie." She grabbed hold of the gate, which was still stuck.

"No, that's what I hear."

"From who?" Klerke asked, slightly offended.

"Most recently from Palsgaard before he suspended me."

Klerke sighed. "Yes, well, when a dummy like Palsgaard has been informed, then there's no telling who else knows."

"When is the reshuffling going to take place?"

"In a few days. Helge Sundvald has been lined up. The government officials have started briefing him on the sly. Preparing the gallows for yours truly," she said with a stiff smile.

"I'm surprised you didn't manage to remove him."

"Well, you weren't very helpful in that department," Klerke said haughtily.

"No, but I assumed you had others besides me to take care of that sort of thing."

"All the rats have abandoned the sinking ship."

"Guess I'm the last rat on board."

"Probably more like the captain who goes down with his sinking ship, if we're to stick with the maritime metaphors."

Cecilie smiled cautiously. "I need your help more than ever."

"Haven't you been listening?" Klerke asked, shaking her head.

"Yes, but . . ." Cecilie said, taking a deep breath.

Cecilie briefly told Klerke about the leads they had discovered, which indicated that Ryan was the perpetrator.

"I've met him only once," Klerke said disapprovingly. "He is the National Police Commissioner's creation. It would be quite a blow to the old fatso if one of his own were to get lynched." She was smiling and her teeth glowed in the dark.

"Which won't happen if the Travel Team takes over. And there'll be more victims as a result," Cecilie attempted.

Klerke wetted her lips. "I wish there was something I could do. What about your own people? Can't they interfere before things get out of hand?"

Cecilie shook her head.

"Palsgaard has already got hold of them. They don't respond to my calls anymore."

"I thought you had command over your troops and that they were loyal."

"They are, but they are also fathers, even grandfathers, with families and obligations. Even if I am wrong about Ryan, the perpetrator is going to strike again soon."

"Can't those two women you mentioned get police protection?"

"Not if the focus of the investigation shifts."

The Minister looked at her. "This is very personal for you, isn't it? You are genuinely concerned about what's going to happen."

"Yes, of course," she said, surprised by the Minister's question.

"I envy you that you have a purpose."

"Don't you have one?"

"No, it's a luxury I can't afford. For me, everything's a war that has to be won. And there are always new opponents."

Cecilie looked thoughtfully towards the dark front lawn.

"What if Helge Sundvald was no longer a threat for you? Would that ease things a bit?"

"Absolutely. Right now, there is no one else with the authority to take over."

"If I were to take care of your problem with Helge, will you then help me?" Cecilie asked, locking Klerke's gaze. "Could you get me back in?"

"I admire your persistence."

"Could you?"

Klerke sighed. "It would be for a short time. A few weeks, perhaps less. There are too many that want your pretty head," she said, stroking Cecilie's hair. The sudden intimacy took Cecilie aback, but she politely allowed Klerke to keep stroking her head.

"Regardless of whether you solve that case or not, you're through. To be honest, I don't really want you hanging around either. You're too heavy a burden."

"But you could get me back in? If I remove Helge?"

"Most probably," said Klerke, winking at her.

"You're not giving me the best odds."

"Well, it's probably the best thing you've got going at the moment, Cecilie. Goodnight," said Klerke as she knocked on the gate, which sprang open.

61

Cecilie hammered away at the martial arts dummy in the living room. Bob's big latex body swayed back and forth as she hit him in the face. She stopped, breathless, and leaned up against the punching bag to catch her breath.

"It's always good to have a round, Bob."

She went over and opened the balcony door and stepped outside. It was daybreak and the rising sun painted the city below her with an orange hue. Even Bellahøj looked beautiful. She cast a glance at the tall building where Farida had lived. The dark window on the second floor stared back at her with an extinguished gaze. There should have been light in there.

When, twenty minutes later, she had bathed and put on some clothes, she bent down and opened the kitchen cabinet. She pushed the back panel to the side and stuck her hand into the hollow space. She found Como's revolver and the bag of coke she had stolen from the pusher. It was incredible that she hadn't caved in and taken a few lines. Perhaps it was more due to forgetfulness than actual willpower. She put the gun and the bag of coke into the pocket of her leather jacket and shut the cabinet. A moment later, she was out the door and taking the urine-smelling elevator down to the ground floor.

She didn't know Helge Sundvald. The only thing Klerke had told her was that someone was protecting him. But that was going to be all over with after tonight. Because Helge was the solution. There was no other way out if she was going to prevent the murders from continuing. Helge was and would become her ticket to get back. Helge, who, on Klerke's command, was going to disappear. The question was how. Either by planting coke on him or shooting him through the forehead. Both plans seemed equally crazy.

She took the deserted highway out to Hareskovby, where he lived. The fashionable neighbourhood was about to wake up. She parked her car a few houses down from his residence. It was sheer idyll, like something right out of a Kinder Milk Slice commercial. Children walking to school together. Husbands kissing their wives goodbye under the roofs of their garages. Electric car after electric car zooming past. And then there were the many dog walkers who mostly had golden retrievers at the ends of their leashes. She had landed in the utopia of the middle class, far away from Bellahøj's realism. This was also a ghetto, a La La Land for the truly privileged. She caught sight of Helge, who came walking along in his grey suit, carrying a leather briefcase under his arm. He was heading for a white Tesla with the symbol of an ichthys on the boot. Helge was in his late forties, bald and had a very striking face. He seemed to be in good shape. Ready for action, raring to go. Together with the other commuters, he took the motorway towards Copenhagen.

The clouds gathered and emptied some rain on the morning traffic that moved at a snail's pace. She had no idea how she was going to get him. Or what was going to happen. Cecilie noticed that he spoke on his mobile phone, and she thought about pulling him over for that. A road sign indicated that there was a rest area further ahead. If she was going to get him in there, she'd have to do it now. She hesitated . . . and the next moment they passed the rest area, which had otherwise been deserted. Cecilie followed him all the way through town and into the Parliament at Christiansborg. Helge parked in one of the spaces between the palace and the old riding ground. He placed his leather briefcase on the car's white roof as he talked on the phone and laughed. Helge gesticulated eagerly and looked very much like an ordinary, decent human being. Helge, her ticket. Helge, who was about to disappear. She saw him walk up towards Christiansborg and she parked a few spots further down. Fifteen minutes later, she spotted Klerke's car, which continued directly in front of the main entrance of Christiansborg. "The world is run by monsters." That's what Omar had said, and it was true enough.

For the next seven hours, Cecilie remained sitting in the car until her behind began to hurt and she got out to stretch her legs a little. Her stomach grumbled. This could end up being a long and exhausting stakeout. She still didn't know what she was going to do with Helge. She saw him walking across the car park towards his Tesla. She got back into the car. Helge pulled out of the car park, and Cecilie followed him. It wasn't a long trip. After a few minutes, Helge pulled into Hambrosgade, close to police headquarters. Cecilie continued while keeping an eye on him through her rearview window. She saw Helge cross the street and enter through a gate. Cecilie parked further down. She thought about who he could be meeting. Perhaps the National Police Commissioner himself or the Independent Police Complaints Authority?

Half an hour later, he returned. Helge drove through Vesterbro and further out towards Valby. After she had followed him for about fifteen minutes, she saw him turn into the square in front of the Jesus Church. She pulled in further behind and watched him get out. Klerke had told her that Helge had become religious and had put all his bad habits behind him. *This is fucked up*, she thought, hammering her hand into the steering wheel. If he entered the church, she'd interpret it as a sign from God that she should leave him alone. Not that she was religious, but there were certain signs one shouldn't ignore. Helge didn't enter the church. Instead, he walked around the building. Cecilie jumped out of the car and ran towards the church. When she turned the corner, Helge was gone. There was a pathway that ran towards a small park. She considered going down there but saw that Helge was on his way back, so instead she rushed towards her car. He had either gone for a pee or just held the world's fastest meeting. From where she was sitting behind the steering wheel, she watched Helge walk over to his Tesla. He looked around quickly before getting into the car. If there was anything that decades of keeping watch had taught her, it was that no one looked around unless they were somewhere they shouldn't be or had done something they shouldn't have done. This was definitely a good sign!

She followed Helge through the heavy traffic out of the city to Beltway 3, where he continued heading towards Herlev. Once he had followed the beltway for a while, he turned on his signal lights and pulled into a rest area. Cecilie followed him and watched Helge park his car at the furthest end. She parked behind the toilet block and got out. When he got back to his Tesla, she saw what he was up to. He may have found Jesus, but the drugs had also found him. She knocked on the side window. Helge started and dropped most of his coke in his lap. He wiped his nose and looked at her. She signalled for him to roll down his window.

"Yes, what?" he asked coolly.

"Helge Sundvald?"

"I have no idea what you're talking about," he answered, and was about to roll the window back up.

"Stop it, Helge. Cecilie Mars," she introduced herself. "What are you doing?"

She could tell that her name had rung a bell.

"Not that it's any of your business, but I'm on my way to a meeting, so I'm busy."

"That's clear," she said, pointing to his lap.

"Haven't you been . . . suspended?"

"Yes, thanks to you."

He shook his head. "Thank yourself."

"Yeah, maybe, no one's perfect. I see that you've started again. Or perhaps you never stopped?"

"You should be the last one preaching. I have seen the list of all your criminal activities."

"I'm not preaching. I'll leave that to the priest. What I can do, on the other hand, is pass a drug test. You can't."

His eyes flickered. "It's just a pick-me-up."

"I don't think the prosecution will look at it that way."

He bit his lip irritably. "Do you think you can threaten me? Do you even know who I am? You're through, bitch! We took the badge away from you, we got you suspended, and soon we'll have you charged and behind bars. So go fuck yourself and enjoy your freedom for as long as it lasts. Go home to your ghetto, where all the other losers are."

"Get out of the car," she said, taking out her phone.

"What?"

"Get out of the car. You're not driving under the influence. I'm calling a patrol that can arrest you. Then you'll be driven to police headquarters, where you'll get a blood test. How does that sound?"

"Go fuck yourself."

Before she could react, he had put the car in reverse and put his foot on the accelerator. He drove over her foot with one of his front wheels and Cecilie fell to the ground. She saw him laughing behind the steering wheel as she tried to get back on her feet. Her vision tunnelled and a buzzing sound filled her ears. Helge was going to get away. Helge was going to win. She looked in her pocket for Como's pistol. Hell no. She took the safety off the gun, but Helge was already on his way out of the rest area.

62

Cecilie limped back to the car. When she got her shoes off, she could see that her foot was swollen and that her two middle toes were crooked. She carefully put her sock and shoe back on but didn't tie the shoelace.

"Fuck, fuck, fuck," she mumbled in pain. The whole thing had gone from bad to worse. Fortunately, she hadn't had a chance to shoot at the car, otherwise it would have been game over for her, and there was no guarantee that she would have managed to stop Helge. Her phone buzzed, and she saw that a message had come through. *Harassing a member of Parliament is punishable by law and won't help your situation.* The sender was anonymous, but she had a long list of individuals who could have sent it. It was Helge's way of emphasising that he had his connections. What the hell could she do? She drummed her fingers against the steering wheel. Helge was untouchable. Whoever had sent that text message must be sitting high up in the food chain. Any attempt at getting at Helge by way of an arrest would be futile. She felt the pain in her foot start to flare up as she stared through the windshield. Where the hell was Helge on his way to? She opened her Facebook app on her phone and found his profile. Facebook: every politician's preferred social media platform, and apparently also Helge's. In his most recent post, it said: *Looking forward to the meeting with the constituency tonight. It's always great meeting up with the local members.* Followed by a note indicating the time and place of the event. Cecilie punched in the address and started heading towards Herlev Community Centre. A plan was starting to take shape in her mind. A desperate plan that was pretty fucked up, but it was the only thing she could come up with.

It was 10 p.m. by the time Helge walked out of the red building. He said goodbye to some of his constituency members before he walked over to his Tesla. He remained sitting in his car and checking his phone as he cast a sidelong glance at those who drove off. When he was finally alone, he put his phone away and took out a small rolled-up ball of aluminium foil. He unwrapped the ball and sniffed the leftovers. At that very same moment, his car door opened and Cecilie got into the seat next to him.

"You again?" he asked indifferently, rubbing the remaining bits of coke into his gums. "Thanks to you, I wasted most of this today."

"Sorry about that," she said, staring back at him vacantly.

"Didn't you receive the message telling you to stay away from me? Are you demented or what?"

"I thought you had found Jesus."

He laughed. "That was my public relations manager's idea. Apparently, you can win a lot of votes among the Christian population. Everyone loves the story about the Prodigal Son."

He crumpled up the tin foil and flipped it with his two fingers in her direction. It hit her on the chin, and he laughed. "You really looked like a toppled cow, the way you were lying on the ground before."

"You ran over my foot."

"Guess you weren't fast enough. Don't you understand?" he asked, squinting his eyes. "You can't damage me. No one can."

"Let me guess, your constituency has just voted to make you our new Minister of Justice?"

"Oh yeah, baby," he said, laughing. "Beatrice, that dyke, is on her way out, just like you. You can go fuck each other now." The coke made him grind his teeth.

"I guess you're the one who I should ask for a pardon?"

He broke out laughing. "That's a good one. You're funny, you know that? I wouldn't count on it."

"Well, it was worth a try," Cecilie answered as she turned towards him. "When I woke up this morning, I didn't know whether I was going to shoot you or what."

"Like you did with that gangster they found?"

"Yup." She pulled up her shirt so he could see the handle of the gun.

"Damn," he said, moving closer to the door.

"Calm down," she said, pulling her shirt back down. "It no longer makes any sense to knock you off. You've clearly won."

His eyes fluttered. "It took you a while to realise that."

"I probably should have gone to you earlier rather than going to Klerke."

"You can't win every time. But if you've got something on her, you could try sharing it with the prosecution. See if that helps your situation."

"Yes, perhaps," she said, lowering her head. "I might just do that. I was lying last time we talked, by the way."

"About what?"

"When I said that I could pass a drug test." She took out the bag of coke from her pocket.

"What the hell is that?"

"Top ghetto shit. Coke of the best kind that I nailed from an unfortunate pusher."

"You're crazy."

"Wanna share a line?"

Helge stared at the bag. "I . . . I think you better go now."

"Okay," she said, shoving her pinky down into the bag. "I didn't think anyone could hurt you. Wasn't that what you said?" She took a little bit of coke up and sniffed it. "Wow," she said, smiling. "Definitely first rate, but you've found Jesus, huh?"

Helge looked quickly out the windshield to make sure the area was still empty.

"Jesus can wait," he said, waving his hand impatiently. "Let's cut it."

Helge didn't exactly hold back. In the next twenty minutes, they sniffed five lines each. Cecilie sensed her heart pounding against her chest. It had been a long time since she had taken coke. Even though the effect was good, she sensed how her body went into overdrive. Her brain felt like it was about to explode.

"Are you okay? You look pretty cooked."

"I . . . I . . . I . . ."

Helge took the bag from her and leaned across her. For a brief moment, she thought he was going to attack her, but all he did was open her door. "You'd better get out. I've gotta go now," he said.

She staggered out of the car. Helge watched her with a manic gaze. "Of all the crazy bitches I've come across, you win first place. But the coke's good. Ciao."

He slammed the door and drove out of the car park. Cecilie stood swaying back and forth as she watched him. The cold sweat broke out as her teeth chattered and she felt as though her legs were about to give way under her. Behind her two men emerged.

"Are you okay?"

She slowly turned around and tried to focus. The young man smiled at her.

"I . . . I'm okay. Did you get it, Dennis? Did you get it?"

The older, hunch-backed photographer waved his camera, which was equipped with a huge telephoto lens.

"We got the whole thing."

"Let me see," she said, reaching out to them with her shaking hand. They showed her the pictures the photographer had taken. They had all been edited so that only Helge was visible. Helge sitting with a bag of coke. Helge cutting the lines. Helge sniffing the coke. Helge laughing manically. "And those are . . . all the pictures, right? There aren't any with me?"

Dennis shook his head. "No reason to go after the little fish when you can catch a big shark. I won't let you down."

"Good. Remember, I was never here. Remember that, Dennis," she said, her teeth chattering and her body shaking.

"You sure you're okay?"

She nodded. "So, what's the plan? Tell me the plan again."

"We'll put it online in about an hour. It'll be breaking news. All the other media will then catch on. In the meantime, we'll go out to Helge's residence so we can get his arrest recorded for the morning news."

"Cool," she said, and started limping towards her car.

"But I thought I heard rumours that you were supposed to be suspended!" Dennis shouted after her.

"Don't always believe what you hear," she answered back.

The next morning, she woke up in her bed, wearing all her clothes. She didn't have any clear memory of how she had got home. She pulled the gun out of her trousers and put it on the bed. She was lucky she hadn't managed to shoot her private parts, she thought. Her head was pounding. Had she really taken cocaine with Helge? And had she on that same occasion invited *Ekstra Bladet* to come by and take pictures of the session? It was a kamikaze attack, the outcome of which she still didn't know. She got up from the bed and felt a piercing pain shooting through her right foot. The idiot had run her over, she remembered as she limped over to get the remote. She turned on the TV and found the news channel. It was everywhere. The pictures of Helge with coke on his face. Helge in handcuffs. Helge being driven away from La La Land in a police car. Her phone rang and she limped back to her bed and answered it.

"I thought you were going to shoot him," Beatrice Klerke said half-jokingly. "But this is just as efficient. Where are you?"

"At home," she said, her voice rusty.

"Why aren't you at work?"

"I wasn't sure whether I still had a job."

"Enjoy it for as long as it lasts," Beatrice Klerke said, and hung up.

63

Cecilie supported herself on a crutch as she limped up to the entrance at Teglholmen. She came directly from the emergency room at Bispebjerg, where the doctor determined that she had broken two toes and sprained her ankle. They had supplied her with a pack of Tylenol and a crutch. The guard at the entrance looked at her in surprise but managed to greet her. *So far so good*, she thought. She continued down to Palsgaard's office, where hell awaited her.

"This is an absurd situation! Completely unacceptable!" Palsgaard shouted the moment she stepped into his office. He was standing behind his desk and there was foam in the corners of his mouth. "You are not supposed to be here! You cannot be here!"

"There are others who don't agree with you," she said calmly.

"It's . . . it's political intrigue of the worst kind! The District Attorney is already on the case. The National Police Commissioner himself is also on it."

"He already seemed to be on it earlier. Listen, Palsgaard, I understand why you're complaining as much as you are, but it doesn't change the situation. Shouldn't we just try to get the best out of it? After all, we have a serious murder case that needs to be solved."

She was surprised by her courage, and she considered whether she was still under the influence. Palsgaard stared at her through his small round spectacles. "You may have managed to manoeuvre your way back in here for a short while, but the case has already been handed over to the Travel Team."

"But I'm taking it back now."

"Not without my approval."

She took a deep breath.

"I imagine it's going to be hard for Ryan to investigate anything from a prison cell."

"You are digging your own grave. You do realise, don't you?"

"Fine. Let's see who I manage to throw into it," she said, staring back at him. His eyes fluttered, which was priceless.

"You trapped Helge. You set him up, didn't you?" His hands were shaking. "So that Klerke could remain."

She smiled coolly. "That's quite an accusation. As far as I know, it was *Ekstra Bladet*'s doing. They were at the right place at the right time."

"You contacted them, didn't you? Have you really managed to sink so low?"

She limped a step closer. "Palsgaard, there are no limits as to how far I'm willing to stoop if it means that it'll stop our perpetrator. I have no limits as far as that's concerned."

"You . . . you . . . you're a psychopath," he said with trembling lips. "Get out of my office."

When shortly afterwards she came limping down the hallway towards her division, she took out her phone and called Ismail. He immediately answered. "Cecilie, you're the last person I thought would call. My family is very upset. Everyone is."

"Dry your tears and come into work."

"But you're . . . suspended?"

"Breaking news. The suspension has been lifted. I'm gathering the team, and I need to see your brown ass back in here."

"Am I going to be let off?" he asked, his spirits suddenly raised. "Will there be no charges filed against me? Is it all over with?"

"Yes, yes, for the time being, at least."

"Oh God, for the time being doesn't sound too good, Cecilie. I don't want to get into any more trouble."

"The only trouble you'll get is from me if you aren't here within half an hour."

"But I live in Ishøj. That's a long way . . ."

Cecilie hung up. She continued limping further through the division. Most of the detectives lifted their heads from their work and looked at her. It was completely silent and the thumping sound that her crutch made against the floor created an echo. Cecilie continued down through the row until she stopped in front of Henrik and Joakim.

"You . . . you're back," said Henrik, sending her a small smile.

"Good to see you," said Joakim. "What happened to your foot?"

"I dropped a vase when I was remodelling the apartment."

"How unfortunate. It must have been a heavy vase."

Henrik shook his head at him. "Cecilie, there are a lot of rumours circulating. The case has been handed over to the Travel Team."

"I've taken it back."

"Oh?" he asked sceptically.

"Where's Heino?"

"He's being interrogated by the Independent Police Complaints Authority," Henrik said, pointing towards the meeting rooms.

"About what?"

"You. We're all going to go through the mill."

"They're threatening to suspend us," said Joakim.

"Can they even do that?" Cecilie sighed. "I'm sorry to have got you into this situation, but no one's going to be suspended. Not as long as I have anything to say." Which could be a short-lived promise. "What room number are they in?"

"Number 3."

Cecilie limped back through the division to the room furthest away. Through the glass window she could see John, Kenneth, Jette from the Police Federation, and Heino sitting with his head bent at the end of the table. Cecilie didn't bother to knock and walked straight into the meeting room. The surprise entrance created the desired effect and they all stared at her. She shut the door behind her.

"You . . . you . . . you've been suspended," said John, who sat with his mouth agape.

"No, and you're not very well informed." She tugged at the cord around her neck and showed her ID card as proof.

"But how did that happen?"

Cecilie didn't answer. It seemed to dawn on John what had taken place. "Helge . . . Klerke. However, that doesn't change anything in regard to this investigation right here."

"It does a little," she said, demonstrating with two fingers how little.

"What do you mean?"

"It's the sequence of events, John. I've already presented you the case that has first priority. The case against Ryan."

"Which didn't hold water in any way, shape, or form. They were the wildest accusations I've ever heard."

"Furthermore, we at the Independent Police Complaints Authority decide which cases are to go forward and when," Kenneth said, crossing his arms.

"Yes, the Independent Police Complaints Authority decides," said Jette.

"Really?" Cecilie said, looking back at John. "As long as I have my team, I'm going to investigate this case, and you and your pale sidekick are going to stay out of my division. Unless you want to explain to the Minister why you're obstructing a case that is close to her heart."

John closed his notebook, as did Kenneth. "You intend to go after the head of the Travel Team?" John asked sarcastically.

"We're already well on our way. Come on, Heino," she said as she knocked the leg of his chair with her crutch.

When they had left the meeting room, Heino patted her on the back. "Good to see you, boss," he said. "Are we going after Ryan? Is he really a suspect?"

"Oh, so you caught on to that, Heino?"

"Have you been in a fight?"

"I was run over by a steamroller."

"I know the feeling," he answered as he wiped the sweat off his forehead. "Thanks for saving me. Fucking John and his little creep of an assistant."

"Of course, you're part of my team."

Heino gave her a guilty look. "I'm sorry for not answering your phone calls."

"Forget it."

"No, it was unforgivable. But Palsgaard said that we risked getting disciplinary punishment if we had any contact with you."

"It's almost like being accused of having syphilis."

Heino laughed, relieved.

Half an hour later, Ismail was in her office together with the rest of the team. Cecilie briefed them about what digital leads Ismail had found against Ryan. She went on to explain that an undercover car had most probably been used to monitor Farida's apartment shortly before her death. Cecilie sensed everyone's enthusiasm, except for Henrik, who remained silent.

"What is it, Henrik?" she asked.

"It seems extraordinary that it would be a police officer . . . that Ryan is behind the whole thing."

"Your point being?"

"Well, what do you suggest we should do?"

"What we always do. Arrest the suspect and seize material."

"But he's at police headquarters. We can't just storm headquarters."

"Now, don't ruin Joakim's big day, Henrik. It'll be the first time he's going to get the chance to see a real police station from the inside," said Heino.

"I don't think we're going to have to pull out our guns, if that's what you mean, Henrik," Cecilie answered, smiling. "I imagine Ryan will go with us voluntarily. Are we ready?" she asked, looking around. Henrik seemed anything but ready, but nevertheless he nodded.

64

The rain was pouring down across the police headquarters rotunda. The last time Cecilie had been here, she had been wearing a skirt and high heels. Now she was supporting herself on a crutch, with Heino and Henrik at her sides and followed by Ismail and Joakim at her heels. She sensed her nervousness now as they approached the National Police Commissioner's division.

"It's infuriating that that asshole Ryan managed to manipulate everyone and strike once again," said Heino.

"We don't know whether it was him," said Henrik.

"He looks like the type who could do it."

They continued along the colonnade and further through the door leading to the National Police Commissioner's division. If Cecilie was hoping to make a surprise attack, she was about to be disappointed. The division was vacant except for Ryan and a few supporters. He sat with his head bowed and the National Police Commissioner standing behind him like a living wall. John and Kenneth were sitting at the table in the background like two shadows.

"Someone's rattled," said Heino as they approached.

"Seems Independent Police Complaints Authority have been at it again. They were fast," said Cecilie. She stopped in front of Ryan, who lifted his gaze from the floor.

"I imagine you know why we've come, Ryan," she said, swallowing.

"This is bullshit," he said, making a fist. "It's our case and then you show up here with your fucking—"

"It's Homicide's case with me as acting boss. And in that capacity, I've come to charge you with—"

"With what?!" he shouted.

The National Police Commissioner placed a soothing hand on his shoulder and coolly smiled at Cecilie. "This is clearly a misunderstanding. An error of some sort."

"I can guarantee you that it isn't and further—"

"And Ryan is of course willing to have this discussion with you in order to straighten things out."

Cecilie smiled back as she tried to get her nerves under control.

"You can call it whatever you like. But we've come to charge Ryan and seize . . . his computers . . ." she said, pointing at the one in front of him, "his phones and to search his residence." Ryan jumped up and positioned himself threateningly close to her.

"You're damn well not sending someone over to rummage through my things."

"Calm down," said Heino, gently pushing him away from Cecilie. Ryan removed Heino's hand and his team formed a semicircle behind him.

"Assaulting a police officer on duty could easily be included in the charges if you don't calm down," said Cecilie, locking his gaze.

"I'll calm down when it fucking suits me," Ryan said, pointing a finger right in front of her face.

Cecilie didn't so much as blink. "It never reflects well for the one who's being charged to resist arrest."

"No one's getting arrested," said the National Police Commissioner, telling everyone to calm down. "Cecilie, you and Ryan are going to find a room where you can talk all this through."

Ryan looked up at him, clearly feeling betrayed. "There will be no searching," the National Police Commissioner continued. "We're one big family. The sooner we put this behind us, the faster we'll be able to use our resources in finding the real perpetrator," he said, extending his arms in a conciliatory manner.

"No!" Cecilie said, shaking her head dismissively. "This is my investigation. And I am maintaining my charge against Ryan, just like I want his computer and phone to be seized. I also want Ole to perform a touch DNA."

They all stared at her.

"Over my dead body," Ryan snarled.

"Ole deals with those as well," Cecilie retorted quickly. "This is standard procedure. There will be no special treatment just because the suspect is an officer. I made a promise to the Minister," she added with a shrug of her shoulder.

"Has Beatrice Klerke been notified about this?" the National Police Commissioner said in awe.

"Of course," Cecilie lied, and turned her gaze to John and Kenneth. "Since the Independent Police Complaints Authority is already being represented, you can confirm that everything is being done by the book."

John looked away. She could feel her heart pounding and was grateful that she had her crutch to lean on. The stakes were high.

"Ismail, will you collect all the items?" she asked, nodding towards Ryan's computer.

"Me?" Ismail said worriedly, pointing at himself.

"Yes," Cecilie answered.

Ismail apologised to Ryan before taking his computer and the phone that lay on Ryan's desk.

"Your private phone too, please."

Ryan got it out and handed it to Ismail.

"And a password," Cecilie persisted.

"Cherie. C-h-e-r-i-e."

"Thank you. And can we also borrow the key to your front door? That way we can save the locksmith bill."

Ryan shook his head as he took his keys out from his pocket. He threw the bunch of keys to her, which she caught in the air. She handed them to Henrik. "Take Joakim with you and contact Dahlstrup and Forensics if necessary."

"Is there anyone at your place?" Cecilie asked Ryan.

"My cat."

"Cherie?" Cecilie asked without getting a response. "Is there an interrogation room vacant?"

Ryan pointed towards the hallway with the interrogation rooms and started heading down there himself as Heino followed behind him. With a gnarled finger, the National Police Commissioner signalled for Cecilie to come over to him. "You're burning all your bridges. Faster than an arsonist. You're going to pay for this and I'm going to personally see to it."

"I know," she answered as she nodded. "Anything else would have surprised me."

65

She looked at Ryan, who sat drumming his fingers impatiently on the table. From the very beginning, he had tried to mock and undermine her position, pursued her mostly to take revenge. Perhaps Klerke had been right when she said this was a war.

"I want to remind you that you have the right to have an attorney present. We can contact the Police Federation so they can send a representative. Jette is supposed to be good," she added.

"Thanks, but I'll manage. For the simple reason that there's nothing to come after."

"We wouldn't be sitting here if that were the case, Ryan."

He gestured with his hand. "Is this all because of a couple of searches in the registry? Big deal," he said, rolling his eyes. "We have had the case. Everything has been approved and gone by the book as opposed to your division."

"How do you know what it is we want to investigate? Who's informed you?" Cecilie asked.

"Rumours spread fast. Learn to live with it."

"What are the names of the people spreading them?"

"The water pipes. You place your ear against them and listen. You should try it one day. If you survive that long, that is."

"Why were you even interested in searching those four victims?" Heino interrupted him.

Ryan sent him a look. "We had a case, buddy."

"There were searches done while the case was in our division," said Cecilie.

"And? Nothing illegal about that. The rest of the team and I had an interest in staying briefed. To make sure that it didn't go off the rails before we took it over again," he said, smiling coolly.

"That doesn't explain why you searched Lizzette three months before her death."

Part of Ryan's self-confident façade started to crack. "But . . . I . . . I didn't do that."

"The login is from your computer," said Heino.

"It must be a mistake."

Cecilie leaned forward in her chair. "A mistake? You mean you logged in and searched her by mistake? Do you really have that many thumbs?"

"You know what I mean!"

"No."

"A system failure."

"A system failure? I've never experienced that before, but okay. Do you also consider it to have been a system failure when the search was placed under the battering ram case?"

"Your case?" Heino added as he took out the copies from his folder.

Ryan stared at the documents before him. "It . . . it . . ."

"Unless Lizzette was involved in your case?"

"I am not familiar with this," he said, leaning back in his chair.

"With what? That she had been involved?"

"With that search, goddammit!"

Cecilie looked at him perplexedly. "It's your computer. It's your case."

"So what?" he snarled. "We use each other's computers. It happens a lot."

"I need to understand this. Who does?"

"What's so hard to understand? Internally in the Travel Team."

"I see. Is that to say that you give out your private password?"

"That's a serious breach," said Heino, crossing his arms. "Who have you given it to?"

"I haven't given anyone anything," he said, looking from one to the other. "All I'm saying is that we use each other's computers. I'm sure you do too." He looked at them quizzically. Neither Cecilie nor Heino batted an eyelid.

"My computer was open while I was present, okay?"

"The search wasn't made by you but by one of your people?"

"I'm not saying that. I don't know how it happened."

"But can you point out a specific colleague who you know has used it?" Cecilie asked.

"No."

"Okay, well then the suspicion returns to you."

"I don't intend to expose any of my men just to satisfy you," he said, looking her up and down.

"It would take more than that, Ryan, believe me. But maybe we'll reach that point."

"A new search made from your computer. This time on Farida," said Heino as he found yet another document and showed it to Ryan. "Several months before her death, and this one's ten days prior," he said, pointing out the date for Ryan.

"A system failure?" Cecilie said.

"I know nothing about it."

"The searches have been placed under yet another one of your cases. Perhaps you could explain what Farida has to do with the stolen goods case that the search is connected to?"

Ryan swept the papers off the table.

"It's you!" he shouted, as the papers flew to the floor, pointing at Cecilie. "You've done all this! You're out to ruin me, ruin my career!"

"Is that your best answer, Ryan?" Cecilie asked.

Without warning, Ryan hurled himself across the table and took a swing at her. Cecilie managed to move back so that the blow only brushed against her cheek.

"I'll kill you!" he shouted, and was on his way across the table.

Heino managed to get between Ryan and Cecilie. "Guard!" he shouted as he tore Ryan's shirt and managed to pull him down to the floor. He placed himself heavily on top of Ryan with his knee to his back as he twisted one of Ryan's arms behind him.

"Kill me, Ryan, like you did the other women?" Cecilie shouted down at him.

"Fuck you, you bitch!" Ryan screamed.

The door opened and two uniformed officers entered. Outside in the hallway, some of Ryan's men were standing and looking in disbelief. Heino loosened his grip and let the officers take over.

"Put him in detention," said Cecilie when they had got Ryan to his feet.

The police looked around quizzically.

"You heard what the head of Homicide said!" said Heino. The officers escorted Ryan out and Heino shut the door.

"He lost it completely," he said, looking at her cheek. "Are you okay, boss? Should we get someone to look at it?"

She shook her head.

"He just grazed me, that's all."

"Are you going to charge him with assault?"

She frowned. "Would you if it had happened to you?"

"No, but he shouldn't get away with it."

"One case at a time."

"What do we do?"

"Wait until Henrik and Joakim come back. We need more than this," she said, pointing at the scattered papers lying on the floor.

"Do you think it might be one of the others? That someone's used his computer?"

"It's a possibility. We ourselves aren't great about logging on and off."

Heino nodded. "There might still be a perp within the Travel Team?"

"Yes, perhaps."

About an hour later, they met up with Henrik and Joakim in the rotunda. There was no reason to have the meeting inside where the walls had ears.

"What did you find? Say that you found something," said Heino.

Henrik shook his head dismissively. "There was nothing."

"The cat was about to run off," said Joakim, "but I managed to catch it."

"Good job, Joakim," said Heino, applauding.

"How about on your end?" Henrik asked. "Did he say anything?"

"It got a little rowdy," Cecilie said, pointing to her cheek.

"Damn, did you get into a fight?"

She shook her head. "It's nothing. Ryan denied having made any of the searches."

At that moment, her phone rang. It was Ismail.

"What have you got for me?" she asked, putting the phone on speaker.

"I put the program with my algorithms through his computer."

"Your algorithms?"

"Yes, it searches for various words and types of files that could be interesting for the investigation. I wasn't able to find anything on the hard drive or in the search engine aside from the information we already have."

"Well, at least it shows that someone made a search on the victims," Heino said.

Cecilie shushed him. "What else do you have, Ismail?"

"I also opened his phone. He's on Grindr and a couple of other dating sites for men."

"Is Ryan a homo?" Joakim asked.

"You're fast, Joakim," Heino said ironically as he looked at Cecilie. "It could still be him. Maybe Nikolaj could help us make a profile of him."

"Yeah, maybe," Cecilie said. "Anything else, Ismail?"

"There is one small thing."

"What?"

"The last search on Farida happened on the same day that Jeremy's corpse was retrieved from the lake. Wasn't Ryan out of the office that day?"

"No idea," Cecilie lied. She clearly remembered that Ryan had been strutting around out there on the lake shore.

"Well, he could still have made the search before or after," said Henrik.

"Or taken his laptop with him," Heino added.

"Of course, I just thought I'd mention it," Ismail said on the phone.

"We have to find out where he's been," said Cecilie.

"I'm already searching for telemetry and tele-information on him. I expect to have it ready tomorrow."

"Thank you, Ismail," she said, and hung up.

"What about Ryan?" Henrik asked.

"What about him?" Cecilie asked, limping off. "I think a night in the slammer'll do him some good."

66

The next morning, Cecilie was on her way to NC3's headquarters in Glostrup. Ismail had called and said he had something important to tell her but that he didn't wish to discuss it on the phone. Judging by the sound of his voice, it wasn't necessarily good news. Twenty minutes later, she was standing with Ismail in what she imagined would be a hacker's wet dream, but for everyone else it was a messy computer workshop. Open hard disks and spare computer parts were lying all around. In the rubbish bin next to him, the contents indicated that the lowest rung on his food chain consisted of Red Bull.

"Explain to me one more time why we can already release Ryan. Because that's really fucked up."

"Not for him," Ismail took the liberty of saying. "But the tele-information doesn't lie. He was not at Teglholmen that day. He spent most of the day in Utterslev Mose. See how the signal jumps from tower to tower," he said, pointing at the diagram from TDC.

"And his computer? Did he have it with him?"

"It was at Homicide the whole time. It can't possibly be him who made the last search on Farida."

"It has to be one of the other members of the Travel Team, someone whom we've overlooked."

Ismail shook his head. "I've checked them. They were all out at the bog that day. The Travel Team is off the hook."

"Fuck," she said, hammering her hand into the table.

"Easy, Cecilie, the equipment here is very sensitive."

"Sorry, but someone must have had access to his computer. Someone must have known his password."

Ismail nodded. "It's not that hard. Either he gave it out or someone looked over his shoulder. Or . . ."

"Or what?

"Ryan's password is so easy that decrypting it would also have been a piece of cake. Like this one."

Ismail took something from the table that resembled an enlarged iPhone with a USB cable hanging from its side. "You can buy it on the internet for twelve hundred kroner. It throws two hundred thousand passwords through the system in a minute."

"If it's not Ryan and it wasn't the Travel Team either, who else? One of my detectives?"

"You don't think it's someone from your division, do you?"

"I don't know, what am I supposed to think, Ismail! That's why I need you to tell me. Can we get tele-information on all the detectives to see where they were in the period in which the search was made?"

"Um . . . yes, but it would take months to go through."

"You did it with Jeremy's phone."

"Yes, but that was different, that was only one person. We could be talking about over a hundred employees."

"Not if you narrow it down," she said, looking at him.

"To your team? Do you mean you want to spy on them?"

"Well, we've got to start somewhere, so take the ones closest to me and then expand the parameters."

"But how likely is it that it's one of them, Cecilie?"

"Do you know that Nik and Jay song 'One Day Left'?" She took out her phone and showed how many unanswered phone calls there were from the National Police Commissioner and Palsgaard. "Guess what's gonna happen when I release Ryan? The lyrics of that song will be fulfilled. It's now or never if we're going to track him down. There's gotta be a faster way, Ismail."

Ismail shut his eyes as his chin sank to his chest.

"What?"

"There is a faster way, but . . ."

"But what?"

"It would need numerous approvals."

"That's no problem. I'll see to those. Tell me what you need."

"We'll need access to the security gate in the reception in your division. They register who comes and goes and when."

"Go for it!"

"Go . . . for it?" he asked in disbelief.

She nodded enthusiastically. "I'll get the approvals while you arrange it."

"No, no," said Ismail, lifting his index finger. "It has to go through the Danish Data Protection Agency and a court first."

"That sort of thing can take days, Ismail. We need that information now. As in today. Otherwise, it's game over."

"But that'll mean that I'll have to hack into the system again."

"Yes, cool!" she said, thumping his back.

He rolled his eyes. "Do we even know what the minimum penalty is for this?"

"No, but what we do know is that if we don't do it, we won't stop our perp."

"Okay, move over, then," he said, nudging her with his elbow. "I'm gonna need some workspace."

"I'll give you all the space you need. I need to get back to Teglholmen. Send me the list as soon as you're ready."

"Will you come visit me in jail?"

"We'll do our daily walks in the prison yard together."

67

She took the highway towards town as Britney Spears sang "Toxic" on the radio. Cecilie changed stations and got some horrorcore hip-hop rapping about giving head, which was more suitable for the drive past the projects south of Copenhagen. Twenty minutes later, she was limping through the security gate in reception. Ismail had got back to them with a preliminary list of those who had been present at Teglholmen when the search on Farida was done. Her entire team had been there, and Palsgaard's and Jane's names appeared on the list too. Cecilie reached the division as she continued scrolling through her phone. She saw that both John and Ole from Forensics had paid Teglholmen a visit that day. As she entered the division, she looked towards the team. She had a hard time imagining any of them being perpetrators. They just didn't have it in them. On the other hand, most murderers appear to be ordinary men and women until they suddenly lose it. The D-factor, as Nikolaj had taught her. The dark sides that live in us all.

She looked over at the vacant spots where the Travel Team had been sitting before. It would be very easy for someone to use Ryan's computer for a moment. Or hang around after hours if you had his password. She slowly limped through the division. Which one of them was particularly good at navigating his way around the registry? She looked at Henrik, who sat using two fingers to punch away at the keyboard. He was able to navigate around digitally, but concealing his searches in the system behind old cases seemed to be above his level. Heino, on the other hand, had a flair for that sort of thing. He didn't like having to leave the capital. Was that why he had chosen his victims from around here? She looked at Heino, who was dressed in a wrinkled workman's shirt and sat yawning. He hardly resembled a sadistic serial killer. But what did she, in fact, know about Heino's personal life? Nothing. Then again, she didn't know anything about Joakim's either. What was Joakim hiding behind his goofy attitude? A bestial assailant? She doubted it. She checked Ismail's message again. Palsgaard's name lit up. Did he have a potential serial killer in him? Absolutely! What with his numerous little psychopathic tics. Still, she had a hard time seeing him as the perpetrator.

"What's up, boss?" Heino asked, getting up and walking towards her. "What did Ismail say?"

"We're going to have to release Ryan."

"Damn. But that means it has to be someone from his team. What about that chubby guy, Kjellberg?"

She shook her head. "They were all out that day to watch the divers pull Jeremy out."

"Are you sure about that?"

"Ismail has given me a list of everyone who was here that day. Don't ask how he came up with it."

"Okay. But weren't we all here?"

"Yes, and so was Ryan's computer."

Heino took a quick look around and lowered his voice. "Do you think . . . it's someone from our division?"

"The computer was here. We were here. The search was done here. How can that be explained?"

"I have no idea, but it can't be anyone from the team. I mean, Henrik, that old teddy bear?" He shook his head. "Or Joakim? He can't stand the sight of blood for the life of him."

"Did somebody say something about me?" Joakim asked, looking up.

"That your mum turns me on."

Joakim shook his head and returned to his work.

"What about you, Heino?" she asked with a sly smile.

"Nah, there's far too much math and not enough rape for my taste."

"Huh?"

He extended his arms apologetically. "If I were a serial killer, I'd rape them first. At least get laid. The rest of it just seems like far too much work."

"You're a sick individual, Heino."

"But what about Nikolaj, the doctor? Doesn't he come off as a little asexual?"

"I haven't really noticed," she said, looking away. "But I don't think he was around that day."

"What about Ismail himself?"

"He wasn't either. But Ole was, on the other hand. And the Independent Police Complaints Authority was also registered."

"Those two bastards were probably busy jerking off in Palsgaard's office. But I haven't seen Ole for a while."

Cecilie nodded. "He dropped by with Lizzette's report that day. It was on my desk when I got here. He had been here early."

"You don't think that Ole . . . ?"

"No, no, definitely not. I've known him for years."

"So? He could fit the profile, you know."

"How?"

"As a doctor he could easily gain their trust and convince them to let him in. More so than a police officer. He's always given me the creeps."

"It's not Ole."

"Who is it, then? It's either one of us or someone who dropped by that day. Which only leaves John and his assistant."

She tossed her head. "The only woman they want to see dead is me."

"Well then, we're back to Ole."

"Or one of the many others," she said, pointing to the rest of the division.

"Ole's got the skills."

"Which our man didn't have in the beginning."

"That's just according to Ole. He may have been deceiving us with that shit."

"Cecilie?" Henrik called. Cecilie limped over to him.

"What?"

"Does Bella Grill ring any bells?"

"Um, yes, why?"

"Because we're searching for businesses in the area that have registered their surveillance cameras."

"Which Bella Grill has?"

"It seems so, yes. According to this information they've been set up there since 2007."

Cecilie smiled. "I'd be surprised if they work."

"Want me to go out there?"

"I'll talk to Kurt myself. Do you have the surveillances of Vinnie and Helle under control?"

Heino nodded. "We've got patrols in the area."

68

Cecilie looked at the surveillance camera that was placed below Bella Grill's neon sign. The camera was dusty and there were old cobwebs hanging from it. She doubted that it worked but turned around anyway to see the direction it was pointing. The camera was able to capture most of Bellahøjvej but unfortunately in the wrong direction, away from Farida's complex. Furthermore, there were three other ways to enter the neighbourhood of Bellahøj. The probability that the camera had captured the perp was minuscule. But either way, she thought she might as well grab dinner while she was here, so she went inside. There were no other customers in the grill bar when she told Kurt about Farida's murder and the reason for her visit.

"It's such a tragic story. It's all people are talking about right now," he said, brushing his hand through his thin, greasy hair.

"And your surveillance camera? Does it work?"

"It should . . . as far as I know. I don't check the recordings all too often. I put it up back in the day when there was a lot of vandalism."

"Do you know whether it saves the recordings?"

"Yes, definitely, I bought it with the big hard disk," he said, nodding. "I think it's every three months that it starts recording on top of the old recordings. You can just go out back and look through them if you want," he said, pointing to a back room.

"Thanks, Kurt." Cecilie went behind the counter and continued to the little back room. She manoeuvred her way past the many boxes and over to a small table. The monitor stood on the shelf above it and the surveillance equipment stood next to an old transistor radio. There was also a picture of Kurt on a motorbike with an Asian woman sitting on the back. She didn't know that Kurt rode motorbikes or had a girlfriend.

"Just take down the system and make yourself at home," said Kurt, placing a Carlsberg and a portion of French fries next to her.

"Thanks, Kurt, for everything."

Cecilie placed the hard disk with the control buttons on the table together with the monitor. She rewound the recording, which ran extremely slow.

"Can't it rewind any faster?"

Kurt pressed the button a few times, which made the machine rewind considerably faster. They heard customers entering the shop and Kurt went out to serve them. Cecilie ate a few French fries while keeping an eye on the time code on the screen. She slowly approached the night Farida was murdered. At that moment, her phone rang.

"What's up, Heino?"

"So, is the surveillance camera working out there?"

"I'm just watching the recording right now."

It was silent on the other end.

"Are you there?" she asked.

"Yes, yes . . . cool. By the way . . . Ryan stopped by after you left. He was furious."

"What did he want?"

"Mostly to vent. He threatened to sue us all. And he wanted to get hold of you personally."

"Did you ask him to wait in line? Anything else?" she asked.

"We're soon going home, boss."

"Okay."

"I searched Ole, by the way."

"Really?" she asked, surprised. "Find anything?"

"Charges of domestic violence four years ago."

Cecilie nodded to herself. "I remember when he got divorced. That was when he started running marathons. Do you know how the case ended?"

"The charges were dropped. Night, boss," he said, and hung up.

She thought Heino sounded strange. Maybe Ryan had shaken him up? Or perhaps there had been something else? She concentrated on the recordings on the screen where the dark road was replaced by a glowing light every time a car drove by. Half an hour later in the recording, a Golf identical to hers became visible. She stopped the recording and rewound it, until the car was outside Bella Grill. The small antenna on the roof indicated that it could be an undercover vehicle. It was impossible to see who was driving it or how many passengers there were.

She rewound a little to see if she could identify the licence plate, but the glow from the headlights made it impossible. She leaned back in the chair, which creaked, and took a sip of the beer. It could have been the car that Allan had seen. According to the timecode, it had been 11:08 p.m. She started fast-forwarding it. Several different cars were coming in the opposite direction, but none of them looked like the Golf. Until . . . She checked the time code again at 1:17 a.m. It was the same Golf as before with the tiny antenna on the roof. There was just a single passenger in the car. Cecilie moved closer to the screen and squinted. It was hard to see the licence plate, but it ended in either 824 or 524. She called Ismail and hoped he was still at work. He was.

"Ismail, I need a list of police vehicles whose licence plates end with 824 or 524 . . ."

"At least you're asking me to search for something legal. When do you need it?"

"NOW!"

"Just a sec." He sighed. "Let's see . . . 824 or 524."

She could hear that he was punching away on his keyboard.

"There is no 524, but I've found a registered black Golf VW that ends in 824."

"Whose is it?"

"You mean which division?"

"Yes, yes, who does it belong to?"

"The police headquarters. The National Police Commissioner's office."

"Are you sure?"

"Yes, but . . ."

"But what?"

"It's been lent out to the Independent Police Complaints Authority." She felt a knot in her stomach.

"Why do you want to know that? Where have you seen that car?"

"Close to the scene of the crime when Farida was killed."

"Shiiit . . . you don't think that . . . ? It's gotta be a coincidence."

Cecilie found the email from Ismail on her phone. It hadn't dawned on her until now that Kenneth wasn't on the list.

"Wasn't John's assistant with him?"

"Hold on," Ismail answered.

"No, I only see John's name as registered."

"Perhaps you overlooked Kenneth? Those two are always together."

"I don't know."

"Try searching again!"

"Then I'll have to go back into the system," he said irritably.

"Obviously, yes."

"Goddammit, Cecilie . . . It's illegal as hell. Like the first time that I did it."

"This is important."

It took a little while before Ismail returned.

"He isn't registered. John was alone that day," said Ismail. "I can also see that he went through the security gate alone today as well."

"Can you see when?"

"An hour ago."

She was about to drop the phone. "An hour ago? Are you sure?"

"Um . . . yes," he responded indignantly.

"Can you see whether he's still there?"

"He hasn't checked out yet, so I assume so."

She quickly got up and left through the back room.

"Keep watching the system and call me if you see him going through the security gate."

"But I risk being discovered."

"Do it, Ismail!" She hung up and smiled at Kurt, who was dipping some frozen fish into the deep fryer.

"Did you find what you were looking for?"

"Yes, don't erase anything. See you, Kurt."

Cecilie limped out to the Golf and drove off towards Teglholmen. What the hell was John doing? And at this time of night when the division was usually deserted? She called Ismail back.

"Is he still there?"

"I assume so."

"Can you see who else is there?"

"Then I'll have to reboot and start all over again."

"Okay, forget it." A thought suddenly struck her. "Can you see whether he's logged in to anything?"

"Not from where I am. And anyway, that's not so straightforward, Cecilie," he answered.

"Well, get your ass moving then and find out whether anyone's logged themselves in there. Find out what's being searched."

She ran through a red light at Vesterbrogade and was about to get torpedoed by a white moving van. The driver honked at her, and she turned on the blue flashing lights. When she had passed Fisketorvet Shopping Mall five minutes later, Ismail called back.

"He's left the building."

"Fuck!" she said, sending the car at lightning speed down Sluseholmen. "Two minutes, two minutes, then you'll be there," she mumbled to herself. Soon after, she turned down on Teglholm Allé. The office was on the right-hand side and the car park just across from it. The tyres screeched as she stopped right in front of the entrance. She got out of the car and looked across at the car park. It was empty.

"Fuck, fuck, fuck."

Her phone rang. It was Ismail. "Did you reach him in time?"

"No. Were you able to see what is being searched right now?"

"There is a single search from Palsgaard's computer even though Palsgaard hasn't been there himself."

"And what was the search?"

"Vinnie Pettersson."

"Thank you, Ismail," Cecilie said, hanging up and jumping back into the Golf. With a bit of luck, she'd reach Høje Gladsaxe at the same time as John. If John had just begun researching his next victim, then he was still in the planning stage. Unless Ryan's release had accelerated his plans. In which case he might go after Vinnie sooner. Tonight, even. She floored the accelerator.

69

Cecilie pulled into the car park in front of the high-rise concrete buildings. She looked for John's Golf among the parked cars but couldn't see it anywhere. She continued down to the opposite end and parked across from the apartment complex where Vinnie Pettersson lived. Cecilie noticed that the light was on in the apartment on the second floor. She heard a car door slam and saw a figure further down between two cars. It was John! John was looking in the direction of Vinnie's apartment. Cecilie crouched down in the seat and tried to conceal herself. John's phone lit up in the darkness and she could see that he was writing something. Perhaps a few notes to himself? she thought. Then he put the phone away and started walking towards the little lawn that ran in front of the tall buildings.

Cecilie checked her pistol in her holster and then Como's little gun in the pocket of her jacket. She was about to get out when John suddenly stopped under a tree. She considered whether she should move to arrest him before things developed further. On the other hand, what was she going to arrest him for? If Palsgaard was protecting him, she couldn't even nail him for making an illegal search. She saw that John was urinating against a tree. Imagine if she had managed to arrest him while he was holding his dick! A moment later, he returned to his car and drove from the car park.

She followed him from a distance, down Gladsaxevej and further to Søborg Hovedgade, where he made a turn towards Hellerup. There were no other cars on the road and Cecilie kept her distance from him so that he wouldn't discover her. Ten minutes later, they reached Bernstorffsvej, on which they continued. Where the hell was the bastard going? Perhaps home? She had no idea where John lived. Maybe in a cave or under a stone, which would have suited a creep like him. John signalled further down and Cecilie followed. When she turned the corner, she saw that his car was parked further ahead. She pulled to the side of the road as she saw him enter a garden. Cecilie got out of the car and started limping along the pavement. Even though it was pitch dark, the neighbourhood with the stately houses seemed familiar. She looked for a street sign and found one on the next corner, which said VALEURSVEJ. This was where Klerke lived.

She picked up the pace and limped past John's car and continued further to the garden gate. She noticed that Klerke's front door was open and that the lights in all the windows were on. Was something going on between John and Klerke? It didn't make any sense. John loathed Klerke. Damn! Cecilie grabbed her service pistol and limped along the garden pathway. He was going after Klerke! She was going to be his next victim! She continued up the small staircase towards the open front door and went into the hallway. Britney Spears's "Oops!… I Did It Again" could be heard coming from the stereo system. It didn't exactly seem like Klerke's taste, Cecilie thought. She continued through the rooms with herringbone flooring and expensive furniture. She found the B&O stereo and turned off the music. A silence that couldn't be escaped spread throughout the house. Cecilie limped back to the hallway and looked towards the staircase leading to the first floor. She released the safety catch of her pistol. Sensed the metallic taste in her mouth, the blood that rushed through her ears. Now she had tunnel vision. She slowly limped up the stairs. She stopped at the landing when she saw John standing by the door to the bedroom.

"STOP!" she roared, aiming at him with her pistol. John looked at her, paralysed.

"Ce-Cecilie . . .?"

He slowly lifted his bloody hands in front him. She also noticed the blood on his trousers and on one of his shoes.

"What have I done? Noth-nothing," he stammered. "It . . . it wasn't me."

Cecilie pushed him away from the bedroom door. "Sit down!" She grabbed hold of his collar and pressed him down towards the floor. John collapsed like a rag doll.

"She . . . she . . . she . . ."

"Shut up!"

Keeping half an eye on John, she opened the door slightly ajar. Beatrice Klerke's corpse was tied down to the bed and she was wearing a maid's uniform. Her throat was cut open and she had elongated lacerations on her face. Her sex had been mishandled just like the other victims. It resembled a bloody version of Vinnie Pettersson's pose in the September issue from 1976. Cecilie turned towards John, who was sitting on the floor. "You killed her just like you killed the others."

"I-I . . ."

"Why did you come back?"

He looked up and wiped the corner of his mouth. "It wasn't me . . . I had nothing to do with this. You don't think that—"

"Liar!" she snarled. "Did you really detest Klerke so much that she had to take Vinnie's place?"

"Vinnie who? I don't know any Vinnies."

He was about to get up, but she aimed the pistol at his chest. "Don't get up. You know perfectly well who. The Vinnie Pettersson who you just visited out in Gladsaxe."

"I didn't visit anyone. I received a message from an informant to meet in Høje Gladsaxe."

"Liar."

"It's true."

"Who? Who were you going to meet?"

"I . . . I can't say. It's none of your business."

She poked him with the barrel of the pistol. "That's damn well not the right answer. Tell me right now or I'll pull the trigger." She placed the pistol against his shoulder.

"Como. I was going to meet Como!"

"Bullshit." She cocked the gun. "Say goodbye to your shoulder."

"He sent me a text message, anonymously, but I knew it was him. He said he had new information."

"About what?"

"A-about you," he stammered. "He said he had something he wanted to show me."

"What?"

"I have no idea. He never showed up."

"You're so full of bullshit, John. You came out here to Klerke's place instead; why?"

"Como sent me an address. I didn't know that the Minister lived here. When I saw that the front door was open, I went inside and found her"—he swallowed hard—"like that," he said, pointing towards the bedroom.

She shook her head at him.

"Como sent you an address in Hellerup and you fell for it?"

"Yes!"

"Even for the head of the Independent Police Complaints Authority, you're way too DUMB!"

"I swear," he said, taking his phone out of his pocket.

"Stop!" Cecilie said, and moved the pointed gun from his shoulder to his chest.

"My phone. I just want to show you my phone."

"Okay, take it out, then."

John first checked one pocket and then the other. His sense of panic slowly started to spread on his face.

"I . . . I forgot it in my car. We'll go down and get it."

She shook her head. "That's precisely what we aren't going to do. I don't need to look at some message that you could just as well have sent to yourself." She could feel her anger starting to take over. "Why did you do it? Do you hate women so much? Or is it just a certain type, huh, John? I know Farida's father, you fucking bastard." Without warning she hit him with the handle of her gun.

John took hold of his jaw. "It . . . it wasn't me."

"Shut your dirty mouth. When you lie, you're smearing their name. I want the fucking truth."

"I swear . . ." She hit him again with her pistol. John spit blood on the carpet.

"What with all the time you spent going after me, you must have a pretty good idea of what I'm capable of." She twirled the pistol in front of him. "You think I shot Jeremy Cox, don't you?"

He looked at her like a submissive dog without responding.

"A monster, just like you. You think I put a bullet through his head, don't you?"

"I . . . I don't know . . ."

"Oh yes you do. And you know what? You're right." She lifted the gun and aimed at his forehead. "Boom." John's eyes blinked. "There you have it. My confession, John. Enjoy. How close do you think I am to shooting a bullet through your forehead right now? As a just punishment for torturing and killing innocent women? And who could blame me? And who would ever find out, for that matter?"

She rested the muzzle of the gun against his forehead, below his retreating hairline. She sensed the heat that filled her body. Excitement mixed with satisfaction. Like what a cheetah must feel when it closes its jaws around an antelope's neck and squeezes the life out of it. She no longer had any sense of fear.

"Stop, stop, I'm begging you," he moaned.

"Admit that you killed Klerke. Admit that you killed Farida. Admit that you killed Lizzette. Admit that you killed Tine. Admit that you killed Kristina."

"It wasn't . . . me." He started crying. "You've got to believe me—I had nothing to do with it," he said, holding his hands out in front of her.

"John, John, John," she hushed him. "I've got you recorded on the surveillance camera out in Bellahøj the night Farida was murdered. Your car."

"I wasn't there . . . I don't know what it was you saw."

"I've got all the registrations of your visits in my division, both when you borrowed Ryan's computer and Palsgaard's this evening."

"What?"

"Yes, too bad for you that you aren't better at covering your tracks."

"I . . . I haven't been to Teglholmen. I swear. I was at home when I received the message from Como."

She pressed the pistol harder against his forehead. "You had your chance. I gave you a chance to get through this alive. The world will be a better place without you. Goodbye, John."

"Okay, okay, okay. It was me. I admit it . . . I don't know why I did it. Revenge, I guess. I'm sorry, I'm a pig."

She noticed that he had peed in his pants and was sitting in a pool of urine.

"Why, John?"

"I don't know . . . because, because I'm sick."

"Sick?" she said, shaking her head. "Are you already aiming for a spot in Nikolaj's yoga class?"

She took out her handcuffs and threw them on the floor in front of him.

"If it's up to me, you'll end up in a proper jail. Put them on."

John did what she asked him to and Cecilie pulled him up from the floor. She pushed him in the direction of the staircase while she looked for her phone in her pocket. It was time to send for the whole circus. She didn't notice the door behind her being opened. She also didn't notice the figure who stepped forth dressed in white coveralls. Or the cloth with ether in his gloved hand. The next moment the hand closed around her nose and mouth. For a moment she was gripped by panic. She wanted to spin around. She wanted to lift her pistol. There was a lot she wanted to do, but she fell into a deep black hole instead.

70

The clinking, knocking sounds woke Cecilie up from her daze. She tried to focus on the objects in front of her and sensed the shiny knife that hit the side of the glass jar with a screw-on lid. In the glass lay some elongated bloody pieces of flesh. She tried moving her head, but the heavy plastic strip prevented her from doing so, and she almost strangled herself. She had been placed on the floor with her hands above her head, firmly tied to the bedposts with cable ties.

"What do you think of my latest specimen?" he asked, lifting the glass up close to her face. His voice echoed and she felt the ether-triggered migraine envelop her.

"Aged and with an uneven and leathery surface and a full-grown clitoris. An old female," he added, and it sounded like he was describing a captured insect. "Magnificent, isn't it? Perfect for my collection." He removed the glass and held up another one. It contained a couple of cut-up labia in a transparent liquid. "Fleshy, with a black-and-pink contour, it belongs to a big, invasive species," he chuckled. "I knew that the black girl was going to be a rarity in my collection."

"Fucking bastard," Cecilie snarled as she tried to break loose. He put the glass jar aside and she attempted to focus on his face. "You," she moaned, her head feeling like it was about to explode.

"Yes, me. Concealed in the darkness. Camouflaged like the Silver Y. *Autographa gamma.* Always at one with its surroundings, which is an especially efficient weapon, both in terms of keeping your enemies at bay and hunting for prey. You never did see me, did you, Cecilie? The pale sidekick—wasn't that what you called me at our last encounter?"

She stared at Kenneth. His face merged with the white coveralls, and he resembled a reptile more than anything else. A human-sized lizard. Kenneth was right; he was the last one she would ever have suspected. He had gone under the radar, living in John's shadow.

"Why didn't you kill him?" asked Kenneth with his squeaky voice as he pointed behind him. Cecilie looked over at John, who was lying close to the dresser, still handcuffed. His lips were trembling, and she imagined he was still conscious.

"I'm a little disappointed. I was counting on your mad mind. If you had killed him, everything would have been perfect. It would have closed the case for good and you would have been put away for life, maybe out to your little fuck buddy?" He clearly sensed her reaction and nodded. "That's right, I've been keeping an eye on you. Just like I've kept an eye on all the other bitches. You aren't exactly stingy when it comes to that, are you?" he said, grabbing her crotch through her jeans. She squeezed her legs tight, and he removed his hand.

"Why did you change your modus operandi? Why Klerke?" she asked, sensing the dryness in her throat.

"Can't you see the irony of it? Of displaying her among the other bitches? The mother of all bitches. Every collector knows that there has got to be a certain edge to his collection if it's going to be of any significance. She is my edge. My most courageous capture."

"You're not getting away with this, Kenneth."

"Who's going to stop me? You?" He grazed the knife against her cheek and left a small cut. He watched the blood run a little before licking it off her cheek.

"My men will find you."

"Your men are just as incompetent as the Travel Team."

"Why did you choose to put the blame on Ryan?"

He shook his head. "You of all people must know how his arrogance follows his amateurism. He was sloppy with his password. It was so easy for me to conceal my searches through his. It was too bad that he had an alibi." Kenneth shrugged his shoulders.

"But just as you like to make use of rotten politicians, I make use of incompetent police officers." He pointed back towards John.

"You were the one who searched on Palsgaard's computer?"

"I had to leave a small trace of crumbs for you and your brown IT friend. Copying John's card was as easy as pie."

"You kept us under surveillance?"

"The good thing about working for the Independent Police Complaints Authority is that you learn about all the loopholes. You see all the offences taking place in the various divisions, which equips one with all the necessary skills to navigate the systems. Abuse them. If you're skilled enough, that is," he said, pointing at himself with his knife.

"Which you are?"

"I'm the only one who's going to come out of this alive."

"Are you sure about that?"

"Oh yes," he said, straightening his neck.

"The only thing up for discussion is which one of you is going to go first." He got up and looked around thoughtfully. "I am thinking we need to create a new tableau: John is busy with Klerke, little Britney can be heard through the stereo, maybe singing 'Toxic' or 'I'm a Slave 4 U.' Isn't it funny how one's taste in music changes? Before I started on my collection, I hated Britney, but now I think she's just wonderful. Events form you, don't they?" Kenneth bent down to Cecilie. "Back to the scenario. You and Klerke are supposed to meet. Probably to make a new strategy. You notice that the front door is open and fear the worst. You run up here, but unfortunately, you're too late. John's been a bad boy. He's been at it with the knife. You shoot but only manage to injure him. John attacks you with the knife and kills you. John gets away," said Kenneth, pointing towards the door. "John makes it down to the lawn, where he dies. Forensics tries to search for these things but in vain," he said, taking out the glass jar containing Klerke's labia from his pocket. "They never find them," he said, and smiled. "And that gives the whole thing a tiny hint of mystery, wouldn't you say?"

Cecilie didn't answer. Even though she was tied down, she desperately tried to find a way out. The only positive thing was that she could feel the weight of Como's gun in her jacket pocket. If only she could get one of her hands free.

"Where should I shoot him so that he doesn't bleed to death too fast?" Kenneth asked, getting out her service gun.

"How good a shot are you?"

He walked over to John and aimed at him. "Should I shoot him in the stomach? Or in the balls? I'm thinking that you, Cecilie, wouldn't mind shooting him in the balls. Just say the word."

John crouched.

"Please don't."

"Or should I shoot him in the back? Are you that type, Cecilie? Or is that too cowardly?"

John started sobbing loudly.

"I'm tired of all your whining," Kenneth said, squatting down. "Tired of receiving all your ridiculous orders." He looked over his shoulder towards Cecilie. "Do you realise how much I've had to tolerate from this guy? You're not the only one who hates him. Should I shoot him in the cheek? Remove his jaw? Then everyone in the force could talk about what a hideous corpse they found. And how vile he looked, even in death."

"I'm begging you . . ." John moaned. Kenneth looked back at him. "I heard you and it won't help." He cocked the trigger. Cecilie realised she had to do something.

"Was that why you battered them?"

"What?" he said, placing the muzzle against John's jaw. John moved his head, but Kenneth found it again.

"I have no idea. Why do you set fire to a kitten? Because it looks funny, I imagine. Because you can? Because it can't defend itself, just like this guy."

"You're just a sick little freak."

"No, I'm a collector of rarities, a connoisseur."

"You're a nothing and a nobody. Was that the only way you could get attention? Don't the chicks like you, Kenneth?"

"I don't expect you to understand or appreciate what I have done. It's way above your little head."

"Oh? I've experienced plenty of creepy guys like you. Little pathetic men. Let me guess, you've never had a girlfriend. You've never slept with a woman. You probably tried once with some poor whore, but your dick is only good for peeing. Am I right? Is that why we haven't found any sperm at the crime scenes? Did the girls laugh at you? You call yourself Mr. Troglodyte on the internet, but you should have called yourself Mr. Impotent."

Kenneth got up on his feet and waved the pistol at her. "I wouldn't go on if I were you. You don't know me at all."

She smiled scornfully. "Did Mummy catch you jerking off? To old porno magazines? Is that why? Did she spank you and say you were a dirty boy, Kenneth?" Kenneth bent down and hit her hard in the face. She tasted the blood in her mouth and her ears were tingling. But at least she had got him away from John. Away from John, free the arm, grab Como's gun. That was the plan.

"I bet you have a pathetic past of some sort. Did someone fiddle around with little Kenneth? Something that you never got over because you were a loser."

He pressed the pistol against her cheek. "That sounds more like your past, the rape victim who became a cop and shot her gangster boyfriend."

"Fuck you, Kenneth."

"Maybe you and John were fighting over the pistol, and it went off in your face? Want me to remove your face, bitch? I was going to show you a little mercy. But that could change. So don't mess with the plan, okay?"

"Okay, Kenneth, your plan is important," she mumbled.

"Enough talk," he said, letting go of his grip on her. He turned towards John.

"Come on, on your feet." He grabbed John and pressed him against the wall. Cecilie tore at the strip that held her hands firmly above her head. It cut deep into her wrists. Even though she had managed to move her arms further down, she still couldn't get her hands loose. This was simply impossible. She had to think of something else. Her fingertips touched the strip that was fastened around her throat and the bedpost.

A new idea popped into her mind. Albeit a truly desperate one. At that same moment, Kenneth turned around to face her.

"What the hell are you doing? Do you think you can get loose?"

She had a hold of the very end of the strip and pulled it. With a couple of clicking sounds, it slowly tightened around her neck.

"Don't injure yourself. That's not part of the plan." He looked back at John. "You remain standing there."

John looked at him tearfully. "I beg you, please don't kill me . . ."

"Fuck you, Kenneth!" she shouted, pulling hard on the strip. It locked itself around her neck and she gasped for air.

"What the fuck are you doing, bitch?" Kenneth shouted.

Her air passages were blocked off. She could hear gurgling sounds from her mouth. Felt her body go into spasm. Felt her eyeballs protruding out of their sockets.

"You crazy bitch!" she heard him say as he came rushing over. She blacked out. She felt her body giving way. She was going to die now. She descended into a deep darkness and a sense of calmness settled within her. No fear. No panic. It was like slumbering in an eternally lukewarm bubble bath. Cecilie felt the heavy kicks to her side. She opened her eyes wide and gasped for breath. Kenneth loomed above her, holding his knife in one hand and her pistol in the other. She coughed and put her hand to her mouth. He had cut her loose. Finally! She was lying on the floor next to Klerke's bed.

"Crazy bitch, you were about to ruin everything. I'd better start with you." He bent over her, holding the knife. Her hand reached inside her pocket in search of Como's gun. It was gone! Had Kenneth taken it? She cast her head to the side and looked around desperately.

"Where do you think John would cut you? In the liver or in your stomach?" Kenneth asked, squeezing the knife, ready to start slashing. She caught sight of Como's gun under the bed. Cecilie stretched out her arm and tried to reach it, but it was too far away.

"What the hell do you think you're doing?" Kenneth asked. She stretched her arm further but still couldn't reach it.

"Ready to die?" Kenneth asked. She kicked her foot, pushing herself halfway under the bed. Kenneth laughed. "Are you trying to flee like a little child? How pathetic." He put the knife aside and pulled the legs of her trousers. When he got her out from under the bed, Cecilie lifted her right arm towards him. She had Como's gun in her hand. Kenneth stared agape into the barrel. The first shot hit him in the chest and made him stagger. The next shot hit him in the shoulder, which made him drop her gun. Kenneth swayed against the wall.

"You . . . you . . ." She aimed at his forehead and pulled the trigger. He slowly slid down towards the floor, leaving a bloody trace on the wallpaper. Cecilie let her arm fall as she tried to catch her breath. She could hear John sobbing.

"Thank you . . . thank you, God."

"It sure as hell wasn't God who saved your ass, John," she mumbled.

71

Cecilie took a sip of her coffee as she watched the news on TV. The coverage of Klerke's murder had filled all the various media the last week or so, and she herself had received a deluge of phone calls from what seemed to be the entire corps of Danish journalists. But she had remained silent. Cecilie was already late, but she stayed glued in front of the screen. The news channel was transmitting from the press meeting with the newly appointed Minister of Justice. She saw Palsgaard standing in the crowd behind the Minister in his most official uniform. The new Minister, a younger man with Dumbo ears, talked about cleaning up the agency and his own ministry. And how generally the morale in the country was going to be improved, just like proper action was going to be taken against criminals by way of harsher punishments and more jails. "We are a law-and-order party," he added. With Beatrice Klerke's and Helge Sundvald's list of sins in mind, Cecilie had her doubts about that statement, but she was in no position to judge anyone. However, it wouldn't surprise her if the new Minister had a couple of skeletons in the closet, either metaphorically or literally.

The next moment, the Minister called Palsgaard forth and thanked him for his efforts in connection with the investigation of the tragic murder case that had cost the former Minister of Justice her life. He praised Palsgaard for his excellent piece of work and handed him the Ministry of Justice's medal of honour for his noteworthy efforts. Cecilie turned off the TV and put the cup aside. In the week that had passed, Palsgaard hadn't even been to her office once. *Fuck him*, she thought, and went out the door.

When a little while later she was standing in the car park, she noticed the moving van further down. Omar was sitting on a chair by the open back door and staring vacantly down at the asphalt as his family carried their belongings into the van. He seemed dejected. She felt like saying goodbye to him and telling him that she had managed to kill the man who had murdered Farida. But she knew that it wouldn't mean anything to him. That Omar would blame himself until the day he died that he hadn't taken better care of her. Maybe it would help the family to move away from the neighbourhood?

Cecilie got into the car and drove across the square. A couple of troublemakers on scooters glared at her and gave her the finger. The thugs had taken back the neighbourhood. All the ones wearing black tracksuits had the gang's symbol on their chest. She hadn't seen Allan for a long time either and she hoped he was smart enough not to frequent the park or the courts. Omar's grim prophecy seemed to be coming true. The neighbourhood was well on its way to getting on the ghetto list and there wasn't a single thing she could do about it.

When Cecilie entered the division half an hour later, she greeted Heino, who was talking on the phone. Both Henrik's and Joakim's seats were empty. Henrik had taken sick leave due to stress and would most likely not be returning before he retired. Joakim had gone on vacation, but the HR department had informed her that he had requested not to be employed in her division again. She understood if the whole thing had taken its toll on them. She had only wished that they had both come to her first before leaving.

Cecilie entered her office. All the boxes with the many case files had been removed and the place looked clean for once. She herself had not overseen the cleaning up. Instead, it had been Ryan and his team who had requested all her previous cases, which they could use in their investigation. The flame of hatred, or perhaps it was more the flame of revenge, was still burning passionately within Ryan. At that moment, Heino knocked on the door and stepped in.

"Seems it's just us two from the old team," he said, placing a file on the conference table.

"Yes, it's a bit strange."

"Nonsense," he said, smiling. "Now we'll finally get to be partners."

"Heino, you know perfectly well—"

"Yeah, I know, you don't have a partner. I've made a report of everything we found at Kenneth's place. He had quite a collection of porn magazines."

She nodded. Kenneth's collection of vintage magazines had filled up most of the space in his two-room apartment in Tårnby. That and an impressive number of butterflies displayed in glass frames that hung everywhere. They had also found various hard drives, which Ismail and NC3 had decrypted: gross things like torture videos of women being killed in the cruellest manner fetched from the darkest corners of the internet. Among the films were also some of his own. Cecilie had been the only one who had managed to watch all of them from beginning to end. She felt that she owed it to the victims.

Heino looked around in the half-empty office. "Will you be able to keep your head above water?"

"Nah."

"But John . . . I mean, you saved his life . . . Have you heard anything from him?" She shook her head. "He at least ought to put in a good word for you."

"Are we talking about the same John?" she asked, smiling.

"If he had just a little bit of character, then he'd stop the investigation. It all depends on him."

"Well, a case has been filed."

Heino rubbed his goatee. "You mean by Como?"

She nodded.

"Como's no longer alive."

"What?" she asked, looking at Heino in surprise.

"Como was shot last Monday while he was at the barber's in Tingbjerg. They've arrested two fifteen-year-old boys who were carrying pistols and everything. Case closed."

"That's quite a tragedy," she said, and meant it.

"But lucky for you. If the Independent Police Complaints Authority back down, Ryan and the Travel Team can go fly the fuck off."

"Ain't gonna happen."

"How's your neck? Is it okay?" he asked, looking at her. She untied her scarf. Heino wrinkled his nose at the sight of the deep red mark.

"Is it true that you tightened it?"

The rumours had clearly circulated fast.

"I didn't have much choice."

"You could have ended up killing yourself."

"It was fifty-fifty."

"Fifty-fifty? You're crazy."

"I knew that no matter what, he couldn't continue with his set-up. You guys would discover that something didn't add up and you would have found out the truth."

Heino laughed and patted her on the back. "You have great confidence in us, boss."

"Always. I trust you guys. I trust you, Heino. You're a good officer."

He looked down at the floor and smiled awkwardly.

"Are you okay, boss? I mean, with the whole thing?"

"No, I'm going to see a psychologist."

He nodded in agreement. "Yes, that's probably a good idea."

"Tonight, actually," she said roguishly.

Heino flashed a big smile. "The doctor?"

"Yup. I've got a date with Nikolaj," she said, giggling like a schoolgirl.

"Good for you, boss. He's damn lucky."

She looked away.

"I'll try to behave myself."

"Seriously, boss, he's a lucky man," Heino said, meeting her gaze.

"Thanks, Heino."

72

Cecilie was having a clothes crisis, and most of her wardrobe lay spread across the bed. She didn't even know if she owned anything that could even remotely be considered "date-like." Her wardrobe consisted mostly of everyday clothes. An exceptional number of jeans and T-shirts. Finally, she managed to choose a pair of black jeans and a blouse with a light blue pattern and silver threads, which she had bought by mistake but which now came to good use. After the clothes crisis was over, a new one emerged. The last time she had worn make-up was at the National Police Commissioner's get-together and it hadn't exactly been a success. She threw on some blue eye shadow and red lipstick. She looked at herself in the mirror. She looked like a clown, so she removed it all again. Nikolaj would have to make do with her natural look. She grimaced in the mirror. Her self-confidence was at an all-time low and she hoped the wine would appear on the table quickly, and that it would be strong.

Cecilie took a taxi to Taverna Kreta on Jagtvej, where she and Nikolaj had agreed to meet at 7 p.m. Even though it was a quarter past the hour, she was the first to show up. The waiter showed her to a window table and asked if she wanted anything to drink. She thought she'd wait for Nikolaj, but when he still hadn't shown up after ten minutes, she waved the waiter over and ordered a glass of wine.

"What kind of wine?" asked the tanned waiter.

"White, please, but not the one that tastes like resin."

"No Retsina for you. I detest that cheap stuff myself," he said, winking at her.

When he returned with the wine, she quickly took a couple of sips, which helped her nerves. Why was she so nervous? It was only Nikolaj. At 7:30 p.m., he came rushing into the restaurant. He looked around for her and she waved him over to the table. "I'm sorry for the delay."

"Did you have to work overtime?"

"No, I was having a clothes crisis. What the hell do you put on when you're going on a date?"

In Nikolaj's case it ended up being a wrinkled T-shirt with a picture of a surfboard on it.

"You look very cool. Do you surf?" she asked.

"Only on the internet," he said, and ordered some wine.

It consoled her to see that he was just as nervous as she was. They ordered some dinner and more wine. While they ate, they talked about this and that. About how good the food tasted. And how good the wine was. About the fact that neither of them had been to Greece but that it could be very nice to go there someday. Cecilie enjoyed talking about things that didn't have anything to do with work. It was almost like being on vacation. But just like vacations, the pleasant part of the conversation eventually came to an end when Nikolaj asked about Klerke. "Pretty tragic, huh?"

Cecilie nodded. "Yes, she didn't deserve to end her days like that."

"And what about you?"

"What about me?"

"Are they going to leave you alone?"

"I'm afraid there'll be no such luck. This is just the calm before the storm."

Nikolaj took a sip of his wine and nodded.

"What?" she said. "You look as though there's something you want to ask."

"It must have been terrible, what you endured. I don't even think I can imagine what you've been through . . ."

"But . . . ?"

Nikolaj looked down at the table before continuing. "I had a look at the criminal report and the one from Forensics. Out of professional curiosity," he said, smiling.

"You have connections."

He nodded.

"And what did you get out of reading them? Did you get a better understanding of Kenneth?"

"No, I don't think so. But I noticed that . . . that you shot him three times."

"Sounds about right."

"Once in the chest, once in the shoulder, and once in the head. In the forehead, to be more specific."

"Bull's-eye," she said coolly, and sensed which direction the conversation was heading.

Nikolaj looked at her for a long time. "It's a good thing that you managed to stop him."

"He would have continued if I hadn't done it."

"Yes, no doubt about that," he said, looking back down at the table.

"But . . . ?" she said, searching his gaze.

He looked at her. "The shot to the forehead. You had managed to pacify him at that point, hadn't you?"

"He had to be neutralised, which he was."

"I'll say," Nikolaj said quietly. "What drove him to do it? Have you and your team learned anything about his background?"

"No, and I really don't care. I'm sorry for not sending him out to you," she said, and took a sip from her glass.

"No, you're not."

"No, I'm probably not."

A wall of silence emerged between them. Both were turning their wine glasses in their hands as their eyes were drawn to the windows, through which they could see the traffic on Jagtvej. Nikolaj took a deep breath.

"Listen. Cecilie, I—"

"It's okay, Nikolaj. You don't have to say anything."

"But I feel that I must," he said, leaning forward. "The shot to the forehead . . ."

She emptied her glass. "Do you see a modus operandi, Nikolaj? Are you eager to know whether I killed Jeremy in the same way?"

"Did you?"

She smiled without answering. He leaned back in his chair. "You need help, Cecilie."

"I know. So help me," she said, reaching for his hand on the table.

"I'm not the right one," he said, moving his hand away.

"You're a psychologist, aren't you? In fact, I told Heino as a joke that I was going to see a psychologist tonight."

"Okay," he said, uncomfortably.

"Maybe I just need someone who's there for me. Someone whose shoulder I can cry on occasionally."

"I'm not the right person. I'm sorry."

"Why not? You don't have to pack it in for me, you know."

"Because you need professional help and to be honest, you scare me."

"I scare myself sometimes," she said, looking down at the table.

"I can recommend this guy. He's good." Nikolaj took out a pen and wrote a name and a phone number down on his napkin, which he handed to her across the table.

She stared down at the napkin without taking it.

He took out his wallet.

"Forget it," she said, waving her hand dismissively. "This is on me."

"Okay, thanks." Nikolaj got up, fumbling both with his jacket and the chair before he rushed out the door. She remained seated and looked out the window towards the traffic.

"Dessert?" the waiter asked, taking her plate.

"Apparently not in this lifetime. Just the cheque, please."

73

Cecilie was sitting behind her desk and staring straight ahead of her. The last few days she had ensconced herself in her office and only ventured into the division if it was necessary. It was as though the detectives knew that her fate was sealed. She had become a burden on the division, and everyone was counting down the days until her dismissal. They could stop counting. Someone knocked on the door and John entered. He smiled awkwardly and she nodded to him. He had a plaster across the bridge of his nose and the bruises were still clearly visible on his face.

"John, I was expecting you."

He extended his arms. "Well, it was inevitable, wasn't it?"

"Have you found a new assistant?"

"I imagine that HR is working on it."

"In which case they'd better do an extra background check on the individual in question. Who else did you bring with you?" she asked, looking towards the door, which stood ajar.

John shook his head. "I came alone. Though Ryan would have liked to have searched your office."

She smiled. "Were they all standing in line to join you?"

"Yes, but I thought that this was, after all, a gesture I wanted to extend to you."

"Or else it was to have the victory for yourself."

He chuckled. "You know me too well, Cecilie."

"No, or I would have let you die in Klerke's bedroom," she said half-jokingly.

"Let me die?" he asked with indignation. "I rather think that we managed the hardship together. Teamwork despite our differences. That we stood by each other when it was most important."

Cecilie had a hard time concealing her smile. "Is that the story you go around telling people?"

"It's a version that could also temper the waters for you."

"I see," Cecilie said, thinking back on how pathetic John had acted. "So, does that mean you intend to bury my cases together with the other versions of your story?" she asked probingly.

"You don't have that much leeway," he answered coolly.

"You saw for yourself what I'm capable of, John. How efficient I am out in the field. Why won't you let me do my job? In my way?"

"Your way? I think most people would like to avoid your way."

"It gets things solved."

"That almost sounds like you're begging me."

"On my knees if I have to. This is the only thing that I can do. It's the only thing I want to do," she said, extending her arms. "And it's all in your hands, John."

He nodded and smiled. "That's true. In that sense the Independent Police Complaints Authority practically holds divine power. But it's not going to happen, Cecilie. We've got to clean up the rotten culture that you and Beatrice Klerke stood for. A culture that has spread down the ranks. There are already cases that have been opened against members of your team."

"What team? Henrik is on sick leave. Joakim has asked to be transferred . . ."

"No one escapes the Independent Police Complaints Authority," he said, folding his arms in front of him. "Should we start heading out to police headquarters?"

"It's not fair on them."

"We need a purge. Unfortunately, there'll always be victims," he said, shrugging his shoulders.

As he escorted her through the division, he placed his hand on her shoulder so that no one was in doubt as to what was taking place. She let him get his little triumph and voluntarily went along with him. Heino looked like he was about to burst into tears, and she winked at him when she passed his desk. "See you, Heino."

"Boss?"

A few minutes later, they reached the car park and the black Golf.

"Have you got the car back after Kenneth borrowed it?"

John opened the car door for her, and she got into the passenger seat.

"Yes. But they say I'll soon be getting a brand-new Passat."

"Congratulations," she responded ironically, and he slammed the door shut.

John had got a new car while she herself had been rewarded with a direct ticket to jail. John sat down behind the wheel and started the Golf.

"Didn't you ever sense anything? Wasn't there at any point something that set your alarm bells ringing?" she asked.

"In relation to Kenneth? No. That's almost the scariest thing about it. Incredible that you can get tricked by a trusted colleague. We're all in shock."

"So, this current purge doesn't include self-examination of any kind?"

He sent her a sullen glance and drove down Teglholm Allé. When they reached the traffic light at Vasbygade, they saw that the traffic towards the city centre wasn't moving due to rush-hour. So, John took the route across the Sjællands Bridge and Amager instead. Cecilie leaned back in her seat. Her last bit of freedom would be wasted on a trip to Amager, Shit Island. What a damn shame.

"There's something I'd like to ask you," said John.

"Perhaps we should just drive in silence. I imagine there'll be plenty of opportunities to talk in those small windowless rooms."

"It's just a single question, out of personal interest."

"What?" she moaned.

"Were you thinking of Jeremy when you blew a hole in Kenneth's head?"

"Funny you ask. My psychologist wanted to know the same thing. Is it some sort of vaginal thing with men and holes?" she answered ironically.

"Seriously, Cecilie."

"That would require that I admit to having killed Jeremy."

"Which you did to me. As you were holding a gun to my head."

"There are many versions of exactly what transpired that night, aren't there, John?"

"Perhaps, but they all end with you behind bars."

They approached Langebro Bridge, which would take them to police headquarters and the prison on the opposite side of the dock.

"I wanted to neutralise him, make sure that he wouldn't pose a threat to anyone again."

Which was true. She had got at least that far in relation to the killing of Jeremy. The killing of Kenneth had been cleansed of hatred. It had been completely pure. Progress had been made when it came to her mad mind. She realised that now. That had to count for a little something in her D-factor scala. Make her one of the good ones.

They were getting closer to the bridge and John sped up. He seemed eager to get to National Police Headquarters. Deliver her to the National Police Commissioner and the whole boys' club. She would spend the night in jail while the assholes stood around drinking port wine in his office. Fuck that! That wasn't going to happen! Not if she could prevent it. There had to be a way out. Fifty-fifty. She was, in fact, willing to settle for worse odds if she could escape, just this one last time. She looked at John, sitting there with that arrogant look on his face. That the cases brought against her were entirely in John's hands was most likely an exaggeration. But if he wasn't in the equation, it would gain her more time. Time in which the top brass couldn't touch her before the reshuffling had taken place. Time to rectify everything. Time to clear her neighbourhood of all the gangs. Time to reassemble the team. Time to stop yet another maniac. She glanced at John and noticed that he wasn't wearing a seat belt. They drove up onto the bridge in the inner lane. The speedometer displayed 129 kilometres per hour. She looked out the side window at the railing. It was 15 metres down to the dock from there. Probably the same percentage rate she had for surviving a fall over it. Perhaps a great deal less. But at any rate, the odds were much better for her than for John.

"So, there's nothing I can say that will stop you?" she asked.

John looked at her with a scornful smile. "You're fucked, Cecilie."

"That makes two of us." She grabbed hold of the steering wheel and pulled it. A howl could be heard from John, whose smile froze. The Golf made a curve across the bicycle path until it hit the railing with a crash. The crash was so intense that the car's back end lifted, sending it in a somersault across the dock. John was hurled through the windshield while Cecilie continued with the car, heading directly for the glistening surface of the water. She closed her eyes and felt free.

ABOUT THE AUTHOR

Michael Katz Krefeld (b. 1966) is one of the most-read Danish crime authors, and his critically acclaimed books have been awarded several fiction prizes. He is best known for his bestselling crime series featuring Detective Ravn, which has thrilled readers across the globe. Having begun his career as a screenwriter, Krefeld tends towards fast-paced and highly unpredictable thrillers. The fight against evil and personal sacrifices made for the greater good are typical recurring elements of his work.

DISCOVER
STORIES UNBOUND

PodiumAudio.com